THE WAINWRIGHT BOYS

THE
WAINWRIGHT BOYS

PAUL WEBB

Copyright © 2024 Paul Webb

The moral right of the author has been asserted.

Apart from any fair dealing for the purposes of research or private study, or criticism or review, as permitted under the Copyright, Designs and Patents Act 1988, this publication may only be reproduced, stored or transmitted, in any form or by any means, with the prior permission in writing of the publishers, or in the case of reprographic reproduction in accordance with the terms of licences issued by the Copyright Licensing Agency. Enquiries concerning reproduction outside those terms should be sent to the publishers.

This is a work of fiction. Names, characters, businesses, places, events and incidents are either the products of the author's imagination or used in a fictitious manner. Any resemblance to actual persons, living or dead, or actual events is purely coincidental.

Troubador Publishing Ltd
Unit E2 Airfield Business Park,
Harrison Road, Market Harborough,
Leicestershire LE16 7UL
Tel: 0116 279 2299
Email: books@troubador.co.uk
Web: www.troubador.co.uk

ISBN 978 1 80514 222 5

British Library Cataloguing in Publication Data.
A catalogue record for this book is available from the British Library.

Printed and bound in Great Britain by CMP UK
Typeset in 11pt Minion Pro by Troubador Publishing Ltd, Leicester, UK

This is for the good friend who first brought me to the Lake District and has been my uncomplaining walking and sailing companion for the last thirty years – she also happens to be my wife.

The usual caveats apply:

No one portrayed in this book is based on anyone living or dead but in the unlikely event of someone identifying with one the author's characters they should probably seek medical rather than legal advice.

Similarly, all events and situations described here are fictitious but if a reader thinks any of them could be based on a personal experience of their own they would probably be well advised not to advertise the fact.

Real place names and locations have been used. The Cumbrian towns of Cockermouth and Keswick have been reasonably faithfully described, and the author is also fairly confident of the accuracy of his descriptions of the Lakeland fells and mountains, although some eagle-eyed fells man bent on the task will no doubt manage to catch him out.

However, liberties have been taken elsewhere: residents of Douglas and the Isle of Man may not recognise their town and island from some of the author's descriptions, and the topography of the St Bees seashore, as described here, may seem unfamiliar to those who know that coastline. However, there should be no cause for offence, certainly none is meant, and this is after all a work of fiction.

PW

ONE

'So you've found them, all of them? And alive,' she added, sounding slightly surprised.

He steepled his fingers and did the peering over the glasses thing. 'Yes, eventually; some were easier than others from what we gather. One in particular, well, let us just say he seems to be living something of an alternative lifestyle. And another appears to have adopted a different name, ahem, without going through the usual formalities.' His disapproval and suspicion filled the pause. 'But yes, we now know where and how to contact all four of the, er, gentlemen. We understood that was your wish?'

'Oh yes, that's the idea. Now I want to meet them, all of them, and at the same place and at the same time.'

If he was at all curious the solicitor hid it professionally well. He had, after all, had stranger clients with stranger requests and this attractive and confident young woman seemed reasonably balanced, a bit intense perhaps, but sane at least. 'Will you be requiring any further services from us?'

'Of course. I want your firm to write to each of them asking them to attend a meeting and...'

'Forgive me for interrupting,' he removed his glasses and placed them carefully on the blotter in front of him, 'but what makes you think they will respond favourably to such a request? As we have understood it, until very recently you did not know of these individuals, so presumably they will not know of you.' He paused, cocking his head slightly in query. 'Quite. So perhaps we should also point out that quite apart from the complications created by the, er, unorthodox gentleman's domestic arrangements, the other parties are spread far and wide. We have one living abroad and the other two in very different parts of this country. Trying to arrange any simultaneous meeting is bound to involve all of them in some travel, not inconsiderate inconvenience and of course, expense.'

'I've thought of that. In your letter I'd like you to tell them that if they attend it will be something like... *in their interest*, or they'll learn *something to their advantage*. Isn't that the sort of bait you lawyers usually dangle?'

The solicitor looked pained and replaced his glasses before speaking. 'We do not...' he said firmly, '...and cannot, make statements or imply some benefit, pecuniary or otherwise, unless such a benefit actually exists and there is a genuine legal entitlement.'

The woman frowned and pursed her lips thoughtfully. 'I could make it worth their while,' she said slowly. 'As you are well aware, my husband left me a considerable sum.'

The solicitor gave a sharp intake of breath and looked alarmed. 'We could not possibly advise…'

'It would be worth it.' She sat perfectly still, her hands in her lap, her eyes locked on the solicitor's greasy spectacles and her mind made up.

He fidgeted for a moment under her gaze before returning the glasses to the blotter and sitting back in his chair. 'Well, with the necessary undertakings and so on, but the amounts involved would have to be reasonably significant, not just a peppercorn. Are you sure that…' He spread his hands. 'Perhaps if you would tell us a little more about your aims in this matter we would be in a better position to give you the full benefit of our advice.'

The woman flapped an impatient hand, the relentless legalese was starting to irritate her. 'It's money, just money and it's *my* money. And as I've said, it'll be worth it. At least to me,' she added quietly.

The solicitor sighed and reached for a lined yellow pad. 'Very well then, we shall need some details.' He slowly unscrewed the top off a fountain pen. 'Where and when do you propose to stage this… gathering, and how much do you propose to, ah, give away?'

The woman thought for a moment then named a figure. 'That should do it.'

The solicitor winced. 'But…'

She repeated the figure and reached down for her handbag. The solicitor watched her for a moment then started to scribble. 'And when did you have in mind?' he said, still writing. She was studying a small diary when he looked up and gave a date for about four weeks hence. 'So soon.' He flicked a couple of pages and pedantically made a note in his desk diary. 'And where exactly?' She told him. He carefully laid his pen along the spine of the open legal pad and re-steepled his fingers. 'Most unusual,' he murmured.

TWO

'Anarchy…?' It came out "an*arkie*" with the emphasis heavily on the last two syllables and accentuated by the southern drawl. '…I don't have a problem with a bit of anarchy, shows these kids've got a bit of spunk. I like that.'

Barry looked dubious. 'Well up to a point, yes, but since your predecessor, er, moved on, some of the more…'

'Spunky?'

'I was going to say "spirited", but anyway, yes, the more confident amongst them seemed to have more or less taken over some aspects of camp life.'

'Well fine, c'mon, Baz, lighten up, it makes our life easier, eh? Less work for us means more time to take in this grand weather, maybe a glass or two, eh?' He nudged Barry, 'And these mountains of yours, great views and… hey, pretty girl!'

Barry looked at him suspiciously. The remark seemed to fit with the Hawaiian shirt but made the dog collar more incongruous than ever. 'Ah yes, Mary, Mary Wainwright, a nice girl, popular with everyone, perhaps doesn't always keep the best of company but well liked, especially by some of the boys.'

The girl turned towards the two men sitting under the canvas awning, flashed a half smile and fluttered a hand in greeting before turning towards the pebble beach where a mixed group of boys and girls had gathered at the water's edge. Both men watched the bikini-clad figure sway across a patch of parched grass, the swing of her hips and bottom emphasised by the swish of the long dark hair hanging halfway down her bare back.

Pastor Jeremiah Spogel gave a whistling sigh. 'Yes, sirree...'

Barry leapt to his feet and clapped his hands together. 'Right, time we got you settled in, properly introduced and shown round.' He spread his arms and with a slightly nervous smile cried, 'Welcome to the Keswick Gospel Brotherhood annual camp, 1976!'

'Yeah, sure, thanks.' Pastor Spogel gave one last glance towards the group of semi-naked youngsters at the lakeside and heaved himself reluctantly to his feet. 'Gotta bottle of JD in my bag, maybe time to crack it... long time since breakfast.'

Summer 1976 and the remarkable drought and soaring temperatures that were desiccating the country had even reached the notoriously sodden Lake District. The fells were hazy in mute shades of orange, yellow and brown and constantly at risk from a carelessly discarded bottle, cigarette or malicious fire-raisers. Most of the lakes had retreated to levels not seen in living memory, exposing long-forgotten villages flooded by grasping utility companies, and previously unknown islands studded with petrified tree stumps. The fore shores had become treacherous and smelly aprons of algaed pebbles and the shallows and inlets just stagnant, fetid puddles.

The annual flood of visitors came regardless, of course, and while the elderly and frail cowered sweatily indoors, the young and fit relished the days of uninterrupted sunshine, dry paths, warm waters and balmy evenings. To the tourist industry the weather was a mixed blessing; brewers of the heavy, dark, local ales were left with unsold stock, while chilled lager sales soared, ice-creams replaced cream teas leaving many tea-rooms largely empty, and walking shops pushed aside their racks of boots and anoraks and scrambled to restock with sunhats and sandals. Meanwhile "*No vacancies*" signs had appeared in lacy windows, caravans clogged the lanes and tents, tepees and marquees sprang up around the lake shores. It was business as usual. Semi-permanent organised camps and "canvas villages" were everywhere; unsightly but tolerated by the authorities for a strictly limited number of weeks in the interest of the local economy. Most were occupied by university mountaineering clubs, Scouts, Guides, and rambling associations. But there were exceptions, and oddities.

Amongst these was the Keswick Gospel Brotherhood camp, which for some years had been allowed to pitch a large circular marquee and attendant cluster of sagging bell tents at the northern end of Derwent Water, where the camp occupied a little grassy spit with its own tongue of pebble beach reaching out into the lake. The KGB, as it was dryly referred to by the council department responsible for issuing the annual permit, was believed to be a loosely religious youth organisation with a vague and unspecific Christian ethos. Over recent years it had brought together youngsters of both sexes for summers of wholesome outdoor activities and fellowship: fell walking, sailing, kayaking and swimming were on offer, but attendance at an occasional prayer meeting or bible class was also expected.

The "campers" were a cross section of youngsters of secondary-school age from around the country and all social backgrounds. The only requirements for a child to attend camp were that the family had some sort of association with a church, or at least claimed to, that the child in question could swim, and that his or her parents' cheque cleared. Having met this criteria, most parents assumed their offspring would then spend the summer being vigorously exercised, both in body and soul, while making "suitable" friends in a morally healthy and closely supervised environment. And in previous years this had more or less proved to be the case. But this year, with the arrival of a nervous new camp leader and a fresh intake of keen but inexperienced helpers – mainly earnest young Sunday school teachers and theology undergraduates – some of the more worldly youngsters, sensing weakness, had asserted their control, with a corresponding decline in behaviour… and morals. The naïve leader and her unworldly assistants seemed to be blissfully unaware of the main preoccupations of the modern teenager, not least the sexual frisson that develops when a mixed group are largely left to their own devices and the weather provides a legitimate and God-sent reason for wearing next to no clothes. After a couple of chaotic weeks, and despite the best efforts of some of the more robust staff, including Barry, anarchy had indeed reigned. The appointed leader promptly left, taking with her several tearful helpers who, overwhelmed by the highly charged atmosphere, had worried they too might succumb to the increasing number of temptations and compromise future vocations or current vows.

Enter Pastor Jeremiah Spogel. This had not always been his name and it certainly wouldn't have been recognised by the string of recently bankrupted pyramid investors he'd left scattered across the Bible belt states of the USA, or the Internal Revenue Service of that country. And outraged members of some small-town congregations, who'd suddenly found themselves embarrassingly young grandparents, would claim never to have heard of him. No recognised church had ever owned up to him and his interpretation of the scriptures, particularly his ideas on pastoral care, were unorthodox to say the least. But he did have a certain brash charisma, his references were almost implausibly glowing and anyway, the agency didn't really have a choice: it was either a recently defrocked prison chaplain, Jeremiah Spogel or no fee.

'This is Pastor Spogel.'

A mixed group of young adults sitting on benches at a trestle table and nursing mugs looked up with hopeful interest. Their initial facial reactions were mixed, but it was clear the billowing shorts and floral shirt had made an impression. After a long pause there were a couple of muttered "hellos" and one of the more confident rose and offered a hand. 'We're so pleased you're here,' he said fervently. There were nods round the table. Barry sat down at the far end leaving their new leader standing at the other. Spogel looked round the marquee and waved at a bunch of boys hunched conspiratorially over a far table who'd turned to look suspiciously at the newcomer.

'Hiya fellas, howya doin'?' The boys turned back to their plotting. 'Guess I got a bit of ice-breaking to do, huh?'

Barry quickly went round the table rattling off names.

'Dandy,' Spogel said when he'd finished, clearly none the wiser. 'So how's it goin'? Anything I should know?'

The hand shaker half put his hand up. 'Two more kayaks have gone missing, that's six this week, and we haven't got enough paddles for the rest. Oh, and someone's drawn breasts on all the life jackets.' He looked meaningfully over at the table of boys.

'And have you seen what they've written on the bottom of the kayaks?' someone else chipped in. 'It started with "OOPS" and "SOS" but yesterday I saw an "OH SHIT" and… I'm sorry, Pastor, but… well, an "OH FUCK". And I'm sure they capsized on purpose!'

Spogel gave a snigger, but before he could respond further a plump blonde girl with acne and a heavy wooden crucifix slapped the table making everyone jump. It was clearly harder than she'd intended and she squeaked an apology before carrying on. 'It's just not good enough. No one will help, the kitchen is a disaster, people keep helping themselves and we haven't had a hot meal since that…

well, that hash thing you did, Barry, and that was two days ago. And the washing up still hasn't been done, they just point-blank refuse to do it and… oh, I can't do it all.' She was struggling to hold back tears. 'And the cockroaches are back too, they're everywhere… and flies and… ohhh,' she finished with a wail.

Apart from the girl's sniffy sobs there was silence while everyone looked up at Spogel, including the group of surly boys from the other side of the marquee. Spogel looked thoughtful, then beaming widely said: 'Well, you know how it goes… hey, kids will be kids. Say, let's go meet some, that gang down on the beach looked like a fine bunch. I just gotta dip into my tent for a moment then see y'all down there.' He turned quickly and lumbered out of the marquee.

Unbeknownst to Pastor Spogel the group of youngsters on the beach were in fact the inner cabal, the "in crowd", the more confident and assertive of the campers who, regardless of any attempts at discipline, had effectively hijacked the camp for their own pleasurable ends. By the time Spogel had finished "dipping" in his tent and met Barry on the beach, the group had long gone, piling into a couple of dinghies and heading for one of the islands for an afternoon of sunbathing, cheap cider, pot and skinny-dipping.

Mary Wainwright was amongst them. Although not part of the inner circle, her lustrous dark hair, smoky grey eyes and full figure made her an unsurprising favourite with the mainly male alpha group. She had a ready smile, a quick but not unkind wit and would gamely join in with any suggested activity, while cheerfully accepting that she wasn't particularly good at any of them. The ability to down a tin of cider in one, roll a two-skin joint, and her unashamed enjoyment of sex also endeared her to the less morally constricted. Uninspired in the more conventional arts, Mary's joyful enthusiasm and creativity in the matter of love-making created experiences and memories which some young men would carry through into middle age – and still not have bettered.

Dwindling camp discipline and a depleted staff of naive mentors meant opportunities for sun-drenched al fresco love were plentiful. Boisterous water fights in the lake often camouflaged several pairs of coupling teenagers, while numbers would steadily decrease during fell side rambles as couples slipped away into heathery hollows. Through the early summer, Mary had embraced this free-loving atmosphere, happily laughing and loving her way through the baking days and sultry nights taking lovers on a whim, but in recent weeks her affections seemed to have settled on just a small coterie of favourites.

She was lying on her back watching the dusty rays of sun filtering through the tangled canopy of leaves that projected a changing kaleidoscope of shadows on to her naked body. It was late afternoon, the group had the island to themselves and Mary could hear the distant voices of the others on the beach. Something tickled her left nipple and she turned her head to find him propped on one elbow gently stroking her breast with a fern frond. She chuckled and smiled.

'The others are packing up, how about we stay on for a while?'

'Yes, that'd be nice, our very own island.'

'They'll all manage in one boat, I'll go and tell them.' He stood up, pulled a ragged pair of cut-off jeans over his nakedness and disappeared barefoot into the undergrowth.

Mary shut her eyes and listened to the birds. There was chatter and laughter from the beach and someone was singing. She heard the scraping of a boat being dragged over pebbles, some splashing, muffled calls of farewell and then the voices faded. The undergrowth rustled and he reappeared, a large plastic bottle of cider in one hand and an old blanket tucked under his arm. 'Life's essentials,' he grinned and wriggled out of his shorts. Stretching out beside her he resumed the fern tickling, then taking a swig of cider leant over her and let some of the golden liquid dribble out of his mouth onto her breasts before covering her mouth with his and letting the rest flow between them. 'Well, what do you think?' he whispered wetly into her hair.

'I think it's all up to you,' she said quietly, slipping a hand down between them. 'Hmm.'

'It's nearly dark.' He was crouched between her legs sitting on his heels still panting slightly.

Mary stretched and groaned luxuriously. She closed her eyes and gently massaged her breasts. 'That...' she murmured, '...was very special.'

He leant forward and kissed her stomach. 'There's some moonlight, how about a swim?'

They slipped off a convenient rock, gasping with full immersion. Despite the heat of the day the water was chill, particularly out deeper where they turned and swam parallel to the shore for a while before returning to the shallows where, too tired to play, they gently washed and caressed each other in the moonlight.

The cooling lake set the usual evening breeze tumbling down the fell-side and the little boat bent to it skimming over the moon-flecked wavelets of the lake's surface.

'Mary...'

'Hmm?'

They had pulled the boat up the beach and were sitting side by side on the gunwale looking back down the lake.

'Are you still... well, what I mean is, now you and me seem to be... oh never mind, it's nothing.'

Mary stood up, put her hands on his shoulders and kissed the top of his head, then turned to walk up the beach and disappeared amongst the shadows of the tents.

The summer of searing days and sticky nights rolled on and started to take its toll; across the country the old and frail succumbed to the heat in headline-grabbing numbers, moorlands blazed and farmers predicted imminent ruin – and for once people believed them. At the KGB camp, enthusiasm for any activity which didn't involve total immersion had waned to nearly nothing and the morale of the remaining helpers was at rock bottom. The arrival of Pastor Jeremiah Spogel, far from inspiring them, had in fact led to the swift departure of several more of their number. Spogel himself was rarely seen, at least not in the camp. The rumour was that he was spending most of his time at a smart hotel at the other end of the lake, where, posing as a wealthy Jewish real-estate agent from Boston, he'd befriended a rich, sexually frustrated widow from New York.

In the meantime, despite the best efforts of Barry and one or two loyal lieutenants, the camp was steadily disintegrating: while the younger children, dirty, bored and surviving largely on sweets and "tuck" from home tended to stay around the site, many of the older youths had gravitated to the town with its pubs, chip shops and shop-lifting opportunities. An additional fascination had been provided by the recent arrival of several biker gangs in the town. This was an annual migration of "chapters", some bitter rivals, who converged menacingly on Keswick every summer. They drank and fought late into the night, knives down their boots and sharpened chains round their necks. By day, bristling and sinister behind the regulation sunglasses, they stalked the tourist-choked streets in their scuffed leathers and greasy "colours" filling any confined space with a miasma of sweat and petunia oil.

Indirectly, it was the bikers who finally settled the fate of the Keswick Gospel Brotherhood camp. When at three o'clock one morning the daughter of an Elim Pentecostalist from Cheltenham came roaring into the camp on the back of a huge Harley-Davidson, naked except for bikini pants and too drunk to stand, Barry decided something had to be done. He would call a meeting.

'Right, guys, listen up.'

There was immediate quiet in the marquee. Barry looked round and grinned. He was fairly sure he had full attendance, at least of the older campers, which after recent days was an achievement in itself. He'd employed two lures: alcohol – he'd placed a case of lager and another of cider on a table by the entrance flap and encouraged everyone to help themselves – and secondly, himself. Barry was well liked by all the youngsters, he listened, didn't patronise and treated them all, boys and girls, as equals. It was known that he ran a boys' club in a rough area of south London where he coached boxing, which gave him kudos with the boys, while his muscular good looks and easy nature made him a favourite with the girls. The fact he was a black man also gave him a certain cache, particularly with the more provincial youngsters.

'OK, everyone got a drink? Don't tell on me, will you?' There was general laughter, and now they were fellow conspirators. 'OK, I wanted to get you all together because we're not here much longer, some have gone already and some of you are going home very soon. And I know things have been a bit… well, chaotic recently, meals and things…' There were some wry chuckles in his audience and a 'Too right!' from somewhere near the back. '…and then there not being enough kit for everyone,' Barry continued, looking stern for the first time. A few boys, also near the back, looked quickly at their knees. Barry held the silence for several moments. 'Right, well here's the plan; we're in the Lake District, you've probably noticed the lakes, what's left of them…' Missing equipment was forgotten, tension relieved, and there were laughs all round. '…but you may also have noticed the odd mountain…' More chuckles. '…and you've probably also noticed that some are quite big and some are quite small. Well, we're going to climb one, all of us, together… and it's going to be a big one! One of the biggest!' There were actually a couple of cheers in the marquee. 'I'm not going to tell you which one, it's a surprise, but the day after tomorrow I want you all here at eight o'clock.' A few groans. 'I'll make sure there are picnics, OK? That's a promise. Right, any questions?'

One of the girls near the front put her hand up. 'Are we walking from here or what?'

'Good point. No, we need to get to the starting point. I would have suggested the mini buses but... well, there seem to be some parts missing, quite a lot actually...' The same heads near the back looked down again. '...so they're knackered. We'll have to get the bus. Fares covered,' he added quickly. 'Any more questions? No, good. Help me finish the booze then, and go and polish up those boots!' There was the odd whoop and general laughter, almost an air of excitement.

Barry hoped it would last.

It didn't.

During the twenty-four hours prior to the planned walk, Barry was presented with a diverse and imaginative rash of health-related excuses, a rash indeed being one of them, of the heat variety. Amongst the others, athlete's foot was apparently rampant, there was an epidemic of sprained ankles, an outbreak of food poisoning (actually quite plausible), a nasty groin strain – that was the Pentecostalist's daughter – and one self-diagnosed case of legionnaires' disease. Other refuseniks had simply reconsidered, and emboldened by their forays into the real world of carousing holidaymakers, brawling Hell's Angels, pubs, drugs and casual sex, simply refused to turn up.

In the end, less than twenty turned up at the appointed hour to hear Barry explain that they'd be catching the local bus to a village called Threlkeld from where they would set off up the mighty mountain of Blencathra. He had, he said, chosen one of the more "interesting" routes. 'A real challenge,' he assured them, an achievement to be proud of and a fitting end to their summer adventure. As they traipsed towards the bus stop, and unnoticed by Barry, two girls slipped away from the back of the crowd and dived into a convenient cafe. Half an hour later it was just sixteen youngsters who disembarked from the crowded bus and stood peering up through the hazy morning light at the dizzying ridges that converged on the distant summit. There were urgent muttered conversations going on and after a moment, with much head shaking and not a word to Barry, a group of four crossed the road to the opposite bus stop and stood staring pointedly in the direction of the recently departed bus.

Barry watched impassively, shrugged and fixed a smile, then made encouraging noises to his depleted band, turned and set off up the parched mountainside. The path was obvious and he made a point of not looking back, setting a steady pace and not stopping until he reached a small grassy plateau about twenty minutes later. He turned and looked back down the line of panting teenagers; another one gone… no, two.

'Everyone all right?' He got a few grunts in response and did a quick head count – ten left. 'What happened to Jake and, er…?'

'Matt.'

'Yes, Matt.'

'Twisted ankles.'

'What, both of them?'

No one bothered to reply.

'There's the bus,' one of the girls suddenly shouted.

'It's coming back. Going to Keswick,' she added. Everyone turned to look down at the twisted lace of distant road and the toy vehicles that wound along it.

'We'd never make it,' someone muttered.

'Right,' Barry slapped his thighs, 'a quick sip of water everyone, not too much, then onwards and upwards.'

An hour later, at the start of a vertiginous rocky edge that would eventually lead to the summit, four more deserted. Barry had given up asking for reasons and none were offered, although one girl did sweetly thank him for a "nice morning" before setting off down the mountain. Barry looked round the remains of his expedition. There were now six of them; four boys, who Barry was fairly sure were only there because Mary Wainwright was, Mary herself, pleasant and friendly as usual but a bit quiet he thought, distracted; and another girl, who seemed fiercely determined not to let one of the boys out of her sight.

'Well,' Barry turned and looked up at the near vertical crag which started the ridge and tried to swallow his nervousness, 'this is it, the best bit. Now the fun starts.'

'I told you! Wasn't that brilliant? We've done it, we've bloody well done it!' It was rare for Barry to swear, and only then when he was in the grip of some fierce emotion – on this occasion, relief. A back-street city boy, he'd never attempted anything like this before, an actual mountain, and more than once in the last hour he'd not only doubted the whole thing but been outright terrified. 'Come on, up you come.' One of the boys had appeared over the edge and Barry held out a hand, which was ignored. Mary Wainwright was next and allowed herself to be helped.

'Welcome to Blencathra.' Barry patted her on the shoulder. 'Well done, you've done it, we've all done it!'

The summit proved to be a large, smooth dome already occupied by quite a crowd: picnicking families, chattering rambling clubs and wistful lone hikers wishing they had the place to themselves. Barry led his little group away from the highest point to a parched grassy patch looking to the south and west where they sprawled gratefully in the dust and ate squashed sandwiches, fragments of crisps and bruised apples.

One of the boys flipped his apple core over the edge. 'We're not going down the same way are we?' he demanded.

'No, no, there's a much easier way, over there somewhere, where those people are coming up now.'

The boy stared at him for a moment. 'Then why the fuck didn't we come up that way?'

'Language,' Barry said mildly, 'I thought the challenge, the adventure, you know… don't you feel a sense of…?'

'No.'

'Nor do I.' It was the sulky girl.

'Well, there we are,' Barry said soothingly, 'we're up here now and look at this.' He swept his arm around the horizon. Revived by food and enthused by relief he started to point out the smudged outlines of various distant peaks, unerringly misidentifying them. 'After this,' he patted the parched turf affectionately, 'we could all climb any one of those. What do you think?'

This was met with surly dismissals by most of the boys, a sulky frown from the jealous girl and a politely disinterested smile from Mary. She was sitting a little apart from the rest of the group, sometimes glancing over at them thoughtfully but apparently happier today with her own company. After a few moments she got up and drifted quietly away to a craggy outcrop near the edge of the steep slope and stood quite still for some minutes gazing towards the distant town, lost, invisible behind the shoulders of lesser mountains, only hinted at by its own heat shimmer. Slivers of the languid lake reflected the early afternoon sun. When she returned to the group she quietly told them she'd be leaving the camp tomorrow; her parents were driving up and she was going home for what was left of the holiday. To those who'd noticed, this explained Mary's slightly sad and distracted air. She would be leaving behind many friends. Her announcement prompted the usual promises of letters, calls and reunions but Mary had clearly decided this was the moment to make her goodbyes; she gave Barry a sisterly hug, smiled reassuringly at her would-be rival and chastely pecked each of the boys carefully on a cheek… the summer was over.

The next day she was gone.

THREE

'Haven't you had enough?'

Dom flinched but filled his glass to the brim anyway, then waved the bottle at the rest of the table in offer... or defiance. Either way he managed to deposit a generous slug on the tablecloth. 'Who's for more? Go on...' There were weak smiles and shaken heads around the table, hands were placed over glasses. An embarrassed silence descended on the company broken only by the hisses escaping from the corner of their hostess's mouth as she dabbed fiercely at her damask.

'Oh, go on then, just a splash, keep it in the glass if you can, ha ha...' The speaker half rose from his chair and proffered his glass. 'George!' the woman on his right snapped, and he sat down again with a bump. 'I think we've all had enough, don't you? Of everything, I mean,' she added hurriedly. 'It's been a lovely evening thank you, Beverley.'

There were muttered affirmations from round the table.

'Oh for Chrissake! Don't be all so bloody tight-arsed, c'mon have a drink.'

'Dom!'

'Go on, George old mate, you have a port, never mind the old... well, never mind. Here...' Dom tried to slide the bottle across the crumpled cloth. 'Oh well caught, Deird! Go on, help yourself, love, then George, he's on your left, got to follow the eti... wotsit.' Dom gulped down half his glass spotting his shirtfront.

'Etiquette,' George said.

'S'right,' Dom nodded sagely. 'Better pass it, Deird, doesn't slide very well... goes to the left,' he mumbled.

Deirdre carefully placed the bottle down the table out of reach of Dom or her husband and a new silence settled.

'Oh, come on,' Dom pleaded, 'the night is yet young.' He suddenly brightened. 'An' it's a celebration. *I'm* going on holiday, gotta little trip to make... bon voyage and sod the rest of you,' he cackled, and drained his glass. 'Well, if you're not going to... c'mon Deird, hand it over.' He lunged across the table and snatched up the bottle. 'Been summoned, I have,' he continued, 'all very mysterious, something "to my advantage", so they say.' He refilled his glass, took a large swig and looked thoughtful. 'To my a'vantage,' he repeated slowly, savouring the words with the solemn concentration of the very drunk.

The dinner guests had already heard all about the mysterious letter earlier in the evening, several times, but some of them managed polite nods and smiles while napkins were crumpled and chairs pushed back.

Dom topped up his glass. 'Bev thinks it's a woman, don't you, dear heart? Chance'd be a fine thing. Wouldn't mind a bit,' he mused, 'gone a bit short on the old shaggy-waggy front recently haven't we, sweetness? The old pork sword hasn't seen a lot of…'

His wife slapped him… hard. The full glass of port flew neatly into Deird's lap and, ducking to avoid another blow, Dom cracked his lower jaw on the table edge and crumpled to the floor.

Beverley grimaced apologetically at Deirdre whose lap was being piled with discarded napkins, then rose briskly to her feet, taking the opportunity to grind one heel into the back of her husband's outflung hand, and started to usher her guests around his unconscious body and into the hall.

As usual, the morning after, Dom awoke in a daze of contrition – and the spare bedroom. Then he rang in sick and started calling round the previous evening's guests. And, as usual, he tried to excuse himself on the grounds of having had a "lousy day at the office" which, increasingly, was true. In fact, the day before had been beyond "lousy". As he'd bemoaned to the loyal George over "a couple of swift ones" in the Cock 'n' Cat on the way home from the station, it had been "fucking shitty".

Dom already knew he'd failed to hit his target again, and probably by a bigger margin than last month, so he was half expecting a summons. But usually these "performance reviews", as they were innocuously titled, came with plenty of notice, so that day's post-lunchtime call had completely caught him off guard. Apart from anything else there was his breath. Lunchtime drinking wasn't exactly banned at the bank but it was frowned upon, and having cupped a hand over his nose and mouth Dom was wishing to God he'd stuck to vodka.

The meeting had been even worse than he'd anticipated. He'd held his breath a lot and sat well back in his chair but had still felt skewered by the bumptious young manager's tight-smiled disapproval. During a brisk thirty minutes of convoluted management-speak it was explained that after his latest returns someone, somewhere on some upper floor had some "concerns". Furthermore, HR had concluded that Dominic (his tormentor pointedly refused to use the familiar diminutive) was almost clientless, technologically inept and a "non-team-player". It was begrudgingly acknowledged that "apparently" Dominic had given long and loyal service, however, the boy-manager explained with his only genuine smile of the meeting, the corporate landscape had changed, there were reviews in the pipeline and some "streamlining" was inevitable. Oh, and he'd asked for a report on Dominic's pension status.

Dom had felt something cold clutch his stomach and the skin prickle hot on the back of his hands. He thought of the years of mortgage still to pay off on the Surrey house (actually it was in Sussex but Bev had settled for a Surrey postcode), the two university loans he was subsidising and the outrageous lease/purchase agreements on the two BMWs.

His smirking tormentor had allowed himself a few seconds of sadistic pleasure at Dom's obvious shock, then without another word had sprung to his feet and strode briskly from the glass-fronted "interview booth", leaving Dom to consider his immediate future. Oblivious to the curious glances of passing colleagues and minions he wasn't sure how long he'd remained there, slumped and miserable in a haze of Polo mints and stale Scotch.

As usual, pre-dinner party, Dom's homecoming had been greeted by an atmosphere of bad-tempered panic and impatience.

'Where the hell have you been?' was the snarled greeting. 'As if I didn't know!'

'Honey, I'm home,' Dom muttered in a fake mid-Atlantic drawl.

'God, your breath!' Dom slunk mumbling up the stairs. 'And make sure you change your shirt,' she shouted at his retreating back, 'and gargle some bloody mouthwash!' She picked his jacket up off a chair and threw it into a cupboard. 'Or weed-killer!' she bellowed as an afterthought.

Dom had made his ablutions last as long as possible so it was only a few minutes before the first guests arrived when he'd crept down into the hall and started opening his post. He didn't bother with most of it, anything brown or with a window was put straight back on the pile, but the stiff white envelope with a London postmark and the franked name of a firm of solicitors caught his eye. Dom didn't get letters from solicitors very often, usually only when he'd misjudged the timing on settling a bill.

Bev stalked out of the kitchen just as he inserted his thumbnail under the flap. 'So what have you done now?' she demanded.

'Eh?'

'Solicitors. How much do you owe now? (It was always "you", never "we".) Why else would they be writing to you?'

He stopped ripping. 'Have you been looking at my post?' he demanded.

'Still sealed, isn't it?' she snapped, and disappeared back into a cloud of steam to berate the new caterers.

Dom hadn't understood the letter at first. Although fairly used to "business-speak" he'd found himself bemused by the almost punctuation-less legalese and unfamiliar phrasing. And the content seemed so unlikely, it was only after a third reading and a careful examination of the embossed list of partners that he started to believe it wasn't some sort of scam.

'Have you sorted the wine?' She didn't wait for a reply and dived back into the kitchen fog.

Dom decided it was probably best not to mention the letter to anyone until he'd rung the advised number for verification in the morning – well, maybe he'd just tell George. Then the doorbell rang.

* * *

'Don't shoot!'

The girl's arms shot straight up and she tried to get to her feet but got tangled in the high-heeled sandals she'd kicked off under the desk and ended up sprawled across the work-station sending half a beaker of warm Coke flying across the room in the process. The two *Guardia Civil,* their pistols holstered, stopped uncertainly, taken aback by the hysterical reaction. The one nearest the desk started dabbing at his wet trouser leg. Seconds later, several grim-faced men in suits, waving badges and crumpled documents, shoved aside the remains of the splintered entrance doors and charged towards the inner office.

'*Sientate!*' the last one shouted at the girl, who had managed to gain her feet, arms still straight up.

'*Sientate!*'

The girl shrugged and shook her head nervously, 'I don't… *No hablo…*' she started.

'*Callate!*'

The girl burst into tears.

Shaking his head in disgust the suited man snapped some orders to the *Guardia* and headed after his colleagues. At the door he turned and stabbed a finger at the tearful girl. 'No phone, no e-mail!' he shouted in English, and shoved his way on into the inner office, already snapping orders and commands.

The *Guardia* with dry trousers tried to get the girl to sit down with gentle patting motions. She eventually got the message and sat, arms still straight above her, fingers spread. The *Guardia* continued with his patting motions, smiling uncertainly, before finally reaching over and taking one of her hands, which he lowered to the height of her shoulder. He pointed at the other and carried on patting. The girl placed her hands in her lap. The *Guardia* nodded his approval.

Another figure appeared in the outer doorway, a plump, rather masculine woman also in the uniform of the *Guardia Civil*, her tunic straining over an ample bosom and stomach and her hand resting on a small black holster at her belt. The two men immediately deferred, they stepped away from the desk and Damp Trousers stopped dabbing.

Even so, the woman eyed his crotch, gave a twisted smile and sneered a sharp remark in Spanish. Damp Trousers reddened and nodded towards the girl.

'*Nombre?*' the woman snapped at the desk.

The girl looked at her uncertainly. '*No hablo…*' she ventured again and looked hopefully at the kinder *Guardia*. He cleared his throat nervously and muttered something to the woman. She paused for a moment stroking the holster, then grim-faced turned to the girl again.

'English?'

'*Si…* yes, yes I am,' the girl blurted with obvious relief. 'I don't know what's happening,' she wailed, indicating the shattered doors, 'and…'

'Passport!'

'Er… I…'

'Passport! You speak English, yes?' The woman held out her hand.

'It's not here. I can get it.' She started to stand up. 'It won't take…'

'*Sientate,* sit down!'

'But I…'

'Shut up!'

The girl started to cry again and the kindly male *Guardia* looked uncomfortable. The woman went round the desk, unnecessarily shoving the girl on the way, and started pulling out drawers and tipping their contents onto the floor.

'There's nothing here,' the girl sobbed, 'I just answer the phone… and make the tea. I could get some tea?' she offered hopefully.

Sounds of filing cabinet drawers being slammed, raised

voices and general ransacking had been coming from behind the frosted inner doors for a while, when several of the suited men reappeared carrying computers, heavy boxes and polythene bags full of papers and files. As they went out through the shattered outer doors one of them said something to the woman. She nodded back, banged the drawer she was holding down on the desktop and grabbed the receptionist by her blonde ponytail, forcing her head back and her breasts forward. The girl squeaked in shock. The woman stared down at the exposed cleavage for a moment: 'Where is Willer?' she snarled. 'And Jack's son?'

'I don't know, I don't know any Willer, or Jack... or his son.'

The woman snorted but let go of her hair, the back of her hand brushing the girl's breast on its way back to the holster. She said something in Spanish to the two male *Guardia* and stalked out snapping her fingers over her shoulder for them to follow.

'So, you think it would be a good idea to get out of it for a bit, is that what you're saying?'

'Yeah, that's about it, Gav. And so does *Senor* Gomez here.' He nodded at the slim grey-haired man sitting tight-kneed and expressionless on the black leather sofa. Gomez had not reacted to the sound of his name or any of the previous conversation, although unbeknownst to his client and his Spanish-speaking aide, the lawyer spoke perfect English.

'Back to the UK, d'you reckon?'

'Doesn't really matter, just out, and don't leave a

forwarding address for the moment. Gomez and I will manage things here 'til this new mayor gets the hang of things. And he will,' he added reassuringly. 'They all play the anti-corruption card during the elections...' Unnoticed, the Spanish lawyer had given the tiniest wince at the "C" word. '...and it's always the developers who get it in the neck first, especially the time-share boys, and especially the Brits. One or two might get an early morning visit, then a few ex-pat pensioners end up with a pile of rubble and a fat legal bill and our new boy can claim he's carried out his manifesto pledges. Then... well, it's never long before it's business as usual, you know how it always goes.'

'Yeah, I do. So what's so different this time, Jacko? Why can't we just lie low for a bit, maybe move out of Marbella for a while? We could stay down at the Puerto villa, pretend we were just renting it; you know, long-term tourists, move the boat down and everything. Nothing's in my name and we're not really known down there. And anyway, I've still got the other passport and...' *Senor* Gomez cleared his throat and Gavin looked at him suspiciously.

His aide ignored the Spaniard. 'It might be best to save that for getting... um, going away,' he muttered. Then, 'Look, Gav, I've just got a feeling, I'm sure it'll be fine but...'

'You really think it's necessary, Jacko?'

'Gav, look, the dodgy planning bit and the bungs to the old mayor and his pals, we can sort that. And the time-share stuff; if some dozy pensioner from Essex gets conned out of his life savings the authorities here don't give a toss. They'll rap a few knuckles, it's all part of the electioneering, and then it'll all be forgotten – until next time. But just at the moment… all this attention, it's not good for the other stuff.' He glanced at the inscrutable Gomez and made long eye contact with Gavin, '…Morocco.'

'What, you think that might…?'

'I'm just saying I think it's time to disappear for a while. And out of Spain.'

'Hello, babe, what's going on?' A flimsy floral wrap had wafted in from the balcony.

'Oh hi, Jacko.' The blonde bob turned in the direction of the sofa. '*Hola, senora,*' she added brightly, nodding at the Spaniard.

'It's *senor,* love,' Gavin sighed.

'Oh, sorry, I mean, *perdon,*' she giggled, and started to settle on the arm of her husband's chair, happily tucking a knot of the wrap down her gaping cleavage.

'Er, this is business, love, all boring legal stuff.'

She pouted and looked little-girl hurt but there was a shrewd glint in the heavily lined eyes as she tousled her husband's hair. 'Oh, babe.'

Gavin sighed heavily again and smoothed his hair back into place. 'Yeah, well OK, I guess as you're here now it's as good a time as any.' Jacko raised his eyebrows in warning but Gavin just gave him a tiny nod of reassurance and carried on. 'Look, love, Jacko and *Senor* Gomez here think it would be good for business if I was to pop back to the UK for a while. You know, keep up the old contacts, put my face round the old manor and keep the investors back there happy… and things. When the boys break up and get here, Jacko will arrange for you all to move down to the Puerto pad while I'm away. You can get the boat moved down in time, can't you, Jacko? Good. Oh, and the new jet-ski? Might as well get it delivered straight there. OK, Jacko? So there you go.' Gavin patted her bare leg. 'You and the kids'll have a ball and I'll get down to you as soon as I'm done back home.'

'It's about that letter, isn't it?' his wife demanded, ignoring the proposed arrangements.

In truth, Gavin had completely forgotten about that; it had arrived earlier that day, he'd flicked through it once, been mildly intrigued and tossed it onto his cluttered desk meaning to discuss it with Jacko later. Obviously his incurably nosey and distrustful wife had found and read it.

'No, that's not…' Gavin stopped abruptly. It suddenly occurred to him he'd just been handed the perfect excuse for returning to the UK, and soon. 'Well look, it's something that needs to be looked at. A bit of business to our advantage it said, that's right isn't it, Jacko?' He winked.

The factotum had no idea what he was talking about. He'd quietly taken a call and been on his phone for the last few minutes, missing the exchange between Gavin and his suspicious wife. His face was grim. 'Of course, Gav,' he nodded. 'Be daft not to.'

Senor Gomez was thanked and dismissed and Gavin showed the letter to Jacko, who was immediately wary, instinctively suspicious of any legal correspondence.

'"Something to your advantage", sounds a bit too good to be true, doesn't it, Gav? I'd better ring around and do a bit of checking.' Gavin picked up the letter again and started re-reading it. 'Never mind that for a minute,' Jacko said, 'that call was from that guy John at St Sebastian's.'

Gavin carried on reading. 'Oh yeah, what the lot that took over our old place, the God squad charity?'

'Yeah. They've been raided.'

Gavin looked up sharply. 'Coincidence?'

'Nope, they were asking for a "Willer" and "Jack's son".'

'You and me.'

'Sounds like it.'

Gavin thrust the letter at Jacko. 'Right, you do that checking and get hold of Bruce and find out when he's taking the Lear over to Blackpool next.'

'He normally takes a batch on Fridays, weather allowing.'

'Hum, doesn't leave much time.' Gavin slid his sunglasses down his forehead. 'Right, I'll go and make the peace,' he sighed, hoisting himself off the leather cushions and heading for the sun-bleached balcony where his wife was sulkily flicking foam off the surface of the jacuzzi.

'Gavin,' Jacko called after him, 'tell her to start packing.'

* * *

'Would you do that at home, WOULD YOU? Is that what you use *your* towels for, eh? No, I bet you don't, even people like you wouldn't…' He shook the bundle of heavily soiled towels he was holding at arm's length then hurled them into the middle of the table, splattering food and spilling drinks. For a moment, apparently appalled at his own actions, he looked down at the mess, then round at the occupants of the table, realised there was no going back and erupted again: 'Yes, actually you probably fucking would!'

There were appalled gasps and other exclamations of genteel distress from around the crowded dining room but Greg couldn't stop now: 'Yes, I can see you lot living in squalor like… like pigs!' He picked up an eggy fork and stabbed at the pile of soiled towels. 'No, no, pigs at least have the good manners to clean up after themselves and kick their own shit out the door, which is more than you lot…'

'Just oo the 'ell do you fink you're talking to?' Predictably it was the matriarch of the clan who'd reacted first. Her husband was still gawping and struggling to free his belly from under the table edge, hampered by the pile of spilt crockery which had collected in his lap. She'd heaved herself to her feet and Greg found himself peering down into a sunburnt chasm of livid freckles and blurred butterflies. 'I said, oo the bleedin' 'ell do you…?'

'Mam, I got egg all over.' The top of a small stubbled head was just visible above the pile of filthy towels. He, or possibly she, was ignored.

'Eh, eh? Oo djer think yer talkin' at? Take our fuckin' money quick enough. In advance,' she added disgustedly, 'so we expec' some service, yeah?' She swept the whole pile of laundry onto the floor taking most of the breakfast setting with it. 'Service!' she snarled. 'We pay, you fuckin' clear up, that's 'ow it works, *sweetie*,' she finished, with a simpering sneer.

'Yeah.' His wife's abrupt table clearance had allowed her husband to release his paunch and he too had lumbered to his feet. 'Yeah, 's'right, don' you speak to my family like that!'

'Ma…am!'

'Shurrup, Tyson, yer dad's gettin' goin.''

'Eh?' The man of the moment looked startled. There

wasn't anything else, that was it, he'd shot his load. He looked round the room desperately, perhaps hoping for support, but no one was going to meet his eye. After the initial shock, the other diners had adopted the usual British approach to an ongoing embarrassment and were pretending nothing was happening. Most were concentrating hard on rearranging cutlery and cruet sets or had suddenly become absorbed in the six-item breakfast menu – apart from a middle-aged Japanese couple who were watching intently from the bay window, fingering their cameras hopefully.

'Well, yeah…' the father eventually managed, looking aggressively round the room again. 'I's a dump anyhow,' he sneered, sending heads ducking back into empty cereal bowls and prompting further feverish cutlery fiddling. '… *and* the chips are crap!'

'Get out,' Greg said quietly. 'All of you, get out, now!'

But Tyson's dad was on a roll; he might have already played his "chips" trump card but now he was really ready to "get goin". 'So what about all this poncey old stuff lyin' about then, what's that all about, eh?'

'Sherlock Holmes,' Greg muttered. 'Now just *get out.*'

'Bleedin' old 'ats and pipes an' those cloak things.' The man waved a podgy blue arm round the room. 'And them stupid old film posters… wha's all that crap then? Ain't even got *Star Wars*, 'ave yer? And books, bleedin' books everywhere!' he added in disgust.

'It's our theme, sir.' The voice was firmly polite, soothing. 'The Sherlock Holmes novels of Arthur Conan Doyle and the films made from them, it's the theme for our establishment. But I don't think that need concern you or your family any longer. As my partner has suggested, I think now it would be best if you would all go back to your room, pack your things and vacate the premises immediately. I will prepare your bill.' He looked down at the debris of the breakfast table. 'We'll deduct the price of this morning's breakfast… I suppose.' He turned and gently steered Greg towards the kitchen.

'Fuckin' poofs!'

'Martin…' Greg whispered, more a plea than a warning, but his partner was already moving slowly back towards the family group. He glanced briefly at the mottled bosoms thrust aggressively at him and wrinkled his nose.

'Yeah? Go on!' Her lips were twisted viciously, the porcine eyes blazing as the chin and breasts competed to jut the furthest.

Martin ignored her. He collected the last few items remaining on their table and was headed back towards the swing doors when he stopped suddenly as if he'd just remembered or heard something. He turned and looked past the Japanese couple sitting in the bay and stared intently at something outside the large bay window. Most heads in the room instinctively turned to follow his stare and when the woman followed suit Martin neatly flipped a large ramekin of Mr Colman's finest and hottest English mustard into the gaping outraged cleavage.

'I can't believe you did that, it was… well, it was fantastic, magnificent!' Greg sat slumped in the old wooden chair in the kitchen while Martin gently rubbed his shoulders and neck.

'I'm sorry, Mart, I shouldn't have let it… let them, get

to me. I actually said "fucking", you know? It was just...' He suddenly jerked upright and his voice quivered. 'Oh my god, Tripadvisor!'

Martin gently pushed his head forward again. 'Never mind, it doesn't matter, they'll brag about it down at their local for a few days then pick another fight and move on, that sort always do. Don't worry, now relax.'

'I know, but... Christ!' Greg's head was up again. 'Did you see the shit on those towels? What were they thinking of? Bloody animals! And why? God knows we put out plenty of toilet paper, and tissues, and they had loads left, I checked. It was disgusting, unspeakable, uggh!' He shuddered. 'I need a shower and those bloody towels, well, we'd better burn them. And we'll send *them* the bloody bill, and they won't pay of course but then we'll bloody sue and then we'll bloody well...'

'It was chocolate.'

'What?'

'Those stains, the brown marks on the towels, it was chocolate.'

'But I thought...'

'Yes, I know what you thought. And so do most of our guests now,' Martin added dryly, 'but it was chocolate. One of their porky brats left a couple of those giant economy bars on the storage heater when they all went out to get pissed last night. Anyway, that was the mess and that was their attempt to clear it up.' He gently pushed Greg's head forward again and started to knead up the back of his neck.

'Oh God.'

Martin had felt the tremors of misery through his

fingertips even before Greg's despairing wail. 'C'mon, Gigi, c'mon, it's all right. It'll be fine. What you need's a break, get away from this bloody madhouse.'

'What, mid-season? I can't. I couldn't, how would you manage? It wouldn't be fair on you, you work just as hard, what with the cooking as well…'

'Look, we'll manage, I'll manage, for a while anyway. Of course you'll be missed but we *will* manage.'

'Really? I…' Greg swallowed a developing sob.

'Of course, I'll get Derek in.'

'Derek! Are you mad? Look what happened at Easter, he nearly killed that bloody American woman.'

'Be fair, it was her poodle he nearly killed.'

'Whatever, the insurers said we were never to let him on the premises again… not even as a guest. And the microwave was never the same again either,' Greg added with a sudden giggle.

'That's better. C'mon, let's plan to get you out of here for a few days. Lisa's home from uni at the end of the week too; she's quite good when she turns up, and she always needs the money. We'll miss you but we'll cope. Look, what about that meeting in Keswick, in that letter. Why not get away and tie it in with that?'

'Oh that's a scam, Mart,' Greg interrupted, 'you know it is. Come on you're the one who always smells these things out. God knows what sort of mess I'd have got myself into without that nose of yours. Remember that Spanish time-share thing?'

'Yes, well, that could have been a good buy… if the island had existed.'

'Exactly. So doesn't this ring your alarm bells?'

'Funnily enough, no it doesn't. Go and get me the letter again and I'll get these towels in the machine.'

Two days later it was settled. Martin had quietly rung the London solicitors and assured himself, and in turn Greg, that the firm did exist, the invitation was genuine and if Greg turned up at the mysterious meeting he really would find it to his advantage.

In the meantime, Greg had obviously been giving his prospective break some thought. To Martin's surprise he'd announced that rather than just take the car or the bus and check into a nice lakeside hotel or spa for a couple of days, if it was all right with Martin, he'd take a little longer, maybe four or five days, and hike to Keswick. He planned to follow a zigzag route up through the Lakes taking in some of their old favourite walks and summits on the way. It would also be a bit of a business trip, he suggested to Martin; he could carry out market research en route, checking out other guest houses: how busy they were, new menu ideas, current trends and fads and interior design themes – maybe their Sherlock Holmes thing had had its day.

Martin was dubious. He was even more sceptical when Greg added he'd also be taking their old tent and camping gear and, weather allowing, would spend the odd night out on the fells, 'Like we used to in the old days.'

'Are you sure, Gigi? It's a different world since we used to do that, you know.'

It was Greg's turn to be reassuring. Eventually a date was set, frayed maps and guidebooks were rooted out and Martin was persuaded to join in with the planning and preparations.

*\ *\ *

'OK, Robbie?'

'Yeah, thanks, guys. Look, I'm really sorry… again.'

'No problem, *sir*, that's what we're here for but do take care and…' the lifeboatman glanced along the pontoon and lowered his voice, '…do us all a favour, Robbie, get that fucking engine fixed and buy yourself a depth sounder.' The RIB started to pull away. 'Oh, and by the way, they're on you in The Mermaid later, and the box'll be on the bar, notes only!' He gave a thumbs-up and the huge twin outboards roared away.

Robbie braced himself against the wash and grimaced after the boat. He'd barely be able to afford a round of drinks for the lifeboat crew let alone a respectable donation to the RNLI – and they'd all be watching. And as for getting the engine sorted, well, forget it. He looked round the chaotic cockpit of the old boat. It was the inevitable tangle of dripping ropes and bundled sails which always followed one of his regular mid-Solent emergencies. God, he couldn't even make it over to the Isle of Wight without getting into trouble these days. The stained decking and grey woodwork exposed by chipped and peeling varnish ("*brightwork*" my arse!) seemed to mock him as he surveyed the battered remains of his dreams of independence and adventure. This was all that was left, this ancient, scruffy little wooden capsule, all that was left after years of ill-advised Green business ventures and expensive experiments in free love and marriage. This was it, his sole asset, security, and for the moment his home – as long as he could keep finding the marina fees.

Robbie shrugged, he supposed it could be worse. He slid back the hatch. 'OK, love, you can come up now.' The sweet smell of marijuana wafted up the companionway followed by a tousled blonde head. Robbie reached down. 'Give us a drag, I could do with something. Don't suppose you've left any wine, have you? No, thought not.'

'Got plenty of something else left though,' the blonde pouted, ''s long as you've got...' Her voice tailed off dreamily and she watched Robbie, shaggy and dishevelled, absent-mindedly coiling a frayed rope, '... you know.'

'Oh yes, I know.' He tossed the rope into a corner, breathed out slowly and passed the limp remains of the joint down to the girl. 'And that's the best offer I've had today,' he grinned, 'apart from those guys towing us off Grimble Bank, of course.' She slapped playfully at his calves and peeled off her soiled T-shirt.

'You sure about that?'

Robbie glanced along the pontoon. 'Get them down below,' he said, gently pushing her head down below the level of the hatch. 'Go on, I'm just coming.'

'Shame!'

'Go on!' The bared breasts and blonde mop disappeared. Robbie lifted the lid of a locker, scooped the frayed rope into it and plucked out a half-full bottle of whisky. He took a long pull, dropped it back in, and quietly closed the lid. His secret stash. 'Coming!'

'Ooh, you!'

The marina was one of the less salubrious on the south coast. It was tucked up a muddy, rarely dredged tributary of one of the larger rivers, which spewed its polluted sediments out into the English Channel, and housed a disproportionately large number of derelicts – not all of them boats. Even those craft still afloat rarely left their moorings, at least not intentionally. The general air of decay and neglect also seemed to have infected the few staff. They moved listlessly around the scruffy sheds and yards, and the office administrators were notorious for their rudeness and casual unhelpfulness. So when Margo Cox-Robinson stormed in, slammed a huge handbag down on the counter and demanded attention it was inevitable she would be ignored.

'Excuse me!'

A hand flapped. 'Just a minute.'

Several passed. 'I said, "Excuse me!"'

'I heard, we all heard.'

'So?'

'So, just a minute.'

'Look, all I want to know is where I can find Robin Cox-Robinson's boat. I don't know what he calls it these days.'

'*Her*, not *it*; boats are *shes* and *she's* called *Idler*.'

'How bloody appropriate!'

The marina manager put down the catalogue he'd been poring over and spun his chair round to look at Margo for the first time. 'Hmm.' He reached over the desk. 'Here, if he's on board you can give him these.' He proffered a bundle of envelopes. 'And make sure he gets that brown one, it's our bill. Overdue.'

Margo Cox-Robinson snorted her lack of surprise, snatched the package and stalked out. She probably heard the shout of, 'Pontoon F,' which followed her out of the door but was unlikely to have caught the muttered '...and *do* take care, it's slippery.'

Idler was not a large boat, perhaps thirty feet long, and despite a generous beam any vigorous movement on board caused her to rock and sway. It was obvious from some way up the slimy pontoon that there was someone on board, and it was equally obvious that he/she/they were engaged in some form of vigorous activity.

'Robbie, you randy two-timing bastard, get your sorry arse out here! Now!'

'Uh oh.'

'Wha's happening?'

'My bloody wife, that's what's happening.'

'Oh… that all, thought it might be something serious,' the blonde mumbled happily, snuggling into his chest.

'It *is* serious, believe me. Potentially fatal in fact.'

'Thought you had some sort of "open" marriage.'

'Well, yes, I do… but I might not have got round to mentioning it to Margo.'

'Cox-Robinson, if you're not out here in one bloody second flat I'm coming in and God help you if…'

'Whoa, whoa, Margie, what's all the shouting? And swearing. Think of the neighbours.' Robbie stood at the top of the companionway grinning nervously and trying to knot a threadbare sarong round his waist.

Margo Cox-Robinson glanced right and left at the deserted and abandoned boats ranged either side of her husband's own wreck and snorted. She was in no mood for irony. 'Oh my god! What…? Who…?'

Robbie winced. He had a shrewd idea what and who

and turned to find her emerging into the cockpit, lazily ruffling her hair and quite naked.

'My god! You're screwing kids now, she can't be half your age... and probably less than half my IQ!'

'Margie, now that's not nice.'

Robbie's mistress tapped him on the shoulder and pouted. 'Is she being rude about me?'

'Don't listen.'

Meanwhile, his wife stamped her foot on the rickety pontoon and waved the bundle of envelopes at him. 'Where's my money, you bastard? It's three months overdue and it's taken me two to find you.'

'Coming.'

'Yeah, I bet you were!'

Robbie rolled his eyes wearily, what was it with the women in his life and double entendres?

'I'll sort it out.'

'Make sure you do, and here!' She hurled the envelopes into the cockpit and watched with malicious satisfaction as several fluttered into the oily water. 'And make sure I get paid before these do. Oh, and don't bother changing the name of your wreck again, I'll find you. And next time it'll be with my... the bailiff.'

Robbie could only manage a grunt from his inverted position, bent over the transom trying to hook his correspondence off the marina slicks, but he registered the threat: "my... the bailiff" was in fact his brother-in-law, Margo's brother. He'd always hated Robbie. At family gatherings he'd sidle up within range and flick or tug at Robbie's hair repeatedly hissing 'fucking hippy'. He was six foot four and fifteen stone of solid muscle and was indeed a bailiff. Robbie knew if he came calling, whether in a private or professional capacity, it would be unpleasant and probably painful.

By the time he'd managed to retrieve the last of the envelopes, his wife was already stomping off down the pontoon. Robbie straightened up and looked after her, just as she skidded sideways flailing wildly and crashed heavily onto the algaed planking. He winced – that wasn't going to help – grabbed his soggy mail and quickly ducked below. The blonde was left in the cockpit, still naked but with a modicum of modesty provided by the logbook on which she was fiddling with the makings of their next joint.

It didn't take Robbie long to catalogue his mail. Most went unopened into the crusty bucket under the sink, condemned out of hand, the postmarks giving away not only their origins but also their likely contents. There was little to bring him any joy, a smug postcard from St Lucia from a previous and now unaccountably rich business partner, a graphically illustrated leaflet offering Viagra in bulk, no doubt spitefully ordered by an earlier dissatisfied lover, and… oh God, a solicitor's letter. Who did he owe that much to? Margo wouldn't have come marching all the way down here to do her own dirty work if she'd already instructed solicitors; the marina would have just impounded *Idler*, they'd threatened before, and none of his other multiple dribs and drabs of debt would singly even cover the cost of a letter from a fancy firm of London W1 solicitors. Robbie opened the letter warily, smoothed out the stiff paper and read. He finished the letter and carefully put it on the table, only to immediately pick it up again. He turned the single sheet over and studied the blank reverse, tilted the paper towards a streaked porthole and tried to make out the watermark, then with trembling hands re-read it.

'We're out of Rizlas.'

Robbie had forgotten the blonde was still in the cockpit. 'What d' you think of this?' He passed the letter up the companionway and followed it, snagging his sarong on the way and arriving naked.

'Nah, too thick, might make a roach though, I suppose,' she added doubtfully.

'No, I meant read it, not smoke it. Go on, what do you think?'

The blonde reluctantly put aside the logbook and peered suspiciously at the letter. She read slowly. 'Real, do you think?' she said eventually.

'Dunno. What do you think?'

'Give 'em a ring.'

'Nothing left on the phone,' he shrugged.

'Yeah, of course.' She wasn't surprised. 'Could be OK, I suppose,' she said, carefully folding the letter. 'Anyway, it doesn't really matter does it?'

'What do you mean?'

'Well, you've got to go, haven't you? To "your advantage" it says. Might be true, it's a solicitor that says so.' Robbie snorted. 'What's to lose?' the blonde asked simply. She replaced the logbook on her lap and started teasing two crumpled cigarette papers flat.

'Well, there's the train fare to start with, or petrol money if I can blag a car off someone. Then there's somewhere to stay, meals...' Robbie paused and looked out over the estuary. 'And anyway,' he said quietly, 'I'm not sure it's a place I want to go back to.'

The blonde looked at him curiously, stroked the pink tip of her tongue along the edge of the tiny paper tube and said solemnly: 'The wind is free, Robbie, that's what you're always telling me.' She flicked the lighter and inhaled deeply. 'And *there's* your hotel,' she added throatily, pointing down the companionway.

Robbie sat thinking, staring down at the letter without seeing it. When he looked up again the blonde had sprawled across the bench, arms stretched out along the coaming, figurehead breasts thrust up towards *Idler's* frayed rigging. Her eyes were closed in apparent ecstasy and twin trickles of smoke snaked from her nose. 'It's an idea,' he said slowly, and slipped a hand under the logbook. 'I was just wondering...'

FOUR

The fallout from the disastrous dinner party had been the worst yet. It wasn't unusual for Dom to be relegated to the spare bedroom for a night or two after one of his "indiscretions" but he hadn't seen the inside of the marital suite for nearly two weeks now. He'd realised it was serious when he'd returned from the Cock 'n' Cat, still nursing the remnants of an appalling hangover, and an inexplicably bruised hand, and found the contents of his half of the wardrobe dumped on the spare room floor. This was a worrying new development. Whilst he'd become increasingly ambivalent about the state of his marriage he certainly didn't want the inconvenience or expense of a divorce just at the moment. Dom decided the best thing was to make himself scarce for a week or so and the curious invitation from the London solicitor seemed to provide the ideal excuse. Beverley could pursue her fling with the tennis coach uninterrupted and perhaps things would calm down a bit.

Work raised no objections, in fact his line manager was worryingly indifferent, and Beverley was predictably disinterested, even when he said he'd use the trip to drop in on the children at their respective universities. This suggestion had been greeted by a similar lack of enthusiasm from his offspring, a wary politeness from his son in Birmingham and a typically nonchalant "whatever" from his daughter in Manchester. Both made it clear they expected his visit to be brief and it would have to fit in around their usual "uni" activities, which, he suspected, were very different.

These arrangements left him with a brief void if he was to absent himself soon, which he decided to fill with a couple of nights' stay with a spinster aunt in the Cotswolds. Dom had always been her favourite and he had high hopes of some sort of inheritance in the not too distant future; her impossibly pretty cottage in the chocolate-box village of Piddle-Mallow had to be worth at least three quarters of a million alone, probably more to some weekending London banker or stockbroker. Yes, it was definitely worth keeping in with the old bird and anyway, it could be fun; she could be quite lively, if a little vague. Dom left the house without any goodbyes, the smaller of the BMWs piled high with luggage containing clothes for every occasion, including an ancient rucksack and pair of walking boots, and set off round the M25 in surprisingly high spirits.

'Auntie, lovely to see you again.'
'Hello, dear, what a lovely surprise, have you got time for a cup of tea?'

'Um, I'm here to stay for a couple of nights, Auntie… I rang last week and then dropped you a card, remember?'

'Oh, how lovely. I'll make some tea.'

The following day had been spent in a genteel meander around the Cotswold lanes, which took in the usual honey-coloured model villages and best-of-bloom winners. After two tea room stops Dom had persuaded the old lady that a pub would be a treat for her and they'd pulled up at a 'traditional' coaching inn where they'd lunched on partially cooked baguettes and orange juice – Dom's discreetly laced with vodka.

'Lovely, dear,' the old lady belched gently into a lacy handkerchief. 'And I've got another treat for you later.' She clapped her hands gently in delight. 'We're having one of our gatherings. I've told the major you're staying and he says he'll be delighted to welcome a new believer.'

'Believer?' Dom didn't like the sound of this. 'Er, Auntie…'

'Oh, and you'll love Madame Tilblush… well, perhaps "love" isn't quite the right word, but you'll see. She's Armenian.'

During the drive back to Piddle-Mallow things became a bit clearer. Madame Tilblush was apparently a well-respected medium, conductor of seances and dispenser of apparently plausible mumbo-jumbo to the well-heeled gullible. There was to be a meeting that night at his aunt's cottage and Dom was expected to attend.

'We have high hopes for this evening, dear, there's an especially powerful force at the moment. Something or other is aligned, I never can quite remember what, and Madame says: "the atmosphere will be charged".'

'Yes, it probably will, there's a storm on its way, it was on the radio.'

The weather forecasters had been gleefully predicting the arrival of an unseasonable Atlantic storm, named Philomena by the Americans, for several days now. The wind had been rising all day and now distant rumbles of thunder and large splatters on the windscreen suggested the forecaster's computer models might actually have got it right this time.

Madame Tilblush was no more Armenian than he was and Dom also suspected "she" was actually a man – the veil helped but the sideburns were a bit of a giveaway – but this didn't seem to matter to the little group of believers gathered in his aunt's best room. They were clearly bewitched. A bluff elderly man of vaguely military bearing was introduced to Dom as "the major". Dom thought he probably had an artificial leg, or was drunk, or possibly both, but he took charge of dispensing his aunt's sweet sherry. Inevitably candles were lit, the medium went through the conventional pre-seance rituals and warnings and hands were linked. Madame, eyes tightly shut, muttered to herself for a few suspenseful minutes then, trembling dramatically and in a high falsetto, started her routine.

'Yes, yes, it's coming, there's someone approaching, they've been allowed across… The atmosphere… so charged… yes, yes, their way is open… They are here!' She muttered and mumbled for a moment then with a last emphatic nod growled, 'They have not long left us.' She cleared her throat and resumed the falsetto, 'Has anyone in the room lost someone recently?'

There was a long silence punctuated only by the noise of the rising storm and the medium's heavy breathing.

'Well, it could be my Vivian, I suppose…' one of the younger women, who seemed a bit bewildered by the whole thing, eventually ventured.

Madame Tilblush's breathing became even harsher and she resumed trembling. 'Yes, yes, the mist is clearing… The atmosphere… I can see her now!' She gave a violent shudder. 'She is among us!' There was a dramatic pause broken only by a perfectly timed clap of thunder while the medium continued to vibrate.

'But he was a *him*.'

'Er, yes… yes, I can see *him*. He misses you, he wants you to know the strength of his love…'

'But we were getting divorced.'

'Um, yes… yes, but now he's passed over to the other side he's realised…'

'But he's in Bournemouth.'

Dom tried unsuccessfully to suppress a snigger.

'No, no… it's going… the storm, it's the storm, too much interference, I'm losing her… him.'

The act might have been hopeless but nature was doing her best with the special effects. As Madame Tilblush's exhausted head dropped onto her lumpy, crushed velvet bosom, there was a vicious crack of thunder and lightning flared behind the heavy curtains. There was a loud pop from somewhere in the cottage and the slivers of light around the door to the hall disappeared abruptly. The major lit a match and suggested pouring everyone another sherry, while Dom went off to try and follow his aunt's directions to the fuse box. He was still in the under-stairs cupboard when he became aware of the curious crackling sound from upstairs… and then an acrid burning smell. A sudden pounding on the front door made him start and crack his head. He struggled out of the cupboard, located the door and started fumbling with the numerous security devices. There was more pounding.

'All right, all right! Yes?' he snapped at the torch shining in his face.

'Your thatch is on fire! Get everyone out quick, the whole roof's going up…'

* * *

Gavin's departure from the villa had been bad-tempered on his part and sulkily suspicious on that of his wife. Friends at the spa had convinced her that any communication that included the expression "to your advantage" was bound to involve another woman. Gavin was tense and snappy; he didn't like leaving the business, even in the hands of the trusted Jacko. He had a gut feeling that his right-hand man, and their Spanish legal representative, may have underestimated the impact the new mayor was going to have on his ongoing operations.

As usual, they'd arrived quietly at the airport in the blacked out Mercedes and quickly made their way to the VIP lounge, where Gavin moodily sipped a beer and Jacko took endless phone calls.

'Well, that confirms it, just as well you're pushing off for a bit, Gav.'

Gavin sighed wearily. 'Go on then, what's happened now… have they invaded Gibralta?'

'Not quite, but this bloody mayor's proving a bit of a handful. According to Gomez his latest idea is an investigation into possibly bent *Guardia*...' Jacko looked meaningfully at his boss, '... and the customs guys.'

'Hmm, that could slow things down a bit.'

'Yeah. Look, you go and have your little break and we'll sort that out, might have to start buying some new friends when you get back.'

'And you, you gonna be OK here, Jacko?'

'Yeah, yeah, I'll keep my head down, I've got a few boltholes.'

'OK, but make sure Bobby and the kids are priority, OK? I want them kept well away from all this shit.'

'No sweat, Gav, they'll be fine down in Puerto... and there's always the *finca* up at Ronda.'

'Not a lot of jet-skiing up there is there, Jacko? The kids'd hate it and if they're not happy... well, Bobby won't be happy. And then...'

'Yeah, well it won't come to that.'

Gavin glanced at his watch. 'Where the hell's Bruce?'

'You know what he's like: flight plans, clearances and all that, he does it by the book.'

Gavin snorted, 'Yeah, until it comes to the cargo manifest and the passenger list!'

Jacko grunted non-committally. 'So you're definitely going then, up to the Lake District?'

'Yeah, why not? Keep a low profile you said, and anyway, I haven't been up there since I was a kid. My parents thought it'd be good for me, wholesome they said... if they'd only known! Anyway, I'll go and see what all this "to your advantage" is about and then get on down to London and catch up with a few things.'

'Low profile things, Gav, all right?'

'Yeah, yeah.'

'OK, I'll be off then, have a good trip and we'll catch up later.'

Bruce, an amiable Australian, came ambling into the lounge a few minutes later and shook Gavin's hand. 'Sorry about the delay, mate, just doing some extra checks on the weather; bit of a dicey low coming in off the Atlantic, should be OK though.'

'We're going then?'

'Yeah, sure, no worries… anyway, all the stuff's on board now. We'll be fine.'

As the little jet taxied out onto the late afternoon runway Gavin helped himself to a beer from the chiller and took his usual seat. He was the only passenger, the rest of the cabin being taken up with various boxes, crates and parcels. Apart from Bruce, the only other person aboard was the "co-pilot", an enormous, tough looking character who Gavin very much doubted had a clue about flying the plane and was more likely Bruce's "protection". The man had never uttered a word in Gavin's earshot and was rumoured to be ex-SAS – but then every heavy working in southern Spain made that claim.

The flight was smooth enough. Gavin had tried to concentrate on an English newspaper but after a couple of beers and the slow release of tension after the frantic activity of the last couple of days he'd relaxed enough to doze off. A bad dream intruded; he was falling into a bottomless void, light-limbed and helpless, almost weightless except for a vice-like claw across his groin. As the fall was reversed, the vice relaxed but his limbs took on an oppressive weight, pinning him down. Unable to move he panicked and tried to force his way to the surface, waking suddenly to find the small aircraft bucking and plunging across the sky. A red light glared at him from above the cockpit door and he was sure he could hear buzzing alarms coming from behind it. Gavin gripped the white leather arms of his seat and wondered where they were and, irrationally, how high they were.

The cockpit door suddenly opened and the co-pilot appeared, bracing himself casually against an empty seat as the plane banked steeply to the right. 'Bruce is gonna divert.'

'Is that a problem?'

The big man shrugged. 'Who for?'

'Well, all of us, the plane.'

'Nah.'

'Where to?' Gavin asked, bracing nervously as the plane lurched further onto its side.

'Biggin.'

'Biggin Hill, Kent? Bloody hell, that's the other end of the country.'

The co-pilot shrugged again and returned to the cockpit, shutting the door firmly behind him.

Gavin considered this change of plan. Despite his initial reaction it could have been worse; south London and north Kent had been part of his old stomping ground, he knew it well and more importantly, he knew people. This gave him options. Someone would put him up and lend him a car for the journey north, or he'd hire one, and if Bruce could somehow call ahead there might even be a friendly face waiting for him at the airfield. Yes, it could have been a lot worse… Luton, for Chrissake!

The change of course seemed to do the trick and after just a few more minutes of turbulence the plane settled down, level and stable. Bruce appeared, filling the cockpit doorway. 'Sorry about this, mate, bloody weather system came in early; fuck-all visibility, sixty knots steady off the Irish and gusting more at "GL" in Blackpool.'

Gavin wasn't really any the wiser. 'No problem, Biggin's not too much out of my way.'

'No proper customs or passport checks either, well, not likely anyway.'

'There is that,' Gavin nodded. He never liked using his "alternative" passport if he could avoid it.

'We'll be there in a couple of hours, anything you need?'

'Couldn't make a call ahead for me could you?'

'Yeah, no worries, gimme the details?'

Gavin had decided to try one particular old acquaintance. They'd been quite close once, known each other since their teens and done several jobs together back in the crazy eighties. Last he'd heard, Billy was more or less retired, had a nice pad down at Tunbridge Wells and played a lot of golf. If he was around, Gavin had no doubt his accommodation, transport and "meet 'n' greet" problems were over.

It was a smooth landing and as Bruce had predicted, officialdom was notable by its absence. And there was

Billy, lounging against a black Range Rover and grinning delightedly.

'Long time, no see, Billy.'

'Yeah, good to see you, Gav. How's it going?'

'Good, good.' Neither of them expected to give or get any embellishment on this. 'Just a flying visit, bit of business up north and then back to town for a few weeks, then… well, I'll see.'

'Yeah, the message said something about Blackpool. Wondered why you were going up there… Yorkshire, isn't it?'

'Nearly.'

Billy turned and indicated a whiskery youth sitting in the passenger seat of the Range Rover, wires dangling from under his lank hair. 'Remember Dwayne?'

'Blimey, he was knee high to a dachshund last time I saw 'im.'

'Yeah, well they grow,' Billy conceded ruefully. 'Daft bugger but he's all right, aren't you, son?' He reached through the window and yanked one of the wires. 'Aren't you, son?'

'Yeah.'

'C'mon then, Gav, we'll stop off for a "Ruby" on the way, best curry house in Kent. Actually, you turning up is a bit handy, I've got something I wouldn't mind running past you. 'Aven't we, son?' he bellowed at the nodding youngster.

'Yeah.'

* * *

Until this last week Greg had still been struggling with his guilt at the prospect of abandoning Martin at one of their busiest times of the year with only the gormless Derek and flighty Lisa as help. But after constant reassurances from his partner and a slight slackening in bookings he'd started to relax and was now enjoying making the preparations for his expedition.

Partly to appease Martin, Greg had planned a fairly easy first day, long but flat – until the end anyway. His route took him west from Windermere and zigzagged through man-made forests to the holiday village of Coniston, arriving around late afternoon, from where he'd head up into the wilderness to a spot amongst the ruins of an old copper mine, which he and Martin remembered from one of their earliest hikes. There he would set up camp for the night.

Things started well. Greg positively trotted down the ramp of the ferry, bold and intrepid, and set off briskly through the gloomy woods. He'd forgotten how dull and damp these dense Forestry Commission plantations were, the natural habitat of voracious horseflies and mountain bikers; grim-faced, mud-splattered maniacs who hurtled along the narrow pathways snarling last-minute warnings – if you were lucky. Greg was almost grateful when he got lost and found himself on a small but busy metalled road. He'd no idea where he was but all his instincts told him he needed to turn left. A mile or so later he came to a crossroads with a helpful four-fingered signpost. He promptly turned round and started to retrace his steps, passing the spot where he'd earlier emerged from the woods and cursing his treacherous instincts.

As far as Greg could tell, the two Coniston pubs that faced each other across the main road hadn't changed at all since he and Martin were here last. He chose the one which would have had the afternoon sun if it hadn't been buried in banks of lumpy grey cloud, bought a cold lager and took it back outside. He eased the sweaty rucksack off his back and decided to call Martin – not that he was lonely he told himself – just there probably wouldn't be reception up at the mines.

'Mart? Hi, it's me. I didn't recognise your voice for a minute. Everything OK?'

Greg listened carefully for a full two minutes without saying anything.

'So is the ambulance still there?'

The answer to this was clearly not straightforward and there was at least another minute of explanation.

'Are we insured for this?'

Another lengthy explanation was clearly underway when Greg exploded, 'and where's Derek now?' There was a brief murmur. 'So he bloody should! What is it with him and Americans?' Greg took a quick sip of his beer while he listened again. 'What! Not all day? Lazy little cow!' He slammed his glass on the bench. 'I'm coming home, Mart, it's not fair. I can get a bus or something… what, yes, OK, I'll hang on.'

While Greg waited he managed to catch the eye of a passing glass collector who reluctantly accepted his order for chicken and chips. He moodily stroked the condensation off his glass and wondered what the consequences of Derek's latest disaster might be – apparently he'd half crushed to death two elderly Americans with their own luggage after losing control of the huge suitcases, which had then tobogganed down the main staircase and ended up pinning their hapless owners against the reception desk.

Martin came back on the line, more cheerful and ready with the reassurances: Lisa had just turned up, full of apologies and "bullshit excuses", Derek had been found and the paramedics had finished treating the Americans in the back of the ambulance, who seemed to be fine. They'd been discharged with a shared bottle of paracetamol for the bruising and seemed remarkably sanguine, treating the whole thing as a bit of a joke.

'So where was Derek? Bloody hiding, I suppose, murderous little sod!'

No, apparently he'd just managed to lock himself in the outside store, but order had now been restored; Martin had some help, no one was going to sue, the insurers didn't need to know anything had ever happened and the reception desk could soon be repaired. Greg was to get on and enjoy his holiday. They'd sack Derek – permanently – when Greg got home.

'Right,' Martin finished cheerily, 'now off you go and enjoy it. We'll chat tomorrow, I'm off to dish out a few bollockings!'

Greg quickly ate the chicken and chips, it was awful, and he remembered now from earlier visits that the food had always been better on the other side of the road. He pushed away the greasy plate, glanced at the darkening sky and couldn't help noticing the 'Vacancies' sign in the window of the pub opposite. He seemed to remember their breakfasts were good too. He swilled a last mouthful of lager to try and un-gum the mushy peas from the roof of his mouth and reached for his rucksack, no, it was the great outdoors for him. The weather could change so quickly in this area, and sometimes even for the better, who knew, there could be glorious evening sunshine by the time he'd slogged the last few uphill miles. He looked dubiously at the sky and wished one of them had thought to check the weather before he'd left.

In fact, as Greg made his way wearily up the old mine road, the sky just got darker and the wind started to gust unpredictably, creating mini, knee-high tornadoes of dust and last year's leaves. He passed the cosy-looking youth hostel where a jolly crowd were unloading kayaks, no doubt looking forward to a hot shower, an evening of companionship and a dry bunk at the end of their day. He trudged on wondering about YHA membership. By the time the huge slopes of spoil and roofless ruins of the abandoned mine came into view, the wind had settled in one direction and was funnelling a steady drizzle down the deep stream gully, which had provided the old workings with its water supply. Greg scrambled in amongst the tumbled masonry and was surprised to find a tent already tucked away there. He wasn't sure whether to be disappointed or relieved. It was a brightly coloured, modern high-tech model, rigid, taut and wrinkle-free, obviously erected by someone who knew what they were doing. There was no sign of occupation but Greg politely moved away to the furthest set of ruins, which wasn't as sheltered as his first choice, but it would do.

For the next half an hour he wrestled with the

flailing wet canvas of the old-fashioned tent as the wind got stronger. Success was partial. The thing was up and relatively dry inside but no matter how Greg tweaked the guy-lines or re-pegged the groundsheet, the tent remained sag-backed and flapped noisily. Apart from that it was surprisingly cosy. He unpacked the rucksack and tuned in his little radio – just missing the weather forecast again – and started to enjoy himself. He found the little stove and a plastic box of pre-cooked chilli, which Martin had made for him, and further rummaging uncovered a small cake, a huge bar of chocolate and finally a half bottle of brandy. Martin! No wonder the bloody pack had been so heavy – bless him!

His meal finished, warm in his sleeping bag and too tired to concentrate on a book, Greg decided he had to defy the storm now howling around him and try to get some sleep. He'd have another chunk of chocolate… and a last brandy, then leave the radio burbling for company and turn off the torch. Exhaustion prevailed and it worked.

Suddenly he was awake, confused and frightened in the pitch-dark. Thunder was rumbling nearby and rain was hammering on the tent. Greg felt clammy folds of canvas slapping wetly against him and the flapping was louder than ever. The murmur of the radio guided him to his torch and by a feeble orange glow he inspected the remains of his temporary home. The home-made pole had clearly given up, the far end of the tent had flopped down onto his feet and the unsupported folds were thrashing uncontrollably. Deciding he needed a pee anyway, Greg reluctantly crawled out of the wreckage and by the light of the dwindling torch found a couple of heavy rocks to dump on the flattened end of the tent – that would at least stop some of the flapping. He turned what he thought was downwind and relieved himself, using a tuft of grass to wipe the wind-blown spillage off his bare legs before scrambling back under cover. With his rucksack as a pillow he curled up in the surviving area of the tent and turned the radio up to full volume for comfort. The news came on and through his own storm he made out something about a fishing boat in trouble somewhere near the Isle of Man, with lifeboatmen and helicopter crews making heroic efforts to rescue the crew, despite Storm Philomena.

'Now they tell me,' Greg said out loud, and jumped as someone replied.

'Are you OK in there? Is there anyone there?'

Greg fumbled with the zip of the tent, poked his head through the flaps and came face to face with a hooded young man crouched at the entrance.

'Are you OK?' the face shouted. 'I had to get up… you know, when a man's gotta go… and saw you'd collapsed. Wondered if we could help.' He stuck his head and shoulders through the flap and shone a torch round. The beam picked out the splintered raspberry cane, obviously beyond repair and the rain pouring through numerous splits and rents in the ancient canvas. Greg was clearly homeless.

The young man introduced himself as Ben, and brooking no arguments, insisted they bundled up Greg's wet possessions and de-camp to his tent. 'It'll be a bit cosy with the three of us,' Ben admitted cheerfully, 'but we'll manage. We've got a sheltered corner over there – safe as houses.'

Ben's partner was a plumply pretty blonde who didn't seem at all surprised that a strange, half-dressed, soaking wet man had appeared in her tent in the middle of the night. Ben introduced her as Cat, and still in her sleeping bag she quickly got a stove going and started to prepare hot drinks. Greg was effusive in his thanks but they were casually dismissed and he was encouraged to make himself as comfortable as possible. Sleep was out of the question and the relaxed, if loud, conversation soon turned to backgrounds and the real world. Greg gathered that Ben and Cat had their own business but didn't quite catch what it was. They lived in the Midlands and had taken this long-planned break to spend a week or two walking around the Lakes, apparently something they didn't think they'd be able to do again for a while.

'That's running your own business for you,' Greg sympathised.

The night passed in a companionable fug. Cat lived up to her name and napped from time to time while Ben and Greg talked mountains and bank loans and sipped endless coffees laced with the brandy retrieved from the wreckage of Greg's pack.

* * *

Robbie had never sailed *Idler* further than Brighton and he hadn't got a clue how far it was up the west coast of Britain to Cumbria, or even the name of any ports once he got there. Whitehaven, he thought, might be one. But while the blonde got dressed, and stung by her scepticism, Robbie assured her that sailing to the Lake District was well within his capabilities and exactly what he was going to do.

'You're going to what!'

That evening Robbie had appeared in the bar of The Mermaid where as promised most of the lifeboat crew had gathered. He'd dutifully bought his round and then casually mentioned his planned voyage. The reaction had been one of predictable hilarity but after ten minutes of good-natured teasing and banter one or two of the crew had started making some serious suggestions, headed by a list of improvements they insisted Robbie would have to make to get *Idler* seaworthy.

'What about crew, you'll need a hand?'

Another debate now started, concentrating on Robbie's shortcomings as a sailor and navigator. There was no malice in it, the lifeboatmen were simply making a professional assessment.

'No offence, mate…'

'None taken.'

One of the younger men took Robbie to one side. 'Look, if you're serious I might be able to help. My brother's just finished uni, he's been in boats all his life, loves it, and he's probably forgotten more about sailing than you'll ever know… no offence.'

Robbie grunted and then listened as the lifeboatman reeled off a list of essential (and expensive) repairs and replacement equipment, without which, he said, he'd never let his kid brother near *Idler*. Robbie agreed to it all, he'd worry about how to pay for it later, but had little choice. A quick study of his AA road atlas had already given him some idea of the distance he'd need to cover, and the offer of a keen and competent crew suddenly made the trip much less daunting. He tried not to show his relief.

Finance was the next challenge, and for once he decided to follow the advice of his bank manager, he would "prioritise his expenditure". Robbie decided to "prioritise" some new ropes, a handful of shackles, a few spares and filters for the engine and two new life jackets. Leaving un-"prioritised" and therefore unpaid: a long-outstanding legal bill, Margo's maintenance, several fines and his marina fees. Robbie just hoped whatever it was "to his advantage" waiting in the Lake District would have a financial element to it.

Within a few days *Idler* was declared, 'OK… just,' by big brother and Robbie had his crew. Little brother arrived on the pontoon before dawn on the day of departure, watched with interest while the blonde got dressed in the cockpit, then stepped aboard and introduced himself as Ed. He said little else, just threw a small duffel bag onto Robbie's unmade bunk and started a silent inspection of the boat. After an hour of fiddling with the engine, tidying up the deck and re-rigging bits of equipment Robbie hadn't looked at in years, Ed announced they were ready to cast off. Robbie didn't seem to have any say in the matter; he supposed he'd have to forego the planned shower and fry-up in the marina cafe.

From then on there was no doubt who was in charge and Robbie found himself more or less redundant, his role on board reduced to tea and sandwich making and grinding the occasional winch. Ed, meantime, had got

Idler finely tuned, heeled to a steady angle and creaming along, throwing out an impressive bow wave and arrow-straight wake. Several days of delightful sailing in fine weather passed uneventfully and despite the lack of up-to-date charts, Ed's knowledge of the south coast ensured they easily found and safely entered, their intended overnight ports. Once anchored or tied up alongside, Robbie would usually retire to the nearest pub, while Ed stayed on board planning the next day's voyage and murmuring endlessly into his mobile phone. From what Robbie could gather, Ed and a girlfriend had recently split and a possible rapprochement was being negotiated.

The trouble-free sailing and benign weather were boosting Robbie's confidence with each passing day, and as he watched Ed's casual mastery of the little boat, he became evermore convinced of his own abilities to take *Idler* anywhere he felt like. Reaching Falmouth was a real milestone and Robbie celebrated by rowing ashore in the gently hissing dinghy and spent the evening swaying from one harbour-side bar to another nodding sagely at the yachty conversations going on all around him. By now he quite looked the part, his rolling gait, stubbly beard and salt-stained clothes all shouted "seasoned sailor", although the image did slip a bit at closing time when he had to borrow a foot-pump to re-inflate the dinghy and then rowed around the bay for several hours looking for his boat. He was eventually pointed in the right direction by a local fisherman who thought *Idler's* anchor might have dragged. He was right, she was now a good quarter of a mile from where he'd left her... and where the hell was Ed? Robbie scrambled aboard and stumbled up to the swaying foredeck to try and re-lay the anchor. Grappling in the dark with the muddy chain and a spinning windlass he found some of his recently gained confidence leaking away.

Next morning Robbie woke up late and found the boat more or less in the same position but there was still no sign of Ed or, it suddenly dawned on him, Ed's few possessions. By lunchtime it was clear the crew had jumped ship. Phone calls to his brother had gone unanswered and when in desperation Robbie rang the marina all he got was aggressive demands for money, threats of impoundment and the news that Margo's brother was looking for him. Going back to the Solent empty-handed was not an option. One way or another he had to keep going – "something to his advantage" – please God, let it be money! He eventually ran out of credit on his phone, tossed it onto a bunk and spread out the AA road atlas on the little chart table to work out his next move. It became clear that getting round the tip of Cornwall, Land's End, was his first major solo challenge. After that he'd have to cross the vast mouth and ferocious tides of the Bristol Channel to reach the west Welsh coast. But he'd cross that bridge when he came to it, first Land's End. He decided the little port of Padstow, "just round the corner", looked reachable and this would be his next overnight stop, then on up the channel to a narrow bit before nipping across to South Wales. With a firm plan for the next few days and no sign of a change in the balmy summer weather some of Robbie's fickle confidence returned.

The rounding of Land's End had gone surprisingly well. The Scilly Isles had confused him for a bit, he'd forgotten there was more land beyond the tip of Cornwall, but once he'd "turned right" a steady southerly wind and advantageous tide had helped *Idler* cover the ground surprisingly quickly. Even so, the light was starting to fade by the time Robbie thought he was probably approaching Padstow and the sudden flashes from a lighthouse couldn't have come soon enough. Somehow his navigation had been spot on. Blissfully unaware of the notorious bar racing by under his keel, he rode the flooding tide close past the lighthouse and into a welcoming channel before heading towards a cluster of already anchored boats. Robbie was exhausted but exhilarated by the success of his voyage and navigating prowess. He decided to stay on board and celebrate with baked beans and red wine.

The next morning there was definitely a different feel to the weather. Robbie was uneasy. Apart from the odd notice pinned to a harbour-master's door and dockside chatter, his only source of weather information came from the radio shipping forecasts, quite a lot of which he didn't understand. The last one he'd heard had talked about "an unseasonal low pressure" heading in from the Atlantic. Robbie suspected that wasn't good and decided to make it a short day, just moving on up the coast to the town of Ilfracombe, from where it would be a quick hop across the fast-flowing Bristol Channel to Wales.

Motoring out of Padstow later that morning Robbie met the biggest swell he'd encountered so far and wind which was coming in ever increasing gusts from all points of the compass. The tide was all wrong too and progress was slow and uncomfortable. By mid-afternoon he'd had his first serious breakage. Without any warning the big wooden boom had suddenly whipped across from one side of the boat to the other and then back again, fortunately missing his head, but snapping ropes and ripping fittings out of soggy deck planks on its way. A tear had also appeared near the top of his main sail, which he was sure was getting bigger. As he tried to get things back into some sort of order the wind strengthened further and changed direction again bringing with it a mixture of spray and mist, which dropped the temperature and blotted out the horizon. The building seas repeatedly lifted the stern and tried to slew the boat round, with an occasional white-topped wave spilling into the cockpit. Robbie pushed the tiller across and quickly let out the sail as the boat took on a whole different motion and heeled alarmingly. *Idler* was clearly overpowered, she was carrying too much sail.

Robbie had never sailed in conditions like this before; he clung to the tiller, pushed the starter button for the engine and tried to work out how to get the out-of-control mainsail down. He needn't have bothered, there was a sudden loud snap and a frayed wet rope came snaking down from the masthead followed by a thrashing mass of dripping canvas, which collapsed heavily onto the side-deck. Passing waves immediately started tugging folds of the sail over the side and Robbie had to abandon the tiller to grab at what was left. Bucking and bouncing on his knees with waves sluicing along the deck, several times he thought he'd lost the tug-of-war as hard-won folds of sail were again ripped from his hands or he was forced to let go to stop himself being dragged overboard. But somehow, with a strength he didn't know he had, born of panic, he managed to finally wrestle the sodden bundle onto the deck and stuff it down a hatch. He tumbled back into the cockpit and lay sobbing with exhaustion and shaking with relief while *Idler* rolled and pitched crazily. Robbie staggered to his feet, heaved the tiller amidships and shifted the engine into gear. Back under power the boat steadied herself and Robbie peered into the murk trying to remember which way he'd been pointing. He wiped the misty compass with a wet sleeve and was just congratulating himself on the way he'd handled the crisis, now it was over, when the engine gave an apologetic cough and stopped. The sea immediately took advantage, the boat slewed sideways and the biggest wave yet slopped over the side. The starter button felt spongy and yielded nothing. Robbie dived below, ripped the cover away from the little engine and started tweaking anything that looked like it might be loose and twisting any joint or coupling that came to hand. The boat heaved and rolled and he could hear water sloshing around in the cockpit. The odd deluge poured over the cabin threshold to drench him where he crouched at the foot of the companionway, head down and feeling increasingly nauseous. A sudden impact jarred the boat throwing him violently to one side and something from the engine came away in his hand. Diving for the hatchway he fumbled his way up on deck.

'You all right, butt? Sorry about the landing.'

Robbie looked in astonishment at the brightly coloured garden shed bobbing up and down next to *Idler*… and was violently sick over the side.

'Need a hand, like?'

The garden shed turned out to be attached to a sturdy

little fishing boat, it was in fact the wheelhouse, and the cheery voice came from a shiny red face poking out of a side window.

Robbie wiped his mouth on his cuff. 'Yes please,' was all he could think of to say.

Another figure, dressed from head to toe in shiny yellow appeared and despite the violent pitching of both boats stepped nimbly over the gap between the two. He fiddled around with a thick rope on *Idler*'s foredeck for a few minutes, stuffed the tattered remains of her little headsail down a hatch and with perfect timing stepped back onto the fishing boat.

'You'll be going our way then. We'll tow you in, butt. OK?'

Robbie raised a thumb, clutched the tiller and was sick over the compass.

It was another two stomach-wrenching hours before a mass of lights emerged from the murk and Robbie felt the motion of the boat ease. He tried to make sense of the lights; some were moving and obviously on the shore, others he was sure were the red and green of buoys and channel markers. Within minutes they were in sheltered waters and Robbie recovered enough to start taking an interest in his surroundings. Ilfracombe was bigger than he'd imagined.

Almost before Robbie knew what was going on, *Idler* had been unhitched and neatly tied up to a stone jetty. 'OK, butt?'

'Yes. Yes, thank you so much... bloody engine... bloody weather...' Robbie looked up at the multistoried lights around the harbour side. 'Um, this is Ilfracombe?'

His question was relayed to the figure in the garden shed whose shiny face appeared grinning delightedly. 'Ilfracombe? You're in Swansea, man, welcome to Wales!'

FIVE

'Didn't see that one coming, did you, Madame?' Dom muttered nastily out the corner of his mouth.

The seance participants were huddled in the lane at a safe distance, watching in fascinated horror as orange flames danced across the thatched roof, hissing and spitting in the rain. Other villagers and near neighbours had also gathered to keep a wary eye on flying sparks. Many of the properties in Piddle-Mallow were thatched.

Dom turned to see how his aunt was taking the destruction of her home and was astonished to find her chatting happily with her little circle, more or less ignoring the drama playing out on the other side of her privet hedge. Meanwhile Madame Tilblush slipped away into the flickering shadows.

'Dominic dear, don't you think you should move your lovely little car?' his aunt said suddenly. 'The major says he's heard the fire engine has been delayed by a fallen tree on the Stow road and it is very near the house.'

Dom clutched at his pockets. Oh God, the keys, they were up on the dressing table in his aunt's little guest room… along with his wallet and mobile phone. He rushed up the drive shielding his face. There was no way he was venturing back into the cottage but he thought he might have left the BMW unlocked. He found he had, and for one desperate moment wondered whether it could be pushed clear. A brief assessment of the slope on the drive and the frailty of the available pushers soon disabused him of this idea, but he remembered some of his luggage was still in the boot, mainly his ancient walking gear stuffed into an old rucksack but it was something. He grabbed this and an old Barbour jacket and retreated back to the lane. Minutes later the cottage's timbered porch, now well ablaze, fell away in a shower of sparks and engulfed the bonnet of the car.

Dom and his aunt spent the remains of the night at the home of one of her friends. Dom slept fitfully on a sofa, waking regularly to the smell of wet soot, which had pervaded everything after the fire brigade's "damping down" operation three doors away. Come the morning, his aunt kindly pressed two twenty-pound notes on him, 'to help you on your way', apologised for having to cut his visit short and cheerfully set off on the bus to see her insurance broker. Dom took another bus, which deposited him in the middle of the town of Cheltenham, where he spent most of his aunt's forty pounds on a National Express ticket to Birmingham. While waiting, he used up some of the precious change ringing his bank to try and arrange some sort of line of credit and replacement cards. They had been suspicious and unhelpful but eventually agreed to re-issue a debit card and one credit card, insisting they would have to be sent to Dom's home address. Dom wondered how he was going to persuade Beverley to cooperate but realised he had no choice but to agree. The bank said the process would take at least three working days.

It was mid-afternoon by the time Dom's coach driver had disentangled himself and his passengers from Spaghetti Junction and arrived in Birmingham. Dom's first born, Daniel, Dan to the family, had always been something of an enigma to his father. Father/son bonding hadn't really been invented when Dan was a child but even allowing for that, he and Dom had a particularly distant relationship. Always a solitary child and prone to strange obsessions from an early age – using school exercise books three times over by writing in pencil, then rubbing it out and starting again was one primary school peculiarity – Dan had always been destined for eccentricity. Secondary school had brought a precocious and fanatical interest in eastern religions and now at university, it was fringe politics and protest groups apparently – the more obscure the cause the better. Dan was studying political science. Dom had never been quite sure what that was but dutifully wrote out the cheques every term.

'Oh, it's you, Dad, I was working.'

Dom had had to knock repeatedly at the indicated door, assured by one of Dan's hall mates that Dan was definitely in. 'Nearly always is,' he'd added.

'Hi, Dan, how are you?'

'You've come to stay, haven't you? I remember. I'm *meant* to be working.' After a furtive glance down the corridor he tugged his father into the room, shut the door behind him and indicated the unmade bed. Dom sat down and looked at the enormous pile of books and pamphlets piled up on the desk by the window.

'Busy then? That's good to see, how's it going?'

'I've got a tutorial tomorrow, I'm only two essays ahead and there's a debating society meeting tonight.'

'Sounds like a busy life,' Dom ventured brightly. His son looked at him pityingly.

'And are you... socialising much?'

Dan thought about this. 'I suppose you mean do I have a girlfriend...?' Dom opened his mouth. '...well no, I don't, thank you. And I don't drink either. My meeting's at seven. Where are you staying?'

'Well...'

Dom explained his current financial straits and the reasons behind them. He wasn't sure his son believed him.

'Where's Mum?'

Dan's tone was accusatory and Dom was tempted to tell him that at that hour of the afternoon Dan's mother was probably spread-eagled under her tennis coach, but instead said: 'At home, I expect, it's just me on this trip. Only one to find a bed for, eh?'

Reluctantly, Dan admitted that one of his few acquaintances was currently at home, apparently suffering from nervous exhaustion and genital herpes, and Dan had been left keys to his room. He supposed Dom could stay there. 'But no more than two nights.' Dom decided he would sleep on top of the bed.

'So, tonight, I'll have to owe you, but fancy a curry and a couple of lag... oh no, of course not.'

'I have my meeting.'

'Of course you have. Is everyone welcome?'

The venue chosen by the debating society was some kind of subterranean concrete bunker in the bowels of the university. Multi-coloured plastic seats, enough for about 200, had been arranged in neat rows and by seven o'clock approximately twenty were occupied. Two fierce-looking young women and one man of about Dom's age sat behind a table on a low stage and glowered at the empty seats.

'Is there a speaker?' Dom whispered to Dan.

'Possibly.'

The man on the stage looked pedantically at his watch, stood up and said: 'I pass the voice to Nola,' and sat down again.

The younger of the two women stood and eyed her audience fiercely.

'The speaker tonight,' she started, 'is being detained elsewhere for his own safety while this meeting debates an emergency motion on whether we want to debate *his* motion... or want him here at all.'

Dom tried to make sense of this while Dan stirred excitedly in his seat.

'Dan Cartwright will propose the emergency motion.' Nola sat down abruptly and to Dom's amazement Dan leapt to his feet and started gesticulating. No one else in the hall seemed surprised.

'I propose that Joe Pelser be uninvited and no-platformed on the grounds that whilst he claims to have been a friend of Nelson Mandela he is in fact an apologist for the original colonial oppressors and a stooge of the neo-colonialists.' Dan had started to sit down but added: 'He's also white, which we didn't realise when we invited him.'

The crowd may have been small but it was enthusiastic in its condemnation of the hapless Mr Pelser and became increasingly incensed as successive speakers tried to outdo each other in righteous outrage. The girl on the stage who wasn't Nola became almost hysterical with rage. No one, it seemed, was prepared to give their proposed guest speaker the benefit of the doubt or right to reply. It was conceded that he had indeed been outlawed by South Africa's apartheid authorities, imprisoned for many years, quite probably tortured and then victimised on release; but there was apparently also overwhelming evidence in his writings and previous speeches of unreformed and latent imperialist sympathies. Furthermore, he had also once spoken at the Tory party conference. Most of the audience had a say but the debate was short and the conclusion inevitable. A motion was duly proposed from the platform, which would send Joe Pelser packing and demand repayment of his travelling expenses.

Dan had become increasingly excited during the "debate". Dom had never seen his son so animated, not since he'd accidentally nailed the child's pet tortoise to the lid of its hibernation box.

'What happens now?' Dom whispered, once Dan had finally sat down, but the man on the stage was already on his feet.

'I… we, take it that no one wishes to challenge this motion,' he smirked.

There were sneers and snorts of laughter from the hall and wry smiles from the two women on the stage.

'Well actually...' Dom had no idea what possessed him to interrupt, he'd never addressed a meeting in his life and didn't really have strong views on anything very much. But the last ten minutes of ill-informed juvenile dogma had riled him. It also happened he knew a little about Mr Joe Pelser. At one time in the 1980s and early nineties you couldn't open a paper or tune into a news broadcast without seeing or hearing his name: he had relentlessly agitated for the overthrow of the South African government, the scrapping of apartheid and release of Mandela, which was to be followed by land grabs from white farmers, an unrealistically high minimum wage and the nationalisation of anything that made a profit. In fact he was demanding the adoption of just about every quasi-Marxist, anti-imperialist policy in the book. Dom also remembered the address to the Tory party conference; the man had been booed off the stage and almost lynched when he effectively accused the whole membership of racism for not supporting sanctions against the apartheid regime. Dom also knew from recent press coverage that Pelser had in no way softened his views. In the interest of fairness and balance, not to mention truth, it was obvious to Dom that these points should have been made during the "debate". But it wasn't this which had got him to his feet, no, what had finally really got to him, was that these young idiots, his son amongst them, hadn't even known that Joe Pelser was a *white* South African.

Ignoring Dan's hissed, "sit down and shut ups" Dom attempted to explain Mr Pelser's biography and political record, rationally and reasonably, amid a rising chorus of howls and jeers from the rest of the hall. The excitable woman on the stage was screaming incoherently at him. Eventually Dom gave up and without resuming his seat shrugged at Dan and left the hall.

Dom found his way to the Students' Union bar and spent five minutes queuing before remembering he hadn't got any money left. He sat sheepishly drinkless at a table in a corner and waited for Dan to find him.

'Hello, haven't seen you around before, you a new mature?'

Dom looked up to find a rather dandified young man with floppy hair and a friendly smile standing by his table. He managed a tight smile back. 'No, I'm visiting my son, Daniel Cartwright.'

'Ah, comrade Dan.'

'Is that what they call him?'

'In certain circles, shall we say?' Dom was slightly alarmed by this rather evasive answer. 'You haven't got a drink.' The young man's voice was cultured and confident.

Dom explained the "mislaid" wallet.

'Never mind, allow me.'

Quickly setting aside any guilt for depriving some impoverished student of a lump of his grant, Dom gratefully allowed himself to be talked into a red wine. His new friend returned with a whole bottle and two glasses.

'Saves having to keep getting up,' he explained and studied the label. 'Ah good, it's my usual. They keep a stock for me in the back, too good for the peasants,' he laughed.

Dom decided this was no normal student. 'What are you studying?' he asked, genuinely curious.

'Ah, good question… well, I started on history but it all got a bit repetitive and frankly, lefty; all women and black people good, anyone with a penis and all white people bad, that sort of thing. Not for me, so I thought I'd have a pop at English lit. That went quite well, actually. I've always enjoyed a good story; *The Great Gatsby* was good fun, loved the party bits, and *1984* was a good laugh, but then we got into Chaucer. Well, in fact I didn't, I mean, *what* is that all about? So, anyway, I'm having a crack at journalism now; thought I might be a war correspondent or something.'

'Dad!' It was not a greeting but a cry of outrage.

'Ah, Dan, your friend here has very kindly treated me to a drink, you'll have to return the favour for me in due course… oh, are we going?'

Without a word, Dan had turned and was stalking towards the door. With a brief thank you and goodbye to his eccentric benefactor Dom hurried after him.

Back in Dan's room the son tore the father off a strip. 'What were you thinking of… showing me up like that?'

'Well…'

'I had to apologise to the committee. It's going to take months before I'm rehabilitated, I'll probably have to attend re-education sessions and…'

'Well…'

'… and do you know who that was, your drinking companion?'

'I don't think he said.'

'That reactionary bourgeoisie bastard is the *Honourable* Sebastian Plunkett-Browne, his father is Lord Plunkett-Browne of Clifton.'

'I thought he had nice manners.'

'They're worth a fortune. And do you know where it came from, eh?'

'Hard work?'

'No,' Dan snorted, 'slavery, that's where!'

'A lot of fortunes did,' Dom said, 'it was a long time ago, a different world.'

'That's no excuse!' Dan snapped and slumped sulkily at his desk. Dom stared at the reflected room in the darkened window and tried to remember who'd taken the iconic photograph of Che Guevara which, predictably, gazed out from Dan's bedroom wall.

'Thomas is back in his room, they've given him Prozac and the herpes has stopped itching, so you'll have to sleep on my floor. If you're staying tomorrow I don't know where…'

'I'll be pushing off tomorrow.'

This was clearly a relief for both father and son.

* * *

Billy hadn't been exaggerating about the quality of the Indian restaurant; the curry was lip-numbingly hot, freshly cooked and delicious. And the bottle of red wine he'd insisted on ordering after the obligatory pints of lager had proved to be of equally high quality. Gavin swivelled his chair at an angle to the table to allow him to cross his legs, dabbed a few crumbs of popadum off his side plate and took a large swig of the wine. 'So,' he said expansively, 'what's this little thing I can help with?'

Billy looked at him over the rim of his lager glass: 'Who said anything about *little*?'

Gavin raised a quizzical eyebrow but showed no other signs of concern.

Billy took a deep breath. 'Well, come next month it'll be Dwayne's eighteenth.'

Gavin looked down to the other end of the table where the hunched teenager was wholly focussed on a small screen, wires protruding from both ears. 'Good on him… happy birthday for next month, Dwayne,' he called down the table, getting no response.

'His own little world,' Billy said apologetically. 'He'll be watching *The Sweeney.*'

'*The Sweeney*? What, the old TV series… John Thaw and what's his name?'

'Dennis Waterman. Yeah, big in the seventies. Dwayne's obsessed with it, even knows some episodes word for word.'

'Oh well, each to his own, I always preferred *Minder* myself.'

'I want to lay on something special for the kid's big one.'

'Sure, I can see that.' Gavin was starting to wonder where this was going. 'What, like a special party or fly a crowd out to Ibiza or something?'

'Dwayne's come up with his own idea.'

Gavin looked doubtfully down the table. 'Oh yes?'

'*Sweeney* themed.'

'Well… that would be different, I suppose, but I don't see…'

There was a sudden commotion at a large table across the room where a crowd of young men, fashionably dressed and well spoken, had been getting increasingly rowdy. 'Oi, Popadum Pete, more beer over here,' a pink polo shirt bellowed.

A waiter came out from behind the counter but instead of heading towards the crowd came over to Billy and spread his hands apologetically. 'Sorry, Mr Billy.'

Billy nodded then turned to Gavin. 'Hang on a sec.' He got up and walked across to the noisy table and said something that Gavin didn't hear, but which was greeted by an abusive jeer. Billy held up his hand and said something else then Gavin saw him lift the front of his jersey. The reaction was immediate. Billy looked round the silent table. 'OK, time to go, lads,' he said quietly. 'Now, who's paying?' He looked round the table again, 'I know, you can.' He rapped the pink polo shirt on the top of the head with an extended knuckle. 'The rest of you out... now! Billy watched the crush heading for the door. 'Rashid...' he called over his shoulder, '... bring this *gentleman* his bill, please. Oh, and the service charge is twenty-five percent... just for this evening and just for you.' He rapped Pink shirt on the head again and walked back to Gavin.

'Sorry about that.'

'You make a habit of that?' Gavin said, nodding at Billy's waistband.

'Can't be too careful, Gav, it's not like the old days. You just can't be sure now, it's all rougher, and some of these East Europeans are right evil bastards.'

The waiter, Rashid, appeared at Billy's side and put an

opened bottle of red wine on the table. 'On the house, Mr Billy.'

Billy nodded his thanks. 'Right, where was I?'

'Er, Dwayne's *Sweeney*-themed party, I think.'

'Oh yeah, well it's not exactly a party, more of... an event. What he really wants to do is his own job, like... well, a good old-fashioned blag.'

Gavin looked at him in disbelief for a moment then let out a bellow of laughter. He couldn't help glancing down the table again before saying: 'Go on! What, with the old sawn-offs, stocking masks, motor running in the street and all that lark?' He shook his head, chuckling.

'Exactly.'

Gavin studied his old mate carefully. 'You are kidding, aren't you? That all went out with... well, *The Sweeney*. And anyway, they always got nicked.'

'Not everyone, Gav. Come on, we've known a few who... well, look at us.'

'Yeah but, Billy...'

'Just hear me out eh, Gav? It would mean a lot to the kid, and if his godfather was along as well, then what better?'

'Yeah,' Gavin looked confused, 'yeah, I suppose that would be a nice touch but...'

'That's you, Gav.'

'Is it?'

When they reached Billy's home, a huge barn conversion in a secluded wooded plot at the end of a rough lane, the fires had already been lit, a cheerful ambience of respectable normality prevailed and a bottle of malt whisky was produced. They sprawled on the huge fireside sofas, reminiscing, while Billy poured the whisky and steered the conversation, before quietly producing a bundle of maps, street plans and architect's drawings, which he spread out on the huge coffee table.

Gavin eyed them and sighed. 'Look, Billy, it's great to see you... and Dwayne, and I really appreciate the hospitality and I'll make sure the kid isn't forgotten on his birthday, but I'm not up for this. I've got too much to lose, mate.'

'Here me out, Gav, just let me run it past you, I'd appreciate your thoughts whatever. Your experience,' he added.

Gavin sighed again. 'OK, go on then.' He helped himself to another Scotch and crouched forward over the table.

Billy gave a surprisingly slick presentation and even his son removed one of his earpieces at one point. Worryingly, Gavin noted, this was when firearms were mentioned. But slowly, despite himself, Gavin found himself being sucked in. He'd always enjoyed the challenge of shaping a plan, anticipating the problems and working out the available bailouts. It was like the old days. He was soon making his own suggestions, which Billy duly noted in the margins of his plans, saying little and allowing his old friend to reel himself in.

'So what would my role be... er, have been, then?'

Billy played it cool. 'That doesn't really matter now, does it, Gav?' He ran his finger down the heavily annotated margin of the nearest map. 'But thanks for all the ideas, appreciate it.'

'Well go on, anyway.'

'Oh you'd hardly have been involved at all,' Billy said apologetically. 'Just standing at the door stopping any last-minute customers coming in. You'd be in disguise, of course,' he added quickly, 'and then driving the Capri.'

'Capri! A Ford Capri? Are you serious?'

'Yeah, it's out the back now; 2.8 V8 turbo-charged, racing suspension, the works. False plates, of course.'

Gavin lolled back on the deep sofa, cradling his glass. 'Young Dwayne's really got it bad, hasn't he?' he grinned.

'Yeah, soppy git.'

'Just out of interest, how exactly am I… is someone, meant to stop customers going into their own bank?'

'Well, like I've said, the whole thing happens right on the point of closing time so there won't be much going on… have another Scotch… and then there's the disguise.'

'Yeah, I was wondering about that; false beard, wig and shades, I suppose.'

'Well you can stick those on as well if you like but this is the clever bit, you'll be done up as a security guard *delivering* cash. Helmet and visor, shades too if you like, full uniform of course and complete with a cash box chained to your wrist. You stop people, politely, by telling them there's a big high-security delivery going on and no one's allowed in until it's finished. And as it's just about closing time anyway, best they come back tomorrow. Good, eh? Have another Scotch.'

'Not bad, Billy, not bad at all,' Gavin mused. 'And alarms?'

'Ah, another clever bit. Every Friday, just after closing, they always test the fire alarm, dozy sods, so it'll be just another drill, no one's going to bother.'

'Link to the police station?'

'Probably, but it's twelve miles away and there's only two of them there. Not a firearms unit within thirty miles,' he added.

Gavin looked thoughtful for a moment. 'Well, you've done your homework, Billy boy. Yeah, OK, don't mind if I do.' He slid his glass across the table.

Billy leant over the table. 'After that, it's like I've explained: Dwayne and his mate do the stuff at the counter with the shooters,' – he glanced down the table at his inert son – 'not loaded of course,' he whispered, 'and I'll keep an eye on things from just inside the door and you out on the steps. Then the lads leg it round the corner and bugger off on a scooter and it's you and me down the alley and away in the Capri with the dough and the guns.'

Gavin shook his head in disbelief and sipped his whisky. 'You're bloody mad.'

'Yeah, but it'll work. Everyone's buggering about with the Internet and cybercrime these days, they won't see this one coming.'

Gavin shook his head again but pulled a street map across the cluttered table.

'Look, Gav, it'll be a laugh. We'll split four ways.'

Gavin let out a snort. 'I don't need it, Billy, I've got Spain. And Jacko will go spare if he finds out.'

'He still with you? Always was the nervy type, I was never quite sure about…'

'Yeah, yeah, I know.' Gavin pulled some photographs towards him and started to study them intently. Billy knew it was time to shut up and let his plan speak for itself. He wandered down the table on the pretext of seeing what Dwayne was doing.

'I'll want to see the car, the bank, the whole set up, OK?'

'Yeah, no problem.' Billy couldn't hide his delight, and relief. He tugged an earpiece out from under his son's lank hair. 'Dwayne, we got our wheelman!'

'Cool.'

* * *

Greg woke slowly, his nose twitching. He uncurled and sat up stiffly in his sleeping bag. Ben's face appeared from within a quilted hood in the opposite corner of the tent and for a moment seemed confused by Greg's presence.

'Oh, morning,' he said eventually.

Greg started to thank him again for his and Cat's overnight kindness but Ben brushed his thanks aside with a yawn, stuck his head out of the open flap and bellowed, 'Coffee woman!'

A minute later a well-bundled Cat appeared at the tent entrance holding two steaming enamel mugs. 'I didn't know how you like it, Greg, so I guessed, it's white and no sugar, is that OK?'

'Spot on.'

'I'll let you boys decide whether you're going to fortify it,' she grinned, nodding at the nearly empty brandy bottle.

'Now there's an idea,' Ben said.

Greg was amazed at how well equipped and organised Ben and Cat were. Crawling out of the tent, still nursing his coffee cup, he found Cat had set up a virtual kitchen in the corner of two tumbledown stone walls; there was an array of plastic boxes and plates, a selection of cutlery arranged on an old roofing slate, two tea cloths draped neatly over the branch of a handy rowan tree and two tiny camping stoves, each sitting on its own flat stone base, one roaring away under a kettle, the other a frying pan.

'Bacon's nearly ready, guys.' The smell on the fresh morning air was tantalising and a minute or two later Greg found himself juggling a plate piled with bacon sandwiches – there was even ketchup – and a fresh mug of coffee.

With breakfast over Ben had wandered off looking for what he referred to as a "dump hole", and returned saying he'd spotted what looked like the remains of Greg's tent. It was about 500 yards down the beck at the bottom of a ravine, out of reach and clearly a write-off. Greg had shrugged ruefully and with an unconvincing sigh, said he guessed it would just have to be B&Bs for the rest of the trip. Then, with more effusive thanks and promises to get in touch, Greg made his goodbyes.

After the storm of the night before it wasn't a bad day, still a brisk breeze but that kept the high white cumulus whizzing across the sky, and there was more sunshine than not. Greg's second day's walking was to take in the lofty heights of the dramatic Wetherlam, which dominates the northern skyline above Coniston, before he descended into the Langdale valley. That would be enough for today. Just the thought of now being able to shed his remaining camping gear seemed to lighten his pack and quicken his steps. He enjoyed his day, it was rugged but rewarding walking and the weather held, but when his downward path at last levelled out, he started looking forward to a hot bath and the crisp bed linen of some cosy Lakeland guest house.

After over an hour of knocking on doors, which had elicited responses ranging from the apologetic negative to pitying disbelief at his optimism, Greg miserably concluded that all the accommodation in the Langdale valley was full. He should have known better, of course; for goodness' sake *he was in the business!* It was getting late and he was very tired. Preparing to knock on one last door, Greg decided that if this was unsuccessful he'd just have to reconcile himself to spending hundreds at one of the country house hotels that discreetly littered the valley – Martin would understand.

The lady who answered the door was kind and sympathetic, but all her rooms were full. Greg wearily thanked her and turned back down the path.

'You could try the Doll's House, I suppose.'

Greg turned round and looked at her doubtful face. 'The Doll's House?'

She frowned uncertainly. 'Well…'

'Yes? Is it nearby?'

'Just down the lane but…'

'Do you think they'll have a vacancy?'

'Oh yes, but…

'Well that sounds promising, which way do I go?'

The woman hesitated and studied Greg for a moment. 'You'll be all right, I expect,' she said finally, and told him how to locate the unmade track off the lane, which led to the house. 'You can't miss it,' he was assured. Greg thanked her profusely and set off down her path again.

'It's a bit… peculiar,' she called out as he reached the gate, but Greg was past caring.

He had no problem finding the track, it was longer than he'd anticipated but there was no mistaking the property, it was the only one in sight. Overgrown hedges bracketed the hingeless gate and Greg had to force his way through before stepping into the front garden. "Peculiar" wasn't the word he would have chosen. Bizarre perhaps, or macabre… perverted even, but whatever it was, it was way beyond "peculiar".

The garden was a patchwork of raw earthen beds and gravelled areas criss-crossed by narrow, crumbling redbrick paths. There were a few flowers and the odd untended shrub at the fringes, but predominantly the garden was dominated by weeds and small plastic figures… or bits of them. Many appeared to be emerging from the soil and gravel, bursting through the surface, or being grotesquely absorbed by the ground as if in quicksand. These were not gnomes; there wasn't one brightly coloured, beaming, fishing or mooning little fairytale character amongst them. No, these mini-manikins and the collection of apparently discarded body parts all belonged to the world of real human beings. Some had obviously been some little girl's baby dolly; large, pink and plump with rosebud lips and unnaturally blue eyes, tufts of filthy synthetic hair still protruding from perforated scalps. But the majority of the collection, and spare parts, seemed to be of the Barbie doll, Action Man type and scale, about nine inches tall and unnaturally thin. Both sexes seemed to be represented and the figures were all naked, stripped of any outfit, costume or uniform they might once have been dressed in. Greg gazed uncomfortably at the exposed nippleless breasts and smooth, moulded hermaphroditic genitalia. Many of the figures were incomplete, the missing limbs scattered amongst the weeds, all were filthy and some appeared to have had crude "tattoos" drawn onto various parts of their little plastic bodies. Greg hesitated just inside the garden and wondered what the inside of the cottage would hold, and what on earth the people who occupied it could be like. Suddenly overwhelmed by weariness he decided to risk it. Supressing his... he wasn't quite sure what, bewilderment, shock, revulsion, he knocked on the door. To his surprise and great relief it was opened by a perfectly normal-looking late-middle-aged couple, cardiganned, slippered and gentle. He was greeted warmly, promised their best room and offered it at a ridiculously low rate. The interior of the house reflected none of the macabre eccentricity of the front garden and Greg's room proved to be traditionally comfortable and charming, as did his hosts. The meal he was served, which he'd eaten ravenously after a quick suspicious sniff, was delicious. Wine was provided without his asking, apparently at no cost, and there were even mints with the coffee.

Making his way through the front garden next morning, Greg averted his eyes from some of the more disturbing figures. They'd made only the briefest of appearances in his dreams and he was leaving well rested and well fed... if none the wiser.

Greg had tried repeatedly to phone Martin from the Doll's House but the surrounding mountains of the Langdale valley had stubbornly refused him a signal and supposedly there was no landline from the cottage. The topography round the town of Ambleside was to prove more cooperative. After a gentle walk, which took him over some of the lower fells, Greg had arrived in the town mid-afternoon. Resisting the temptation to break his journey and simply jump on the local bus and head the few miles home, he checked into one of the larger looking B&Bs – he was, after all, supposed to be doing a bit of market research during the trip.

Nothing much impressed Greg about the place he'd chosen, it all seemed a bit shabby and dirty. He'd collected several fingertips worth of dust from a variety of surfaces while a sulky young woman checked him in, and there was a vague smell of uncleaned toilets about the place. There was a theme of sorts, less sinister certainly than naked, dismembered children's toys, but Greg wasn't impressed by the huge, randomly arranged collection of dusty novelty teapots. Spouted and handled VW Beetles were wedged next to red telephone boxes, a Thomas The Tank Engine threatened to be shunted off its side table by a flowery pig and the Houses of Parliament teetered on the mantelpiece next to The Kremlin. They covered every surface and most were just tackily impractical.

'God, it sounds awful,' Martin exclaimed, when Greg phoned him a little later from the privacy of his room. He'd already been chastised for not ringing the evening before and when he'd described the sinister Doll's House, Martin had nearly had kittens. 'Why did you go in? They were obviously crazy, anything could've happened. Anyone who rips the limbs off naked dolls has got to be...'

'Well, they didn't.' Greg recalled the shuffling old couple in their matching tartan slippers and heavy-pocketed cardigans pottering around making his dinner and together trying to wrestle the cork out of the wine bottle.

'Didn't what?'

'Rip my limbs off...' Greg said, '...and they didn't get me naked either,' he giggled.

Martin snorted. 'Yes, but just think...'

Greg let him huff and puff in this vein for a few minutes before interrupting. 'So anyway,' he said, 'I don't seem to be doing very well with this market research. I suppose we could scrap Sherlock Holmes and start collecting one-legged Barbie teapots... naked, of course. What do you think?'

There was silence at the other end of the phone for a moment, then a giggle: 'Fool!'

'I miss you.'

'I miss you, too.'

'How *are* things at home? Everything OK? You're managing?'

'Yes, yes, of course.'

'Sure?'

'Of course, Gigi, no problems. I fired Lisa yesterday but she's no loss.'

'What!'

'Dirty little cow, I caught her at it in the Windermere suite... on freshly changed bedding too.'

'But what about...'

'It's not a problem, it'll save us some wages and anyway it's gone a bit quiet on the bookings.'

Greg wasn't sure he believed his partner. 'And Derek?' he ventured.

'Ah, Derek, well he's in hospital. A broken leg and an ankle, different legs, can't remember which way round.'

'Christ, what happened? Not our fault, is it? He didn't slip in the kitchen or…?'

'Well, not exactly.'

'Martin…?

'Well, believe it or not, it was Derek giving Lisa one, and when I started trying to unlock the door he legged it out the window.'

'But Windermere's on the second floor!'

'I think he was trying to get down the drainpipe onto the kitchen roof – oh, and he was stark-bollock naked by the way – anyway, the pipe came away from the wall and he sort of went with it, missed the roof completely. Gave the neighbour's cat a hell of a fright.'

'Martin, you're making this up.'

'Honest to God, Gigi.'

There was a long silence then bellows of speechless laughter erupted from both ends of the phone.

* * *

Finding himself accidentally, if fortuitously, on the wrong side of the Bristol Channel had dissolved what was left of Robbie's confidence and he was seriously starting to doubt whether he was capable of sailing on up the coast on his own.

The Welsh fisherman, it turned out, played for the same rugby team as the marina manager and together they'd arranged a cheap berth for him in a corner of one of the older undredged parts of the marina. Robbie was grateful, but decided what he really needed was a competent crew – what he needed was an Ed. This, it seemed, was not to be. Robbie had eventually got through to Ed's brother, who was mortified by his younger brother's mutinous behaviour. He apologised repeatedly on his behalf but explained that Ed's efforts to re-woo his girlfriend had proved effective and he'd returned to town where he'd promptly disappeared into the girl's flat, and apart from the boy who made the twice-daily pizza deliveries, no one had seen them for nearly a week. Ed would not be coming back.

Robbie had prowled round the bars and chandlers of the marina trying to spot a likely recruit or two but his chances had been hampered by not being able to offer any form of payment, nor a particularly glamorous destination. At this time of the season it was only the hot spots of the yachty south coast that were likely to tempt young casual hands, not the abandoned industrial ports of the north-west. Robbie had no takers.

In the meantime he'd got on with the repairs to *Idler's* main sail and replacing the various cleats which had been torn out by the crash gybes during what he now referred to as "the great storm". With a little help, he'd even gone up the mast and managed to re-reeve the halyard. It was fiddly work patching and stitching the frayed fabric of his sail back together, but apart from the tenderised fingertips, Robbie quite enjoyed sitting in the cockpit with the sail spread over his knees and a glass of something close at hand, stitching steadily away as marina life went on around him. Some of the old hands watched his work critically, never commenting, but other friendlier souls would occasionally stop to chat. Late one afternoon he noticed an attractive young couple watching him from a little way up the pontoon. He'd been vaguely aware of them for a few minutes and they seemed shy. Robbie smiled at them, especially the girl.

It seemed to give the boy confidence. 'You have a beautiful boat,' he said carefully, in a polite, heavily accented voice.

'Thank you.' Robbie sounded doubtful. 'Do you sail?' he asked.

'Yes. Yes, much at home.' The boy was doing all the talking but the girl nodded vigorously at this. 'We like to very much.'

'Are you students?'

There was a brief hesitation but Robbie was re-threading his needle so didn't see the glance between the pair. 'Yes,' the girl said eventually, 'we are students but have holidays now.'

'We like travel,' the boy added. 'Where are you go to next?'

'Oh, wherever the wind takes me,' Robbie said airily. 'But north,' he added.

'Ireland?'

'No, why?'

'We have friend in Ireland, in Conk.'

'Conk? Oh I see, *Cork*.'

An idea was starting to occur to Robbie. He put down his needle and thread. 'Are you good sailors?'

The boy nodded emphatically and the girl quickly joined in. 'We win races... often. At home,' he added.

'From where I'm going it would be easy to get to Ireland.

You can get a ferry from Liverpool… or maybe Whitehaven.' Robbie had no idea whether ferries went from Liverpool to Ireland and he was pretty sure they didn't from Whitehaven. 'I could give you a lift, drop you off, and you could give me a hand to sail the boat. Not that I really need it but if it would help you out.' He glanced at the girl. 'It might be a bit of a squeeze down below but we could manage.'

'You pay us?'

'No, no, I give you a lift.'

'Food?'

Robbie was a bit taken aback. 'Well… I expect we can come to some sort of arrangement. Take it as it comes, eh?' he grinned.

'We need time for thinking. We come back later.'

To Robbie's surprise the couple reappeared within the hour, and to his further surprise, both were carrying hefty rucksacks, which they dumped in the cockpit before clambering aboard. 'We come.' The boy held out his hand. 'My name is Stephan,' he said formally. 'This is Michaela… Micky. We come from Romania. Micky is my girlfriend,' he added firmly.

Robbie was a bit taken aback by the abruptness and speed with which events seemed to be overtaking him, but completed his part of the introductions and showed them down to the chaotic cabins. It was agreed he would squeeze into the partitioned-off forepeak to sleep while the young couple would occupy the twin bunks of the main saloon. Back on deck Stephan and Micky showed little interest in the rigging or deck gear. 'How does the engine go?' Stephan demanded. Robbie showed him. 'OK,' Stephan said, 'now we go.' So they did.

The weather was once again benign with helpful southerly winds and they had left Swansea, as luck would have it, at the right state of the tide and lunar cycle. They made steady if unspectacular progress without too many dramas, initially west and then north along the west Wales coast. *Idler* was a kindly boat and in these conditions happily sailed herself with the minimum of human intervention, which was just as well as it quickly became clear to Robbie that his new crew hadn't got a clue.

Most nights they managed to reach the port or harbour that Robbie had planned, and apart from being shooed out of one bay, which was subject to live firing and unexploded ordinance, his navigation had proved surprisingly (not least to him) reliable. There were, of course, onboard tensions; the primitive "sea-toilet" in a curtained-off cubicle within the forepeak was a particular source of niggle and embarrassment, particularly with members of both sexes on board. Any thoughts of a cooking rota had soon collapsed and inevitably the pan one party particularly wanted would be found congealed and discarded in the sink by the other. And it *was* a case of two parties: us and them, or in the Romanians' case, us and *him*. They were making less effort to speak English now, increasingly muttering to each other in their own language and their mobile phones were in constant use. Robbie would occasionally catch one or both of them glaring at him for no apparent reason and felt he was increasingly being ignored, particularly when there was work to be done.

Tensions normally eased when they were all ashore, usually spending their evenings separately, although in smaller, one-hostelry ports this wasn't always possible and one evening, somewhere along the north Wales coast, things came to a head.

Robbie wasn't exactly sure where they were that evening, it hadn't been a good navigating day, but late afternoon he'd spotted a sea wall and they'd been allowed to squeeze into the tiny harbour it protected and then, with some relief, had gone ashore. The size of the port reflected the size of the village and that evening all three eventually found themselves together in the only bar. Already several drinks ahead, Robbie decided to try and thaw the atmosphere with his crew. He invited himself to their table, insisted on buying them a drink and thought he'd try a bit of light chat and banter: he burbled about the weather, assured them they would soon be at their destination (wherever that was), made up wildly exaggerated tales of previous sailing experiences and told smutty schoolboy jokes. All his efforts were met with the same blank, if anything slightly contemptuous, expressions. A moody silence eventually descended.

'So what do you two think about free love then?' Robbie suddenly demanded with a chuckle.

This got a reaction. The two youngsters exchanged glances and looked embarrassed. 'Our love is always free. We do not pay each other,' Stephan said carefully.

'No, no, let me explain…'

'So everyone with everyone?' Stephan eventually ventured, clearly shocked.

'Yeah.'

'But we are Catholics,' Micky said.

'All the more reason then,' Robbie exclaimed illogically.

'So you fuck Micky?'

Robbie missed the outrage in Stephan's voice: 'Yeah, and you too if you like.'

'You fuck me too?'

'Well… that's not what I meant but I suppose…'

Micky's slap was a split second before Stephan's punch and the evening was over.

Robbie finally stumbled back aboard much later that night and was surprised to see the twin humps in the saloon bunks as he crept towards the forepeak. The atmosphere onboard the next morning was predictably tense, but everyone seemed keen to get underway, and for the first time in a while the youngsters actually lent a hand in hoisting the heavy mainsail and casting off. After three hours of conversationless sailing Stephan suddenly pointed towards the north-west horizon: 'Ireland?'

'Yeah, an island,' Robbie mumbled through his swollen lips, not sure which island it was but pleased to break the silence. He disappeared below for yet another visit to the "heads" – the sea-toilet. The closing-time kebab and God knows how many pints from the night before were playing merry hell with his bowels… and guts… and bladder. Not to mention his head.

Squatting uncomfortably in the tiny, nylon-curtained cubicle, braced against the boat's motion, he was startled by a sudden crash on the little hatch above his head. Almost simultaneously the sliding door of the forepeak slammed home followed by a scraping and banging which caused the whole bulkhead to shudder. Robbie squatted, helpless and confused. He was desperately trying to tidy himself up and redress when there was another huge crash and the sound of splintering wood from further aft.

'What the fuck are you doing to my boat?' he bellowed, and grabbed at the sliding door – which refused to slide. 'Hey, help, let me out!'

Then the engine started and the boat heeled sharply as it changed direction. Robbie could hear the headsail flapping above him and pushed at the little foredeck hatch. That wouldn't budge either.

'Let me out, you bastards,' he roared. There was no response. His incarceration was obviously by design, not by accident. He heaved against the hatch and jerked at the door again but both held firm. He could hear their voices, guttural and urgent, and a painful grating and grinding as something heavy was moved across the deck. Robbie thought he knew what had happened, what the crash had been; the idiots had dropped the mainsail without tensioning the topping lift – the line that supports the end of the boom – so the heavy wooden spar had dropped with the sail and crashed onto his coach-house roof. Robbie winced at the thought of the likely damage.

He was having a rest from bellowing obscenities and battering the door and hatch when the engine suddenly stopped. The boat started to wallow and he could hear panicky exchanges on deck. The starter motor whirred time and again eventually fading to a pathetic whine. Great, Robbie thought bitterly, so now a flat battery could be added to the list of problems, along with the empty fuel tank, gunged up filters and smashed rig.

After a few minutes another engine coughed into life. Robbie recognised it as the little outboard on the inflatable tender. And then the voices were suddenly closer, they were in the main cabin, something smashed and there was a giggle followed by the sound of breaking glass and more laughs. Robbie went berserk. He threatened everything from drowning to disembowelment and frantically crunched his already bruised shoulders against the unyielding door as the sounds of ransacking and destruction continued.

Looting Robbie's meagre possessions didn't take long and the voices soon receded, followed a few minutes later by the engine. They'd abandoned him, captive in his own boat, powerless, sail-less and drifting. Robbie had no idea where he was or how close to land he might be; a steep beach, sheer cliffs or jagged rocks might only be a matter of yards away. Every few minutes he made himself listen intently for the dreaded sound of breaking waves, not that there was anything he could do about it; all he could do was sit and wait.

His watch was in the saloon, or at least it had been, so Robbie had no idea how long it was before he heard the approaching engine. It was loud and powerful, this was no tender outboard. He could hear distant hails of: 'Ahoy yacht, *Idler*, anyone aboard?' Robbie hoarsely tried to shout back but three hours of bellowing threats and obscenities had taken their toll. He felt a slight bump and heard heavy footsteps on the deck.

'Anyone on board?'

'Yes, yes, down here. Get me out!' Robbie croaked.

There was a splintering sound from the other side of the door and it suddenly shot back to reveal a bulky figure in the familiar RNLI outfit.

'I was hijacked,' Robbie said weakly and looked round his trashed saloon. He shook his head miserably and sighed.

'Not much better on deck, I'm afraid,' the RNLI man said and patted Robbie kindly on the shoulder. 'What on earth happened?'

'They hijacked me,' Robbie repeated, 'a couple of foreign kids.'

'Knocked you about a bit, did they?' he nodded at Robbie's mouth.

'Um, sort of...'

'OK, don't worry, it doesn't look too bad, we'll sort that out later. Let's get the boat straight again, I need to check the steering and then we can get a tow sorted.'

'Where am I?'

The lifeboatman looked at him in surprise: 'How long have you been stuck in there?'

'I don't know, three or four hours.'

'Where were you heading?'

'Sort of... Blackpool.'

'"Sort of Blackpool"? Well, if you had a date for tonight there you're not going to make it. You're about ten miles south-east of the Isle of Man, we're out of Douglas, and that's where you're heading now. Lucky for you we were out here training.'

'Yeah, dead lucky,' Robbie said vaguely.

SIX

At eight o'clock the next morning Dom found himself clinging to one of Dan's smellier friends, who had been persuaded to give his friend's reactionary father a lift to the nearest motorway slip road on his moped. The friend obviously hadn't been briefed on which direction his lift was heading and Dom had to trudge round the enormous roundabout dodging murderous rush-hour traffic at every exit before reaching the northern slip road. There he found a queue.

Near the top of the slope and about ten yards apart were two aggressive looking men in cheap anoraks holding red and white number plates, twenty yards further down were two young women with an enormous rucksack apiece, and then at the very bottom, where the slip road officially became the M6, a long-haired figure with a collection of beer tankards dangling from his pack waved a hopeful thumb at everything that came down the ramp. Dom decided he was better off where he was and hoisting his old rucksack over one shoulder turned to face the traffic coming off the roundabout and tried to look harmless.

'Oi, and what d'you think you're bleedin' doin'?'

Confused, Dom stopped and turned to find one of the anoraks pointing at him. 'Er, hoping to get a lift,' he called.

The man advanced quickly. 'And what the 'ell d'you think the rest of us are doing? We're not 'ere to collect fuckin' car numbers, are we? And we were 'ere first.'

'Um, well…

'Back of the queue, mate, bottom of the bleedin' 'ill.'

Dom had no idea there was any form of hitch-hiking etiquette, but looking at the man's angry face he decided not to argue and headed down the hill towards the motorway. He'd barely got past the two scowling men before a smart silver saloon, ignoring them completely, skidded to a halt by the two backpacking girls. Clearly well practised, they flipped open the car's boot, toppled in their rucksacks and jumped onto the back seat together. The whole exercise took less than ten seconds and the car took off again in a spray of gravel. The peculiar figure at the bottom of the queue gave the car a cheery wave as it roared past and edged up the slope towards Dom. The two men with the trade plates appeared to have teamed up, which turned out to be a sound strategy as within a few seconds a scruffy box van had pulled up next to them and both managed to squeeze into the cab. Dom saw little point in moving any further down the ramp and waited for the tankard carrier to reach him and claim what was obviously his rightful position, at the head of the slip road.

'We're clearly not doing this right,' the figure panted

as he came level with Dom. He had a broad Birmingham accent.

Dom gave a rueful smile of agreement and tried not to stare. His new friend certainly cut an extraordinary figure; his beard consisted of three beribboned plaits, tattoos crept out from collar and cuffs and he had numerous facial piercings. Apart from a waistcoat, which seemed to be of some sort of skin, possibly goat, he was dressed entirely in faded denim, which seemed to have been patched with floral curtain material. His rucksack was a frayed, misshapen bundle, which apart from the dangling collection of pewter tankards, also sported a mass of patches and badges – everything from CND to Spurs Football Club to Led Zeppelin.

'Helps to be a pretty girl or guys doing a job, I guess.'

Dom nodded and grunted agreement.

'Won't be long though, I bet… I'm Alice, Alice Cooper. Where you heading?'

'Alice Coo… not *the*…?'

'Nah, course not, just his greatest fan. So where you going then?'

Dom explained. 'And you… Alice?' he asked politely.

'As far as possible, man, I'm on a jail break.'

Dom couldn't stop himself taking an involuntary step back. He looked at Alice Cooper warily and tried to remember the name of the prison in Birmingham… something Green, he thought… and whether it was high security or one of the open type. If his companion had absconded from the latter then he was probably fairly harmless; Dom had a solicitor friend who'd served two years for some sort of mortgage scam in a prison of the open variety and claimed it was just like a long bank holiday weekend at Butlins, except with more drugs and fewer fights. Dom thought he ought to say something but could only come up with: 'Oh, that's interesting.'

'Yeah, I need to get as far as possible.'

'Yes, I suppose you would.'

'Scotland would be great, I'm already on over a pound a mile so that'd be worth a few hundred quid.'

Dom had no idea what he was talking about, and it showed.

The supposed ex-con looked at him closely. 'A jail break, you must have heard of them?'

'Well…'

Alice Cooper suddenly let out a bellow of laughter. 'You really think I've broken out of prison don't you?'

'Well…'

'Don't be daft,' he laughed again, 'it's a charity thing. There's a load of us set off from The Rat and Maggot in Solihull at eight this morning and we've got to see how far we can get in twenty four hours, but without spending anything. We're sponsored for every mile – I'm on over a quid already.'

'Of course,' Dom said, as if he'd known all along.

Alice looked up the slip road towards the roundabout. With the rush hour more or less over, far fewer vehicles were now joining the motorway. 'And this isn't getting us very far, is it?' he said, and set off up the hill. 'C'mon, it's gonna have to be plan B.'

Dom wasn't at all sure about plan B. But Alice Cooper had persuaded him that in the unlikely event of being challenged, all he had to do was explain about the "jail break". 'Just tell 'em it's all for charity and we'll probably be given a complimentary ticket and sent on our way. Might even blag a bit of sponsorship.'

Which was how Dom had found himself hurtling northward at 125mph seated on a stainless steel toilet staring at a yellow sign sternly instructing him how to wash his hands. Dom was not enjoying his first experience of "train-jumping", as Alice Cooper had called it. Despite the "engaged" sign, which he knew would be glowing over the door in the corridor, the handle had been tried a few times already and the constant threat of discovery was making him nervously dry-mouthed and slightly nauseous. Dom decided the next time the train stopped, when the corridors would be chaotic with passengers leaving and fresh faces embarking, he would risk the buffet car, break into the five-pound note (borrowed from his reluctant son on production of a signed IOU) and get himself a coffee and a sandwich.

Ten minutes later he made his move, passed quickly through two carriages and was halfway down the third when he heard the shouting and stern voices telling someone to "calm down". Dom slipped into a vacant seat and joined several others in craning his head to look down the aisle and see what the fuss was about. There was a knot of uniforms clustered round the toilet cubicle at the far end of the carriage, mainly railway employees but with at least two policemen amongst them. A loud West Midlands voice carried over the general hubbub, '…look, I've told you, it's all for charity, sick kiddies, I'm not allowed to pay, it's against the rules…'

'Not our rules, it isn't,' the stern voice interrupted. 'Now don't make a fuss, sir, just come with us and...'

'Look, I'm on a jail break...'

There were a few gasps from passengers within earshot and the policemen stiffened. Alice Cooper had not done his cause any good.

'Right, that's it, you're coming with us.'

'No I'm bloody not! Look you heartless bastards, I'm gonna...'

One of the policemen had reached round to the back of his cluttered belt and unhooked some handcuffs. 'No you're not, sir, now just calm down.'

There was a yelp, a loud crash and the whole scrum moved towards an open door, somehow squeezed through as one and bundled onto the platform. The carriage was treated to one last bellow of: 'It's all for fuckin' charity, you bastards...' before the door was slammed shut and the train gave a shudder, as if shaking off the last of Alice Cooper.

Dom stood up, uncertain what to do next, when a ticket collector appeared at the far end of the carriage and started to sway his way down the aisle. Dom headed quickly in the opposite direction until he ran out of carriages. The rearmost toilet cubicle was engaged and Dom impatiently hovered close by until the door opened and a young woman came out. She started, obviously surprised to find someone waiting so close. Dom tried to smile reassuringly and lunged into the toilet cubicle. He sat down and read the sign about washing his hands. Now what? After the discovery of Alice Cooper, the ticket collectors were bound to be checking all the toilets for a possible accomplice. He might be only minutes from discovery. The train must be getting near Manchester by now, but would he make it that far... and how would he get off the platform? Alice Cooper had never explained that bit. No, it was obvious he had to get off the train as soon as possible, and preferably not at a station. Dom put his elbows on his knees and cupped his chin in his hands. God, how had he come to this, squatting, illegally, on a high-speed metal bog seriously contemplating jumping off a moving train? He wasn't Richard bloody Hannay!

As it happened, whilst Dom had been contemplating his immediate future, the train had slowed considerably. There was another sudden deceleration, which almost threw him off his perch and he decided to risk the corridor and see what was going on. Nothing, was the answer, to his relief. The little lobby was empty and looking down the adjoining carriage he could see no sign of officialdom, or anyone else on their feet. It felt as if the train was barely moving now, just vibrating slightly and rattling gently over track joins every few minutes or so. Dom looked out of the left-hand window and straight onto another set of tracks. Beyond these was a steep bank of sharp looking gravel topped by a sooty block-work wall. If he was serious about jumping, and it was a big if, he certainly wouldn't be going out that way. The right-hand side was more promising, if he was quick; a narrow grassy verge became a weedy bank sloping gently down to a broken fence, beyond which was a little meadow bisected by a canal. The train gave a shudder, Dom couldn't be sure it wasn't picking up speed again, but realised his moment had probably come. It was decision time; either jump, probably to a painful but respectable freedom, or sit tight and almost certainly face detection and ignominy. He opened the door and was immediately blasted by a rush of air. The train must be accelerating, the grassy verge, which had looked almost stationary from behind the carriage window now seemed to be whipping past and on closer inspection appeared lumpier and less well covered than he'd thought. The train gave a sharp jolt, Dom grabbed at his rucksack for balance and the door was ripped from his hand, but not before dragging him beyond the point of no return.

* * *

Three days after arriving at Billy's, Gavin found himself standing on the top step of a short flight of weathered stone steps with his back to the partly closed door of an old-fashioned, small-town bank. He was dressed in uniform dungarees, leather gloves and a visored helmet. A scarf pulled tight to his chin and reflective dark glasses further obscured his features. How had he let this happen?

The morning after the Scotch-fuelled planning session Gavin had woken early, thick-headed, dry-mouthed and vaguely aware he'd done something stupid the night before. It wasn't just the hangover, it was like the feeling he remembered from childhood, waking up the morning after being sent to bed early for some misdemeanour. Slowly the fog had cleared, the events of the previous evening started to come into focus and with it the appalling realisation of the commitment he now remembered making. Gavin knew he couldn't back out,

Billy would never trust him again… and word would get out. He'd wandered downstairs, found the maps and plans still scattered across the coffee table amongst the empties and started looking for some irrefutable flaw in Billy's scheme to use as ammunition… or, if he was honest, as an excuse. Billy duly appeared, sploshed the remains of the Scotch into their coffees and proceeded to shoot down every one of Gavin's objections – so here he was.

'Excuse me, may I go in please?'

Distracted by a sudden shout from inside the bank, Gavin had had his head stuck through the door checking everything was OK when the old lady with the tartan shopping trolley suddenly appeared at his elbow. He quickly pulled the door to and gently moved to block her way before explaining the "security situation", throwing in a bit of "health and safety" for good measure.

'Oh I'll be very careful,' the old dear assured him, 'and I'm hardly going to rob the bank, am I?'

Gavin decided to try gentle levity. 'Ah, that's what you say, but I don't know that, do I?'

'Oh you!' she tittered. 'But really, I must…'

'Look, madam, I would if I could, but it's more than my job's worth, see?'

The old lady sighed. 'Oh dear, I really don't like having this much money in the house over the weekend. It's not mine, you see, it's the flower arrangers'.'

Gavin muttered something sympathetic, then suddenly conscious that the tiny woman could see up under his visor, lowered his chin and turned away.

The old lady suddenly gave a little squeak. 'I know,' she

said brightly, 'if you wouldn't mind, you could pay it in for me with yours.' She tapped the aluminium security case chained loosely to Gavin's wrist.

There was no arguing and a moment later Gavin found himself cradling a bulging floral soap bag, which, he was assured, contained a completed paying-in slip and £483 pounds and 27 pence… in cash.

Billy's helmeted head appeared round the door. 'Won't be long,' he said, with a puzzled glance at the soap bag. 'Sweet as a nut so far… oh fuck!' As he'd spoken, the bank's alarm had gone off and a blue stroboscopic light started pulsing angrily over the main door. This was clearly not a fire drill. Billy didn't even have time to duck back inside before there was the unmistakeable double boom of a shotgun being discharged. 'Bloody hell, the little sod got himself some ammo… thank God the Luger's a replica.' His head disappeared and Gavin followed, pushing the door to.

Inside the bank there was chaos. The room was full of dust and chunks of plaster were scattered across the floor. Water was pouring between exposed lathes and joists from a huge hole in the ceiling and everyone in the room seemed to be shouting or screaming. Dwayne was still standing at a serving window waving the sawn-off shotgun in the air. Billy snatched it off him and pushed him towards the door. 'C'mon, for Chrissake!'

'They won't give me any.'

'Bugger that, get out. NOW!'

The other youth, Dwayne's friend and partner-in-crime, was standing at a window further along the counter brandishing a handgun and screaming incoherently at a pen stand, which he'd mistaken for an intercom. Billy headed for him while Gavin, guarding the door, shoved the reluctant Dwayne outside onto the steps, yanking his stocking mask off him as he went. Gavin turned back just in time to see Billy get pistol-whipped by Dwayne's friend.

'It's me, you silly fucker!' Billy bellowed. His visor saved him and he slapped the pistol away and, none too gently, prodded the youth in the stomach with the shotgun. 'Now get going, out, now!'

'We ain't got nothing.'

'You'll get ten fuckin' years if you don't move. C'mon.'

The youngster started to follow, then clearly decided on one last attempt. He shoved the pistol under the glass screen and screamed, 'Hand it over!' at the pen stand. The bank teller didn't hesitate, she grabbed the gun, turning it away from herself, and pulled with all her might. A colleague joined her and the would-be robber found himself dragged across the counter, his stockinged face flattened against the glass screen. 'Leggo,' he mumbled.

'Oh for Chrissake!' Billy spat, between clenched teeth, as he and Gavin turned from the door and watched the woman teller grab the gunman's hand, which had followed the gun under the screen, and sink her teeth into his trigger finger.

'Oww!' The distorted face was turned towards Billy and Gavin now. Suddenly released by the bank staff, the would-be robber then fell off the counter, slipped and landed in a sludgy puddle of water where he sat nursing his finger. 'She's nicked my gun,' he whined.

The robbery now abandoned, the two youngsters, as planned, had taken off round a corner to escape on their scooter. Billy fervently hoped they'd remember where they'd left it… and that they'd put petrol in it… and that they wouldn't break the speed limit, and… oh what the hell, they were on their own now. Billy and Gavin had waited a moment and then left the bank at a brisk but un-panicked pace, only to be intercepted by the little old lady at the foot of the steps. She was breathless and looked excited.

'It's all right, I've called the police,' she said, and looked in confusion at her soap bag.

'Here, you take this, it'll be safer with you.' Gavin thrust it into her arms and quickly followed Billy round a corner and into an alleyway, leaving the old dear to peep curiously round the bank door. After a hundred yards or so Billy led the way through a barbed wire-topped gate and into a working scrapyard. The gate was quickly locked behind them, their uniforms and the gun were shoved into a waiting holdall, which was hurled into the crusher, and they jumped into the Ford. Gavin carefully put his seat belt on and drummed his fingers on the steering wheel. 'I don't know how you ever talked me into…'

'C'mon, wheelman, drive!' Billy whooped, and then collapsed into helpless laughter.

The drive back into the Kent countryside had been careful, sedate, and above all, *legal*. Gavin hadn't broken a speed limit, jumped an orange light or even risked getting too close when overtaking cyclists. As they got further away from their crime scene, and with no sign of a hue and cry, Gavin relaxed and he too started to see the funny side of the farcical stunt they'd just pulled off.

'I can't believe I let you talk me into that… That was the most ridiculous… How the hell we got away with… I hope there's another bottle of that Scotch back at your place, I reckon I've bloody earned it!'

'A whole case, mate, don't you worry.'

Several hours, another excellent curry and half a bottle of Billy's estimable Scotch later, and the two were again sprawled on the low-slung sofas surrounding the huge coffee table where the plan had been hatched.

'He's a good lad really,' Billy was saying, 'a bit bloody thick, but then his mum was no mastermind. Mind you, bright enough to take me for a fair few quid when she finally buggered off.'

'Yeah, I was wondering…'

'Oh, the old story, I had to go and stay with "Her Maj" for a few years, Joycie got a bit frisky, she always was a horny bitch, and well…'

'I thought it was Sharon.'

'Nah, that was the one before.'

'Right, so whose fault is…? I mean, who's Dwayne's mum then?'

Billy opened another bottle of whisky and thought for a minute. 'Sharon,' he said finally. 'I think.'

'So she was the thick one?'

Billy filled the glasses. 'Well, both were really. In fairness, Joyce did have some GCSEs, three I think. Mind you, cooking certainly wasn't one of them,' he laughed. 'What about you then?'

'I've got a Bobby.'

'Blimey…'

'Bobby's a *she*.'

'Yeah, of course. Young?'

'Yeah, a bit,' Gavin said defensively.

'Thick?'

'Oh yeah.'

They sat in silence while rain beat on the high windows set in the eaves of the barn, refilling each other's glasses regularly.

'But he's not a bad lad,' Billy resumed, 'a bit thick... have I already said that?' He took another sip. 'Mind you, I'm no Einstein, am I? But a bit more of the old common wouldn't go amiss with the daft little sod, he's got no savvy, not really streetwise if you know what I mean. At least we had that, eh? But he's a good lad, we're more sort of mates really,' he slurred with a drunk's affection. 'Yeah...' he mused '... sort of mates, good mates... *What the fuck are you doing here?*'

Dwayne had appeared from the shadows at the end of the room. 'Forgot me charger,' he whined.

'I told you not to come near the place for a week or so. You're meant to be up in town with Scot, you silly little bastard. If anyone's got wind of... or seen you... hang on, how did you get here?'

'Came on the scooter. I forgot me...'

'You what? I told you to get rid of that, dump the fucking thing. You stupid little gits, you could drop us all in it.'

Gavin got to his feet. 'Right, Billy, I'm out of here. Dwayne, make me a coffee, strong and black, I'll get my gear. I need a taxi, Billy.'

'Not from here you don't, it'll link you if anyone comes asking. I'll run you across to the station, there's always a couple of late guys sitting around there.'

'You OK to drive?' Gavin looked dubiously at the empty bottle on the table.

'Yeah, yeah, it's only twenty minutes down the road. Where you going, up town?'

'Nope, Gatwick, lots of hotels, people coming in and out at all hours, and I can pick up a car from there in the morning and head north.'

* * *

Greg awoke surrounded by dusty teapots. Amongst others his room hosted a chipped Flying Scotsman, Dumbo the Elephant and the peeing boy of Brussels, mercifully spoutless. Glad to get out of the room, he was treated to an appalling breakfast but a beautiful morning. He stocked up at a sandwich shop in Ambleside high street, avoiding the ubiquitous chains, and with the sun shining in an almost cloudless sky decided to take one of the more challenging routes across to Patterdale, his destination for that night. The walk would take him up and along the western spur of the famous Fairfield horseshoe, onto the whale's back of Fairfield itself and then along the spectacular ridge of the delightfully named St Sunday's Crag, before descending into the village of Patterdale. It would be a challenging walk and Martin would have been tutting and fussing if he'd known, but conditions were perfect and Greg felt rested and confident.

His day's walk started gently enough, with an easy stroll along the side of a valley much trodden by thousands of Wordsworth pilgrims, which brought Greg to Rydal Mount, once home to the great poet. Predictably, it was now a magnet for tourists, and today, like most days, it was packed with crowds of largely disinterested coach-trippers queuing for their postcards, fridge magnets and cups of tea. At the moment the crowd seemed to be predominantly Americans, with a smaller contingent of well sun-blocked Japanese, the former brandishing preposterously large camera lenses, the latter, mobile phones clipped to selfie sticks.

Greg decided to treat himself to a coffee. He joined a queue, then found a seat in the crowded garden where he sipped and listened, unavoidably, to a loud conversation going on at an adjoining table. They were a late middle-aged couple and even if the strong accents hadn't given away their origins, the outfits would.

'So this is it, eh, honey?'

'Sure is.'

The woman looked over her shoulder at the white-painted house. 'Kinda dinky... I guess he never made it rich... not 'til he died.'

'Guess so.' The man was studying his guidebook. 'Picture here shows it with a kinda straw roof. Guess it musta leaked so they changed it.' He shut the book satisfied with his own explanation.

'How come they're so big on these daffodil things?'

'That was the name of his theatre, honey.'

'Oh.' She sipped her coffee and wrinkled her nose, which dislodged her sunglasses. 'Did he write everything here?'

'Sure he did.'

'What, even *Romeo and Juliet*? That's my favourite.'

'Guess so. What better place to write it than in Scotland?'

Greg couldn't help staring… gawping would have been a better description. He couldn't wait to tell Martin this one.

The path steepened sharply after he left Rydal. It got hotter, and with no sign of the top, Greg started to wonder whether he'd been a bit ambitious in his route planning. But five minutes sprawled in the heather and a couple of swigs of warm water revived him, and fifteen minutes later he was strolling along the gently undulating ridge delighting in the crystal clear view and sheer magnificence of the landscape. This is what it was all about. He wished Martin was there with him, which made him think of home. He giggled out loud recalling Martin's description of the now incapacitated Derek flying naked over their yard wall.

The slope steepened again as he got nearer the domed summit of Fairfield and despite the altitude it was hotter than ever. It was a relief to reach the summit cairn and he was glad to shrug off his rucksack and flop onto a flat stone. After a few moments he fished out his crushed lunch, sipped some more warm water and surveyed his limited horizon. Surprisingly for such a beautiful day it was empty. He was just congratulating himself on this when a curious figure suddenly materialised, bustling up the slope towards him. He appeared to be quite a small man but was bent almost double under the biggest pack Greg had ever seen, his face hidden beneath the brim of an enormous hat. His load didn't appear to be the usual walker's rucksack, just a huge square-edged box really, with a long whippy aerial. The man completely ignored Greg but carefully put his load down a few yards away, straightened and stretched, and then started unwrapping the box. Then the aerial started to grow and finally the man started to talk to his box. Greg couldn't hear clearly but a lot of figures were mentioned and the box squealed and crackled from time to time. Greg couldn't resist, and finishing his sandwich wandered over. As he approached, the man looked up and said, 'Ham.'

'Pardon.'

'You were going to ask me what I'm doing, everyone does: ham.'

'Um, I'm not sure what…'

'Amateur radio operator.'

'Oh, I see, I thought it must be something like that. Who are you talking to?'

'You at the moment, can't get a bloody signal for anyone else. Not as strong as it was last time I was up here.' He turned back to the box and Greg edged round him to look at the knobs and dials that now preoccupied the little man.

'Do you do this very much then?'

'Most days,' the man said, without turning round.

'Must keep you fit.'

The Ham just grunted, then after another moment: 'Bugger it! Nothing doing here, we'll give it a go on Red Screes.'

'That's miles.'

The man ignored him, busily put all his equipment back in its casings and without another word or acknowledgement marched off across the rocky dome and disappeared over the rim in an easterly direction.

Greg was left with the vague feeling that there had

never been anyone there at all, and that he'd imagined the whole thing. He must remember to tell Martin about it though.

The walk along the ridge of St Sunday's Crag was as spectacular as Greg remembered it, but by the time he started his descent, the heat of the day had taken its toll, joints and muscles ached and he was looking forward to getting down off the mountains and a hot shower… or maybe a cold one, and a cup of tea… or perhaps a pint of lager? Decisions, decisions.

Unlike in Langdale, Greg was lucky first strike: an attractive stone house with a lively, mossy beck running through the garden had a small single with bathroom across the landing available. He hadn't much liked the man who'd greeted him, presumably the owner, a bit sly and seedy Greg thought, but he was too tired to move on and signed the book. The room hadn't yet been made up, which Greg thought rather odd, but he was told there was a "bar of sorts" to sit in or he could take something out into the garden, while it was prepared. Greg plumped for the garden and a pint of lager. There were several small "rustic" tables dotted around in the dappled shade but all were occupied and Greg had just resigned himself to a grassy bank when a familiar figure turned from the nearest table.

'Greg!' It was Cat. She had a book open on her knees and a teapot and single cup and saucer in front of her on the uneven table. She seemed delighted to see him.

'Hey, Cat, great to see you again. Can I?' Greg sat down at the spare chair. 'Where's Ben?'

Cat grimaced. 'Emergency back at the office. He's had to shoot home for a couple of days, hopefully back the day after tomorrow. Bloody staff,' she added.

'Oh God, tell me about it. What was your business again?'

Cat hesitated. 'It's a sort of agency.'

Greg picked up on the hesitation. 'What sort of agency... oh, I see, don't worry, I've got nothing against estate agents.'

'Oh God, no, it's nothing as bad as that.'

'Well?'

'OK, I'll come clean, then there's something I want to show you.'

Cat explained how she and Ben were convinced they'd spotted a gap in the West Midlands adult entertainment market and had recently started an agency to fill that gap. Apparently, the idea had come to Ben after his stag night (the full details of which Cat still didn't know). She proudly told Greg that they could now supply strippers, kissograms and drag artists for every occasion, and catering for almost every taste – Cat stressed the "almost" – and although the business was proving highly successful it was also very demanding. 'Some of our *artistes* can be a little... temperamental,' Cat grinned.

'Well, there you go.' It was all Greg could think of to say.

'You're shocked.' Greg insisted he wasn't. 'Well,' Cat laughed, 'now that I've proved what a broad-minded, easy-going sort of gal I am, come and see what I do find shocking.' She got to her feet and led Greg back into the house. After a quick check around the other ground floor rooms she led him into a large room laid out with tables and chairs, presumably for breakfast. Quietly shutting the door Cat went straight across the room, reached up and unhooked a small framed embroidery, a hideously distorted version of the *Laughing Cavalier*. She flipped it over and handed it to Greg. 'Get a load of that.'

'Christ!' Greg gasped.

'They're all the same, every picture in the place, at least the ones I can reach.'

'God, that's gross, how did you find…?'

'It fell off the wall at breakfast. I was in here by myself and managed to get it back up double quick so I don't think they know I know. Makes my boys and girls seem pretty tame, that's for sure. I'm not even sure some of the stuff is legal.'

'But, I just don't get it, I mean…'

'No, me neither, but they're a pretty creepy pair who run this place. He's certainly been hitting on me, now that Ben's gone, and actually I'm not too sure about her either. I guess they get some sort of kick out of knowing we're all sitting here tucking into our wholemeal muesli and free-range eggs surrounded by this… stuff. Pervy eh?' Cat nodded at the *Laughing Cavalier,* which Greg was holding tapestry side up, 'and that's not the worst; you want to see what's behind *Mona Lisa* over there.'

'No thanks.'

They went back outside and talked about walking. Greg told her he was heading for Grasmere the next morning, but not sure whether to tackle the mighty Helvellyn on the way or to take an easier low-level path, what he called the Grisedale route. After a tough day today getting to Patterdale, he said he was tempted to take it a bit easy tomorrow.

'What do you mean by "easy"?' Cat asked cautiously.

Greg got out a map and showed her.

'Yeah, that doesn't look too tough.' She looked thoughtful for a moment. 'Look, Greg, if you do go your easy way, would you mind if I came with you… say "no" if it's not OK, I'll quite understand. You're obviously walking on your own for your own reasons and I…?'

'That would be great, Cat, honestly, no problem at all. I'd really enjoy the company, I'm only walking by myself because Martin, my partner, has got to look after *our* business. Really, it would be great.'

'Oh thanks, Greg. I'm really not comfortable by myself in this place, I'm not even sure the lock on my room is working properly.

'No problem, but what about Ben?'

'Oh, he'll be really pleased. I messaged him about these creeps and he wasn't happy. As long as you're sure, I'll let him know this evening. It'll be easier for him to catch up with me in Grasmere anyway,' she said happily. 'Let me get you another beer.'

At that point their host and hostess appeared, him being dragged by a large dog of indeterminate breed with dangerous looking pale blue eyes.

'Can see you two are *hard at it*,' the landlord leered. His wife sniggered suggestively. 'Still two rooms is it, or…'

'We'll both be leaving tomorrow morning…' Greg interrupted, '…together.'

'Well, you're a fast worker, mate.'

Greg ignored him. 'We'll be leaving early, please make

sure our bills are ready.' He didn't wait for a response but turned back to Cat and said loudly, 'We'll get better packed lunches in the village shop.' Then he picked up the map. 'Now, this is the hardest part...' Cat took her cue and placing a random finger on the map started asking unnecessary questions.

* * *

'So you don't know their names?'

'Stephan and Micky, I told you.'

'Their *full* names; and you don't have their passport numbers? In fact, if we're to believe you, you didn't even see their passports – you didn't ask for them. Mr Cox-Robinson, you have heard of people smuggling, have you?'

'Look, how could I be smuggling the sods, they were already in the country... well, Wales anyway. They fucking kidnapped me!'

'No need for language, Mr Cox-Robinson.'

'Well, how would you bloody feel? You get hijacked while you're on the bog, your boat gets trashed, all your gear gets nicked and then you're the one being treated like a fucking criminal!'

Robbie had never been to the Isle of Man before and on the basis of this welcome he wasn't likely to return. The tow in had been rough and too fast for his liking and he'd been seasick, much to the lifeboatmen's amusement. Obviously tipped off, the police were already waiting for him on the quayside and he'd been forbidden from leaving the boat for any purpose. He could see a pub tantalisingly close, but it wasn't just a beer he craved; the Welsh kebab hadn't done with him yet and he'd have given a lot for five minutes in a proper shore-based WC cubicle. But for the moment it seemed he was under boat-arrest.

After an hour's wait, during which a uniformed policeman had stood on the quay eyeing him suspiciously, an aggressive and sceptical immigration officer had turned up. He spent two hours grilling Robbie on the whole episode while several unidentified officials and a spaniel worked their ways from stem to stern turning out the contents of every locker and cupboard that the mutineers hadn't already emptied. Robbie silently blessed the blonde (God, that seemed like a lifetime ago) for having cleaned him out of cannabis before he left the south coast. His cigarettes had been sniffed one by one and a half-empty bottle of duty-free Scotch had been "bagged" as potential evidence. The spaniel had got quite excited at one point, and dangerously close to where Robbie normally kept his stash, but it turned out to be a family of mice nesting in a chewed-up pair of underpants at the back of a drawer.

Eventually, and despite obvious scepticism, the RNLI had been despatched to carry out a search for the "alleged hijackers", the immigration officials had left, with a muttered apology for the dog turd in the cockpit, and Robbie was allowed to go to the pub. On the way, further down the quayside, he met the RNLI crew preparing to leave. 'You can let the bastards drown as far as I'm concerned,' he snarled, 'but there's a pint in it if you can get my tender and outboard back.'

'The brotherhood of the sea, eh, sir?' had been the

withering reply, before the cox shoved the throttle forward and roared away.

Once again Robbie found himself port-bound with repairs to do, and there was a bit more urgency this time. With the calendar flipping over and this mysterious meeting to make, supposedly to his advantage, he needed to get a wiggle on. *Idler* had been tucked away at the scruffy inland end of a long stone quay, with no mention of marina charges. Worried about the cost, Robbie was relieved to be told that as long as he remained technically under investigation he would not be charged for the berth. So, once he'd talked the management of the quayside pub and a nearby chandlers into giving him credit, he'd adopted his old Swansea routine and set about using his meagre resources, tool kit and boat-building skills to once again patch up *Idler* – punctuated by regular visits to the pub.

To his amazement, a couple of days after his arrival, a police Land Rover pulled up on the quay towing a trailer with his tender attached, complete with outboard. It was partly deflated and the bottom seemed to be splattered with what Robbie suspected was sick ('serves the bastards right'), but the boat was basically intact. It had apparently been found on the other side of the island hidden amongst some dunes with no sign of the Romanians, although the woman who ran the nearby village post office had reported two young foreigners asking when the next bus to "Conk" was due. The bad news for Robbie was the police decided this concluded the official investigation and he now had to either move on or start paying for his berth. Another line of credit was negotiated but it added to the urgency of his situation.

'Hey, Robbie, make sure you're in the bar at six, mate, you've made the bloody news.' One of Robbie's regular drinking companions beamed down at him from the top of the slimy wall.

Robbie put down the mastic gun he'd been trying to seal a battered hatch with. 'What do you mean, "The news"?'

'The TV. You were on the news at dinner time, the Beeb no less, you're the new "Captain Calamity".'

'Oh great. Just what I need.'

'They got the RNLI guys from down south talking about you and then our guys here said their bit. They were polite... sort of, but I don't think the coxswain likes you very much.' He grinned and shrugged. 'Now that MP's been jailed and they've got over whatsisname being kicked off breakfast telly, I guess there's not much news about, so they filled the gap with you.'

A thought suddenly occurred to Robbie. 'Did they say where I was?'

'Yeah, of course: Douglas, Isle of Man,' Mike said proudly.

'Oh fucking great!'

'C'mon, Robbie, it's a laugh, gotta be worth a few pints tonight.'

All Robbie could think about was the growing list of people who would very much like to know where he was at the moment, topped by his ex-wife... and her homicidal brother. Nevertheless he did go to the pub in time for the evening news; the item was predictably mocking but mercifully brief. He took the ribbing good-naturedly, let the banter and free drinks flow and started to quite enjoy the notoriety. And with each pint his worries about pursuing creditors eased. After all, he didn't owe anyone enough to warrant the expense of a trip all the way to the Isle of Man. It wouldn't make sense.

In fact, the Captain Calamity evening in the pub proved to be something of a watershed in Robbie's relationship with the Isle of Man and its residents, or at least some of them.

Apart from its distinctly un-nautical name, The Plough was a fairly typical harbour side pub; the decor was predictably maritime in tone, the toilets were referred to as the "heads" and the bar menu was heavy on the fish – which was delivered weekly by refrigerated van from a mainland warehouse somewhere in the Midlands. The clientele was also fairly typical: a hard-core of heavy-drinking "wharf rats", most of whom Robbie had already met at one session or another, a few loud yachties discussing ambitious voyages that would never happen, and a mixed crowd of cheery locals. Fortunately, as far as Robbie was concerned, The Plough didn't seem to be a favourite of the lifeboat crew.

As Captain Calamity, naturally the yachties had ignored him, keeping their superior sneers within their own elite little group. The wharf rats had had their fun, bought Robbie the odd pint and then gone back to their own. It was the livelier of the locals who had adopted him. They were an eclectic set, a mix of couples and singles as far as Robbie could make out, mostly of middle years and all a bit bohemian. They were clearly a pretty freewheeling crowd and there was an easy familiarity amongst them, which was soon extended to Robbie. Despite, as Robbie was learning, different backgrounds and circumstances, they seemed to be a group comfortable with themselves. The drinking was steady but not outrageous, several of the group, including Robbie, regularly slipped outside for a smoke, and a hint of dope had drifted through an open fanlight more than once. This was his sort of crowd.

This evening, the television appearance had put Robbie centre stage. His new friends had been kindly sceptical of the mocking reporting and seemed genuinely interested in hearing Robbie's side of the story. They sympathised over the disasters, gently teased him over his cock-ups and included him in all their conversation and laughter. Inevitably, the conversation got noisier and the laughter more raucous as the evening wore on, attracting scowls from the yachties, and Robbie couldn't remember when he'd last felt so relaxed and enjoyed himself so much.

He spent the later part of the evening in a particular sub-group that was mainly female. One woman in particular, more mature but attractive in a natural untinted way, with a trim figure and proud cleavage, seemed particularly interested in his experiences. But it was a younger girl, auburn hair down to her bottom and flashing green eyes, who held Robbie's attention. The tight skimpiness of her summer dress and obvious lack of a bra made it difficult not to stare, and when she intercepted Robbie's glances, which was frequently, there was always an open smile in return. She seemed to be partnering one of the younger and more bohemian of the men, long-haired and animated, who was dominating the conversation within the group.

'So what do you think, Robbie?'

'Um... well, yeah, I guess so.'

There was general laughter. It had been obvious to all that Robbie hadn't been following the conversation for a while... and why, but no one seemed offended or bothered, least of all the speaker, who was called James.

'Don't worry, man, it was all bullshit anyway,' he laughed. 'So what are you doing tomorrow, Captain?'

Some of his new friends had jokingly adopted Robbie's media rank. He'd got used to it and didn't mind.

'More repairs I guess.'

'No way, have you seen the weather forecast?'

'Er... no, I haven't actually. Should I?'

'It's going to be brilliant, wall to wall. A crowd of us is going up to Cormorant beach in the afternoon for a bit of a party; barbecue, a few beers, all the normal stuff, and then we're going to doss down in the dunes for the night, watch the sunset, do a bit of star-gazing and listen to the sirens calling,' he grinned. 'Then at sunrise... well, we used to sacrifice a virgin but we've run out, so these days it's bacon sandwiches round the campfire. What do you think?'

'Yes, come on, come and relax on terra firma for a change.' It was the older woman who'd spoken but there was a general buzz of encouragement and Robbie found Green Eyes smiling encouragingly at him.

'Sounds great.' Robbie had already forgotten his mastic guns, epoxy tubes and whipping twine.

'Right, be in here at twelve and someone'll give you a lift. Have you got a sleeping bag... yeah, of course you have.'

SEVEN

Dom decided he'd probably got away pretty lightly. Admittedly one knee felt quite badly grazed but his trousers were still intact so it couldn't be that bad. And his left elbow might be throbbing a bit, but clearly he hadn't broken anything, apart from whatever had crunched in his rucksack when he'd landed on it. He levered himself up using his right elbow and sat propped against the rotting fence post that had stopped his roll. Looking up the bank after the now fast disappearing train he experienced a strange sort of elation and an almost irresistible urge to laugh out loud. He supposed he was probably a bit hysterical, but how many people could say they'd jumped from a moving train and lived to tell the tale? Certainly not many in his circle. He couldn't wait to tell George.

Unsteadily rising onto his knees and finally his feet, he had a dust-down and another check for injuries. All seemed well, so he collected his flattened rucksack from halfway up the bank, stepped over the tumbledown fence and headed for the canal. Canals, he knew, had towpaths, which must eventually reach some sort of civilisation. He had no idea how far he was from Manchester, and his total funds were just a few coins and Dan's begrudging fiver, but reaching a bridge, a pub or even a lock, would be a start. The canal looked green and greasy, but as he'd hoped, was accompanied by a narrow cinder track, potholed and dotted with dog turds, but a path, and obviously a well-used one.

Trudging along, lost in uncharitable thoughts about his son, it was a minute or two before Dom became aware of the steady thumping sound behind him. Turning stiffly and looking back down the canal he could make out a brightly coloured narrow boat weaving amongst the shadows of the overhanging trees. It seemed to be coming at quite a rate and struggling to stay within the banks of the canal. As Dom watched, it burst from under the trees and veered sharply towards his bank, prompting an invisible shriek of alarm from the little sunken foredeck, from where a large stripy figure suddenly popped up. A roar of laughter followed by a loud curse came from the other end of the boat, then the bows slammed into the bank and the boat came to a juddering halt. With another squeal, the figure on the foredeck abruptly disappeared again and there was the sound of breaking glass followed by another curse from the stern. An ominous silence followed, broken only by the rhythmic thump of the engine. Dom walked quickly back along the towpath until he could look down into the foredeck well.

'Ah, good afternoon.' A large grey-haired woman in baggy, stained white pantaloons and a striped seaman's jersey lay sprawled in the little triangular area, wedged and apparently inextricably tangled, in the remains of a beach chair.

'Are you all right?'

The woman managed to move one plump, pantalooned leg, then produced a huge wine goblet from somewhere amongst the debris and studied it carefully. 'Didn't spill a drop,' she said with satisfaction, and took a huge swig. 'Hang on a sec.' She straightened her other leg, which had the effect of lifting the frame of the canvas chair. 'Here, get hold of that, will you, and give it a tug? That's it... ow!'

'Sorry...'

'Hang on a sec... that's it. Right, have you got it?'

Dom set the remains of the chair down on the bank.

The woman heaved herself to her feet, glass still in hand, and raised it to Dom. 'Thank you for that.' She stuck her head above the roof of the cabin and bellowed down the boat, 'Ernie, you foolish and reprehensible man, when will you learn?' She turned to Dom. 'You'd have thought after forty years he'd have some idea by now wouldn't you?' She raised long-suffering eyebrows and looked back over the cabin roof. 'Ernie?' Nothing came back except the beat of the engine. 'Ernest, are you all right?'

Suddenly, a battered sailing cap and grey beard appeared in the little doorway, the face in between obscured from Dom's angle by the cap's frayed peak. 'Yes, of course I am, old girl, just had to get a refill. Ah, good afternoon... you don't have a glass.'

Dom acknowledged that he didn't.

'That'll never do.' With a surprising agility, the man gained the side deck and reached out to shake Dom's hand. 'I'm Ernie and this is Nesta. Red or white?'

'Um, that's very kind but don't you want me to push you off or something?' Dom looked down at the dented, muddy bow. 'Is the boat OK?'

'Oh yes, no problem, doing it all the time,' the man said, and hopped back down onto the foredeck.

'One day it *will* be a problem,' the woman said sternly. She looked up at Dom. 'And it costs a fortune in broken crockery.' She pecked the man on the grey beard. 'Go on, go and get my saviour a drink.'

Dom looked down at the woman and then at the retreating back of the man and was struck by how well matched they were; where he was grizzled and paunchy, it would be kinder to say she was greying and full-figured, both were weathered and bare foot; her faded jersey complemented his grubby smock and her pantaloons were almost the twin of his frayed shin-length trousers. Both wore their tops tucked in and sported wide belts, which ignored waistband loops. Curious affectations, Dom thought.

'Come aboard, old man.' Ernie waved his glass, apparently happy to leave his boat embedded in the bank and slewed halfway across the canal.

The temptation of a half-pint glass of red wine was too much for Dom, and once Nesta had ducked into the cabin to make room for him on the foredeck, he climbed down into the boat. Ernie then disappeared through the little double doors, calling over his shoulder: 'Come abaft, the sun's always under the yardarm on *Pilar*.' It became clear that Ernie liked employing nautical terminology, if not always accurately.

The interior of the boat was cluttered and scruffily homely. Books, magazines and used glasses were everywhere, as was nautical bric-a-brac; old storm lanterns and scraps of fishing net hung from the roof, Dom noted at least three ship's wheels, and a huge bronze propeller dominated the saloon. The walls were covered in sepia prints of long-since rotted boats, creased charts – mainly of the waters around Cuba and the Florida Keys – and framed facsimiles of Ernest Hemingway book covers. Startlingly, there were also several enlarged photographs of a much younger but clearly recognisable and totally naked Nesta, laughing and frolicking in the surf on some icing sugar beach. Dom wondered whether when he reached the back of the boat he'd find a "fighting chair" bolted to the deck, and sea rods hanging off the stern. He was partly right, but the chair turned out to be the twin of the one Nesta had recently demolished, and the "tackle", a child's plastic fishing rod and reel propped up against the stern rail, its line sagging into the algae soup of the canal.

'Cheers.' Ernie thrust an enormous goblet brimming with red wine into Dom's hand, took a gulp of his own and nodded at Dom's rucksack. 'What course you steering?'

'Eh?'

'Your port of destination?'

'He means, where are you going?'

'Ah, I see, Manchester,' Dom said, 'to see my daughter.'

'Us too... well, not the bit about your daughter, but we're Manchester bound too. Look, we can slug the grog as we go along, no rules against it out here… well not many, anyway… We'll give you a lift.'

'Well…'

'Splendid. Nesta, get the belaying pin off the poop deck and give us a good shove… and mind Gellhorn.'

'Gellhorn?' Dom said, wondering who else was on board.

Ernie was busy with the engine control and tiller. 'Yes,' he said over his shoulder, 'the tortoise, he… or maybe she …lives on the roof. Weigh anchor!'

Nesta unplugged the boat from the bank and with the engine thumping furiously Ernie bellowed, 'Ready about!' and engaged reverse gear. The boat shot backwards with Ernie frantically swinging the tiller from side to side. They narrowly missed the opposite bank, but the rudder didn't, the tiller was ripped from Ernie's hands and in the ensuing struggle he kicked his wine goblet overboard. 'Bugger!' He heaved on the tiller again, crunched the engine control into forward and finally seemed to regain some sort of control. 'Full steam ahead now,' he shouted down the boat and turned to beam at Dom.

Nesta returned to the rear deck, replaced and refilled glasses and disappeared back inside the boat. There was the crashing of crockery then her disjointed voice came back up the hatchway: 'Anyone hungry?'

Dom realised he was ravenous. It was a long time since he'd finished the stale cereal bar supplied by his son as an excuse for breakfast. Alice Cooper's antics had meant aborting his trip to the train's buffet car and the bucket of red wine he'd just finished had taken his hunger to a new level. 'Oh yes… please,' he called fervently.

'You OK with fish?'

Dom glanced over the stern to where the fishing line trailed along at the head of a frothy green "V". Ernie caught his glance and laughed. 'Don't worry, not out of there, we're talking an Ernesta special – Marlin Munchies.'

'Er, yeah, great,' Dom said, none the wiser and still nervous. He nodded over the stern. 'Have you ever caught anything?'

Ernie reached up on to the cabin roof and lifted down a rusting, tyreless bicycle wheel. 'Warwick, two summers ago, can't bring myself to get rid of it.'

Marlin Munchies turned out to be bulging fish-finger sandwiches smothered in a relish of Nesta's own invention – tartar sauce and tomato ketchup certainly came into it but she wouldn't be drawn on the third secret ingredient. They were stunningly delicious and accompanied by fresh buckets of wine, all white this time. 'White with fish,' Nesta had insisted.

A little later, while Nesta was washing up and Ernie was distracted by re-baiting his fishing line, the boat got wedged under a toppled willow tree. It took half an hour of engine revving and some vigorous hacking with a bread knife by Nesta to get them free. Once on their way again Dom glanced at his watch. 'Er, what time do you expect to get into Manchester?' he asked.

'Nesta's the navigator. What's our EBA, dear?'

'Oh, we should be there in time for dinner... probably Tuesday.'

'Ah.'

'Problem?'

'Well, I'm meant to be there this afternoon.'

'Hmm. Nesta, any ideas, old girl, for our stowaway here?'

'Just before the next lock we run alongside a main A road for a few miles. This close to Manchester there's bound to be buses, we could drop you off there. Any good?'

'That'd be great, thank you.' He fingered the five-pound note in his pocket.

'Right, better luff up and crack on then,' Ernie said and thrust the throttle control forward. There was a loud bang and a puff of black smoke from the stern but no noticeable change in speed. Dom watched the smoke curling over the canal and noticed the little plastic fishing rod had disappeared from its corner.

'Ah well, probably hooked into a big 'un and got dragged over the side,' Ernie grinned.

The main road appeared sooner than expected and there seemed a fairly steady flow of buses of several liveries. When the gap between the road and the canal had converged to one small field, Ernie headed for the bank. Nesta was already at her post in the bow shouting incomprehensible instructions and Dom, suspecting what was coming, braced himself against the cabin and waited for the shock. The impact duly came, Nesta shrieked and Ernie swore and broke another wine glass. Dom thanked them profusely for the lift and their hospitality and after helping Nesta disengage the bows he set off, rather unsteadily, for the road. A half-mile walk alongside thundering traffic helped sober him up and brought him to a small village with a bus stop. Ten minutes later he'd negotiated five pounds worth of mileage with the bus driver and was on his way towards

Manchester. Dom had resigned himself to more walking and hitch-hiking after that, but got lucky; within minutes of being dropped at a busy junction he'd picked up a quick and easy ride into the city centre, albeit in the company of a dour sales rep, who was not only totally lacking in humour, but apparently orders too. The rest of Dom's journey was completed on foot, a tedious trudge dodging pavement-riding cyclists through one of the city's less salubrious suburbs.

At the beginning of term, when Dom had delivered Christine, or "Krissie" as she'd started calling herself, and her mountain of possessions to her student digs, he hadn't been allowed much further than the threshold of the scruffy Edwardian villa. The state of the hall hadn't given him any great expectations for the rest of the house then, and it certainly didn't now. He had no idea how many students were crammed into the place, whether Chris… Krissie shared, had her own room, or what other arrangements she might have made. Five minutes later he was none the wiser. A spotty youth had ushered him into a large dark room, the floor littered with empty cider cans, discarded clothes and full ashtrays. Dom was looking round, slightly bewildered, when three tousled heads appeared from under the duvet on the huge old-fashioned bed. Two of the heads, one of each sex, appeared at the pillow end and were unfamiliar to Dom. The third, the one that popped out at the foot of the bed was that of his daughter. The rest of her followed, slithering onto the floor, quite naked. She reached for a packet of cigarettes. 'Hey Dad, how's it going?'

* * *

As Billy had predicted, there were a couple of taxis still outside the local station, not because any more trains were expected that night but because local late revellers knew to find them there. Gavin asked for a quote from two of the least bored-looking and chose the one who didn't smell of drink. The journey took an hour and Gavin sat in the back, tight to the door behind the driver and out of the scope of the rear-view mirror. He avoided conversation, which didn't seem to bother the cabbie, but the radio got louder as the journey progressed.

Gatwick glowed orange, a neon haze pierced by an occasional bluey-white arc light. Darkened police cars and vans were prominently dotted around the approaches with others discreetly tucked away in the labyrinth of roads and tunnels that ran between the terminals and mass of anonymous buildings. Foot-bound colleagues, bulky in body armour, hung with pouches and holsters and clasping automatic weapons to their chests, prowled around the pedestrian areas. It was 3 a.m. and the last scheduled flight had long since landed but there were still plenty of people around to ensure Gavin didn't stand out: passengers lately disgorged from delayed flights, bewildered family groups delayed by immigration or customs, transferors who'd missed their connections, and the normal mixture of flight crews, ground staff and administrators milling around.

Gavin had himself dropped at one of the modern chain-owned towers that claimed four stars, but once the taxi was out of sight he ignored the brightly lit reception and walked quarter of a mile across the campus to another similar building where he finally checked in. The room was as expected. He resisted the mini-bar, made a coffee and despite the hour rang Jacko.

'Christ, Gav, it's the middle of the bloody night. Where are you anyway?'

After apologising, Gavin explained that he'd moved on from Billy's, but not why. Just that he intended to hire a car in the morning and then take a couple of days to drive north to Cumbria.

'So how's it going then?' There was a long pause on the line. 'Jacko, you there?'

'Yeah, I'm here.' His voice was weary, resigned. 'It's not good, Gav. This fucking mayor is really going for it, much worse than before, the whole place is being turned inside out, and…' There was another silence.

'Jacko, and…?'

'It's fucking Gomez…'

'Go on,' Gavin said quietly.

'They've got to him. I think he's gonna talk.'

It was Gavin's turn to go quiet. 'You got it covered?' he asked eventually.

'I'm working on it, but…'

'But what?'

'Well, I can't be certain, Gav,' Jacko said slowly. They were both silent as Gavin mentally ran through the implications of this latest development. 'Bobby and the kids are fine though,' Jacko said suddenly. 'They're up at the *finca,* it seemed best. The kids are missing all the beach stuff but they've got the pool and there's plenty on in Ronda. Bobby's fine.'

'Well, that's something.'

'Look, Gav, you've really got to keep your head down now. If this goes much further and Gomez... well, you know, then they might take it further and come looking.'

'What, like Interpol or something?'

'Something like that, yes, could be.'

'OK, Jacko, I'll get myself lost for a few weeks. Keep me in touch, OK?' He had a sudden thought, 'are the phones clean?'

'So I'm told... for the moment.'

'OK, I won't call again, you find a clean one or stick to mobiles and call me when you need to, OK?' He rang off, made another coffee and watched the grey Sussex sky start to lighten.

Gavin hadn't bothered with bed; after his conversation with Jacko he knew sleep wouldn't come. Instead he spent the pre-dawn hours reviewing the various escape routes he'd carefully built up over the years as his finances and business had become ever more complicated... and questionable. If things panned out as Jacko seemed to think they might, it was certainly going to involve major disruption, but not necessarily disaster. In a funny sort of way he was looking forward to the challenge. Maybe things had been too easy for too long. But first, the Lake District.

The car hire firm Gavin chose was barely open – computers were still warming up, cleaners were fussing with Hoovers and bin bags, and the staff were unprepared, particularly for a "walk-in" with no booking. Gavin was asked to come back in half an hour. He considered some of the other companies in adjoining offices but most didn't even have lights on yet so he left his details and promised to return later.

Breakfast hadn't been available at the hotel so Gavin wandered into the arrivals terminal looking for a coffee and a pastry. The airport was shaking off its night-time lethargy: floor polishers were humming around, bins were being re-lined, shutters lifted and display stands wheeled out. The smell of fast food wafted through the building. Flights were starting to come in and the barriers at the arrivals area were already lined with drivers holding up hand-written name cards, hopeful taxi drivers and assorted hustlers. Friends and relatives squeezed in around them, most waiting in a state of excited anticipation, others clearly impatient and frustrated, presumably at delays. One man in particular, hooded in an outsized parka and with a scruffy holdall slung over his shoulder, had got himself onto the "air side" of the barrier and was berating a female official in broken English. Some of the taxi drivers watched and listened with cynical amusement; they'd seen and heard it all before. Apparently the man's brother had been detained by the immigration service for questioning; no, the woman could not give any more details, and no, nor could she give any likely time when he'd be released, or even confirm whether he would be at all. She was calm, cold and professional, but her manner was not calming the man. On the contrary, it seemed to incense him. Two armed policemen appeared at the end of the hallway and stood by a column watching closely.

Gavin decided to make use of the gents before an influx of arrivals started causing queues for the facilities.

He edged along the back of the crowd at the barriers and headed for the signs. The woman official had by now managed to lead the protesting man to the right side of the barrier but the haranguing was getting louder and the English more garbled. Gavin glanced at the man in passing and thought he was probably high on something.

He had the gents to himself; that was until, mid-flow, a small plump woman in a shapeless blue uniform appeared at his shoulder and emptied a container of pastilles into the neighbouring urinal.

'Morning.'

'Christ! Er, yeah, morning.' Gavin turned away as far as his limited target would allow but sensed the woman was still nearby. He looked over his shoulder and found her resting her plump bottom on the edge of the newly refreshed urinal, rolling a cigarette.

'I'll do you next,' she said, 'when you're finished.'

'Um… thanks.'

'You gonna be long?'

'Well…'

'You take your time then, luvvie,' she patted him on the bottom, 'I'll go and have a smoke. They ain't never caught me yet,' she added. 'They just thinks it's one of you damn men… likely some damn foreigner, ha!' She disappeared into a far cubicle chuckling to herself.

Gavin finished up quickly, not wanting to be the "damn man" if the smoke alarms went off. He spent a minute washing his hands but before the roar of the hand-dryer could blot everything out he heard a loud noise from down the corridor and then what sounded like screams. He wiped his hands on the seat of his trousers.

Yes, there was definitely something going on just outside and Gavin had a shrewd idea he knew what it would be about. He eased the self-closing door to, and edged down the L-shaped corridor towards the arrivals hall. Elements of the commotion were becoming discernible now; the odd male rumble or female shriek, repeated shouted commands to put something down, and above it all, the voice of the enraged foreign man. Gavin flattened himself to the wall and edged along the last few yards of the corridor. He wasn't sure what he'd expected to find, but as he peeped round the corner it had fallen strangely silent and he felt like he'd accidentally walked onto a film set in the middle of a take. The scene was set: the crowd, like obedient extras, stood gaping and unmoving, two armed policemen crouched motionless about ten yards away, their machine guns pointed in Gavin's direction, and centre stage, between the guns and Gavin, the lead players provided the action. The enraged man, now hoodless and muttering incoherently, had the female official clutched to his chest with an arm round her throat. With his other hand he slashed at the air with a machete that flashed wickedly with reflected neon.

The police had now seen Gavin, as had the crowds at the barriers, and it could only be a matter of time before the machete-wielder realised he was there too. Doing nothing wasn't an option, that much was clear. Abandoned trolleys were scattered around and various pieces of discarded luggage lay on the floor just a few yards from where Gavin stood. With any noise covered by the latest shouted police commands, Gavin stepped quietly forward and picked up a large Samsonite suitcase, then heaving it above his head, took a few steps further and brought it crashing down on the man's head. The noise levels in the hall immediately went up, the freed woman stumbled forward, unbalanced by her sudden release and the man fell to his knees. Gavin kicked him hard between the shoulder blades sending him sprawling, then stepped over the figure and stamped down on the man's wrist. There was a crack and a muffled scream of pain. Gavin flicked the machete away with his toe, back-heeled the man in the head for good measure and quickly stepped away as the police officers rushed in, screaming commands, which as their target was already flat on his face with his arms outstretched and an obviously broken wrist, were largely unnecessary.

The chaos if anything then intensified, which suited Gavin. He slipped under the nearest barrier, scooped up a discarded name-board and tried to disappear into the crowd of drivers. One or two realised who he was. He was patted on the back and at one point his hand was grasped: 'Well done, mate.'

Someone else joined in. 'That showed the bastard. Fuckin' terrorists! Good on yer.'

Gavin feigned bewilderment. 'Not me, son, you got it wrong,' he said, holding up his board. 'The guy you want is over there with the bill. Bloody hero, that's what he is. Ta, anyway.' With that he worked his way through to the rear of the crowd, decided to avoided the car hire office, where there was bound to be a queue by now, and headed for the railway station, dropping the name-board in a handy bin as he went. The name on it was Wheeler. For no logical reason the coincidence unsettled Gavin. It seemed he'd been there to meet himself.

*   *   *

'So you really reckon they thought they were in Stratford?'

'No, they thought they were in Scotland.'

'So how did Anne Hathaway's Cottage end up there?'

'God knows, I was as confused as them by then, but I'd still love to see a version of *Macbeth* written by William Wordsworth… I wandered lonely as… Banquo's ghost!'

Martin giggled. 'How much have you had?' he demanded.

'Oh, only a couple of lagers, it's just been a good day; a great walk, a bit of company and now being able to talk to you.'

'Yeah, it's good, and I'm glad you're having a good time, and that you've got someone to walk with tomorrow. It's quite a relief to me really.'

'I thought it would be.'

There was a short, comfortable silence between them.

'So, business…' Martin said suddenly.

'Yes. How's it all going? Are you…?'

'It's fine, absolutely fine. Fairly busy, but d'you know what? Things run a lot smoother when you're not depending on an unreliable slut and a naked, homicidal maniac who tries to kill your guests and rips parts off your building.'

'Oh God, don't get me going on that again,' Greg gasped.

'Actually, that wasn't the business I meant,' Martin said. 'Your market research, it seems to be taking us into some pretty weird places. So far, I'm getting dismembered dolls – naked, bizarre teapots and now some heavy-duty porn! What do we do with that lot? What kind of place do you think we're running, Gigi?'

'I wasn't suggesting we took any of this crap on.' Greg knew Martin was teasing.

'Well, thank God for that!'

'Actually, I have had an idea,' Greg said.

'This should be interesting after your experiences!'

'Well, I thought, bearing in mind where we actually are, maybe we ought to have a theme that was a bit more relevant to the Lakes, not Victorian London.'

'Oh, not bloody Beatrix Potter!'

'Noo...'

'Or John Ruskin – that arts and crafts stuff is so… so stuffy.'

'Philistine, but no. What about Arthur Ransome, *Swallows and Amazons*?'

'Well… not very original, is it?'

'I haven't seen it done. We could stuff the place with the books and prints, quite cheaply, and then get loads of boaty stuff to hang around the place.'

There was a long pause before Martin said: 'Now that *is* an idea, we could have some fun with that.'

'Good, think about it. Now I've got a challenge for you…'

Greg and Cat walked down to the pub together for dinner. Cat said Ben was really pleased they'd met up and that she was getting out of the B&B and had a walking companion. Greg was still going his "easy route", wasn't he? Greg assured her he was and said how pleased Martin had been too.

Cat slipped her arm through Greg's. 'Sorted then,' she said happily.

'And Martin and I have come up with a little plan for some fun before we say goodbye to the pervy pair at the B&B,' Greg said.

'Oh, I like the sound of this.'

Cat and Greg sat across the stained cloth sipping watery orange juice. They'd ordered an early breakfast, which seemed to be taking forever, and in the meantime had to put up with endless innuendoes from their hosts, to whom a shared pub dinner and a companionable breakfast obviously meant a night of torrid and unrestrained sex must have taken place in between.

'It'll be worth it,' Greg whispered. 'How many did you manage?'

'Ten, then I fell asleep.' She pushed a pad of yellow Post-its across the table.

'I'm about the same. More than enough.' He looked round the room. 'Five in here we can do, I reckon, eight in the lounge and then another six in the hall.'

Breakfast eventually arrived and wasn't worth the wait. Greg pushed his unfinished plate away in disgust. 'Let's pay on the way up,' he said, 'then I'll see you in the hall, booted and bagged, and we'll make a run for it,' he grinned.

Cat delicately spat a bit of bacon gristle onto her fork, placed her napkin over her plate and gave a thumbs-up.

'Finished?'

Cat gave the "A-OK" diver's signal.

'Right, let's get out of here.'

Ten minutes later, by the time other guests had started to drift down to the common rooms of the B&B, Greg and

Cat were well away, already in the village shop choosing their lunchtime sandwiches. What the other guests found prompted several disgusted early departures, demands for heavily discounted bills and a mass loss of appetite at breakfast. By early evening, Internet review sites were full of graphic descriptions, outraged comments and a few heavily redacted photos. As their parting shot, Greg and Cat had worked their way down the staircase and through all the downstairs rooms turning over every reachable painting to reveal its pornographic flip side. And every pornographic image had then been given its own Post-it, placed as strategically as possible, on which was written:

CENSORED
A couple of pervs in the Lakes
Thought it fun to stick porn on their fakes
Most was extreme
All spunk and whipped cream
But not to everyone's taste.

Greg and Cat had been walking for about an hour, mainly in companionable silence. After leaving the village shop and the main road, they'd worked their way through some steeply sloping fields and little copses and were now walking up a gravelled track along the bottom of a long valley. Peaks soared either side of them, while the pass they ultimately had to cross formed the skyline at the head of the valley, a zigzag path making its way to the ridge just discernible.

'Can't wait to see Tripadvisor later,' Greg suddenly laughed. 'Martin said he'd keep an eye on it during the day.

He was a bit worried he might have gone a bit too far with the "spunk" though.'

'I don't see why – did you see the back of The Haywain?'

'What, the nun and the donkey?'

'No, no, that was The Last Supper... anyway, he's quite a poet, your Martin, he should write some more and publish them in a little book. You could flog it to all your guests,' Cat said.

'What, *The Little Book of Obscene Lakeland Odes*?' Greg snorted with laughter.

'Why not? There's Lakeland recipe books, picture books, guide books, ghost stories, all sorts.'

'Yes, but they're not *obscene*,' Greg pointed out.

'There's a market for everything, just look at our business,' Cat said. 'You should see some of the acts. What our girl with the ping-pong balls can do... well...'

'You *are* joking?' Greg turned to look at Cat. 'You're not, are you?'

'Nope. Bet your Martin could come up with a good limerick for her... There was a young woman called Annie... and that is her name, by the way.'

Greg thought for a moment, mouthing words to himself, '...who did peculiar things with her... no, no, I'm not going there!'

'OK,' Cat laughed, 'we'll leave it to Martin. I'll look forward to the book.'

Greg liked the casually familiar way Cat used Martin's name. It was as if they were old acquaintances, which despite Martin's absence somehow made them a friendly threesome.

'Are you OK?'

Cat had stopped walking, thrown back her head and was taking deep breaths. 'Yeah, I'm fine, just a bit puffed. Not fit enough,' she grinned ruefully.

They'd left the track and the valley floor now and had for a while been on a narrow, rocky path that weaved its way between scattered moraines, crossed occasional becks and their tributaries, and was now steepening noticeably. As they scrambled up the last few yards of a particularly rough outcrop a squat little stone hut appeared, tucked against the mountainside on a small plateau of sheep-cropped grass.

'Let's have a breather,' Greg said. 'A proper one, get the packs off and sit for a while. Better have some water too, we probably haven't drunk enough.'

Cat just nodded her agreement and without removing her rucksack flopped heavily onto the grass and lay back with eyes closed.

Greg studied her for a moment, then sat down and dug out a water bottle. 'You look hot, make sure you drink plenty and then why not shed a layer when we start moving again?' Ever since they'd first met, that stormbound night in her and Ben's tent, Greg had noticed that Cat was always well bundled up, whatever the situation and conditions. She was clearly full bosomed and a little tubby round the middle but walking behind her he couldn't help noticing that she had a neat bottom, narrow hips and slim legs. It gave her a rather top-heavy appearance and a curious gait.

Cat sat up. 'I'll be fine,' she assured him. 'Ravenous, though, do you fancy a cereal bar or bit of Mint Cake?'

They shed their rucksacks, sprawled on the grass and crunched energy bars and sipped at the water bottle. Greg kept taking surreptitious glances at Cat; she was breathing quite heavily and still looked very flushed. 'Best get going,' he said, after ten minutes or so. 'The bright lights of Grasmere await us. It's not far up to the tarn now, then all downhill. The first bit's a bit steep and scrambly, if I remember rightly, but after that it's plain sailing.'

Cat got wearily to her feet and Greg helped her on with her rucksack. 'You are OK, aren't you?'

'Yeah, I guess so, it's just that… oh, never mind. We're about halfway now, aren't we?'

'Almost exactly, I'd say,' Greg said. The thought had already occurred to him that they were now about as far as they could be, in either direction, from a road, or a bus stop or any sort of lift. 'St Sunday's Crag and Fairfield,' he said brightly, sweeping his arm up. 'I was up there yesterday. And Dollywaggon Pike up there.' He turned and waved to the opposite side of the valley. 'Great name, eh?'

Cat politely looked where indicated and managed a wan smile.

The path got steeper and the surface looser and rougher, a victim of its own popularity and the thousands of boots that ground away at it year after year. In places, restoration works had been carried out and huge rough slabs had been arranged to form a sort of crude staircase. Cat took these one at a time, treading carefully, her head down, her eyes never leaving the path. Greg had given up any attempt at conversation. He'd taken to walking behind Cat after she'd kept falling behind, but her sudden unexplained exhaustion was worrying him. They still had several hours walking ahead of them and at this pace…

Cat suddenly let out a desperate wail and slumped

onto a bank of heather at the side of the path. 'Oh God!' she groaned and rolled onto her back, her eyes screwed up tightly in pain. 'Oh God!' Her whole body seemed to spasm.

Greg shrugged off his rucksack and threw himself down beside her. 'Cat, what is it… what have you done? What's the matter?' He was already rummaging for his mobile phone. Cat let out another groan and clenched her knees together. 'Oh God, Greg. Oh, that's it, that's a bit better,' she panted.

'What's happening, Cat?'

'Oh Greg, haven't you got it? I'm pregnant… oohh…'

* * *

The beach was almost deserted when their little convoy of cars and vans pulled up amongst the low dunes. About twenty people in all piled out and set about unloading cool boxes, wine and beer crates, sacks of firewood and assorted bags and rucksacks. Everyone seemed to know the geography of the beach and soon there was a heavily laden caravan winding its way through the marram grass, along a narrow path, which finished in a low, natural amphitheatre on the other side of the dunes. Open to seaward, the bowl had views across the width of the beach and down to the incoming tide.

Camp was quickly established, a fire laid for later, the food and drink stacked in the shade of a flimsy beach shelter, and blankets and towels spread. Within minutes everyone had stripped off to beach gear and glasses of wine and beer had been poured. Some quiet acoustic music burbled out from under the beach shelter and people sprawled with their drinks, chatting happily. A small group wandered off towards the sea to swim.

'Not everyone bothers with a cossie later, not once the grockles have gone.' Green Eyes had thrown herself down on the sand next to Robbie.

'Grockles?'

'Trippers, tourists. My name's Siobhan.' There was the slightest hint of an Irish accent. Robbie smiled and nodded and they both turned to watch the little group making their way across the beach. Without breaking stride two of the women casually slipped off their bikini tops and carried on walking towards the sea.

Robbie took a swig of his beer and lay back on his towel, sucking in his stomach and displaying his "sailor's tan"; a brown face, forearms and lower legs, and a "V" of chest, everything else milky white. 'This is my idea of heaven,' he sighed.

'Not bad is it? And it gets better, you'll see.' The girl jumped up and walked towards the beach shelter. Robbie rolled over and watched her. He didn't think he'd ever seen such a tiny bikini.

The afternoon passed quickly; glasses were never empty, conversation and laughter were lively and a riotous beach cricket match descended further into farce and hilarity when a passing Labrador ran off with the ball. Throughout the afternoon small groups peeled away and headed down to the advancing sea for splashing fights or a swim. And Siobhan had been right, by late afternoon most had dispensed with costumes, politely covering up before re-entering the camp, with just a few of the women remaining topless. To Robbie's mild surprise one of them was the older woman from the group he'd been part of the previous evening. Still dripping from the sea, she came and sat down on the sand in front of him, then without a word carefully arranged her legs in the lotus position. Robbie noticed the firmness of her stomach, and the muscle definition in her legs but tried to ignore the taut triangle of fabric between them. Seawater drained from her hair and trickled over her firm brown-nippled breasts.

'Hi, I'm Sylvia. It's taken me years to be able to do this,' she laughed. 'I show it off at every opportunity, causes quite a stir on the bus. Mind you, I can't always get out of it again.'

It was Robbie's turn to laugh. 'God, I couldn't get near doing that!'

'Rubbish, go on, give it a go.' Robbie lifted one ankle and eased it onto the opposite knee with a grunt of pain. 'Right, that's the easy bit, now the other one.' Sylvia lifted her bottom off the sand and "walked" the few feet between them on her knees. She took Robbie's other ankle and lifted it a few inches.

'Ow, no way, something's going to snap,' he gasped.

Sylvia suddenly giggled and let go of his foot. 'OK, how about a swim then?'

'That sounds less painful.'

'With or without?'

'Eh...'

'Clothes, costumes.'

'Oh, well...'

'Oh don't be shy, I've seen most of what you've got already.' She nodded at Robbie's crotch where the yoga exertions had slid a couple of inches of his penis down the leg of his swimming shorts.

'Oh God, sorry!' He grabbed at his crotch and started laughing. 'Come on then, d'you need a hand?' He nodded at her entwined legs. She smiled, uncoiled effortlessly and sprang to her feet. 'Right, I see,' Robbie said. 'I bet the bit about the bus wasn't true either.'

Sylvia helped him to his feet and they walked towards the sea and setting sun, stopping a few yards from the water's edge to shed their costumes.

The fire was lit before the sun was fully set, barbecues appeared, more drinks were poured and someone produced a guitar. The food was better than many restaurants; expertly cooked steaks and whole mackerel, intriguing salads and crisp-skinned potatoes cooked in the ashes of the fire.

Since returning from their swim, Robbie and Sylvia had been re-absorbed into the general company and Robbie found himself on a shadowy side of the fire in a group that included, amongst others, James and Siobhan. After an afternoon of red wine, sun, sea and good company, Robbie felt he'd found a sense of peace he'd previously forgotten. The firelight, quiet music, smoke-scented air and murmur of conversation created an intimacy in their darkened hollow, which he found almost sensual.

'Do you believe in free love, Captain?' James' voice suddenly rose above the general murmur from the shadows.

Robbie looked warily into the flickering light remembering the last time *he'd* tried to start a conversation with that line. 'Er… well, I certainly used to.'

James' smiling face emerged fully into the firelight. 'So what happened, why no more?'

'It got me beaten up…'

'Ah.'

'… and my boat stolen.'

'Ah, a miscalculation perhaps?'

'You could say that.'

'You could always try it again.' It was Siobhan's gentle Irish lilt.

Robbie looked around the fire not sure how he was expected to react to this. 'Um, so is that why you people all hang out together?' he asked warily.

'Oh no, that's just because we all get on, simple as that. But live and let live, that's our motto. There's a load of things we have in common, enough to make us all friends, and there are some things that work for some and not for others. A bit of grass isn't for everyone and nor is sharing.' James laughed quietly. 'And those of us who do share… well, we make sure it's with a like-minded spirit.' He smiled in the firelight. 'That way you don't get beaten up.'

Siobhan suddenly appeared on Robbie's other side and took his hand. 'Do you think it's time to try again, like-minded spirit?'

Stunned but delighted, and a little embarrassed at having been seduced so publicly, Robbie allowed himself to be led away into the shadows and the dunes. In a shallow marram-fringed gully where the firelight only reached the very tops of the enclosing dunes, Siobhan spread a large throw and pulled her kaftan-style dress over her head. She was quite naked underneath. There wasn't much of her body that hadn't been revealed during the course of the afternoon but as Robbie's eyes adjusted to the dim light he still looked in wonder at her fully naked form. Siobhan tossed her dress aside, led Robbie onto the throw and kissed him lightly on the lips. She pulled his shirt over his head and kissed his chest, then dropped to her knees and started to ease his shorts down his thighs. As his semi-erect member emerged she took it in her mouth and held it there as she lifted his feet out of the shorts.

What followed was largely dictated by Siobhan. Initially, Robbie revelled in making love to a beautiful young woman, or at least having her make love to him, but even before they'd finished, he sensed that he was there merely as an accessory, a toy. The sex appeared unhurried but didn't seem to take long, it was adventurous and accomplished but not necessarily erotic, and yes, technically successful, but somehow not fulfilling.

Robbie and Siobhan returned to the firelight. 'Thank you, like-minded spirit,' Siobhan said, and pecked Robbie on the cheek. He watched her drift off towards the far side of the fire and was left feeling rather… he wasn't sure; sheepish, vaguely ashamed? He looked around the hollow, numbers seemed depleted; presumably others had drifted off into the dunes seeking privacy and intimacy too. Robbie sat at the edge of the shadows enjoying the music and the murmur of conversation and occasional ripple of laughter. No one had paid any attention to his return, or presumably his absence. He settled back in the warm sand determined to regain his earlier mood.

'Hi.'

'God, you move quietly, must be the yoga.'

Sylvia laughed quietly. 'Just naturally sneaky, I guess.' She sat down carefully, balancing two glasses of red wine, and ground their bases into the sand.

'You don't strike me as sneaky,' Robbie said.

'I thought you looked a bit sad.' She moved a little closer to him until they were sitting with shoulders almost touching. Robbie didn't say anything. Inevitably their eyes were drawn to the fire and for a few minutes they sat in silence, mesmerised by the dancing flames.

'So where do you fit into this… this scene?' Robbie eventually asked.

'I don't really see it as a "scene", but I love it.' She looked round the hollow. 'We're a funny bunch, I suppose, but somehow all get on. No one judges, each does their own thing, and we all give and take what we feel comfortable with.'

'And the free love stuff?'

Sylvia thought for a moment. 'Yes, I went that route for a while, but then, well… So is that your thing?'

'Not anymore.'

Sylvia nodded her understanding. 'Yes, I saw you with James and Siobahn. They're great people but their ideas aren't for everyone. James can get a bit political and… well,' she gave a little laugh, 'Siobhan is our self-confessed resident nympho.'

Robbie laughed too. 'I'd never have guessed.' It was his turn to look around. 'They certainly are a mixed crowd, aren't they?'

'I think that's why it works. That and plenty of give and take. And not just what you were given in the dunes just now,' she laughed.

'You disapprove?'

'Not at all. Right person, right place, right mood – go for it!'

'Yes, maybe,' Robbie said slowly.

They sipped their wine and went back to gazing into the fire.

Sylvia searched out and found Robbie's hand in the sand. 'Did you enjoy our swim though?'

'Yes, yes, I did, very much.' Robbie thought for a moment. 'It felt so… natural, innocent,' he finished, simply.

Sylvia squeezed his hand and smiled into the fire. Her face was ruddy in the flickering light, her short blondish hair spiked and tousled by sand and salt.

Robbie went and refilled their glasses and they stretched out on opposite elbows in the firelight and talked quietly, learning a little more about each other. Sylvia told Robbie that she was long-since divorced, had a grown-up son and owned a book shop in Douglas, which she'd inherited from her father, who'd also taught her to sail. She lived alone and was happy in herself and with her group of friends. Robbie told Sylvia about some of his early failed ventures, his hand-to-mouth existence on *Idler* and his vengeful ex-wife. He told her the reason for his journey and about its ambiguous promise, said he probably wasn't that happy, had few friends and it was probably time he settled down and changed direction… but he wasn't sure how.

The fire had been allowed to burn down and for a while people had been disappearing into the dunes individually for non-amorous purposes. Bivvy bags and sleeping bags were being unrolled in the peripheral shadows of the sandy amphitheatre. Robbie and Sylvia, with an unspoken understanding, rolled out their bags next to each other in the relative privacy of a shallow depression at the edge of the surrounding dunes and in sight of the dying fire. They lay on their backs and gazed at the stars, undimmed by a mere sliver of moon or any man-made light.

'So what next, Robbie?'

'Well, Cumbria, Keswick, as commanded.'

'And then?'

Robbie didn't have an answer.

'I'd come with you,' Sylvia said, 'help you sail your *Idler* to Whitehaven, but I can't leave the shop, not at the moment.'

'I'd have liked that,' Robbie said quietly.

'You could always come back.'

They lay together on the sand almost touching. Someone put a last huge piece of driftwood on the fire and turned off the music.

'I'd like you to,' Sylvia whispered.

Robbie lifted himself slowly on his elbow, looked at her for a moment then kissed her on the cheek. 'Thank you.'

EIGHT

Krissie had found some sort of wrap and ushered a rather shell-shocked Dom into the kitchen of the student house. The room was another shock; walls and ceiling painted a glossy rose pink, woodwork picked out (badly) in scarlet and on the largest area of vacant wall a huge mural depicting Snoopy, the cartoon dog, eyes shut, feet pedalling in apparent ecstasy with what was unmistakeably meant to be a giant spliff dangling from his bottom lip.

Dom thought he'd try and inject some normality into the situation. 'So, how's it going then?'

'Oh fine.' Krissie put a chipped mug on the table next to him. 'Coffee?'

Dom picked up the mug, looked at the ring of scum just below the rim and put it down again. 'I meant your course.'

Krissie looked confused for a moment. 'Oh that, yeah, fine.'

'What was it again?'

'Oh Dad! It's drama and modern theatre… and media something… no, hang on, modern media and drama and… I know theatre comes into it somewhere. Anyway, it's going really well.'

Krissie changed the subject and asked her father where he was staying. Dom explained his current financial situation and his reliance on the efficiency of his suspicious bank and the cooperation of Krissie's mother to put him back in funds.

'No problem, you can have our "guest suite".'

Dom was delighted, that was until he discovered his "suite" consisted of a stained mattress on the cellar floor.

'You'll have to make friends with Kenneth.'

'Kenneth?'

'Yeah, he lives down there… he's a toad.'

'Oh charming.'

'He's OK, he's the house pet.'

'Yes, but what about… hang on, why Kenneth?'

'*Toad of Toad Hall, Wind in the Willows*, we're putting it on this term, Kenneth Williams.'

'I think you'll find *Wind in the Willows* is Kenneth *Graham*.'

'Oh yeah, Kenneth Williams is the beaky guy from *Carry On*, isn't he? We've got that this year too, I'm playing the washer woman…' Dom was struggling to keep up with Krissie's curriculum, '… in the nude. We were going to do the whole thing naked but Fatima, she plays Badger, said it might cause a few problems at home, so some of us are nude and the rest are playing it as punks. Fatima's a great spitter, she can make the third row.'

'Good God!'

'I hope you and Mum can get up for the first night. How is Mum? Still shagging the tennis coach?'

'Krissie! For God's sake, how do you know about…?' Dom couldn't think how to finish the question.

His daughter lit another cigarette and blew the smoke at the pink ceiling. 'How do you think? I passed him on to her, of course. Right,' she looked at her watch, 'I'd better get something on, pub time, wanna get front-loaded before the party. You can come if you like, we'll find something for you to wear.'

Dom looked down at himself. 'Well, I thought this was…'

'No, no, you'll have to do better than that. No problems, we can sort it.'

Half an hour later, and attended by two of Krissie's male housemates armed with a half bottle of vodka, Dom found himself in the "guest suite" being squeezed into an ancient red wetsuit, which was showing severe signs of perishing at the crotch and armpits, and a pair of white cowboy boots (the first choice of black high-heels having proved too small). A dirty white Stetson was to complete this ensemble. Somewhere between gulps of neat vodka and the wrestling match with the wetsuit, it had been explained to Dom that he was to attend a "fetish party".

'Best we could do,' the friends shrugged to Krissie, leading Dom back into the pink kitchen half an hour later.

'Well it doesn't do it for me,' she laughed, 'but I suppose it might ring someone's bell.'

Dom in turn gawped at his daughter. Her idea of "getting something on" hadn't amounted to much: tiny scarlet knickers and matching bra, a sheer black camisole, fishnet stockings and glossy thigh-length boots made up the total. Dom gulped and finished the bottle of vodka.

There appeared to be about ten people sharing Krissie's house, all of whom were apparently attending that evening's party and were dressed accordingly, to one extent or another. Dom's presence had been cheerfully accepted without question and during the bus journey to the pub, surrounded by laughing, chattering teenagers, he thought back to the humourless few hours he'd spent with his son and *his* friends… or comrades. He grinned to himself – this was fun! Once at the pub they'd all squeezed into a back room where they joined a crowd of leather, rubber and PVC-clad figures. There were also several nurses and schoolgirls in minute costumes, a flabby topless policeman and a tall figure in a flesh-coloured body stocking with a condom on his nose who laconically answered the inevitable queries with, 'Fuck nose!'

The room had its own corner bar, and although he wasn't sure who was paying, Dom cheerfully accepted every offer of a drink and any challenge at the pool table. It turned out he was quite good; he'd already beaten the topless policeman and a girl in a tiny furry bikini with a papier mâché club – Dom knew it was only papier mâché because she'd playfully bounced it off his head during his slightly drunken victory celebration.

Another glass was placed in his hand.

'Can I give you a game when it comes free again?' It was a girl's voice, and a little hesitant.

'Yeah, of course.' Dom turned to look at his challenger.

She was a tall girl, at least as tall as Dom, broad-shouldered and wide-hipped wearing a short leather skirt and a scuffed biker's jacket. Her make-up was predominantly black and inexpertly applied, as if she wasn't used to wearing it. 'Of course,' he repeated, 'I'm taking on all comers.' He swayed against the girl and spilled a bit of his drink. 'Oops, sorry.'

She flicked the wine off the sleeve of the leather jacket and smiled. 'Don't worry, that's one of the beauties of leather. A bit warm though.' She unzipped the jacket, unleashing a massive black-laced bosom, apparently unaware of the effect. Dom blinked and downed his drink. While they waited for the pool table to come free he downed two more, to the girl's one.

The game didn't last long; on her second shot the girl managed to canon the black ball into a corner pocket, losing by default and attracting a lot of barracking from the spectators.

'Bloody hell, Doris, you're useless.'

'You've gotta keep your tits off the table, Doris. One foot on the floor, no tits on the table, that's the rules.'

'Recharge her, Igor.'

'Yes, master.'

The girl smiled apologetically at Dom, shook her head dismissively at the hecklers and moved away from the table, quickly mingling with the crowd.

Somehow, once at the party, the good-natured generation bridge that seemed to have existed in the pub, disappeared. The youngsters who had earlier been happy to chat to Dom as an equal, laugh at his jokes and lose to him at pool, had scattered themselves around the rambling house and been re-absorbed by their own. Dom had no idea where Krissie was. Friendless and ignored he slumped onto a sagging sofa, drank another half a bottle of wine and watched as the younger generation became less and less inhibited. The music was louder than ever, the dancing frenetic and many of the costumes seemed to have become suddenly skimpier; some bare breasts and the occasional bottom danced before Dom's eyes. Dom decided he was drunk enough to dance too. A rare recognisable track was blasting out, The Rolling Stones, and hauling himself unsteadily to his feet he launched into his celebrated Jagger "strut 'n' pout" routine, which had always gone down so well at the tennis club discos. Head thrown back, eyes shut and imaginary microphone clutched in his hand, Dom strutted his stuff, blissfully unaware that he'd managed to clear the dance floor. He was, however, suddenly aware of a cool draft in the crotch and midriff area and dropping the imaginary microphone clutched at his groin where he found crispy ribbons of perished rubber, a handful of crumpled Y-front and one unfettered testicle.

Almost simultaneously the music stopped. 'Ladies and gentlemen,' the disc-jockey howled, 'a cherry has been popped, a rubber split! Watch out, girls, Grandaddy Mick's got his *Yah Yahs* out and *Wild Horses* won't get him back into that skin! But don't worry, Mick, remember, *You Can't Always Get What You Want!*'

The fact the DJ was riffing on songs made famous before most of the crowd were even born, didn't stop the general hilarity, and Dom was at the centre of it. Stranded in the middle of the room, he swayed unsteadily, wetsuit split from crotch to mid-chest and horribly conscious of his grubby pants and noticeably whiter belly. Dom started to shuffle towards the margins of the room, tucking away the rogue testicle as he went, but with cheers and mocking laughter ringing in his ears he soon gave up any thought of a dignified retreat and headed for some open French windows. He snatched a bottle of wine from a near-naked couple entwined on a beanbag as he passed, and lunged out into the garden.

The terrace was unlit, weed-ridden and uneven, and Dom didn't even see the steps down to the overgrown lawn until he was stumbling blindly down them. He missed the bottom step tripped and landed on his knees.

'Are you all right?'

'What?'

'I said, are you all right? Are you OK?'

'Yeah, of course,' he snapped.

'Only asking.' It was a soft female voice.

'Sorry, yes, thanks, I'm fine. A bit pissed, I think.'

'Well, it is a party.'

Dom got to his feet and could make out a figure on a bench a few yards away. 'Do you want some wine, not sure what colour it is?' He held the bottle up to the lights of the house. 'Red, I think… can't see any fag ends either, I think we're in luck.' He moved over to the bench. 'Oh, it's Doris. Hi.'

'Hi, Krissie's dad.'

'Call me Dom.'

'Only if you call me Claire.'

'Why?'

'Because that's my name… with an "I".'

'What happened to Doris?'

Claire sighed. 'They all think it's funny, and I suppose it was OK to start with… Karloff, you see? Boris Karloff, *Doris* Karloff, Frankenstein's monster, get it? It's because I'm sort of big… and ugly.'

'No.'

'"No" I'm not big, or "no" I'm not ugly?'

'Well, just "no".'

'OK, I'll take that. Pass the wine.'

Dom let her keep the bottle and watched a sliver of moon appear from behind a cloud. He clutched his arms around his bare middle and shivered.

'Are you happy?' Claire said suddenly.

'Happy?'

'Yeah.'

Dom looked at her, then back at the moon.

'Krissie says you're very successful, a banker. She's very proud of you.'

Dom turned to look at her. 'Is she?'

'My dad's a farmer,' Claire said.

'So are *you* happy?' Dom said.

Claire sipped at the wine, gave a long sigh and passed the bottle to Dom. 'Not often, but I'm still young. There's time, I suppose,' she said quietly.

Dom thought about this and decided it sounded very sad coming from one so young.

Claire's voice became stronger again: 'So go on, I asked first, are you happy?'

'What, being a banker? No, I'm not a very good one,' he gave a snort, 'and I drink too much, and they're probably going to repossess my car and my wife is fucking her tennis coach.'

'Hmm, Krissie didn't mention any of that.'

'No, I don't suppose she did.'

They sat for a few minutes with their own thoughts, passing the bottle between them and watching the moon glide amongst the clouds.

Dom patted the back of Claire's hand. 'It's been nice but I think I'm going home.' He gave a bitter little laugh at the thought of the basement mattress. 'Well, when I say "home"...'

'I'll come with you.'

Dom turned to look at her. 'OK.'

'Dad!'

'What the...?'

'Dad, you've got someone in there!'

'It's Kenneth.' Dom's voice was muffled by the sleeping bag.

'You lying toad!'

'*Ribbit*,' a muffled female voice said.

'That's him... or her,' Dom giggled.

'Dad!'

Dom popped his head out from under the sleeping bag. His daughter, still in her dominatrix outfit but apparently minus the bra, stood at the foot of the mattress flanked by a grinning Lucifer and one of the Village People.

'It's not what it seems...'

'Yes it is.' Claire's tousled head and one enormous breast appeared next to Dom.

'Doris! Dad, not Doris!'

'It's *Claire* actually, *Christine*.'

'Bloody hell, Dad, what about Mum?'

Dom lifted the edge of the sleeping bag and peered underneath. 'Nope, she's not in here,' and with that he pulled down a giggling Claire and tugged the bedding over their heads. 'Anyone for tennis?'

* * *

'Christ, Gav, is that your idea of keeping a low profile? You've been all over the TV out here, you even made page three of *El Mundo*. The fucking world and his wife know who you are now… and what's more, *where* you are.'

'It had to be done,' Gavin said simply, 'and they haven't found me yet. You just concentrate on sorting things out down there so I can come back with no problems.'

'It's not as simple as that, Gav.'

'Yeah, well I gathered that. What's the latest?'

'We don't really know, all our inside hotlines have gone cold, and that's worrying.'

'And Gomez?'

Jacko gave a snort of humourless laughter. 'Well that's the one bit of good news. We obviously weren't the only ones he was trying to hang out to dry. Someone's got to him.'

Gavin was silent for a moment. 'That could make things a lot worse.'

'Yeah, maybe in one way, but it buys us time. And we need to use it.'

'Like?'

'Consolidate, get out of the Costas, at least for the time being, sell everything we can and pull back to Gib and Morocco.'

Gavin clicked his tongue. 'I never much liked the Marbella pad anyway,' he mused, 'see what we can get for it.'

'Yeah, well, bit of a problem there. I was ahead of you on that but according to our new guy all the permits were dodgy, it should never have been built, probably unsaleable. In fact, we may actually have to pay to have it demolished and...'

'Oh beautiful!' Gavin gave a wry laugh. 'Hoist by our own whatsit.'

'Petard, yeah well...'

'What about Puerto?'

'Well it's legal but the valuation was disappointing.'

'Go on.'

Jacko told him the figure.

'Bloody hell! Are they taking the piss?'

'I'll see what I can do,' Jacko sighed.

'And the *finca*? Go on, give me the worst.'

'No big problem, paperwork's OK and it's gone up a bit. But I think we could hang on to that, if you wanted to... in fact, I'm there now.'

'What're you doing up there?' Gavin snapped. 'We need things to be happening down on the coast, Jacko.'

'Gav, listen, it's too hot down there, and I'm not talking about the bloody weather, OK?'

Gavin was silent for some moments. The phone murmured suspiciously. 'Is Bobby with you?'

'Yeah, she's here, in fact she said if I got through she wanted a word.'

'OK, put her on.'

It was a short call. Bobby, in best baby-doll voice had

pleaded boredom at the *finca*. Not for herself she assured him, she was happy shopping and lunching in Ronda but the boys were restless and fractious. Some friends from school had invited them to Florida, their family had a spread outside Fort Lauderdale apparently, and the boys were pleading to go. Bobby thought they should. It would be a treat for them and she could amuse herself with new friends she'd made in town and stay at the *finca* and wait for Gavin to return to Spain. Jacko would be there for company.

Gavin had agreed, but instinctively he knew something was going on, and not just in his business affairs. He asked Bobby to put Jacko back on the line, told him to make the arrangements for the boys, be generous with the pocket money and to "keep an eye on" Bobby.

'You've got nothing to worry about there, Gav,' Jacko assured him. 'By the way, where are you?'

On hearing Gavin was in London, albeit in an anonymous Victoria hotel, Jacko had urged him to "get the hell out of town" and lose himself somewhere in "the sticks". Gavin decided his fixer was probably right. He'd already stopped shaving and within a couple of days should have a suitably rugged stubble – mainly grey he noted ruefully – and tomorrow he'd find an outdoor shop and pick up some basic walking gear, then take the next train north and get lost amongst the walking crowds of the Lake District. He'd mark time there until it was time for the mysterious meeting, the way things were going he could do with something "to his advantage".

For once, London's black cabbies proved fallible; the

first two shops Gavin was deposited at were certainly "outdoor", especially if you were a site worker – the boots they stocked were of the steel toe-capped variety, the waterproof suits strictly "high-vis" and the hats were of the hard, rather than the bobble variety. But neither shop stocked any equipment remotely suitable for fell walking. Eventually, running out of patience, Gavin ended up in the sports department of Harrods, where at eye-watering prices he was quickly suited and booted. The choice of a rucksack prompted a bit more debate as the enthusiastic assistant tried to steer Gavin towards larger models, which, he was assured, would accommodate a full week's camping equipment. 'One's own home on one's own back,' the assistant had enthused plummily, 'and the freedom and flexibility to move on whenever one wants, even at short notice.' Gavin had no intention of going camping, but he could see some merit in this argument, particularly in his current situation, and it gave him an idea. With a large green and gold bag in each hand he returned to his hotel and started doing some ringing around.

Eleven o'clock the next morning found Gavin in a scruffy Portakabin on a run-down industrial estate under the Hammersmith flyover, scribbling his alternative signature on a seemingly endless pile of disclaimers and pages of small print. Once completed, this would allow him to drive away in the very large and well-worn camper van, which he'd chosen from the limited "fleet" in the yard. As he handed his credit card over, the door to the office crunched open and a large guitar case appeared, neck first, followed by a group of five people carrying a variety of luggage: tent bags, rucksacks, two more guitar cases and an accordion. There were two women and three men. The women both had colourfully dyed hair, assorted face piercings and tattoos escaping from under sleeves and shoulder straps. The men all had long hair and beards, grey to one extent or another, and were also well tattooed, with a selection of rings and studs in their noses and ears. All five appeared to have been dressed by a poorly stocked charity shop. They were loud and excited and from what Gavin could gather were there to collect a camper van they'd booked weeks before to take them to some sort of festival. However, as Gavin was led outside by an oily youth to be shown the controls and quirks of his vehicle the mood seemed to be changing. The rental manager was trying repeatedly to take payment from a series of plastic cards, which the group were taking turns to offer him, and one by one they were being rejected. When Gavin returned to the office after his briefing to sign one last form recording the numerous dents and scratches he'd noted on his van, the group had disappeared.

Five minutes later, as he edged his huge vehicle out of the compound gates, he spotted them standing dejectedly on the pavement, clustered round a pile of rucksacks and guitar cases. One of the women raised an ironic hitch-hiking thumb. For some reason Gavin stopped, he pushed the button to lower the passenger side window but nothing happened, so he found the hand brake, got out and walked round the van.

'Got a problem?'

It was the woman with the raised thumb who spoke. 'No transport, man, that's the problem.'

'That and no funds,' one of the men added with a grimace. He nodded back at the Portakabin. 'Not enough on one card between us to cover their fucking damage deposit.'

Gavin looked at them all for a moment, then said: 'Can I give you a lift anywhere?'

'Well, yeah...' the woman started.

'Yeah, Keswick,' the man said with a bitter laugh.

Gavin slitted his eyes and looked at him closely. What was going on here? How could this peculiar bunch of strangers know...? This had to be more than coincidence. Gavin studied the whole group one by one. There was nothing to indicate they knew who or what he was, or for that matter where he was going. Perhaps it *was* just simply coincidence.

'You all right?' The man looked at him curiously. 'Seriously, thanks, a lift would be great. Just back into town would be fine, if it's on your way.'

Something else was occurring to Gavin. He looked at the men's beards and fingered his stubble. OK, he couldn't match the piercings or tattoos and his clothes might shout Lacoste not Oxfam, but these people weren't much younger than him and there'd be nothing remarkable in six middle-aged scruffs heading for a music festival in an old van. 'Are you really going to Keswick, Keswick in the Lake District?'

'*Were*, yeah, best gig we've been offered in years, even got all the gear on its way up there in a mate's van. Won't play itself though,' he added bitterly.

'As it happens, I'm going to Keswick,' Gavin said quietly.

It was the turn of the group to look dumbstruck.

An hour later the old van was swinging and rocking

along the M4 somewhere near Reading as Gavin tried to master the steering in a vicious crosswind. The group had been ecstatic at the offer of a lift. Hands had been pumped, Gavin had been kissed on the cheek by the woman with green and purple hair and prominent nipple rings, and names had been exchanged. All of which, Gavin had already forgotten, apart from Nipple Rings, who was called Grace, and apparently partnered the accordion player, who might have been called Noel. The men had all scrambled into the back of the van and spent until about Windsor stacking and restacking their luggage and instruments, while the two women had settled onto the front double passenger seat, ignored the seat belts and put their sandalled feet up on the dashboard.

'This is brilliant,' Grace said, rolling a cigarette. 'Just meant to happen, man, meeting you... pre-ordained.'

'Hell of a coincidence,' Gavin agreed.

The women contentedly passed the cigarette between themselves for a few minutes and the one whose name Gavin couldn't remember hummed a tune to herself, which Gavin thought he recognised. 'What *is* that song, um...?'

'Jan,' she said, turning towards him and flicking her long hair away from her face, 'it's Jan.' She smiled. 'Only my mother calls me Janice... and my shrink. And it's "House of the Risin' Sun" – we do a great version.'

'Of course it is. Is that your normal sort of thing then?' Gavin asked, keeping one eye on the articulated lorry currently overtaking them.

'Country Punk,' Grace said. 'I play guitar and do vocals and Jan plays drums and sings along too, don't yer, hun?'

Jan nodded and blew smoke at the tax disc.

'Johnny Cash meets Johnny Rotten, eh? Sounds interesting,' Gavin said.

'Yeah, it's kinda challenging,' Jan confirmed, handing the cigarette back to Grace. 'We're the Shaggy Cracks.'

'Right, OK,' Gavin said slowly, 'and what about the guys?'

Grace gave a snort. 'All of us, we're all Shaggy Cracks.'

'Just theirs are in their faces,' Jan said, deadpan.

Gavin glanced sideways at her. 'You've used that line before,' he grinned.

Right on cue a bearded face appeared between the seats and a hand reached out and flicked the nearest nipple ring through Grace's T-shirt. 'How's it going, babe?'

'Yeah.'

The man (it might have been Noel) put his hand on the back of Gavin's seat. 'How's this thing driving, Gav? Feels like a fuckin' ship in a storm back there. Might have to bring Dave up front for a while, he's gone a bit green. Don't mind if we smoke a bit of weed and tune up in the back, do you?'

'Be my guest.'

The afternoon in the swaying van passed amiably enough. There was an ever-changing rota of front-seat passengers so the racket from the back, which occasionally included a few recognisable chords, varied depending on which instrumentalists were back there at the time. Gavin thought he'd identified a harmonica amongst the twanging of guitars, certainly the accordion and probably a violin. Some sort of percussion, which sounded like it was being beaten out on the flat surfaces of the van, sometimes managed to hit a vague rhythm. Acrid clouds of smoke from cheap rolling tobacco and the sweet smell of marijuana wafted throughout.

During the revolving front-seat conversations Gavin got to know a bit more about the individuals who made up the Shaggy Cracks, and, up to a point, they got to know a bit more about him. The band's gig was in a park in the middle of Keswick at some sort of walking/outdoor festival. They weren't really sure how it had happened; they'd been contacted out of the blue on the Internet, told they'd been "spotted" and then been offered the biggest fee of their careers. Almost too good to be true, although Dave (Gavin was starting to put names to beards), did admit they thought they might have been confused with a more mainstream indie band called Shagpile. But what the hell, a gig was a gig.

Gavin had told them he had a business meeting in Keswick early the following week. He was taking a leisurely westerly route up the country, going to stop overnight somewhere in the Midlands, probably at a riverside pub with a campsite, which he vaguely remembered from childhood, and then drive on to Cumbria the following day. This plan suited the Shaggy Cracks perfectly; they had tents with them, arriving the following day would give them time for their "sound-checks" – probably the first ever in their careers, Gavin suspected – and they would treat him to a meal at the pub that night as a thank you.

The pub, river and campsite were just as Gavin had remembered but, predictably, busier. Leaving the band hidden in the van Gavin had charmed the woman at reception with reminiscences about earlier, youthful stays and duly been allocated a favoured corner of one of several fields. It was directly across from the pub on the opposite bank of the river, a flat site partially screened by a few scattered birch trees and scrubby bushes and with "river frontage". The band was delighted with the arrangement and set about littering the plot, and beyond, with their tents, bedding and instruments. Neighbouring campers and families watched warily – as well they might.

* * *

'Cat, listen, we've got two choices… you've got two choices: I can go for help and keep trying to get a signal, or I can wait here with you and hope someone comes along with a phone that works, or who can go for help.'

'No, don't leave me, Greg,' Cat panted. She reached for his hand. 'Someone will come.'

Greg stroked her hand. He couldn't think what else to do. 'Is anything, sort of… happening?' he asked, looking at Cat's bulging anorak. It was so obvious now, how could he not have realised?

'No, no, I don't think so.' Cat breathed deeply. 'It feels sort of… I don't know, I've never had a baby before.'

'Me neither,' Greg said seriously.

Cat squeezed his hand and managed a strained little smile. 'I don't want to disappoint you, Greg, but you probably never will.'

He grinned at her sheepishly, relieved that at least she was still making jokes.

Then things started to happen. Two men appeared, moving fast up the path towards them. After the usual exchanges and a brief explanation from Greg with affirmatory nods from Cat, they smoothly took control. It turned out they were teachers "shadowing" a group of students on an expedition for their Duke of Edinburgh's award. Both were experienced walkers and had some limited medical training, and critically, they had a satellite phone. Greg was happy to be side-lined while the one man, fresh-faced and reassuringly cheerful, unwrapped an insulated bag and tucked it in all round Cat, then with a flourish and a grin produced a huge flask of tea. The other teacher, older, sterner and presumably the more senior, had started a series of short, intense conversations on the phone.

'Right,' he said finally, 'things are under control.' He squatted down next to Cat. 'Mountain rescue are on their way and so is an ambulance. That'll come as far up the track as it can and the rescue people will get you down to it. It shouldn't take long, these guys really shift, but there's a helicopter on standby too… just in case. How are you feeling? Any more signs?'

Cat said she was fine but grimaced slightly. 'I want Ben.'

The senior teacher waved Greg closer. He obeyed but said: 'Actually, I'm not Ben.'

'Oh, then who…?'

Cat lifted a hand. 'Can I use your phone? I want to speak to Ben.'

Ben, it seemed, was not answering so Cat left a short non-specific message, saying she'd try and ring again later.

She reached for Greg's hand and looked miserable. The two teachers conferred quietly, glancing at Cat from time to time.

The mountain rescue team took just over an hour to reach them. Gruffly kind and professional, they exuded a calm confidence and wasted no time. As two of them, one a woman, set about assessing Cat, another quickly assembled a rigid stretcher. A further member of the team was in constant communication with someone on a radio. After a few minutes the two teachers, visibly relieved at being able to hand over responsibility, wished Cat well and set off up the path in pursuit of their youngsters.

Apart from the odd word of reassurance, Greg had been largely ignored by the rescue team but was finally waved over to listen in to the brief discussion, which concluded that Cat's condition was stable enough for a stretcher-borne descent. The helicopter wouldn't be required but she'd be got to hospital as quickly as possible by ambulance, which would be waiting at the bottom of the path by the time the team had got them down. Cat was eased onto the stretcher and gently strapped in place. One of the men humped her rucksack over his shoulder and they made ready to leave.

'Greg, you will come too, won't you?' Cat twisted her head round on the stretcher. 'Please?'

Greg moved to where she could see him more easily. 'Of course I will, Cat.'

The mountain rescue group, despite their large packs and the clumsy burden of the stretcher, moved incredibly smoothly and quickly down over the rocky terrain. Greg struggled to keep up and was relieved when they reached the valley floor and he could see the ambulance only about another half a mile ahead.

Cat was transferred to the back of the ambulance and Greg was banished while the paramedics made their own examination and assessment. They emerged a few minutes later to say it was fine for Greg to join her, then after a few last words and exchange of details with the rescue team, the ambulance set off down the track, the same track, which just a few short hours earlier Greg and Cat had strolled along making up limericks.

In the back of the ambulance a woman paramedic sat at Cat's head and Greg sat strapped into a sort of jump seat at the foot of the stretcher and looked around at the array of equipment and apparatus. He was intrigued to see, amongst all the state-of-the-art gadgetry, and neatly strapped in its place, an old-fashioned road mender's shovel and wondered what medical application it could possibly have.

The paramedic caught Greg's eye and smiled. 'She's going to be fine, don't you worry,' she said.

Greg looked at Cat's flushed face on the crisp white pillow, and their eyes met. She stretched out a hand towards him. 'Oh Greg, I'm sorry, I should have told you before, shouldn't I?'

'Well, I suppose…'

The paramedic looked at Greg in amazement. 'You mean you didn't know that… that she was… not that it's any of my business, of course.'

Greg looked a bit embarrassed.

Cat managed a little laugh and turned her head to the paramedic. 'Greg and I are just friends, we only met recently, while we were both walking and… ooh.'

Greg started in alarm but the paramedic just muttered a few words of reassurance and placed a clear mask over Cat's mouth and nose, telling her to breathe deeply. Cat closed her eyes and did as she was told.

Greg closed his eyes too. The motion of the ambulance combined with the lack of any substantial food recently, and probably an adrenalin overdose, was making him feel slightly queasy.

It was as if the paramedic knew. 'A longer trip than it should be, I'm afraid,' she said, 'but not long now.' She explained that they couldn't go to the usual, the nearest, hospital: 'Bed shortages,' she shrugged.

The hospital was the usual confused mixture of new and old, endless corridors, confusing signage, bustling staff and bewildered patients. It could have been anywhere in the country, but this was the main hospital for the town of Whitehaven on the Cumbrian coast. After a quick admission procedure and brief chat with a young doctor, from which Greg was again excluded, Cat was whisked away. Clearly not needed and starting to feel he was in the way, Greg hovered uncertainly. A passing nurse took pity and directed him to a bleak little waiting area with several rows of orange plastic chairs, a crumpled pile of magazines and a single filthy window overlooking a chaotic roofscape of water tanks, air-conditioning units and chimneys belching funereal smoke. He had the room to himself and had been pacing around for about an hour, not sure what to do, when a plump middle-aged woman in a straining blue uniform suddenly appeared.

'Right, we've finished with her for a while, you can go on in and see her.'

'Um, do you think I should... is she, well, decent?'

The sister looked at him curiously. 'Bit late for that isn't it?' she said in brusque Cumbrian tones. 'You won't see 'owt you haven't seen before – she is having your baby, pet.'

'No, no, it's not mine. Hasn't she explained?'

'Right, well...' her tone softened, 'OK, that's as maybe but she said she'd like to see you anyway. And yes, she's decent,' she added, disappearing through the swing doors.

Cat appeared to be asleep, her face still flushed, hair spread across the pillow and her swollen belly straining against the bedclothes. Greg shook his head and wondered again how he'd failed to notice her condition before. She drowsily opened her eyes and lifted a hand off the bed cover. Greg went across and took it. 'OK?'

'Yeah, for the moment, they're going to speed things up a bit soon though. I wish Ben was here. I've left a message telling him where I am but...' she gulped back tears, '... it'll take him hours.' A sob escaped. 'He's going to miss it.'

Greg made soothing sounds and stroked her hand and wrist again. 'Um, if you want, if it would help... I know I'm not Ben, but...'

'Oh Greg, you're lovely.' She used her free hand to wipe tears off her cheeks. 'Please, when it happens, I'd love you to be somewhere nearby. Just knowing that would help.' She took his hand in both of hers. 'Go and find somewhere to pace up and down and chain-smoke, I think that's what expectant dads are meant to do, even de facto ones.' She gave a little laugh and winced.

'I'll get someone.'

After tracking down a nurse, Greg returned to the waiting area and watched the late afternoon sun haze over. He looked over the jumble of hospital buildings and other distant rooftops spilling down towards the sea, and thought about Ben, and Martin. He was still gazing out of the window when he heard the now familiar creak of the swing doors behind him.

'Greg?'

Greg spun round. 'Ben, my god! How have you got here?'

'Where's Cat, where is she?'

Greg told him. 'I'll wait here,' he said, but Ben was already through the doors.

He was back within ten minutes, looking flushed and nervous.

'Everything OK? Is she all right?'

Ben nodded and let out a long breath. 'Yeah, yeah, everything's fine. With both of them,' he added with a sort of wonderment. 'They're going to induce her, just to make sure.' He sat down next to Greg and put his chin in his hands.

After a moment Greg broke the silence. 'So how have you managed to get here…? Not that I'm not pleased.'

'I was already well on the way,' Ben explained. 'I'd got things sorted at the office, so I left early and thought I'd surprise Cat by being in Grasmere when you and she walked in. I've even booked a table for the three of us at the Wordsworth for tonight.' He gave a strained little laugh. 'Better change that to four now, I guess. Hopefully.'

'Which one of you is Ben?' A nurse in a full-length gown with a mask hanging from one ear appeared in the doorway. Ben was led away and Greg was left with the rooftops of Whitehaven, the dying sun and out-of-date Mothercare catalogues.

* * *

Robbie had woken in the dunes covered in heavy dew and found Sylvia already rolling up her sleeping bag.

'Sorry, I didn't mean to wake you. I've got to get back to town, there's an order coming in, and I ought to get the shop open anyway.'

Robbie sat up and stretched. 'No problem, I've got things to do as well.'

'Would you like a lift?' Sylvia said shyly.

They didn't talk much on the drive back across the island but when Sylvia dropped Robbie at the harbour-master's house she pecked him on the cheek and said: 'Why don't you call by later for a sun-downer, five-ish? Ask anyone in town where the shop is; Shakespeare & Co.'

'Classy.'

'Not original,' Sylvia smiled, 'but thanks. See you later.'

Robbie had a productive day and managed to tick off a lot of superficial repairs from a long list, but the mainsail was definitely work-in-progress and the damaged boom really needed professional attention, he decided. He'd popped into the Plough for a lunchtime cheese sandwich and pint, and the landlord had told him that a reporter from the local rag had been in the evening before looking for him. Apparently he'd hung around for an hour or so then given up and wandered off. Robbie said he hoped he wouldn't be back. The landlord didn't know.

As predicted, Robbie was readily pointed in the direction of the book shop and jingled his way through the door punctually at five. Sylvia was dealing with a pompous tweedy-looking man at a desk at the back of the shop but she looked past him and gave Robbie a little wave of greeting. The man glanced over his shoulder, then pointedly turned his back and moved slightly to his side to block any direct line of sight between Robbie and Sylvia. He was obviously determined to have her undivided attention. Robbie made a face at his back, and for something to do, picked up a large paperback off an island display stacked with copies of just the one book. It had an intriguing title and the cover showed a quintessential English village overshadowed by a giant wind turbine. Robbie turned it over and started to read the blurb.

'Utter rubbish.' The pompous man brushed passed with a contemptuous nod at the book in Robbie's hand and marched out of the shop. Sylvia puffed her cheeks and let out a long breath. 'God, he could bore for England, he's been in here for hours. Thanks, I think you scared him off.'

'My pleasure. Is it "utter rubbish"?' Robbie held up the book.

'Well, it's not likely you'll find it on a shelf amongst the classics in the future,' Sylvia smiled, 'but it's got its points. A good laugh, dirty as hell in places too,' she laughed.

'Sounds right up my street. *The Smugglers' Fingers*, a

curious name.' Robbie turned the book over in his hands again. 'How much?'

'On the house, as long as you tell all your friends about it. It's a local writer, we like to support them, and they need all the help they can get. Take it.'

Robbie thanked her and she led him through to the back of the shop. The building's hillside position meant the rear sat several floors higher than the front, and from a storeroom a glazed door opened onto a small balcony with views over neighbouring rooftops to the sea. A bottle of red wine and two glasses were already sitting on a low wooden table between two canvas chairs.

'Perfect,' Robbie said, 'all we need now is the sun.'

He was right, the weather was definitely on the change, and in the last few hours lumpy cloud had gathered from the west blotting out the sun by degrees.

'Never mind, let's have a drink.' Robbie put down his book and poured the wine. 'Here's to us.' It was said on impulse and he looked quickly at Sylvia to see what her reaction would be.

She smiled happily, raised her glass and repeated the toast. 'I can keep an ear out for customers from here,' she explained, then went on to apologise, saying she only had an hour or so as she'd forgotten a prior engagement. 'Afraid I can't wriggle out of it either, I'm the host. Got about ten of the BBC turning up here a bit later.' She glanced at her watch.

'Oh,' Robbie said, obviously surprised. 'Can't say I'm exactly on TV people at the moment, not after... you know, that thing the other day.'

Sylvia laughed. 'No, nothing to do with the telly, my

BBC is the Boozy Book Club. A load of ladies who like a glass or two,' she raised hers, 'and a good read.' She tapped the book on the table. 'Actually, that's this month's choice, it'll be interesting to see what the ladies have made of it. I can see one or two of them being quite scandalised. Nothing like a bit of ripe language and gratuitous sex to stir things up a bit, especially after a bottle or two.' She grinned, breaking off to dive inside and answer the phone. When she came back she asked how the repairs to *Idler* were going. Robbie had to admit that some of the worst damage was beyond his shipwrighting skills, and budget. 'You won't be sailing away anytime soon then?' Sylvia smiled. Robbie smiled back. The question of his leaving the island seemed to lead naturally back to the subject of the strange summons to the Lake District. 'Have you been there before?' Sylvia asked.

Robbie paused for a few moments, as if he was having to think about this, then sighed heavily. 'Not since I was a kid,' he said eventually. Sylvia gave him a curious look and watched as Robbie twiddled his glass, spinning the wine almost to the rim. 'My parents used to send us, my brother and me, to a sort of youth camp thing. It was all a bit religious.' He gave a weak smile, 'I suppose they thought it would do us some sort of good.'

'And did it?'

'Well…'

There was a tinkle of the shop bell and Sylvia looked at her watch. 'God, is that the time?' She apologised and disappeared inside, returning briefly to gulp down the last of her wine and explain that the first of the BBC ladies had arrived. She gave Robbie another peck. 'Will you be around tomorrow?'

They arranged to meet in the Plough for lunch.

Robbie was sat in the cockpit working on his damaged mainsail after its latest mauling. A glass of whisky sat within easy reach on a nearby winch and although the sewing wasn't going well, the hour with Sylvia had left him in a lasting good mood.

'Nice evening.'

Robbie looked up at the quayside. A short, plump man in baggy trousers and a quilted car coat stood on the edge smiling down at him.

'Enjoying a drop, eh?' The man nodded at the winch.

Robbie was pretty sure he knew who this was. He looked up at the sky, which was rapidly darkening. 'No, not really,' he said.

The man looked confused. 'Not really what?'

'A nice evening.' Robbie held his free hand out, palm up. 'In fact, it's raining.'

The man looked up. 'So it is, time to get under cover. Can I buy you a drink?' He nodded towards the Plough.

Robbie unsmilingly accepted. His on-board whisky supply wouldn't last forever and he was already pushing his luck with the various lines of credit he'd established round the dock. He decided he'd let the journalist have what he wanted, up to a point, but stay wary and just take whatever was on offer.

Established in a corner of the bar, Robbie said he'd have a pint of bitter, adding, '…and a whisky chaser wouldn't go amiss… double.' The man had cheerfully obliged and introduced himself as 'Doug', a features writer for *The Douglas Crusader*. He bought another round and explained that he was keen to hear Robbie's own account of his recent mishaps. He said his editor had been following Robbie's story with interest and was appalled by the unfair treatment Robbie seemed to have received at the hands of the national press, especially on television. As the voice of a seafaring town, *The Crusader* was naturally sympathetic to all sailors and saw it as their duty to redress the balance and give a true picture of just how difficult and challenging solo sailing really was – and how brave its adherents were. Robbie had shrugged modestly at this, given a wry smile of the hard-done-by, and accepted another drink. The whisky chasers now came as a matter of course. Doug asked if he could take a few photographs a little later and produced a small, sophisticated-looking camera. Robbie pretended to demur but was quickly talked into it. 'A bit later then,' Doug said.

The Douglas Crusader had always prided itself on its campaigning role, it was its *raison d'être,* but had recently produced a few duds; the campaign against topless sunbathing on local beaches had merely resulted in the newspaper's offices being besieged by a hundred or so bare-breasted women and every naturist on the island, creating great amusement and titillation for the rest of the population, and in turn, great copy for the national press. And the crusade to improve domestic fire safety had proved even more embarrassing, literally going up in flames, when a sub-editor, in breach of the office non-smoking rules, and working late, had knocked out his pipe into a wicker waste basket full of rejected copy and burnt down the news room.

The editors had decided they were on safer ground,

so to speak, running a nautically themed campaign. But despite Doug's claims, and his editors' supposed admiration, their latest campaign had absolutely nothing to do with the qualities of solo sailors. After several serious boating and jet-ski accidents already this summer, one fatal, and all reportedly involving alcohol to one extent or another, the paper had decided that too many pleasure-boat users were showing a selfish and reckless, not to mention drunken, disregard for other boat users and bathers. Quite apart from flaunting health and safety rules, their behaviour was "anti-social", "irresponsible" and "downright dangerous". So the latest campaign was to demand more control and testing of those *The Crusader* had catchily christened: "Cruiser boozers".

Robbie was being set up. *The Crusader*'s editorial team had indeed watched his national press coverage with interest, and they'd decided that no sober person could possibly get themselves into that much trouble, even at sea. Robbie washing up on the shores of the Isle of Man had been an absolute godsend, and once some proof had been gathered – or manufactured – he would be held up as a drink-raddled anti-hero, the archetype "Cruiser boozer", who not only risked his own life but also those of many others, including the brave men and women of the RNLI, on whom Robbie seemed to regularly depend.

Doug came back to the table with another round.
Robbie squinted at the frothing pint pot and the half-full tumbler, which curiously, also seemed to be frothing. 'Wassat?' he mumbled.
'I thought you'd like another chaser,' Doug said.

Robbie studied the glass again. 'Oh, awright, a fizzy chaser then.' He belched. 'But only one at a time.'

'Er, there is only one.'

Robbie shut one eye and squinted at the tumbler. 'Oh yeah,' he giggled, 'bottoms up.'

Doug wanted to give this "chaser" a few minutes to work and filled them by trotting out ever more fatuous questions. Robbie gave increasingly monosyllabic answers and was obviously losing interest, not to mention consciousness. The reporter peeped at his watch under the table. It was time to wind this up. 'It must be really frightening out there sometimes, Robbie,' he said.

'Eh, what?'

'Out at sea on your own, weather getting rough, things starting to go wrong, God, I couldn't do it. I bet when it gets really scary you could do with a bit of Dutch courage... Enough to turn any man to drink, eh?' he laughed heartily.

'Christ, yes, you'd never get me out there fuckin' sober!' Robbie roared, joining in Doug's laughter. He took a long pull at his beer and licked the froth off his upper lip. 'Nah, not really,' he was struggling to form his words, 'gotta keep a straight head, never know when yer might need it.' He tried to focus on Doug's face. 'All sorts happens at sea, yer know?' he said seriously.

'Can I quote you on that?'

'Yeah, course.'

Doug quickly scribbled in his notebook: *Quote: "Christ... you'd never get me out there f****** sober!"*

'Right, I think that's me just about done,' Doug said. He suddenly looked down at his feet as if he'd dropped something and bent under the table. Robbie felt something pulling at his trouser leg and began to slide across the shiny leather bench. One last sudden yank and he slid right off the bench, throwing himself sideways at the last minute to avoid the table edge and taking the remains of his pint with him, prompting cries of alarm and anger from neighbouring tables. In the confusion Doug jumped to his feet and, unnoticed, nudged the table over, tumbling the remaining glasses onto Robbie's sprawled form. Confused and temporarily blinded by a faceful of cheap whisky, Robbie was still struggling to disentangle his feet from the table legs when there were two bright flashes in quick succession.

'Cheers, Robbie! Oh yeah, and bon voyage!' Doug pocketed the little camera and headed for the door.

NINE

'Is that you, Dominic? Bastard! Krissie says you've been shagging her friends.'

'Well, not exactly.'

'What d'you mean, "not exactly"? Either you have or you haven't!'

'Well, it was only one, in the singular, and Claire isn't exactly Christine's friend.'

There was a snort from the other end of the line. 'Oh, Clare, is it?'

'With an "i".'

'I don't care how the slut spells it and…'

'Listen, that's a bit fucking rich coming from you.' Dom had promised himself he wouldn't go where he was about to, but with the "slut" remark, Beverley was asking for it. 'Still shagging that macho twat at the tennis club, are you? Sloppy seconds from what I hear… and while we're at it, telling tales, it's pretty rich coming from Christine too. From what I can gather, she's happy jumping into bed with anything that's got a pulse round here.' Dom listened to the electronic silence for several moments; he knew she was still there and could imagine the blazing eyes and pinched lips.

'Dominic, this is over,' she said slowly.

'Yeah, I've got to go anyway.'

'No, I mean it's *over*, we're over, this whole bloody… sham of a marriage. You do what you want up north, you can shag who you like as far as I'm concerned, but keep it up there and I'll stay down here in civilisation. And I don't want you back. I've been seeing a solicitor.'

'God, you're not shagging him as well?'

'For legal advice!' Beverley shouted.

'Oh.' It was Dom's turn to pause. 'Well, I'll need those bank cards,' he said calmly.

'Did you hear what I just said?'

'Yes, Beverley, I did. Solicitor, tennis coach, whatever you want, that's fine.' He was back in control and quite enjoying it. 'The bank cards?'

'They're here.'

'I thought they might be. Can you send them on to…?' He gestured frantically at Claire and put his hand over the receiver. 'What's the address here?' he whispered. Claire scribbled it on a used envelope and Dom read it out to his wife.

'Gamekeeper's Cottage? Oh yeah, who are you shacked up with now?'

Dom decided not to provoke her any further, not until he had his hands on those cards. 'It's a B&B,' he said.

'I thought you were broke,' she said suspiciously.

'They're trusting people, I told them I'd soon have the...'

'Yeah, yeah, OK, the cards are on their way.'

Dom and Claire had emerged from the basement mid-morning and been relieved to find the pink kitchen deserted, still littered with pre and post-party debris, but void of judgemental friends, or daughters. They left the house quickly and found a cafe a few streets away where Claire insisted on buying them both breakfast.

'So, where you off to now?' Claire asked over a second coffee.

Dom explained his curious journey north and briefly described the events which had brought him this far, and left him temporarily destitute.

'Keswick by the weekend, eh?' Claire said. 'I reckon I can help there.'

'Claire, are you sure you ought to be...? Well, last night was great, bloody wonderful in fact, but I'm not sure I should be... I mean...'

'Yeah, yeah, you're old, I'm young and I'm at uni with your daughter. Did it matter to either of us last night? No, and actually it was bloody wonderful for me too.'

This was a different girl... young woman, from the shy creature of the evening before, taunted, bullied and despairing of finding happiness. 'Come on, let's get you to Keswick and have some fun on the way,' she said, jumping to her feet.

It had taken Dom 200 yards of pushing to jump-start

the ancient VW Beetle, and by the time he'd been allowed to slump into the passenger seat he was shattered. His breath came in raw gasps, his head was thudding and it felt like his heart was trying to beat its way out of his chest... but he was starting to enjoy this new adventure.

Claire had explained that she and her sister shared a tiny cottage on the edge of her parents' farm near Penrith in Cumbria, and that's where they were headed. 'Only half an hour from Keswick,' she assured him, 'even in this jalopy.' She patted the steering wheel affectionately. Apparently they'd have the place to themselves as her sister was away backpacking at the moment, the family weren't sure where but the last phone call had been from a brothel in Istanbul. In answer to what Dom thought was a grown-up question about her unscheduled lost study time, Claire snorted and dismissed any pending lectures or tutorials as unimportant to her academic progress, and "a waste of time, anyway". She was studying politics, philosophy and economics with the avowed intention of becoming the future president of the National Union of Farmers. 'They need a bloody good shaking up,' she explained, 'a woman's touch... nothing feminist, mind you. I'll get there, you'll see.'

Dom looked at the fierce eyes and set mouth and believed her.

The plan was that they'd stay at the cottage over the weekend, Dom could look round the farm if he liked, and Claire would take him over to Keswick on Monday morning on her way back to Manchester.

'What about your parents? They might not like... you know?'

'Oh, I shan't bother telling them you're here. If we bump into them, no problem, they're pretty relaxed.'

'As long as you're sure, I wouldn't want to cause any...'

'Look, I told you, no problem. I'm a bloody angel compared to Steph; she was making homemade porn films and flogging them at school when we were fifteen, and then turned the bloody attic into a cannabis farm. It's only because Dad knows the chief constable that...' Dom was starting to think the picture of the humble hill-farmer he'd formed from Claire's description the night before might have been a bit wide of the mark. '... and anyway they like me having boys around.'

'That's my point really, boys.'

'Oh stop banging on about the age thing or I'll start calling you "Krissie's Dad" again, or "*Grandad Mick*",' she grinned.

'I thought you were in the garden when all that happened.'

Claire roared with laughter. 'Not until after your balls dropped out.'

'Only one,' Dom sniffed.

The cottage was like a beamed version of the student accommodation they'd just left, but less cluttered and slightly cleaner. There were the usual posters on the walls promoting aspiring bands or advocating revolution, frayed throws covering even more frayed furniture and surfaces cluttered with grimy ashtrays and wax-caked Chianti bottles – and an empty fridge.

Claire showed Dom her bedroom – it seemed there was no question of them not sharing a bed. Then she found a warm tin of lager at the back of a cupboard, put it in Dom's hand and said he was to make himself at home while she went out "foraging". She returned an hour later, beaming happily and lugging two enormous hessian shopping bags. 'Mum never does things by half, we're certainly not going to go hungry. Or thirsty,' she added, producing two bottles of red wine and a half-full bottle of whisky. 'Dad insisted,' she explained.

'You're a whisky drinker?'

'Not particularly, but he thought you might be.'

'You mean you told him?'

Claire hesitated for a moment. 'Yeah, he asked.' She was suddenly the shy, awkward girl of the night before again. 'He's pleased,' she said quietly, 'I haven't got... had, many friends, especially not to stay. You don't mind, do you?'

Dom tried to imagine how he'd feel if Christine brought home a near fifty-year-old man and installed him in her bedroom. He supposed after the last forty-eight hours he wouldn't be that surprised, and probably wouldn't bother taking a stand one way or the other. What the hell. 'No I don't, not one bit,' he said, and picked up the bottle of whisky. 'Single malt... and I guess your father doesn't either. And your mother?'

Claire reached into one of the bulging bags and pulled out a huge foil-covered dish.

'She says she hopes you like anchovies in your fish pie.'

While the pie was warming in the oven they sat over the kitchen table and sipped red wine. Dom stretched and yawned. 'I won't be late to bed tonight,' he said, 'not that I mean...'

'Don't worry,' Claire laughed, 'I'm knackered too. It's been quite a day and we didn't exactly get a lot of sleep last night, did we?' She leant across the table, her shirt gaping, and took Dom's hand. 'Bloody wonderful,' she smiled.

It was Dom's turn to be shy. He couldn't remember when, if ever, anyone had complimented him on his lovemaking before. He was still struggling to reconcile the tangle of emotions Claire stirred in him: a sincere and growing affection, and raw lust, were juxtaposed with a slightly uncomfortable paternalism and the niggling feeling that somehow this just wasn't right. But why not? Simply because of convention, the fear of disapproval, a scandal? They were both adults, and it felt good. And it was making him happy, her too it seemed, and yes, the sex *had* been "bloody wonderful". He lifted her hand to his lips, a gesture he'd never have dreamt of before.

Claire served out two huge portions of the fish pie and poured some more wine. 'Should be white with fish, I suppose,' she said through a mouthful.

'No, no, it should always be red with anchovies,' Dom said seriously, 'ask any sommelier.'

'Ask any what?'

'Sommelier, wine waiter.'

'Oh. Don't get many of those in the uni bar.'

'You surprise me,' Dom grinned, thinking of his son's "Honourable" friend, and then asked about the farm. It sounded huge judging by the areas of land Claire was talking about, and was apparently a "mixed" farm. To Dom's surprise Claire said she'd be taking it over at some point in the future, when her father eventually decided to retire. 'My brothers aren't interested,' she explained.

'The older one wants to be an international banker, more money, and the younger one, Matt, says he'd rather dish dirt than shovel shit. He's going to be a journalist.'

'So why PPE,' Dom said, 'I'd have thought agriculture or something to do with farming would have been more useful?'

'I already know it all,' Claire said simply. 'I've been working with my dad since I could walk, but I thought the PPE would help set me up to make it in the union.'

'That's quite an ambition.'

Claire shrugged. 'It's doable. Anyway, I'll show you round properly tomorrow, give you a crash course in farming. We'll leave out the form-filling bit though.'

* * *

'Man, look at this!'

Gavin was on his own inside the van enjoying a relatively quiet glass of wine and flicking through a well-thumbed copy of the NME, which he'd found lying around amongst the band's debris. He'd already registered the gentle throbbing of an engine but at the exclamation from outside he got up and stuck his head out the door. Coming across the field at a sedate rumbling pace was a huge, long-forked, three-wheeled motorbike. What wasn't chromed was painted matt black, and the rider was dressed to match, in scuffed black jeans and T-shirt. Everything was huge about him: the belly, the beard draped over it, the saucer-like dark glasses and the two foot ponytail swinging in his slipstream. The only exception to the funereal colour scheme was a grubby white skull and crossbones stretched across the rider's chest. He weaved the machine between the three tents of the band (Gavin had yet to work out the sleeping arrangements but suspected they were fluid) and pulled up a few yards from the van.

'Good afternoon,' he said in an unexpectedly refined voice. There was the hint of a Welsh accent. 'I'm Jock Evans, owner and landlord.' He nodded across the river at the pub. Still astride the "hog" he turned the dark saucers on Gavin. 'My young lady hadn't gained the impression that your group was, er, so large.' He looked around. 'Three tents, hmm, there's some owing if you're going to stay, but we do have a policy here against large groups.' It was a statement mildly made, not a threat.

Dylan, the third male of The Shaggy Cracks, was sitting cross-legged in front of one of the tents cradling a guitar. He strummed the first few chords of "House of the Risin' Sun". Jock Evans looked down at him and then cast his eyes around the chaotic site, noting the other instruments and their cases.

'You folks in a band?'

Dylan played another few chords, which the landlord seemed to accept as an affirmative. 'Well, that's different then.'

It seemed that live music was the *raison d'être* of the pub, particularly in the summer months when a marquee, which Gavin had assumed was for a wedding, was set up in the riverside garden as a semi-permanent venue. Musicians and bands from around the area were encouraged to just turn up and strut and strum their stuff – subject to a brief audition. The riverside fields were opened up to music-loving campers from all around and most evenings something was going on in the marquee.

'You guys any good?' the landlord asked bluntly.

Gavin assured him they were.

'I haven't got time for a listen but if you want to do a set this evening it shouldn't be a problem. Amps, PA and drum kit are there if you need them. What kinda stuff do you do?' he added as an afterthought.

On being told, he looked thoughtful and scratched his enormous stomach. 'Hmm, the country bit should be OK, if you can make it a bit rocky, but I'm not sure about the punk. That was never big round here. What are you called?' Grace told him. The landlord said 'Hmm,' again and looked doubtful. 'Won't do, we get a lot of families in our crowd.' Grace muttered to herself and the landlord, still astride his "hog", tugged at his beard thoughtfully. 'Don't want to upset the regulars,' he concluded. 'We'll call you The Shaggies. No *Cracks*, OK?'

None of the band responded so Gavin broke the awkward silence with a: 'Yeah, sure.'

'Right, well we don't expect something for nothing, there'll be fifty quid behind the bar for you, after that you buy your own.' With that, he eased the clutch on the huge machine and trundled off towards the gate.

'Looks like you've got yourselves a gig,' Gavin said, from the steps of the van. 'Need a hand with the gear?'

Dylan looked up from his guitar, which had just shed a string. He was the surliest one of the five. 'Know anything about it?' he challenged.

'I spent a few years setting up PAs and turntables and amps in clubs,' Gavin said mildly. 'Don't worry, I know my way round a roll of Gaffer tape.' This was largely true. Gavin could have added that he owned the clubs in question, which were spread along the resorts of the Costa del Sol, but for the moment it suited him to play the humble "roadie".

The neutered Shaggy Cracks had not taken their censorship well. They spent the late afternoon on a hidden pebbly beach they'd found round a bend in the river, where they muttered sulkily amongst themselves, endlessly tuned their instruments and stoked their resentment with cheap cider, endless joints and a jar of multi-coloured pills – sort of narcotic Liquorice Allsorts. Early evening, leaving Gavin in the van, they'd trooped unsteadily across the little stone bridge to the pub side of the river and headed straight for the bar in one corner of the marquee, where they'd set about their ration of free drink. It didn't last long. By the time Gavin arrived the pot was dry.

Out in the garden, a large brick-built barbecue was belching smoke over a hungry queue. Little gangs of children scampered and squealed between the guy lines of the marquee and swung on the protective swags of rope that fenced off the riverbank. The marquee was already packed with a noisy throng, long hair and denims were much in evidence, but it was an eclectic crowd, with family groups and loud knots of local youngsters cheerfully mixing in with the middle-aged hippy contingent. Straw bales and battered trestle tables were scattered around, and electric reproduction storm lanterns hung from the roof. The small bar in the corner was permanently besieged.

Gavin took his plastic beer glass and weaved his way around the perimeter of the marquee looking for the band. They were on next and he had to admit to a certain nervousness, which wasn't diminished by their appearance and behaviour when he eventually ran them to ground. They were huddled in a corner to one side of the stage, more dishevelled and scruffier than ever, apart from Grace, surprisingly demur in a full-length creation of cream frills and flounces. Predictably, or rather unpredictably, the afternoon of excess was clearly catching up with them, taking the various band members in different ways; Dylan, particularly drunk or stoned, had not lost his surliness but was now more belligerent with it; Noel and Grace were giggly and conspiratorial, Dave seemed a bit bewildered, obsessively tuning and retuning a violin, and Jan had gone hyperactive. She rattled her drumsticks on every available surface, occasionally jumping up and down on the spot like an athlete warming up. As it turned out, there was very little setting up for Gavin to do. Several other bands had already made use of the equipment before The Shaggies were due to be introduced, and although Gavin fussed importantly round the stage, changing a microphone stand here, twiddling an amplifier knob there, and adjusting speaker angles, none of this was strictly necessary. The stage was already set.

The first band of the evening, a wall-of-sound guitar trio, had not gone down particularly well. They'd been followed by a Bob Dylan impersonator who'd been received politely enough, but by far the most popular, the hit of the evening so far, had been the group who'd just finished playing. At the end of their set they'd been persuaded to play an encore, always a good sign, and the crowd were happy, receptive and obviously eager for more of the same, many remaining on their feet waiting for the next danceable number. The Shaggies couldn't have asked for a better audience. But Gavin still sensed trouble. As the band started to clamber onto the low staging he caught Noel by the arm – there was no band leader as such but Noel seemed the "straightest" at the moment – 'I'd stick to the rocky country stuff like the man said if I was you,' Gavin said. 'That's what they seem to like.' Noel just grinned and nodded, stroking one of Grace's breasts distractedly. Gavin helped pick up Dave and boost him onto the stage, then retreated to a corner of the marquee and watched. And waited.

He didn't have to wait long. As Gavin had predicted, Noel took the lead, but it was Grace who grabbed the microphone stand and straddling it suggestively bellowed: ''Ello, we're The Shaggy Cracks and we're gonna fuckin' rock you!' In a staggered start the whole band then crashed into a frenetic, just-recognisable version of "Me and Bobby McGee". The speed they all played at, apart from Dave who'd sunk to his knees and was trying to play his violin with his teeth, meant they thrashed through the song in a bare minute and a half. So they started again. At least some of them did, the rest caught up in their own time, which made for a slightly longer version but meant the finish was even more ragged than the start. The guitars stuttered to a halt first, Jan went for a last drum flourish next, then Dave's violin contributed the terminal squeal as the last string snapped and whipped him across the face. By this time most of the audience had given up trying to dance and returned to their straw bales and beer. Somebody near the back clapped, it might have been politeness but was probably irony. In the rest of the tent there was a discontented muttering. This was even worse than Gavin had feared. But the band seemed oblivious, and with Dave now back on his feet and re-armed with a fully stringed guitar, they launched into "Hotel California". Their treatment of this classic was not too radical and some of the audience even got to their feet and tried to sing along. Gavin was relieved to see that Jock Evans, who he'd noticed over by the bar nursing a pool cue just a few minutes earlier, had disappeared again. The band's choice of song was fine, and the treatment acceptable, the problem was the execution; their instruments were ill-tuned, their timing hopeless and the singers kept forgetting the words, and couldn't hold a note when they did. They were irredeemably awful.

A clod of earth landed on the stage, then a plastic beer glass. Jan leapt out from behind the drum kit, scooped them up and hurled them back into the audience with a snarl. She returned to her stool and started flailing around wildly, hitting out at any drum or cymbal and frequently missing both, making no attempt to set up any sort of beat or tempo. More missiles started to fly and one by one the other band members stopped playing until all that was left was Jan's thrashings and a chorus of boos and jeers. A sod of earth hit Grace.

'You don' fuckin' like that, eh? Try a bit of this then,' she screamed.

Every expletive brought an ever-louder burst of outrage from the crowd and Gavin saw the landlord had reappeared, pool cue in hand. And he'd brought reinforcements.

'Wayne County and the Pink Pussy Cats,' Grace yelled, 'this is a tribute!' She started to count the band in, pausing on three as Noel, with a leering grin, stepped up behind her and literally tore the dress off her back. Left clad in nothing except stockings and a tiny G-string, Grace thrust her bare, nipple-ringed breasts at the crowd and howled into the microphone. Taking their cue, the rest of the band launched a frenzied attack on their instruments and started pogoing round the stage. Even Jan left her stool and bounced round the drum kit lashing out at whatever was in reach. Unheard above the amplified racket the staging started to groan and there were several ominous cracks. Dave had dropped to his knees again, head slumped on his chest but still clawing at the remaining strings of his guitar, when with a silent wail, he suddenly disappeared through a splintered hole in the staging. No one seemed to notice, the noise remained deafening, the crowd outraged and missiles rained down on the disintegrating stage. Gavin watched as the landlord and his posse started forcing their way through the crowd and decided it was time he wasn't there. The Shaggy Cracks would have to fend for themselves; their roadie had just quit.

* * *

Left alone in the waiting room Greg didn't really know what was expected of him, or even whether he should stay at the hospital. After all, *he* wasn't the father, or even a relative. Was his being there a welcome show of support or an intrusion? He decided for the moment he'd stay, at least until he'd seen Ben again to say good luck and goodbye.

The swing doors suddenly flew open and a large man in jeans and a rugby shirt came barging in looking anxiously at his watch. His beard and head were shaved to a uniform length and he looked cross.

'I told her,' he said, 'any day she liked this week, I said, just *not* today. So what does she do? Leaves it 'til this evening, half an hour before kick-off, and then *she* bloody kicks off!' He looked at his watch again, threw himself down on the row of seats and studied Greg. 'First time?'

'Well, it's…' Greg couldn't be bothered to go through the full explanations again, 'I'm just a friend,' he said.

This seemed to satisfy the man. 'I've spent half my bloody life in here.'

'Not your first then?' Greg said.

The man snorted. 'Bloody hell, no, this is the fourth… no fifth, I was forgetting Kane – little sod.'

'You obviously like children then,' Greg said politely.

'No, not particularly, it's her you see.'

'Ah, your wife, er… partner, she's keen on a big family?'

'Nah, it's her bloody awful memory.'

Greg thought this was a bit rich coming from a man who couldn't remember how many children he had. 'What, she can't remember…?'

'Yeah, whether she's taken her bloody pill or not. Hopeless!' The man smiled ruefully.

'So have you been at all their births, all, um, five of them?' Greg asked.

'Bloody hell, no! The first one was enough; all that legs in the air stuff, everything gaping and her hollerin' fit to blow the windows out, no thanks. So long as I'm in here though, that's enough for 'er and she's OK about it.'

An attractive young woman in a white coat with a stethoscope hung round her neck appeared at the door. 'Ah, Mr Hardwicke, here again. Well that's it, all over, another boy for you. And everyone's doing well,' she added.

'God, she's getting quick,' the man said. He looked at his watch. 'Might just make the second half.'

The doctor sighed. 'Mrs Hardwicke did say she'd try her best before half-time. She asked if you'd just pop in before going back to the pub, she wants to pick a name… and not another footballer, she said.'

The man glanced at his watch again. 'Cunning mare, she knows I haven't got time to argue.'

Greg had sat in bewildered amusement throughout this exchange. The man suddenly turned to him. 'What's your name?'

'Er… Greg, Gregory, why?'

The man nodded. 'Yeah, not bad, that'll do.' He disappeared through the doors.

The doctor smiled at Greg, helped herself to a beaker of water from a dispenser in the corner and went to stand at the window. Greg watched her reflection in the window, turned mirror by the night sky. She had slightly curled shoulder-length hair and gentle eyes. Greg thought she was probably a good doctor.

The doors crashed open again. 'Right, that's done, Greg it is. Sorry, not the full *Gregory* though,' Mr Hardwicke said apologetically.

Greg shrugged and smiled.

Greg desperately wanted to speak to Martin. He had so much to tell him, but most of all he just wanted the calm reassurance of Martin's voice after the high drama of the last... God, was it only six hours or so! He fiddled with his phone, which had run out of power up on the fells after his repeated attempts to summon help, and felt a bit tearful. Maybe he was in shock; no one would blame him, Martin wouldn't. Greg hadn't wanted to move too far from the waiting area looking for a payphone, and all he'd found during his one quick foray had been a couple of vending machines, no phone. But as he was there, he thought he might as well get something to eat and drink, it might provide a bit of comfort. Not much, the coffee machine just gave him a puff of powdered milk and a squirt of tepid water for his pound, and for another two, an almost empty machine spat out a chocolate bar with a torn wrapper. Back in the waiting area Greg sipped some water and ate most of the chocolate – he left the chalky white bit under the torn wrapper. Bored with Mothercare he then arranged himself over four or five of the moulded plastic chairs, tucked his rucksack under his head and tried to get some sleep. He had no great expectations.

'Greg! Oh Greg, I had no idea, the doctor only just told me you were still here – well, that there was someone in walking boots sound asleep on a rucksack in the waiting room, I figured it could only be you.'

Greg had no idea how long he'd been asleep but he felt groggy. He swung his legs to the floor, sat up rubbing his eyes and tried to straighten his back. 'I couldn't just leave,' he said, smoothing down his hair, 'and I didn't really know whether... or what...'

Ben patted him on the shoulder and sat down next to him. 'Well I'm glad you didn't, Cat will be too.'

Greg looked at him. There were lines of strain etched from the corners of his mouth and grey smudges under his eyes, which looked pink and moist. He wondered whether Ben had been crying. 'Umm…' Greg tried to read something in the tired face but knew he had to ask.

Ben looked at him and saw the uncertainty. He smiled and put his hand on Greg's arm. 'Everything's fine, Greg. And thank you.'

'Well I didn't really…'

'You did, you did more than you realise. You've been a true friend.'

Greg suddenly felt tearful again. He put his head in his hands, bit his lip and thought of Martin.

Ben put his arm round Greg's shoulders. 'Right,' he squeezed Greg gently. 'C'mon, there's someone I want you to meet.'

Cat was propped comfortably on a mound of crisp pillows. Her hair was brushed, her cheeks glowed healthily and her eyes sparkled. She looked fresh, relaxed and happy and in a considerably better state than either of the men standing at the foot of her bed.

'Greg, you *are* still here.'

'Hi, Cat.' Greg suddenly felt inexplicably shy. 'Yeah, I didn't quite know…'

'Oh, I'm so glad, look.'

Since he'd entered the room Greg had barely taken his eyes of the little blue bundle cradled on Cat's chest. She eased a fold of blanket to one side, 'Come on, come and say "hello",' Cat said quietly.

Greg hesitated and Ben gave him a gentle push. He

looked down at the tiny, puckered face and then as Cat gently tugged aside another fold of the soft blanket the baby stirred slightly and a minute clenched hand appeared. 'My god!' Greg breathed. 'It's just… wonderful.' He straightened up and wiped the corners of his eyes with a grubby thumb and forefinger.

'We're both so grateful to you, Greg,' Ben said seriously, 'being there, handling things like you did and sticking by Cat.'

Greg made dismissive noises.

'And there's something else,' Cat said.

Relieved at the opportunity to lower the emotional temperature, Greg said: 'Don't tell me, twins?'

'Please!' Ben laughed.

'No,' Cat smiled. 'Come here, Greg. Now, shake hands, go on.' She held up the blue bundle and Greg stretched out a tentative finger and touched the tiny fist still peeping from the swaddling. 'Greg… meet Greg,' Cat said.

'Seemed like a good idea,' Ben said casually, 'it's a name we've always liked and, well, with all you, *input,* it just seemed right.'

'I don't know what to say. I can't wait to tell Martin.'

'I knew you'd say that,' Cat laughed. 'When you do, would you ask him something?'

'Not a dirty limerick?'

Cat laughed again and winced. 'Well that too if you like, maybe for when little Greg's a bit older, but meantime, would you and Martin be godparents? We'd love that.'

'But you don't even know Martin.'

'Oh, I think I've got to know him well enough over the last few days,' Cat said.

'Gentlemen, perhaps you should let this lady get some rest now.' The young woman doctor had quietly appeared at the door. She smiled gently at Cat. 'Get some rest while you can. You're going to have a lot on your hands from now on, for quite a while, say about eighteen years or so.'

Cat smiled back and snuggled the little blue bundle even tighter into her chest. The doctor held the door open; there were to be no arguments. Ben gave Cat and the bundle a quick kiss and Greg gave a little wave from the door. 'See you soon, take care.'

'We'll be in touch soon, Greg,' Cat called. 'We won't forget, promise.'

The sky was lightening as Ben and Greg made their way down to the hospital reception area and the flow of human traffic in the corridors was steadily increasing. In a cafeteria area tables were being unstacked, there was the hiss of coffee machines and the faint smell of hot fat mixed with that of floor polish.

'God, I'm starving,' Ben said, 'what about some breakfast? Better get our own today, I guess – never a woman around when you need one. I don't know, just lolling about in bed.' He grinned happily.

After the biggest and most comprehensive full English the cafeteria could manage Ben and Greg sat over coffee, each pondering aloud what to do next. Ben didn't think Cat would be allowed to travel for a couple of days, particularly as they had such a long journey. He said he'd find a B&B in Whitehaven and see Cat and little Greg as often as he was allowed until they were given the OK to go home. 'Can't wait,' he added.

Greg said he'd get himself to Keswick on public transport. His meeting was the day after next and he was too exhausted to resume his walk. Having made the decision, it was quite a relief.

'I'd drive you over,' Ben said, 'but...'

Greg wouldn't hear of it. 'You stay with Cat, and little Greg.' He couldn't help smiling as he said it, adding, 'Don't worry, there are loads of buses in this part of the world.'

They'd exchanged contact details, shaken hands and Ben had insisted on giving Greg a hug, then they went their separate ways. Ben headed for the lift, Greg for the main entrance.

Greg was too tired to concentrate on bus timetables, so to get him where he wanted he'd largely relied on the advice of fellow passengers, all well-meant but not always correct. Consequently, he'd found himself zigzagging across West Cumbria making lots of unnecessary stops and changes. Late morning brought him to the bustling little town of Cockermouth, famed as the birthplace of William Wordsworth and for flooding spectacularly every five years or so. It was one of the few remaining towns in the area which hadn't been swamped by outdoor shops and craft jewellery studios. Instead, its streets were lined with shops actually useful to the local people: butchers, green grocers, bakers, hardware stores and the odd clothes and shoe outlet. Greg stumbled off his latest bus and went to find a coffee, if nothing else just to keep him awake. He sat in a bustling, noisy cafe of scrubbed wooden tables and eclectic chairs, and admired a huge collection of sticky-looking cakes arranged under plastic domes. He liked the small-town atmosphere; the friendly familiarity, the comings and goings and the good-natured gossip and banter that filled the room. As another wave of exhaustion swept over him, he decided to try and find somewhere to stay in the town. After all, Keswick was in striking distance now, a mere half an hour away – as long as he got on the right bus. Wandering up the main street past pubs and antique shops he crossed a narrow bridge, stopping halfway to look down on the benign rippled surface of one of the two rivers that converged on Cockermouth and periodically created mayhem. He was running out of town centre and about to turn round when he found himself at the end of a wide cobbled street lined with handsome Georgian-style buildings. Dominating one row was a pleasant-looking old-fashioned coaching inn.

A room was available, and although check-in was usually two o'clock, after Greg had explained that he'd been up all night. 'I've had a baby you see.' The receptionist, a smart young woman with a ready smile, took pity on him. He was shown straight up to a spacious room on the first floor and half an hour later, fresh from a shower, had stretched out on the large bed, just for a moment, still intending to ring Martin, but despite the traffic rumbling over the cobbles, had promptly gone straight to sleep.

* * *

Robbie needed help to get back on board *Idler* later that night. The operation wasn't helped by the fact the tide was out, widening the drop between quay and deck. Finally, left alone on board, he spent ten minutes trying to find his keys and then another five trying to force open the locked hatch. Nauseous and on the point of collapse he eventually gave up and crawled under a sail bag in the cockpit. Curled up into a defensive ball, Robbie screwed up his eyes, and still struggling to regain control of any of his senses or the kaleidoscope that was his mind, slipped into unconsciousness. And then the voices started:

The Blonde: We're out of Rizlas, but the wind is free, Robbie.
The Chorus (loudly): Hooray, it's Captain Calamity!
Robbie (his voice echoing): On the bog, trashed, how would you fucking like it?
Man in suit: No need for language, Mr Cox-Robinson.
BBC voice: Dogger, German Bight, Humber…
The wife: Robbie, you're a sorry-arsed, two-timing bastard.
Man in suit (firmly): No need for language, Mr Cox-Robinson's wife.
A fisherman (laughing): Welcome to Wales, boyo!
Chorus: Oooh, Captain Calamity! Yakee dah!
BBC voice: Low 250 miles west of Sole deepening 996 by eighteen hundred…
A foreign voice: You fuck Mickey, I fuck Mickey? When we get to Conk?
Man in suit: No need for language, Mr Cox-Robinson's hijacker.
Man in orange helmet and life jacket: It's no better on deck, get that engine fixed. The box will be on the bar, we'll throw you a line.
James: Do you believe in free love, Captain?
A female foreign voice: Our love is always free, we are

Catholics.

Sylvia: How about a swim, with or without?

Chorus: Hooray for naked Captain Calamity!

A female Irish voice: Thank you, free spirit.

The bailiff (hissing): Fucking hippy!

Man in suit (getting angry): No need for language, Mr Cox-Robinson's brother-in-law.

BBC voice: ... force 8 backing and increasing force 10 later. Run, Robbie, run!

Man in orange helmet and life jacket (sarcastically): The brotherhood of the sea, eh sir? Mind how you go.

The reporter (slyly): Enjoying a drop, eh? Don't let the bubbles get up your nose. Must be scary out there, bon voyage!

Sylvia: Did you enjoy our swim? You could always come back... here's to us.

A spaniel with sad eyes: Sorry about the turd.

Then everything went silent and blank. Apart from vital life-sustaining functions, Robbie had effectively shut down.

Rain woke him at dawn, the rattle of it on the sail bag adding to his confusion. Slowly Robbie reset his mind, and to some extent his memory, and some of the events from the previous evening started to swim into focus. He crawled stiffly out from under the canvas, dousing himself with puddled rainwater in the process, and found his keys already in the lock. He'd obviously forgotten them in his haste to get to the pub the night before. Staggering below, he managed to put the kettle on, then flopped onto a bunk and promptly fell asleep. The urgent whistle of the kettle finally brought him round, he rescued it and shakily made half a mug of coffee with the water that remained, then slipped under a sleeping bag and sat listening to the rain drumming on the coach-house roof. There was a heavy thud and the boat rocked slightly.

'Robbie, are you there, mate? Anyone aboard?' The voice was hoarse and Robbie recognised it as that of one of his regular drinking companions. He groaned quietly. All he wanted was to finish his coffee and curl up for a few hours of dry, warm sleep, but his friend was obviously already aboard.

'Yeah, come on down, Mike.'

A red unshaven face under a fraying blue woollen hat appeared in the companionway. 'Cor, that coffee smells good.' He shook the droplets off his hat onto Robbie's sleeping bag.

'Help yourself, you'll need to put in more water.'

'Ta. How d'you feel?'

'Bloody awful.'

'Not surprised, that bloke was pouring them down you like there was no tomorrow. How did he get you on the floor like that? One minute you were there, next thing... crash! Fucking chaos. George was none too happy but we got you out before he could actually bar you. That other bloke didn't hang around either; journalist from *The Crusader* someone said.' He poured hot water into a mug and sat on the other bunk.

Robbie groaned. 'I'm sure he gave me something.'

'Yeah, about six pints and half a bottle of Scotch,' Mike laughed.

'No, no, he slipped me something, put something in my drink, I'm sure of it.'

'Oh come on, Robbie, this is Douglas not LA. He got you pissed, plain and simple. What did he want, anyway, stuff for their boozy cruisers campaign?'

'Their what?'

'"Cruiser Boozers", haven't you seen it? They're always on about something; *crusading*, see? This year they've got it in their heads that everyone who goes out in a boat, unless they're a fisherman, is a complete piss-head.'

Robbie just stared at him.

'Ah,' said Mike, 'you didn't…'

'I suppose he got some photos?' Robbie sighed.

Mike grimaced and nodded, 'Yeah, once you were on the floor, covered in spilt booze and broken glass.'

Robbie ran his fingers through his sticky hair. 'Oh that's just great.' He suddenly thought of Sylvia, and was glad he'd be seeing her before that evening's paper came out. He'd be able to explain. Right now, he badly needed a shower.

'Anyway,' Mike said after a sip of his coffee, 'thought you'd like to know, there's a couple asking after you. Not sure whether they're TV people or something, but they're dead keen to speak to you.'

Robbie was immediately alert, or as alert as his hangover would allow. 'What? Who are they?'

'Dunno.' Mike took another sip from the mug. 'George at the pub might know, someone said he'd spoken to them.'

Robbie put down his mug and pushed the sleeping bag aside. If the strangers had been rash enough to speak to George at the pub, the landlord would know all. Moments later Robbie popped his head over the stone sill of the jetty and glanced warily each way like a nervous pensioner crossing the road, then scrambled up the last few rungs and hurried over to the pub. Five minutes later he was back, diving over the edge of the quay and crashing onto the deck on all fours after losing his footing on the slimy ladder.

Mike appeared in the cockpit still holding his mug. 'You all right?' Seeing Robbie was unhurt he grinned, 'So what is it then; *This is Your Life, Panorama, Blind Date*?'

'My ex-fucking-wife, that's what it is,' Robbie snarled.

'Christ, mate, she can't be that bad.'

'Believe me, she is, and she's brought her enforcer with her. I could be dead by opening time.'

Mike kept up a chatter of meaningless reassurances while Robbie quickly ran through his options. It didn't take long, he only had one – cut and run. On local advice, he'd already decided on Whitehaven as his port of entry to Cumbria, a safe haven in more ways than one, and a mere forty nautical miles away. With the threat of severe pain and humiliation possibly only yards and minutes away, Robbie decided now would be a good time to go. The weather was reasonable, a bit blowy perhaps but from the west, he knew his boom was damaged but it should be OK, and the mainsail repairs seemed to be holding. He'd managed to cadge a few litres of diesel, so could run the engine for an hour or so if needed, and was fairly sure there was an almost full bottle of Scotch in a galley locker for emergencies. So all in all, he was about as prepared as he could be.

'Right, we're off!'

'Eh?'

'I'm off. Get the lines, will you, Mike?'

'What about me coffee?'

'Bugger your coffee, what about my balls!'

'Nice.' Mike reluctantly started up the ladder, stopping halfway to hand down his coffee mug. 'See you then.'

Robbie waved distractedly and started the engine.

TEN

Dom and Claire had woken each other up shortly after dawn and lazily made love before falling asleep again. It was late when they woke next and Claire was obviously keen to get on with the guided tour of "her" farm. Dom looked at her over the enormous farmhouse breakfast she'd magicked up from her mother's bulging bags and cooked on the little range. She was bubbly and enthusiastic, laughing a lot and humming happily to herself. Dom was again struck by the transformation from the sad, introspective young woman he'd shared a garden bench and a bottle of wine with only two nights before. He remarked on it.

'I'm home,' Claire said, 'this is me, my world, it's where I belong. And being big and ugly on a Cumbrian farm is the norm,' she laughed.

'You are *not* ugly, or big for that matter,' Dom said fiercely. 'Forget all that crap!'

Claire smiled at him, 'And I've got a new friend, a lovely one.'

Dom huffed and muttered something inconsequential and shovelled in another forkful of sausage and tomato, secretly pleased.

'Right, come on, washing up can wait, you can do it later,' Claire grinned. 'I'll see if I can find you some wellies that'll fit.' She ducked into the under stairs cupboard and reappeared clutching a huge pair of boots caked in crumbling red mud, a greasy canvas satchel and a double-barrelled shotgun.

Dom eyed the gun warily, 'I thought you got on with your parents.'

Claire snorted. 'I thought we might take out a few crows on the way. I hate 'em.'

They left the cottage and started gently uphill on a cinder track, overhung by a tangle of woodland on one side and flanked by a verdant, head-high hedge on the other. An occasional gate-opening let into a field, thick with grass and dotted with buttercups.

Claire strode out breathing deeply, a satisfied half smile on her face, while Dom wallowed along in his wellies and tried to keep up. 'So what have you got against crows then?'

'Vile things: noisy, filthy and you want to see what they do to the lambs given half a chance.'

'Do I?'

'No, probably not. But imagine being eaten alive, starting with your arse...'

'God!'

'... whilst having your eyes pecked out.'

'Really?'

Claire nodded.

'God, that's revolting. OK, I take your point. Fine, go ahead and shoot the bastards.'

And right on cue Claire suddenly threw the shotgun to her shoulder, swung it in a short left to right arc and fired both barrels in quick succession.

Dom managed to jump and flinch simultaneously at the double explosion, but recovered in time to see a tattered bundle of black feathers tumble from the sky to land with an audible thud in the field beyond the hedge.

Dom was impressed. 'I expect that was a good shot, but I wouldn't really know.'

'Not bad,' Claire grunted.

'So what do you do with it now?'

'Oh just leave it to rot. Or sometimes, if we can be bothered, we stretch 'em out on the fences as a kind of warning to the others.'

Dom wrinkled his nose. 'Does that work?'

'Probably not but at least it pisses off the ramblers.'

'Can't you eat them?'

'What, ramblers? No, I think it's against the law but Dad did once...'

'You know what I mean. Maybe make a rook pie or something.'

Claire looked at him pityingly. 'You can if you like, I'm more of a pheasant girl.'

'My first pheasant plucker!'

'Yeah, very funny, now try saying it quickly ten times... no, don't!'

Dom put his arms round her, carefully avoiding the gun, and kissed her on the lips.

'Hmm,' Claire sighed and nibbled his ear, 'even better than pheasant.'

'Oh, praise indeed!' Dom mumbled into her neck. 'Do you know, I don't think I've ever had pheasant?'

Claire pulled away and looked at him in amazement. 'You what? Well, we've got to sort that out before you get much older.' She turned and scowled at the tangled woods. 'Trouble is it's the closed season and I shouldn't, but… look, take this.' She picked up a whippy stick, jagged on the end where it had been slashed from the hedge in the spring, and thrust it at Dom. 'Now hop over that gate and then follow the track until you reach the fence at the edge of the copse, it's only a few hundred yards, go left for fifty yards or so, then turn into the trees and come back here, but through the woods. And make a lot of noise on the way, beat the bushes with that,' she nodded at the stick, 'and give the odd shout.' She let out a loud whoop, part tally-ho, part rebel yell. 'Right, off you go, you're gonna have to earn your supper today, city-boy.'

'Whoa, just a second, where are you going to be?'

'Over there,' Claire nodded at the hedge on the other side of the track, 'in that field.' She snapped open the shotgun, pinging out the empty cartridges and started back up the track towards an open gate, the "broken" gun over the crook of her arm.

'Claire, hang on just a minute, this is legal, isn't it?'

She turned to face him and grinned, then slipped two fresh cartridges into the gun. 'Well,' she gave him a wink, 'almost.'

The layout of the copse was as Claire had described and Dom was quite enjoying his first time beating. He assumed that's what he was doing. The undergrowth wasn't too dense and weaving his way through, obediently thrashing and rather self-consciously whooping, he'd almost forgotten the point of the exercise when a rhododendron to his left suddenly erupted. Dom let out an involuntary oath, tripped backwards and landed heavily on his backside. Distracted by the damp ground rapidly soaking through his trousers to the skin, he never even saw the two panic-stricken cock pheasants crashing their way through the low branches and bursting out of the treeline. Before Dom could get up there was the double boom of the gun again, and much closer than he'd expected. Although still on the ground, he ducked involuntarily and there was a pattering like that of light rain on the foliage around him. Looking up through the canopy at the almost cloudless sky Dom realised with a shock that it must be spent lead shot from Claire's gun.

He found his way back to the track and as there was no sign of Claire, he headed through the open gate and found himself in an enormous field of freshly mown grass. Claire was on the far side and appeared to be poking around at the base of a hedge. As he watched, she straightened up and catching sight of him waved a floppy multicoloured bundle in his direction. 'Over there,' she shouted, pointing across the field with the gun. 'I got 'em both. Go and get him.' Dom set off as directed, fidgeting with his clammy underwear as he went, and only vaguely heard Claire's next shouted instruction but thought it might have been something to do with "stretching necks". Dom didn't like the sound of this at all and fervently hoped that if he found it, the pheasant would already be dead. It was, and when

Claire caught up with him he was gingerly holding up the corpse by one scaly, spurred foot.

'Brilliant,' Claire panted, 'almost two for the price of one. What a left and right, I wish Dad had seen that.' Dom had no idea what she was talking about but she certainly seemed pleased with herself. Claire took Dom's bird from him and gave its bloody beak a rough tweak. 'Hmm, a bit old but it'll have to do; a pile of buttered potatoes with shredded parsnips, a few bacony sprouts and some Cumberland sausage patties with a good splash of red wine jus and you'll be in fucking heaven.'

Dom looked at her in surprise but couldn't help grinning at her enthusiasm. 'I seem to have spent a lot of time there since I met you,' he said with a laugh. 'God, that sounds corny.'

'Yeah, it does,' she kissed him, '…but I think it's lovely.'

As they walked back across the field Claire explained she was going to stash the gun and pheasants in the copse for later collection. 'Don't mention the birds to anyone, OK? And what's wrong with your bum?'

'You shot me.'

'Did not!'

Another few hundred yards along the cinder track, beyond a low rise, brought the farm into view; a collection of large barns and assorted sheds, mainly of stone and slate, with a handsome pinkish stone house at their centre, all nestling in the bottom of their own shallow valley with gently sloping fields rising on three sides. A single-track road led from the open end of the valley to the farm and appeared to go no further. From the opposite direction an ever-widening stream, or beck, ran from the head of the valley and after winding around the buildings, started to meander its way across the valley floor roughly following the course of the track.

'It's beautiful,' Dom said.

'It is, isn't it?' Claire said. 'Well drained too, some of the best land around here. Our production figures can't be beaten locally.'

Dom smiled at her. 'It's really in your blood, isn't it?'

'Yeah, it is,' she nodded. 'Come on, let's see what's going on.' As they walked on down the track Claire pointed out individual fields and described their present usage, crop or animal occupants, adding her own explanations and opinions on the health and growth rates of the grass, cereals or young animals. Dom learned that this year's lambs were unlikely to make the same price as last, fleeces were worth less than it cost to shear the sheep, but it had to be done for the animals' welfare, and that winter feed stocks were looking promising. 'Could always be better of course,' Claire added, with a farmer's characteristic pessimism.

As they approached the first buildings Dom again wondered nervously what Claire's parents' reaction to him would be. But although they bumped into various overalled characters around the buildings and yards, all of whom Claire greeted with a gruff familiarity or friendly insult, clearly none of them was her mother or father. Dom was shown the overnight quarters of a vast flock of free-range chickens, a row of pigsties where an enormous sow contentedly suckled a tumbling pile of frantic piglets and behind one of the stone barns a small paddock, home to two enormous rams. "Tups" Claire called them. They were huge creatures with ugly Roman noses, malevolent eyes and scrotal sacks that swung close to the floor. 'Show winners every year,' Claire said.

From a passing hand they learned, to Dom's secret relief, that Claire's father was out on a task in some remote corner of the farm and her mother was "up town" at the WI market, where apparently she was begrudgingly acknowledged as the chutney queen.

'No point going to the house then,' Claire said. 'Never mind, we'll see them tonight.'

'You what?'

'We're going to supper.'

'What about the pheasants?'

'A ruse.'

'Right...'

* * *

Gavin wasn't sure whether it was the strangulated hiss of air brakes or the violent swaying of the van that woke him but further sleep was clearly out of the question. One way and another it had been quite an eventful night; apart from the riot "his" band had started back in the little Shropshire town and his precipitous escape, he'd nearly come to blows with a drunken, foul-mouthed farmer who'd insisted Gavin moved on from the gateway he was parked in, and then the camper wouldn't start.

Eventually, misfiring badly, the van had spluttered back onto the main road but it had been another hour before Gavin found a likely lay-by. It was already partially occupied by several overnighting HGVs and Gavin felt reasonably confident he should make it through to dawn without being disturbed, at least not by an irate landowner.

Fully awake now and still dressed from the night before, he stretched and swung off the bunk. While the kettle came to the boil on the little gas stove he flicked back the windscreen curtains and surveyed the lay-by. It was the usual pot-holed, litter-strewn ox-bow. Trucks were parked haphazardly around the crescent, detritus spilled from several battered plastic bins and an unshaven man in a lumberjack's shirt squatted under a hedge, trousers rucked down over his rigger boots and a cigarette tucked in the corner of his mouth. The man was apparently engrossed in reading *The Morning Star* until another use became more urgent and he started to tear it into strips. Gavin hastily looked away, re-drew the curtains and made himself a strong coffee. The side door of the van faced the thundering main road and Gavin sat on the top step sipping his coffee and wondered what had happened to the Shaggy Cracks. After his desertion he decided perhaps it might be best if he made sure he didn't bump into them in Keswick. He needn't have worried.

Gavin's escape had been fairly straightforward; after the stage had collapsed, he'd ducked out of the marquee, crossed the car park, made his way round the side of the pub and then back over the bridge to the campsite. Once in the van he'd scooped up the band's spare instruments, any incriminating paraphernalia and other assorted possessions, and hurled them out onto the grass. Meanwhile, the police had obviously arrived at the pub, no melodrama spared, sirens blaring and blue lights pulsing. This prompted an increase in the screaming and shouting, with Grace's gravelly, foul-mouthed epithets clearly distinguishable above the babble, which was then followed by a lot of loud splashing and panic-stricken shouts from the far bank of the river, suggesting possible escape attempts, or drownings. This, and the arrival of at least one more emergency vehicle, had sent Gavin diving for the cab of the camper. Without lights or seat belt he'd slithered across the campsite, spun the wheels noisily getting out of the gateway and taken to the road. He tried to remember whether anyone at the pub had taken the van's registration number.

Meanwhile, those of the Shaggy Cracks not too incapacitated one way or another, continued to try and dodge the outraged crowd and avoid arrest by fleeing or floating their way to freedom. The situation had reached the point where it was every man or woman for him or herself, and it was some weeks before the band were reunited and could compare stories.

The surly Dylan had probably fared best, he'd managed to hang on to his guitar and taken the same escape route as Gavin back to the camp. Once there he'd wasted no time in stuffing a tent and other random possessions into a rucksack, and ten minutes later was 200 yards down the road, where almost immediately he managed to thumb down an obliging late-night delivery driver.

Despite the mayhem, when the landlord and his pool cue arrived on the stage Jan was still pogoing around the remains of the drum kit lashing out at anything or anyone that might make a noise. The cue versus drumstick battle was always going to be a one-sided affair and Jan was soon overwhelmed and handed over to two burly WPCs.

Noel, his accordion, and the almost naked Grace got themselves cornered by the river and decided to swim for it. They soon discovered two things: firstly, accordions don't float, and secondly, the current was much stronger than it appeared from the bank. Within seconds they'd been swept under the bridge and didn't regain dry land until they were almost another quarter of a mile downstream where they washed up at the edge of an expansive lawn. A stilted summer house seemed to offer an obvious refuge and proved to be surprisingly well equipped. Giggling like naughty school children they stripped and wrapped themselves in beach towels, then sprawled on a scattered pile of cushions, and with an abandon born of relief, launched into a wild session of noisy sex. This roused the householder's dog, which dutifully roused the householder, who promptly roused the local police – those that weren't already upstream at the pub.

Dave wasn't found until much later when an attempt was made to salvage and re-erect the debris that had been the stage. He was discovered tightly curled up clutching the remains of his violin and mumbling an obscene schoolboy version of the Lord's Prayer. An ambulance was called and he was hospitalised, but flummoxed doctors had to delay meaningful treatment while a team of fascinated microbiologists tried to work out exactly what was in the cocktail frothing through Dave's bloodstream.

The Shaggy Cracks never got their gig at the Keswick festival.

Gavin's disturbed overnight experience, compounded by the early morning sight of a crapping Marxist trucker, the unreliability of the vehicle and the possibility of future identification, had decided him that the camper van had to go – and quickly. The London rental company had not been happy, but for a fee they agreed to him leaving the thing with a car-hire firm an hour up the road, where he also arranged to hire a more conventional vehicle.

Gavin got to Ambleside late in the afternoon, tired and bad-tempered. He'd originally planned to book himself into a modest, unobtrusive B&B or guest house in some back street, but as he thought sourly of the over-friendly and inquisitive Cumbrian welcome he'd probably receive, he had a rethink. Eventually, with the minimum of personal exchanges and in relative anonymity he'd checked into one of the larger lakeside hotels and taken a top-floor suite. After a shower and a room-service meal he poured a large drink and dialled for an outside line.

Jacko answered the phone on the second ring and sounded wary.

'Yeah, hi, it's me,' Gavin announced.

'Gav! Where've you been?'

Gavin thought Jacko sounded nervous and ignored the question. 'You OK?'

'Yeah, well...'

'What's going on, Jacko?' Gavin said wearily.

'It's got worse. They've shut us down, completely.'

'What, everything?'

'Yeah, some sort of confiscation order that's come down from Madrid. Looks like you've made some enemies in high places, Gav.'

'We, Jacko, *we've* made some enemies in high places. So what's left?'

'I think the *finca* will be OK, and there's a bit of cash left in Gib...'

'What about Morocco?'

'Don't even think about it, much too dangerous.'

Gavin let out a long sigh, his mind racing. 'They haven't come looking up at Ronda then, at the *finca*?'

'Er, I don't think so.' Jacko's voice was a hesitant drawl.

His factotum's evasiveness was starting to irritate Gavin. This was not what Jacko was paid for. 'What d'you mean, you don't think so?' Gavin was suspicious, he knew he wasn't getting the truth, or at least not all of it. 'Have you had a knock at the door or not?' he snapped. 'I think you'd have noticed, they'd have been big guys in smart green uniforms carrying big guns, talking Spanish and probably not very friendly.'

Jacko spoke quickly to someone else at his end, then back on the line muttered,

'Well, I haven't heard...'

'Haven't heard... Hang on a minute, where the fuck are you?' The immediate reply was just a vague static hum. 'Jacko, you there?'

'Er, yeah, Florida.'

'Florida! What the hell... where's Bobby?'

'I'm here.' The voice was shrill, brittle and aggressive, no hint of the little-girl-lost baby talk that Gavin was usually subjected to. 'We were fed up with sitting around in the arse end of nowhere just waiting for...'

'We? Who's we?' Gavin demanded.

There was a long pause. 'Me and Jacko. We decided

to… and anyway, the boys were here… and we've got the beach and Jacko's got us a speed boat and they've got a multiplex and malls and… oh lots of really cool stuff. He's looking after me, Jacko is.'

'I bet he is,' Gavin snarled.

The sarcasm was lost on his wife. 'Yes, he is. And he's nice to me and lets me do things, and see people, fun people. And we go to parties and he likes shopping…'

'Oh, well then, shopping…'

'And *he's* not on the run from the police. The police *everywhere,* he says.' She'd lapsed into her baby-talk lisp but the voice suddenly hardened again. 'And he says you've really screwed it up big time in Spain and it's all your fault that we're here and if it wasn't for him…'

This was enough, too much, for Gavin. 'Right, put Jacko back on. NOW!'

There was some distant muttering then: 'He says he's gone out, he'll call you later.' The line went dead.

Gavin called down for a large Scotch and while he waited he gazed out of the window at the mountains, now silhouetted by the dipping sun. He turned at the knock, signed the chit without letting the waiter into the room and took his drink back to the window. In those few minutes the sky had transformed itself and the mountains were now backlit by multi-layered streaks of glowing pastel.

Gavin sipped at his whisky and thought about the last fifteen minutes. Not so long ago what he'd just heard would have sent him into a towering rage. He'd have gone berserk. Bobby, her many shortcomings catalogued with cruel sarcasm, her ego shredded and self-image mocked, would have been left reeling and hysterical. He knew how to hurt her. Gavin wouldn't have wasted much time on Jacko; a few curt questions to see if there was anything to be salvaged from the apparent melt-down of his business, a verbal savaging for his treachery and finally, coldly, he'd have terminated the relationship with a veiled but unambiguous threat of future physical harm. But that was then. Now, somehow, things were different and he just couldn't be bothered. It wasn't worth the effort; they weren't worth the effort.

Gavin was in no doubt that most of what had been his just a few short weeks before was now irretrievably lost. And he also knew that if he'd bothered to look, the signs had been there for some time. But he'd been too comfortable, complacent, bored even, to do anything about it, his business or his marriage. And now they were gone. He sipped his drink and looked out at the darkening mountains. It was strange, he almost felt relieved, liberated even, and with this realisation came a surge of excitement, a thrill at the prospect of a new challenge. He didn't know exactly what, or how, but something would turn up. Perhaps this mysterious appointment in Keswick would be the catalyst.

In the meantime, he had a day to kill.

The green and gold bags containing the newly acquired walking gear, still tagged, folded and wrapped as it had left Knightsbridge, sat neatly arranged on the luggage stand where the porter had left them. Gavin looked at them. Well, why not, that's what people came to the Lake District for. It had been a long time, maybe fresh air and some exercise would prompt fresh ideas, a fresh start.

* * *

It was mid-afternoon when a particularly noisy tractor and its bouncing empty trailer roared past Greg's hotel and jerked him reluctantly to the surface. He'd been dreaming vividly, and in those few moments before full wakefulness the thundering of the tractor became the soundtrack for the fleet of whoomping helicopters, which crowded his subconscious as they swooped amongst a swarm of giant babies in blue nappies hovering like tethered barrage balloons. Greg shivered and slowly opened his eyes. The dream was of the recallable type, the images still vivid, and he stared at the ceiling and tried to make sense of it. The baby characters were obvious, Greg smiled slightly remembering the little blue bundle resting peacefully on Cat's chest, but where had the helicopters come from? Mountain rescue maybe? After a few minutes he decided it really didn't matter; it had been a dream, the usual nonsense, confused, illogical and surreal. More to the point, where was he?

He swung his legs off the bed and looked round the sunny room, noting with professional approval the decor, the furnishings and the general impression of well-ordered cleanliness. A comfortable room, what the brochures would describe as "well-appointed". It all came back to him now; the bus journeys, the coffee shop, the coaching inn, the sympathetic young woman receptionist. He stood up and stretched, then examined the tea and coffee-making paraphernalia neatly arranged on a dresser but decided more was needed than a lonely cup of tea and a couple of chocolate chip cookies. He was hungry, fancied a glass of wine and felt in sudden need of some company.

Greg sat at a low table in the bar and crumpled his paper napkin onto the empty plate. It had been an excellent omelette and he was enjoying the glass of white wine but the bar was devoid of any other life. Apart from exchanging a few words with the young woman who'd taken his order and brought his food, he'd been left with his own solitary company. A large window looked out onto a broad sunny pavement where a steady flow of busy people hurried to and fro. Watching them, Greg suddenly felt very lonely. Silly really, only an hour or so from home where he'd be in a few days anyway, but he couldn't help it. Greg was homesick. He missed the cheerful brashness of Bowness, the shabby familiarity of their guest house and even the infuriating customers. And, of course, Martin. Just a phone call would help; he really couldn't remember when they'd last managed to speak, and so much had happened. One day had blurred into the next, night and day had become interchangeable and Greg's body clock had all but given up. He'd rung home before leaving his room and been surprised to get their professional answering service and, although less surprising, Martin's mobile was also only taking messages. Greg had left a message telling him where he was and asking Martin to ring as soon as possible.

In the meantime, what to do – tomorrow he'd move on to Keswick, and if for no other reason than to satisfy his and Martin's curiosity, be there ready for the conclusion of this silly goose-chase, as he'd come to think of it – but what about the rest of today?

Greg decided to kill time by exploring Cockermouth. Down a narrow side street he found a footbridge over the river leading to a pleasant park with a riverside path and benches. Although the benches were mainly occupied by necking, uniformed school children there was a high turnover rate, presumably as tongues tired and homework demanded, and Greg soon managed to claim one, still warm and in a prime position. He sat for a few moments gazing at the river, then watched passing dog-walkers, none of whom looked anything like their pets, but all at some point obliged to stoop and scrape a canine turd or two off the cinder path with little multi-coloured bags.

Greg returned to the main street via a road bridge and found himself outside a smart-looking hotel whose riverside garden he'd noted from his bench on the opposite bank. He took a glass of wine to a table at the river's edge and carried on watching the dog-walkers from a distance. He decided they were more interesting close up and turned his attention to a pair of courting ducks while he finished his wine. Regaining the main shopping street, he wandered vaguely in the direction of his hotel, glancing in shop windows as he went. He admired prints of panoramic Lakeland views in the windows of galleries, disbelieved the prices being asked for patent junk displayed in some antique shops, and was tempted by the cleverly themed display in the window of an old-fashioned book shop. The smells of late-afternoon cooking and "prepping" from a variety of restaurants mingled and swirled above the street. At pavement level Greg enjoyed the aromas wafting from a bakery and several small coffee shops, but stepped into the road to avoid the queues and sickly sweet airborne gloop that hung around the chain junk-food outlets.

Standing on a central island under a statue of someone

he'd never heard of, Greg watched the pavements get busier with people, probably homeward-bound, and the traffic become sluggish with cars queuing to leave town. It made him feel lonelier than ever. He checked his phone – nothing from Martin. Greg shrugged and rather miserably decided he might as well have another glass of wine. He was still scanning the several pubs he could see from the middle of the road, looking for one that didn't advertise Sky Sport, when a double-decker bus appeared at the top of the street. Greg watched it ease its way through the traffic, wait for an illegal parker to vacate the bus stop and then edge up to the kerb immediately opposite him. Greg crossed the road and found the driver leaning up against the side of the bus having a cigarette.

The doors were already shut when Greg got back to the bus stop. The driver had said he would be leaving in twenty minutes and wouldn't wait, but when Greg waved from the pavement he got a begrudging nod of recognition, the doors were re-opened and his fare was taken. 'Yer cut that fine, pal,' the driver growled. Too breathless to reply Greg gave him a grateful nod, squeezed his lumpy rucksack under the stairs and flopped onto a vacant seat.

'Derek!'
'Oh, hi, Greg.'
'What are you doing here?'
Derek looked pained. 'Helping out, of course,' he sniffed. 'Martin asked me to cover for a couple of days, while you were away. Someone had to,' he added pointedly, then swept a hand across his lower body taking in the

frayed, graffitied plaster cast encasing his left ankle and a brace contraption clamped to his right leg, 'even with all this.'

Greg ignored the injured martyrdom. 'Is Martin upstairs?'

'No, he's with you.'

'Derek,' Greg said slowly, 'you can clearly see he is not with me.'

Derek craned his neck and looked over Greg's shoulder into the hallway. 'Not just out there then?'

'No.'

'Hmm, well he said he'd be with you, said he'd be back some time in the morning. That's why he asked Lisa to come in and help with breakfast.'

'Lisa! Has he gone completely mad?' Greg took a deep breath. 'So where did Martin actually say he was going?'

'Like I said, to see you...' Greg was about to interrupt. '...in Cockermouth. He said he'd got a message from you and as it's quiet here tonight he'd take the car and surprise you. Nice, eh?'

'Yes, very.'

'So was it?'

'What?'

'A surprise.'

'Derek, I haven't seen Martin,' Greg said patiently. 'I'm here, in Bowness, and Martin, if you're right, is probably now in Cockermouth. We haven't seen each other.' He gave a wry snort, 'We probably passed going in opposite directions somewhere on the road, but that's about it.'

'Oh well, at least that's something then,' Derek said vaguely.

Greg didn't bother to reply and started for the stairs seeking sanity and privacy when something suddenly occurred to him. 'Derek, what are you doing with that fire extinguisher?'

'Oh this, putting it in the yard to be collected.'

'Why?'

'Cos it's empty.'

'Why?'

'Cos I've been using it.'

Greg used to think that when conversations with Derek sunk to this level it was the sod being deliberately awkward, but he'd come to realise that even obtuseness was beyond Derek, he was just thick.

'Now, Derek, think about this very carefully, why has it been necessary for you to empty a fire extinguisher?'

Derek shook his head dismissively. 'Oh nothing really, the barbie just got a bit out of control.'

'So no guests involved?'

'Oh no, nothing like that, just me and Lisa.'

Greg gave a little sigh of relief. 'Right, so is it under control now?' He looked out of the window and saw it was raining.

'Yeah, pretty well.'

'Are the fences all OK?' Greg asked suspiciously, 'and the shed?'

'Oh yeah, no problems like that... one or two of the beams are still smoking a bit but it's not a problem.'

'Hang on, what beams?'

Derek looked thoughtful and studied the various doors leading off the entrance hall. 'Under the breakfast room I reckon, probably.'

'Bloody hell, where did you have this barbecue? No, don't tell me, not in the…?'

'In the basement, yeah.' Derek looked out of the window. 'Knew it was going to rain,' he said smugly.

'What exactly do you mean, you've had a baby? Go back to that for a minute.'

Greg had started to explain but had gone off at a tangent, jumping between topics as he tried to recap everything that had happened since he and Martin had spoken last.

'Well, it's not actually mine.'

'Well that's a relief.'

'Look, it's probably best I explain when I see you.'

Martin agreed, but added, 'Just tell me again though, briefly, where does the other baby Greg come into it?'

Greg started to explain again but was quickly interrupted.

'So which one am I godfather to?'

'Greg number one,' Greg giggled.

There was a long silence at the other end of the phone finally broken by Martin clearing his throat. 'Have you been drinking?' he demanded.

'Well I've had a couple,' Greg admitted, 'but that's your fault.'

'My fault?'

'Yeah, leaving the bloody A-Team in charge here!'

The conversation had been going on for well over an hour. Martin was sitting in the bar at the Cockermouth hotel Greg had vacated only hours before, Greg, having soaked the charred joists under the breakfast room, smothered the smell of wet soot with air-freshener and discreetly checked on the well-being of their two guests, was sprawled on a sofa in their top-floor flat, a large glass of wine at his side. When they'd finally made contact, resigned laughter had eventually replaced the initial disbelief and frustration at the ludicrous situation, but they'd reluctantly decided it would be best if Greg stayed at the guest house. He could supervise the kitchen in the morning, significantly reducing the risk of a salmonella outbreak or any other Derek/Lisa-generated disaster, and the breakfast room joists really ought to be checked regularly.

Initially Greg had been a little hurt that Martin wasn't proposing to turn straight round and head back to Bowness to join him. 'It'll take under two hours at this time of the evening, Mart, and I can't wait to see you,' he'd pleaded.

But Martin was gently adamant. 'Greg, I've been doing a bit of thinking while you've been away…'

'Oh,' Greg said warily. He was suddenly frightened.

'Good stuff,' Martin said quickly, 'stuff about our future, how to make things better for us, together. Changing the business so we're running it and it's not running us; giving us more time to do the things we want to do. Maybe some travel, our walking trips again, I've really envied you your trip these last days… well, the bits I understand, anyway. Look, there's something going on up here in Cockermouth, call it luck, serendipity, whatever, but I think it might be an opportunity for us. And the timing – and I mean *this evening* – couldn't be better. I want to look into it a bit. Trust me, Greg, have another glass of wine, get an early night and I'll tell you all about it tomorrow.'

Martin couldn't be persuaded to say any more, but although frustrated, Greg was largely reassured. He'd always deferred to Martin when it came to the more worldly aspects and business side of their lives and trusted his judgement completely. Then, to Greg's surprise, Martin had proposed that they met in Keswick first thing next morning. 'Let's just get away for the day,' he'd said, 'it'll give us a chance to talk and we can do some fun things together at the same time. You can tell me all about the baby Gregs and who knows, maybe I'll have found us a sort of baby of our own to talk about.'

Greg had gone through the familiar chores of checking and securing the old house for the night and was now lying in bed thinking about the events of the last week or so. Martin's palpable excitement had been contagious and although Greg didn't know exactly what about yet, he decided these last few days had somehow changed things, perhaps he too was ready for a new challenge.

* * *

Robbie had never been so glad to feel wet sand and slimy pebbles between his fingers. He managed to struggle to his feet, weighed down by his saturated clothes and waterlogged life jacket, then another breaking wave punched him in the small of the back and sent him sprawling back into the surf. He crawled into the shallows, fighting the vicious backwash that sucked at him and rattled pebbles back down the steepening beach. Finally breaking free from the waves, he slithered over some larger weed-covered rocks, rolled onto his back and lay panting and blinking salty water from his eyes. Foam still lapped round his lower legs but he was too exhausted to move. Robbie wasn't sure how long he lay there, but it was a while before he recovered sufficiently to sit up and take stock of his injuries; nothing appeared to be broken but he felt shockingly bruised all over and his hands were bleeding from clutching at barnacle-covered rocks. He wiped them on his torn trousers and looked out to sea where *Idler* lay on her side in a tangle of canvas and broken timbers with wisps of smoke still drifting from the foredeck.

As soon as Robbie had left the shelter of the Douglas seawall he'd seen what Mike had meant; in the open the wind was far stronger than it had felt snug against the quay, and the sea was rough and confused. It soon became clear that *Idler* was totally unprepared for any voyage, let alone in near-storm conditions; deck equipment was chaotically unsecured and down below nothing had been put away or "lockered" for days. The saloon was a jumble of unwashed crockery, empty bottles, and discarded clothes. As the little boat pitched and rolled her way into deeper water there were repeated thuds and crashes from down below as Robbie's few possessions were tossed around. One particularly shattering crash was followed by the overwhelming smell of spilt whisky, which increased Robbie's growing nausea, but he didn't dare let go of the tiller to go below to clear up.

Idler battled on, more spray flying over the coach-house roof now, and Robbie prayed there was enough fuel to motor the whole way and he wouldn't have to climb out onto the deck to hoist any sail. It was a forlorn hope.

The mainland coast was reassuringly close by the time the engine spluttered and died, but there was no sign of the lighthouse Robbie had been told to look out for, and more worryingly, there was still no sign of a harbour wall. *Idler* was now at the mercy of the elements and even as Robbie wrestled with his tiniest storm sail, struggling to hoist it, she drifted closer and closer inland. By the time he'd crawled back into the cockpit and regained the tiller it was possible to make out figures walking along a low cliff, and even the breeds of their dogs.

Robbie was never sure which gave way first, the boom or the mast – '…probably simultaneous cause and effect,' the loss adjuster suggested later – but the end result was the same and both splintered spars toppled over the side dragging the broken rigging and collapsed sails with them. Before a stunned Robbie could react, the keel touched bottom causing *Idler* to judder and tip to an alarming angle. He desperately clung to the redundant tiller as a series of larger waves raced under the boat, lifting the hull and letting it slam back down on the seabed. The crashes shook Robbie into action. He forced himself to go below, emerging quickly with a frayed life jacket and an ancient flare, praying someone was watching from the low cliff or the rocky beach. The flare fizzled out of its tube, rose ten foot in the air and then dived onto the foredeck where it disappeared into folds of the bundled headsail. There was no way Robbie was going to risk going forward to deal with it, not with *Idler* grinding and bucking along the bottom at this crazy angle. Despite the flying spray and an odd breaking wave, a plume of greasy black smoke soon appeared from the foredeck. This latest disaster rammed home the stark reality of his situation and it suddenly dawned on Robbie that he was actually going to have to make the decision whether or not to abandon ship; should he take his chances, lash himself to the helm and possibly go down with *Idler*, or should he take to the boats… or in his case swim for it. In the end the decision was made for him; the rudder suddenly hitting the bottom whipped the tiller across the cockpit, which caught Robbie behind the knees and neatly flipped him into a backward somersault and straight over the side.

'Y'all right, lad?'

Robbie had slumped back onto the beach; he wasn't even sure he hadn't passed out momentarily. He opened his eyes now and looked up into a wrinkled face, which funnily enough, he thought, would work either way up. A mat of curly grey hair framed top and bottom of the face, the flattened and shapeless nose and bright blue eyes were more or less central and the mouth was invisible, lost in the grey curls at one end or the other. Robbie struggled up onto an elbow.

'Steady, lad, no need to rush.' The voice was rough but gentle. Then the face rotated and with a wheezy sigh the old man eased down onto his knees at Robbie's side.

A woman's voice spoke from over Robbie's shoulder: 'Oh, you poor thing, look at the state of you… and your lovely boat.'

Robbie sat up fully and looked from face to face. Apart from the quantity of facial hair they were remarkably similar. Then he looked back out to sea where the helpless *Idler* rolled in the surf.

The old woman followed his gaze. 'We watched you swimming in,' she said. 'I was going to call the coastguard but you seemed to be managing and Jack said not to bother them.' She gave the old man a reproachful look.

'Don't you worry, *we'll* get you sorted, lad. And your boat. Leave it to me.'

'Don't you go making no rash promises, Jack Wells.'

'Nothin' rash about it,' the old man said firmly, patting Robbie on the shoulder.

The woman patted his opposite knee. 'Are you all right?'

Robbie gingerly stretched all four limbs, one at a time. 'Yes, yes, I think so.' He looked at his bloodied hands. 'A few scratches and...' he rubbed his knee, then the opposite shin, then an elbow and then his left buttock, '...a bit bruised here and there.'

'Look me in the eyes a moment,' the woman said.

Startled into obeying, Robbie stared into the slightly watery but piercing blue eyes and tried not to blink.

'Yer all right, no sign of concussion there.'

'Used to be a nurse,' the old man said, nodding at the woman. 'One of the best,' he added, with simple pride.

'Hush you.' The woman was looking out to sea again. 'Such a shame, it looked like a nice old boat.'

'Never want to get yerself so close on a lee shore, lad,' the old man said. 'Engine trouble finish you, did it?'

'Um, sort of, yes, and just bad luck really.' Robbie shrugged, releasing a fresh trickle of cold water, which found its way between his buttocks and made him shiver.

'You should get out of those wet things and get dry. Do you live far?' the woman asked.

Robbie looked out at the wrecked *Idler* and suddenly felt very lonely. He was close to tears.

'Did you live on your boat?' the woman asked gently.

Robbie just nodded.

'Oh dear, that's awful, have you lost everything?'

Robbie swallowed hard. 'Pretty much,' he mumbled, and produced a clear waterproof pouch from somewhere under the life jacket. 'Wallet and passport at least, and my phone's in here somewhere,' he said.

'Cheer up, lad, all is not lost. Me and Wi…'

'Jack! Not now.'

'Is this Whitehaven?' Robbie asked suddenly.

The old man looked startled. 'Not by a long shot, lad, you're near St Bees, Whitehaven is way up there.' He pointed northwards up the coast. 'Now then…' He turned and looked out towards *Idler* and muttered thoughtfully, 'Tide's well on the ebb now.'

'What, going out?' Robbie said vaguely.

The old man looked at him wide-eyed. 'Of course, I mean you do know which way the…'

'Not now, Jack!'

The old man mumbled something, got to his feet and obviously decided it was time to assert himself. 'Right, Mother, let's get this lad home and you can look at some of these scratches and get him warm and dry.'

Robbie didn't seem to have much choice in the matter and didn't have the energy to resist anyway. The old couple helped him to his feet and for the first time Robbie realised a little crowd, bubbling with curiosity, had gathered a respectful few yards back up the beach. It was mainly an elderly gathering with dogs outnumbering humans.

Robbie turned to look out at *Idler* again. She appeared to have settled quite firmly on the bottom and only the occasional wave moved her now. The smoke had disappeared from the foredeck. The old man gave the woman a hard look and held up a warning finger, then gave Robbie's shoulder a reassuring pat and said: 'Not to worry, lad. It's like this…" He paused to sniff the wind and turned his face from side to side, '…the wind's backing now, knew it would, calming down nicely, and it'll be a millpond by the time the flood starts.' He slitted his eyes to look out to *Idler*. 'And you've had one bit of luck, lad, dumped her on one of the sandbars, you have. Not many of them out there but you've found one and it'll go gentle on her.' He looked Robbie square in the eyes. 'We'll get her off for you, lad,' he said simply.

The woman gave him a little smile and a nod. The old man nodded back and turned to the little crowd, who obviously all knew the old couple and each other. The old man singled out a youth at the front of the crowd who was heaving back at some sort of bull terrier with a studded collar. 'Frank, you got anything on for a couple of hours, pal? Good lad, you stay here then and anything that comes washing up from that,' he nodded towards *Idler*, 'you stack it up here and keep an eye on it. Mother and me'll get this lad fixed up and I'll be back presently.'

Robbie allowed himself to be led across the beach, up a steep but thankfully short path, and on to a cinder track, which ran along the edge of the low cliff. They soon reached a row of neat bungalows, large picture windows looking out over the Irish Sea, and each with its own brightly painted gate giving access to the cliff-edge path from manicured gardens. Robbie was ushered through a bright yellow gate and down a weedless garden path, which neatly bisected the garden. The old man, Jack as Robbie had been instructed to call him, pointed out two old-fashioned fisherman's anchors, both brightly painted and each propped up on its own island of marble chippings centred in each half of the velveteen lawn. 'Off my old boats,' Jack said wistfully. He walked over and patted the smaller of them. 'We'll be needing this later,' he said, grinning happily. The old lady, who had by now been introduced as Florrie, Jack's wife, caught Robbie's eye and rolled hers. 'Nothing personal, pet, but he's loving this. He's been waiting for something like this to happen for years, ever since I made him come in off the boats. He'll be on the phone to his Willie, his brother, soon as we're in the house – he's still got a boat up at Whitehaven – and they'll plot and plan and talk tides and the like and Willie'll be down here like a shot, you'll see. They're as bad as each other.'

The inside of the bungalow was predictably pristine but with the characters of both occupants well represented; the feminine domesticity of Florrie by carefully arranged sprays of silk flowers, family photographs and a glass-fronted cabinet displaying floral paperweights and a hundred years of royal memorabilia; while Jack's influence was obvious from a collection of black and white photos of roll-necked fishermen posing awkwardly on rugged-looking boats, several well-used framed charts of the local coastline hanging in the hall, and a brass-bound telescope in pride of place on the mantelpiece. The overall effect was comfortably homely and Robbie allowed it to envelop him. His repeated and effusive expressions of thanks were all brushed aside by both of them with a casual: 'Nay bother, lad.'

As Florrie had predicted, Jack disappeared as soon as the door was shut and could be heard in another corner of the bungalow making animated phone calls. Florrie, in the meantime, had bustled; she'd run Robbie a bath, started laundering his clothes and then, while he was still wrapped in just a towel and despite his protestations ('For goodness' sake, pet, I was a nurse for thirty years, I've seen it all before.') she creamed and dressed his various cuts and abrasions. Robbie was then provided with a sort of shapeless tracksuit, which smelt faintly of mothballs, and steered to a wing-backed chair next to the coal-fired back boiler. He'd lost count of how many mugs of tea he'd been obliged to drink during these various processes but the latest one was accompanied by a huge serving plate piled high with eggs, bacon, sausages (Cumberland, he was assured), baked beans and half a loaf of toast. After a hesitant start Robbie wolfed the lot. And then promptly fell asleep.

Jack came into the room, his eyes sparkling. 'All sorted,' he said, his voice unconvincingly casual. 'Our Willie's on his way, he'll make it by the flood no problem and a couple of the lads are coming over to give me a hand to get the anchors out. We'll get him off,' he concluded happily.

His wife looked at him and raised her eyebrows. 'You're loving this, aren't you, you old goat?'

ELEVEN

'Ah, there you are, what do you think of that?' A huge wooden spoon was thrust under Dom's nose. 'Go on then, give it a lick.'

Dom tentatively stuck out his tongue and Claire's mother stabbed at it with her spoon. 'Horseradish, chilli and banana,' she said triumphantly, 'what d'you think?'

Dom gasped and felt tears welling up. 'Lovely,' he croaked.

Claire's mother nodded approvingly and turned back to a huge copper pan on the range, which was where she'd been when Claire had shoved a nervous Dom into the room a few minutes earlier. Even from the back it was obvious her mother had once been the same shape as Claire, but with extra inches accumulated over the years covering bottom, hips and bosom, she'd acquired a plump, homely figure. It went with the kitchen, a huge, low room, beamed and flagged, everyone's image of the typical farmhouse kitchen. There were pans everywhere and the room was full of steam and cooking smells, particularly hot vinegar.

Claire indicated a couple of old wheel-back chairs with greasy cushions, beside a little pot-bellied grate built into the wall opposite the range, and they sat down. Despite the season, a couple of logs glowed in the basket and a fan of grey ash spilled across the floor from beneath it.

'Do you make chutney?' Claire's mother called over her shoulder.

Claire nodded at Dom. 'Er, no, not something I've ever tried.'

There was a grunt from the range and another hiss of vinegary steam. 'More horseradish, I think... We'll eat in the dining room, Grandma prefers that, especially when there're guests.'

'Grandma?' Dom whispered.

Claire winked at him. 'Dad's mum, mad as a drunk badger.'

'Is that a big problem round here?'

Claire kicked him gently. The outer door suddenly flew open and a tall young man with longish hair and a wispy beard bounded into the room slamming the door behind him. 'Oh, hello both,' he said to Claire and Dom. 'Hi, Ma, what's fer dinner? Bloody starving, I am.' He went across to the figure at the range and peered over her shoulder. 'Christ, what's that? Horseradish, is it? Beef then.'

'No, pork.'

The young man shrugged and turned to Dom and Claire without any obvious curiosity at Dom's presence.

'This is Dom, Matt,' Claire said, rather defiantly Dom thought.

Matt nodded amiably. The back door opened again and a burly figure hunched in. Holding on to the doorjamb for balance he kicked off a pair of filthy boots then looked across to the fireplace and started peeling off a torn nylon boiler suit. 'You'll be Claire's friend then. Welcome to ye.'

Dom started to thank him.

'Well, let's be 'aving a look at you then.' He stepped out of the remains of the boiler suit and moved across the room.

Claire used her eyebrows and a slight nod to indicate that Dom should stand up. Suddenly realising his lack of manners he jumped to his feet and proffered his hand. Claire's father took it, turned it over and ran a coarse fingertip over the palm. 'Hmm.' He dropped the hand and walked round Dom.

Dom sucked in his stomach and cheeks and tried to look young and sleek. He'd had a second shave just before leaving the cottage and spent ten minutes in front of Claire's dressing table mirror experimenting with his hair; he'd slicked it back, brushed it forward and moved a parting to and fro before eventually, at Claire's insistence, returning it to its usual arrangement.

Claire's father sucked his teeth. 'Hmm.'

'Dad! Dom's a guest, not a new tup.'

'He'll do. Good in the hay, I daresay,' he looked enquiringly at Claire.

'Dad!'

'Dinner's nearly ready,' Claire's mother called from the range.

'Got any kids?' Dom nodded dumbly. 'Good. Not been…?' The farmer made a vicious snipping action with two fingers.

Dom started. 'Um, no…'

Claire's father nodded and turned towards the range. 'Sounds all right, Mam.'

'It's pork.'

'He made the last one drop his trousers,' Matt chipped in. 'Looks like you're gonna be OK though.'

'Matt, shut up.'

'Do like your sister says,' Claire's father said, turning back to Dom. 'Have a whisky.'

Dom was obliged to have several before Grandma finally appeared; a stooped figure dressed in shades of grey with hair to match, who peered at the world through tiny round spectacles and walked with a stick, which sported a huge carved ram's head for a handle. She looked at Dom without interest, only nodding briefly when Claire introduced him. The old lady's appearance was the signal that supper could be served and Claire led them all into the dining room, seating Dom next to Grandma, before returning to the kitchen to help her mother. Dom looked round the large, gloomy room, austere and formal in a dark-wood Edwardian style. There was a baby grand piano pushed into one corner, which was covered by numerous silver photo frames of varying sizes, every one of them displaying the grinning head of a pig. Matt caught Dom staring and winked across the table. 'Better looking than any of the relatives… or us kids,' he laughed. 'Winners every one of them, Dad's pride and joy. Claire's too, that's the competition you've got.'

'Matt,' his father said threateningly and poured Dom another whisky.

Dom was starting to feel the effects, and rather enjoying them. Warmed and cheerful, confident and convivial he turned to Grandma. 'Have you always lived here on the farm?'

She looked at him in surprise, as if not expecting anyone to talk to her. 'That I have,' she said slowly.

'I expect you've seen a lot of changes over the years.'

Grandma thought about this for a moment during which Claire slipped into the chair on Dom's other side, and a carving platter with a huge joint of meat was placed in front of her father. 'I've seen lots of things,' Grandma said eventually.

Dom nodded solemnly. 'Especially in the woodshed, I expect,' he said, suppressing a grin.

Claire glanced at him quizzically and the old lady looked at him as if he was mad.

'What would I be doing in the woodshed?'

'He's talking about *Cold Comfort Farm*,' Matt called across the table. 'It's a book by... can't remember her name, Stella somebody, but it's about a loony farming family, even loonier than this one.'

'Loony, eh?' Claire's father said, now on his feet and slashing a carving knife along the length of a steel.

Dom felt his face colouring. 'I didn't mean that...'

Claire's father let out a bellow of laughter. 'Loony's not the half of it,' he roared, 'stark staring mad's more like it, especially come the end of haymaking! And as for my brother...' The whole family laughed at this and even Grandma managed a tight smile. Dom joined in, relieved, and Claire squeezed his leg under the table.

Glasses and cups were filled. Claire's mother seemed to have a pot of tea to herself, Grandma had a small glass of something milky and effervescent, which went pink when she added something from a tiny hip-flask, and Claire and Matt passed a bottle of wine back and forth. Dom, it seemed, was expected to help his host demolish a bottle of single malt.

'Now, let's see what you make of this leg of pork of ours, young man.' A plate stacked with thick slabs of meat was passed down the table to Dom. Others were passed round, vegetables were distributed and then several reverential minutes of silence followed as the first few mouthfuls were taken.

'That do ye then? Good eh?' Claire's father called down the table, brandishing his cutlery. Dom, with a full mouth, tried to smile without letting anything drop out, and nodded dumb appreciation.

'Home-grown this is, one of our own.'

His attention focussed on his host's semaphoring cutlery, Dom didn't notice the exchange of raised eyebrows between Claire and her brother.

'Oh aye, one of our best,' the farmer continued. 'You saw our Duchess today, didn't you?' Dom looked blank. 'The Duchess, our grand sow, the big lass weaning the little 'uns.'

Dom swallowed the last of his mouthful. 'Oh yes, yes, I did, a magnificent animal, and all the piglets…'

'Didn't see her stand up though did you?'

Dom was confused. 'Er, no.'

'Only three legs, yer see.'

'Oh… oh that's a shame, but still I…'

'That's the other one.' Claire's father pointed at Dom's plate, then swept his knife round the rest of the table before tapping the remains of the joint in front of him. 'See, when you've got an animal of that quality you don't want to eat it all in one go, best to make it last… and keep it fresh.' He shovelled another forkful into his mouth and concentrated on collecting the next. There were serious nods around the table, apart from Grandma who made a curious little cackling noise. Dom pushed a piece of crackling round his plate, suddenly feeling slightly queasy, but aware that everyone round the table was watching him.

Suddenly Claire burst out, 'Oh, Dad!'

Her father threw back his head and let out a roar of laughter, which sprayed his end of the table with partially masticated meat and veg. The rest of the family ducked and chuckled dutifully.

Claire picked a piece of carrot out of her hair and kissed Dom on the cheek. 'Don't listen to him, Dom, it's a load of old bollocks.'

'Claire…' Her mother tutted and rattled her teacup in its saucer.

Claire ignored her. 'This isn't the Duchess, it's not even one of ours, comes from Cranston's, the local butcher. It's Dad's party piece, he likes to wind up any newcomers, especially… well, never mind.'

Dom had managed to deflect some whisky top-ups but was still a bit unsteady on his way back to the cottage. Claire held his hand and flashed a torch on the track ahead of them. 'They are all a bit barmy, I suppose,' she said suddenly.

Dom's silly *Cold Comfort* crack still troubled him. 'Look, I'm sorry, I didn't mean to...'

Claire squeezed his hand. 'Don't worry, they liked you. Better be careful though, you might not be allowed to leave,' she giggled, 'not now Dad's got you down as good breeding stock.'

* * *

Gavin had slept remarkably well, despite the overnight bombshell from Florida, and was pleased to find he'd retained his previous evening's mood of optimism and anticipation, which had replaced the initial shock and anger at the news of his double betrayal. He'd only thought about it briefly since waking, but realised it was the disloyalty of Jacko, his erstwhile right-hand man, which riled more than the fickle unfaithfulness of his wife. He supposed that didn't say much for any of them.

He ordered breakfast in his room and while he waited reread the solicitor's letter summoning him to Cumbria, again experiencing that little frisson; there was something here, he was sure, an opportunity, a new door ready to open. He shrugged and tossed the letter onto the bed, creased and crumpled next to the crisp new map of the North Western Lakes. If nothing else, the letter had got him out of Spain at an opportune moment, and in a curious way had contributed to bringing his previous life to this abrupt, if not wholly unexpected, juncture.

Gavin turned to the map and smiled at childhood memories of poring over similar maps with long-forgotten friends planning impossibly long walks and climbs, which would never be started, let alone completed, once a shot of adult reality had been injected. The memory reminded Gavin that he was no longer that lithe, agile teenager of years gone by, and in fact he had no idea just how fit or otherwise he really was these days. He flexed his knees, which creaked slightly, and slowly lowered himself into a squat position. After crouching there for a moment he reached for the edge of the bed and heaved himself upright again – it had been a long time.

He took the remains of his breakfast coffee to the window and looked out at last night's silhouetted mountains. Now spotlighted by the low morning sun they presented a dramatic backcloth of deep shadows, glistening crags and sparkling becks. Regardless of his protesting joints Gavin had a sudden urge to be part of that landscape. Pushing aside the breakfast debris he spread out the map and ran his finger randomly from peak to peak, tracing paths and skirting lakes. Where to go? After his experimental PE, nothing too challenging he decided, but definitely involving a climb – he wanted to stand on a summit. It would be good to look down and see if he could remember it as it had been and get things in perspective again. He went back to the map and various names of fells and peaks caught his eye: the famous, the notorious, and a few still holding memories from years ago. One in particular stood out. Gavin remembered it as always being the first afternoon or a Sunday morning walk; an obvious path, safe, not too high and relatively easy, but offering fine views. Although it would mean going to Keswick first and involve a short boat ride across the lake, Gavin decided he would climb Catbells.

An hour later he emerged from the narrow spiral of stairs onto the empty top deck of the Keswick bus and instinctively looked towards the vacant rear bench. On the school bus that had always been the bad kids' domain, where they'd teach each other to smoke, play pontoon and roll joints. God, was that really the last time he'd been on a bus? He smiled at the memory but turned to the front instead, put his crisp new rucksack on an adjoining seat and sat back to enjoy the novelty and the views. He enjoyed the short launch ride across the lake too, despite remembering too late that it didn't need much of a chop for the bows to toss showers of spray over the first half dozen rows of benches, where he'd joined other unwary tourists.

Leaving the jetty, Gavin made his way up the pebble beach tugging experimentally at the straps hanging from his rucksack, then set his shoulders and followed the crowds. He was surprised just how busy it was, and although a lot disappeared off along a lakeshore track, it was still quite a crowd which headed for the well-trodden uphill path. Slowly the crowd thinned and spread, redistributed according to fitness and ability; the hares, younger and fitter, racing ahead, taking short-cuts where the terrain allowed, the tortoises, heads down, deliberately picking each footfall, trudging relentlessly upward. Of the rest, the stop-starters and the photo fanatics were the two biggest sub-groups.

Gavin didn't remembered the path being so loose and rugged, or so wide and ill defined. Years of erosion he supposed, millions of boots and countless deluges must have hammered and sluiced away at the path since he was on this mountainside last. After about half an hour he reached a sort of sub-peak and took a breather and a few sips from his water bottle. Despite a slight burning in his chest and the suspicion of a blister on a little toe, he was pleased with his progress and quite enjoying the unfamiliar tightness he could already feel in his thigh and buttock muscles. Further adjustments had also made more sense of the multiple straps on the rucksack, now sitting fairly comfortably against his back. A last sip of water and he set off again, slightly slower and no longer kidding himself that all his halts were to admire the view, but steadily enough. With the topography already having made several false promises and the path reduced to a craggy scramble, Gavin was too busy concentrating on picking a route and keeping his footing to worry about how much further he had to go, so when he did finally emerge on the top it came as something of a surprise.

The summit proved to be crowded and noisy, the cairn besieged by the photo junkies, and people darting from one vantage point to another calling and exclaiming loudly to each other. Just about everyone seemed to have a camera or a mobile phone in their hands. Gavin had to admit he was disappointed, he hadn't anticipated crowds on this scale, and moved away from the peak, the magnet for the masses, hoping to find a quieter vantage point nearby. Spotting a small, craggy outcrop a little way down one slope he decided to scramble down and see if he could tuck himself away there. Apart from anything else he was hungry and looking forward to investigating the enormous paper sack, which was his hotel's idea of a packed lunch.

'Oh sorry, I didn't realise...'

The woman looked up at Gavin and gave a deep sigh before turning back to the view with a scowl. She was sitting on a folded anorak, her back against the slab of rock which was the downhill face of the crag, and had been quite invisible from further up the slope.

'I was just looking for somewhere to...'

'Yes, so was I,' the woman said, not taking her eyes off the distant line of fells.

'Yes, sorry, I'll move on.'

'Is it always like this?'

'Sorry?' Gavin was taken aback by her abruptness.

She looked up at him again. 'Your famous Lake District, is it always so bloody busy?'

The woman had an accent Gavin couldn't quite place, slightly guttural, Germanic, Dutch maybe, or South African. He eased his rucksack straps with his thumbs and leant against the crag.

'I wouldn't really know, I haven't been up here since I was a kid but this was always a favourite,' he patted the rock. 'And yeah, from what I've read, I think the whole area's always pretty busy these days. It's a beautiful place,' he added.

The woman snorted. 'Too small and too many bloody people. Well are you going to sit down or not?'

'No, I wouldn't want to...'

'Look, just sit down.'

Gavin unhooked one rucksack strap then hesitated and looked down at the woman again.

She caught him looking at her. 'Go on, sit down, I don't bite.' She waved at a flattish rock a few feet from her. 'Maybe some company'll do me good, teach me some bloody manners.' She sighed and her voice softened to a husky drawl, 'Look I'm sorry, I'm not usually this crabby, it's just all these bloody crowds... and I guess I'm homesick. Go on, be my guest.' She waved at the rock again.

Gavin finally took off his rucksack and sat down on the proffered rock. Adopting her bluntness he openly studied his new companion. She was probably older than him, he decided, lean, tanned and lined – weathered would be kinder – with blonde hair scraped back into a long ponytail streaked with silver. Her clothes, at a glance, were an outfit of crumpled well-worn beige, and somehow incongruous. She certainly hadn't been fitted out by any of the Keswick walking-gear outlets.

Gavin got out the huge lunch bag and put it between them. 'So where's home?'

'Eh?'

'You said you were homesick. Where for?'

'Well, I was born in Sweden,' she smiled to herself, 'but it's Africa I miss.'

'Africa?' The incongruity of the crumpled beige made sense now, more safari than fell. 'What do you do out there?'

'Chimps... amongst other things. I've got a small bungalow in Nairobi, it's in a bloody awful neighbourhood but it's fine for me, and got a good yard and room for my sanctuary.'

'Chimps?'

The woman nodded. 'I rescue chimps, like I said, amongst other things. I spend most the winter in Tanzania, Serengeti... my rich countrymen can't get enough of the great outdoors and the "big five", but they do like the bathroom arrangements explained in their own language, preferably by a blonde… or ex-blonde,' she laughed, tugging at her greying ponytail. 'Then in my spare time I have this friend in Uganda. Carlson, a crazy Dane but a bloody great Dane!' She gave a short laugh. 'He has his roundels, little huts, which he lets out to the tourists, and I have my tours. We pool any profits and split it between my chimps and his girls.'

'His girls?'

'Single mothers, foundlings, hookers, orphans… he feeds them, pays for some basic schooling, gets them medical care… You've probably heard of AIDs,' she said dryly, 'well it's rampant in our parts.' She shrugged, 'They need all the help they can get. We do what we can.'

'And does it work?'

The woman looked at him in bemusement and then turned back to the distant purple fells. 'No one's ever asked me that before,' she mused. 'Fair question, I suppose.'

'I'm sorry, I didn't mean…'

She ignored him. 'As far as it goes, yes, I guess it does. A drop in the bloody ocean of course, but something needs to be done and someone needs to do it, or at least try.'

Gavin decided he was on safer ground with chimps. 'So where do they come from, these chimps?'

'Oh, rich men's whims, Chinese mainly; they buy them illegally as babies, get lots of photos for their social media sites, then when the ape gets a bit bigger, not so cute, and starts crapping everywhere, and maybe someone gets bitten, and it tries to hump the family dog… well, the novelty kinda wears off and it gets dumped, completely helpless.'

'Lucky not to end up in the chow mein.'

'Oh, some do.'

'God, I'll never order a number thirty-seven again.'

'A what?'

'Thirty-seven… well, it could be any number, I just chose that one at random.'

The woman looked blank. 'What are you on about?'

'Ordering food, you know, from a takeaway menu, people just use the number of the dish.'

'Can't say I've ever tried. Not very imaginative, is it?'

'No, I suppose not,' Gavin conceded, and decided it was time to change the subject again. 'So anyway, what brings you to this part of the world, clearly not the delights of the Lake District?'

The woman snorted and explained that she'd been visiting an aged aunt and uncle, who '… for some bloody reason…' had decided to settle in Carlisle back in the sixties. The aunt was rapidly losing a battle with dementia and had wanted to see her niece while she still knew who she was.

'And did she?' Gavin asked.

'Almost, she thought I was my twin sister but that's near enough. Right, that's enough about me, you've got all you need to know. I want to hear something about you.' She studied him shrewdly, 'You look like a man with a back story.'

Gavin wasn't sure how to take this but tentatively started to offer vague scraps about his past and background, while the woman rummaged around in the paper lunch sack. 'Don't mind, do you?' Gavin shook his head and told her about Spain.

The woman listened attentively and demolished a round of sandwiches. 'Sounds dodgy,' was her only comment. She extracted a piece of game pie and sniffed it suspiciously. 'What the bloody hell's an egg doing in there?' She took a huge mouthful.

Gavin mentioned his marriage.

'You're married?' she mumbled through a mouthful of pie, 'never have guessed that.'

Gavin thought for a moment. 'Well, until last night.'

The woman swallowed and coughed. 'Tell more.'

Gavin did, at length, and was surprised to find he was quite enjoying opening up to this extraordinary woman. He supposed this was what some people got from therapy.

Eventually, taking advantage of a pause in the monologue while Gavin bit into a sandwich, the woman advanced her own conclusion: 'So let's get this right; your marriage is screwed, your business is a car crash and basically you're a bloody crook.' It was a statement not a question but Gavin treated it as one. 'Well, yes, I guess so,' he grinned sheepishly. She grinned back.

They walked down the mountain together, the woman scowling at other walkers and dismissive of the landscape, comparing it unfavourably with the plains and *kopjes* of East Africa. Sitting wedged together near the stern of the launch they finally exchanged names. The woman was called Annie. They parted company on the Keswick beach and Gavin set off into the town to locate the solicitor's office where the next day's meeting was due to be held.

On the bus on the way back to Ambleside he saw Annie again. She was sitting at a slatted table in the raised garden of a small roadside inn. There was a book propped up against an ashtray on the table and a half-full pint glass at her elbow. Gavin had a sudden urge to stop the bus and get off.

* * *

There was no sign of Martin when Greg got off the bus outside a busy supermarket in Keswick. He scanned the milling crowds for a few minutes and wondered what to do next. Then a nudge in the back, which he'd taken as just another shove from some impatient shopper, became a pat and he spun round to find Martin grinning happily. Greg smiled back and felt inexplicably shy – ridiculous, how long had they been together now? 'There you are,' he said, then glancing down at the large hessian shopping bag at Martin's feet, 'and you've done the shopping.'

'Is that the best you can do?' Martin said. 'Come here!' They hugged and Martin led the way to a far corner of the car park where, lacking change, he'd left the car in the hope of avoiding the attentions of any prowling traffic warden. He'd been lucky.

'Right, here's the plan,' Martin said, immediately taking control. 'We're taking the whole day off, just you and me together… we've got loads to talk about, wait 'til you hear… well, you'll see.' He pulled down the sun visor. 'And even the weather's playing ball. Right, I'll drive and you can talk, then I'll do the talking while you row.'

'Row?'

'You'll see. Now let's get the real-life stuff out of the way; how did you leave things at home?' Martin threaded the car through the tourist traffic towards the lakeside while Greg reported that the basement had not spontaneously combusted during the night, breakfast had gone smoothly and, against his better judgement, he'd left Derek and Lisa in charge. But with dire warnings of the consequences if they set fire to anything, or killed, maimed or harmed a guest in any way.

'Best we can hope for,' Martin agreed.

Once parked up in the lakeside car park, duly paying and displaying, Martin explained his plans for their day. The shopping bag turned out to contain the makings of a huge picnic: cold chicken and meats, cheeses, a French stick, salads and fruit, bottles of ridiculously strong Belgian lager and both red and white wine.

'Completely over the top, of course,' Martin admitted cheerfully.

The picnic was to be eaten on one of the islands that dotted the lake and Martin had booked one of the old-fashioned wooden rowing skiffs that were available for hire to get them there.

'I've brought a towel from the hotel so we can have a dip too if you like.'

Greg looked dubious. Martin shrugged, 'Whatever, we can just chill out and catch up. Then I've got something to tell you.'

'I thought you might,' Greg said. He didn't need to be told that Martin was very excited about something.

'Right, look out for some of the idiots in the electric

boats, keep out of the way of anything with a sail and watch out for rocks round the edges.' With that, the young man with blue arms and calves gave the boat a hefty shove.

Almost jerked off his bench Greg fought to keep his balance and in the process let go of one of the oars, leaving it tangled under the legs of the pontoon. The young man scooped it out of the lake and dropped it neatly back into its rowlock. 'You'll be needing that,' he said, and turned back down the pontoon.

After a few minutes Greg managed to tame the oars and set up some sort of a rhythm. Martin, lolling on the stern bench, wasn't getting splashed quite so often and they'd managed to get clear of the beach and the general chaos of other boats, paddling toddlers and indignant swans. Greg let the oars dangle in their rowlocks for a moment and rubbed the palms of his hands together.

'So come on, Mart, what's going on? Something's happened hasn't it? I hope it's good.' Greg paused. 'Your call, you had me worried, I thought… well, I wasn't sure, you know?'

'Oh Gigi,' Martin reached forward and patted both Greg's knees, 'don't ever…' The boat suddenly bucked violently, Martin was thrown back onto his bench, there was a crash as the picnic bag slid off the foredeck and Greg had to dive for an oar, which had jumped its rowlock and was threatening to float off. Unwittingly they'd drifted into the regular lane used by the launches ferrying trippers between the various landing stages scattered around the lake's edge, and one had just passed close by, leaving a huge wash.

Once order had been restored, the picnic bag checked for breakages and spillages, and Greg reunited with his oars, it was agreed the serious talking could wait until later. For the moment they'd concentrate on the rowing and avoiding getting swamped.

For the next hour Greg zigzagged them up the lake while they chatted easily, admiring the view and trying to remember the names of the fells. They had fun mocking other boaters for their incompetence but still kept a wary eye on the launches. Greg had learnt the trick of turning the bows into the waves to ride out the wash and they'd started to quite enjoy these roller coaster rides, but it was still a relief when, with Martin rock-spotting from the bow, they'd eventually crunched the boat gently up a shingle beach on one of the islands.

An assortment of craft was already pulled up on the pebbles and their occupants had set up camps and staked claims in the various inlets among the rocks. A large group of schoolchildren, who'd obviously arrived in a fleet of open canoes, played noisily in the shallows.

Martin frowned. 'Hm, busy,' he grunted. 'Come on we'll go round the other side, it's rockier but it'll be quieter. The boat'll be safe enough here.' He tied the painter to a large bit of driftwood then they each took a handle of the big shopping bag and set off across the wooded interior of the island. Voices drifted through the undergrowth along with woodsmoke and the smell of barbecued meat. Suddenly emerging from the trees they found themselves on a craggy outcrop ten or fifteen feet above the surface of the lake. Working along the top of the crag in the opposite direction to the distant voices they came across a narrow crevice, which Martin disappeared down, emerging a few minutes later to pronounce it the perfect spot.

'There's a little beach just round to the left, plenty of room for the two of us, and all to ourselves.'

Ten minutes later a bottle of white wine lay partly buried, cooling in the gritty sand at the water's edge, the picnic bag was wedged in the shade behind a large rock and Martin and Greg sat comfortably shoulder to shoulder sipping lager from plastic beakers. They looked out across the lake where a variety of boats and boaters were passing: arm-pumping kayakers, couples in open canoes sedately dipping their paddles, one with a dog in a life jacket perched up at the bow, and a small wooden boat with a full red sail frothed past. Away to their left, near the top of the island, a group of youths in a skiff howled and hooted and scooped handfuls of water over each other.

'It's your meeting with the solicitors tomorrow,' Martin said suddenly.

'Yeah, I know.'

'Well, you don't sound very excited.'

'Can't say I am really, I just want to get home now. I'll go and see what it's all about, I suppose. Probably a scam anyway.'

'I don't think so, *to your advantage*, remember?'

'I know, I know. But never mind that, why are you so excited… and mysterious?'

Martin took a deep breath. 'Right, you know what I was saying last night about us somehow getting more from life, not letting the business run us anymore?'

Greg nodded. 'What are you thinking, we try something else, or get something smaller?'

'No, bigger!'

'Bigger?'

'Yeah, something big enough to support a proper staff; cooks, cleaners and decent management.'

'Christ, not Derek and Lisa?'

Martin gave one of his snorts of laughter. 'No, but I do have someone in mind. Cheryl.'

'Who's Cheryl?'

'She's the manager at the hotel where you stayed yesterday in Cockermouth, where I stayed last night and where we're both staying tonight.'

'We are?'

Martin nodded.

'You're going to have to explain, Mart. I agree, if your Cheryl is who I met, she seems like a very nice girl... woman, but I don't understand.'

'The hotel is for sale, Greg. I found out last night when I met the owner, Val, in the bar. She wants to retire as soon as possible and is really keen to do a deal. We even talked price.' Martin described how he'd spent the previous evening checking out potential rivals, visiting as many of Cockermouth's hotels and pubs as he could get round before closing time, and he was dismissive of the competition. 'Val filled me in on her main clientele. She gets plenty of business people all year round from the nuclear place at Sellafield, then lots of Wordsworth groupies in the spring when the daffs are out, especially Americans. Apparently quite a few Japanese turn up who think Beatrix Potter was born in the town – Cheryl said she even had one group who thought she still lived there – and then the same mix of tourists as we get down in Windermere. It's a good business, Greg, I'm convinced of it, but it could be a hell of a lot better. I think we could really make something of it…' He looked out across the lake to where the little boat with the red sail was racing downwind and smiled. '…with a fair wind.'

'Do you really think…?' Greg started, '…I mean what about the money? The place is huge, it must be worth a fortune.'

'I think we could do it. I've even got a theme worked out, we'll rename it "The Bounty".'

'"The Bounty"?'

'After the ship, you know, the mutiny, Captain Bligh and all that.'

'Yes, yes, I know that stuff but what's it got to do with anything?'

'Fletcher Christian.'

'Yes?'

'He was the bad boy, or the hero, depending on whose side you're on, anyway the ringleader of the mutiny. Well, he was born in Cockermouth.'

'Oh, right.' Greg looked thoughtful for a moment. 'What about calling it "The Pitcairn"; that's where they ended up, didn't they, and it's a bit classier for a hotel? Then we could have a Bounty Bar with all the nautical stuff and film posters and things… Marlon Brando, wasn't it?'

The ideas started to flow and Greg quickly caught Martin's mood of excitement. It was mid-afternoon before the picnic was remembered and the bag raided. Fresh beakers were produced and Martin paddled out to retrieve the white wine, which had floated off unnoticed. The food and wine were consumed hungrily but largely untasted as they continued to bat ideas back and forth.

Choosing his moment, with Martin temporarily

gagged by a mouthful of quiche, Greg finally brought things back down to earth. 'Mart, are you sure we could do this, I mean afford it and then… well, cope?'

Martin swallowed quickly. 'Yes, I do, I really do. It'll be incredibly hard work to start with but once it's all set up I think it'll give us the flexibility we need, and that'll give us the time and the space to think about the other things in our lives, the really important things.'

Greg thought about the people he'd met and the experiences he'd had in the last week or so and nodded. 'Yes, that would be good.'

They both looked out over the lake, the shadows had lengthened and the breeze had dropped. The far treeline was reflected almost perfectly in the mirrored surface of the undisturbed, now boat less lake.

In the meantime, up at the end of the lake near the boat-hire pontoons a last grand water fight was going on between two boatloads of rather drunk youngsters, the action punctuated by girlish squeals, bellows of laughter and laddish insults. The group had set off together in one boat, but finding a second skiff adrift on the lake, untended and with no obvious claimants, they'd decided more fun could be had by splitting their number between the two. It didn't occur to them to look for the original hirers, or that some accident or tragedy may have befallen them.

By the time all the boats were eventually returned, the hire people had long-since forgotten exactly who'd taken out what; their numbers tallied, they had all their boats back and it was time to lock up after a busy day.

'God, we're going to be late, we're meant to get the boat back.' Martin scrambled to his feet and started stuffing the remains of the picnic into the bag. 'C'mon, Gigi, let's get back to the hotel, *The Pitcairn*,' he smiled. 'I want you to meet Val and we can look around together, properly.'

The initial reaction to the empty beach had been one of confusion. Greg was convinced they were in the wrong bay but when Martin identified the piece of driftwood he'd tied the boat's painter to, and with the thin cord still firmly attached, there was no doubt. Martin found the other end of the painter, which had obviously once been a neatly spliced loop but was now a couple of frayed tails. He held them up in disgust. 'Snapped! And all those waves from the launches must have washed it out.'

They both looked out across the lake but there was no sign of any boat of any description. Not really knowing what else to do they set off round the island to check every beach and inlet. 'It might have been washed back up, I suppose,' Martin said. It hadn't. Next, they crisscrossed the inland paths, but it was clear the island had been deserted. Then they shouted and waved the towel in the direction of the far shore where cars on the road had started turning on their lights, but got no reaction.

'You'd have thought someone, you know...' Greg shrugged.

'I don't understand the boat people not worrying. Where's your phone?'

'At home, I forgot to charge it, where's yours?'

'In the car.'

'Great!'

With the light fading by the minute it was clear they

would be spending the night on the island. Martin quickly warmed to the idea but Greg was less sure. A whiff of woodsmoke led them to the smouldering remains of someone's campfire, which Martin managed to rekindle making the little clearing dance with orange light and restless shadows. The addition of light and warmth to the proceedings cheered Greg considerably. Then, with a flourish, Martin produced an unopened bottle of red wine from the picnic bag. 'We hadn't finished talking anyway, had we? Seems like the perfect opportunity, don't you think?'

Greg looked at the fire and the wine and Martin's glowing face and nodded happily.

And talk they did, well into the night. Hunched by the fire with the bath towel over their shoulders, sipping wine, they almost forgot where they were as the talk ranged over hotel management, and babies and staffing rosters, and god-parentage, and wine lists and menus and marriage and love.

* * *

'I've made you a brew, lad.'

Robbie smelt the tea before he saw it. He slowly ungummed his eyes and tried to remember where he was. The old lady, Florrie, was standing in front of him holding an armful of clothes, his clothes, and things started to come back to him. 'All ready,' she said, piling the clothes carefully on a nearby pouffe. 'I'll make myself scarce while you change, I know how shy you are.' She gave a cross between a snort and a chuckle. 'Now, what about something to eat, you're going to need your strength?'

Robbie sipped the scalding tea, which was unbelievably sweet. 'No, no, I'm fine, thank you,' he mumbled, still not fully awake.

Florrie shook her head reproachfully and left the room, calling back: 'I'll make you a sandwich or two anyway, in case you change your mind.'

Robbie stretched gingerly and groaning quietly eased himself out of the warm chair. God, he ached, and he could feel the sticky edges of various dressings tugging at the fleece lining of the loaned tracksuit. He walked slowly across the room and looked out of the big picture window across the garden and out to sea. It looked calm and the sun was shining with just a few small, fluffy clouds drifting by. The shadows were starting to lengthen across the garden and Robbie noticed that the smaller of the two brightly painted anchors was missing from its marble chip island. He came back to the armchair and picked up the pile of clothes. They were still warm and had been carefully stacked in order; underwear on the top, then trousers, shirt and finally jersey, all neatly folded, and, to Robbie's amazement, the trousers and jersey neatly repaired. Florrie came back in just as Robbie was pulling his jersey over his head and gave her handiwork an approving nod. She was carrying a plate stacked high with sandwiches.

'Jack and some of the lads are down on the beach,' she said and glanced at a clock on the window sill. 'He popped in for a cuppa 'bout an hour ago and told me to wake you now. It'll be high water in a couple of hours and he thought you might want to go down.' She put the sandwiches down in front of Robbie. 'Wouldn't bother though if I were you, better off staying here for a nice cup of tea and letting me drive you up to Whitehaven a bit later. Jack and his Willie know what they're about and reckon they'll have her floated off no problem. Loving it they are, the old buggers. Anyways, no real need for you to go getting wet and cold again.' She gazed out of the window at the sea for a moment then turned and her eyes met Robbie's. 'But then I know you sailors…' She gave a sigh and left the rest unsaid.

Robbie thought it was probably something she'd been repeating all her married life. He spoke for the first time since he'd woken up. Plucking gently at the front of his freshly laundered jersey, he simply said, 'Thank you.'

Florrie waved a dismissive hand but looked pleased. 'If you really want to go with them, I suppose we'd better be getting you down there then.'

Robbie wiggled his toes in his warm newly darned socks and looked longingly at the little coal stove glowing seductively on the scrubbed hearth. It was his turn to sigh, but he knew if there was any realistic chance of salvaging *Idler*, however small his contribution, he ought to be involved. 'I should,' he said, sounding more reluctant than he'd meant to. He looked out of the window and a thought suddenly occurred to him. 'Could I use your phone, please? Just one quick call?'

'No need, pet, I've charged yours up for you. She darted out of the room and returned with his phone and his wallet, both safely back in their waterproof pouch.

'Um…' Robbie took the phone out and fiddled with it for a moment.

'No credit, eh?'

'Nope.'

This, like everything else, was "nay bother".

Robbie was left alone in the hall and to his surprise got straight through to Sylvia at the book shop. Her greeting of: 'Oh, it's you,' was not encouraging, nor were her monosyllabic responses and the long silences, which had Robbie repeatedly checking whether she was still on the line. Eventually his rambling account of the whys and wherefores of his precipitate departure and subsequent disaster was interrupted by a curt: 'So where are you now?'

Robbie told her.

'And what happens next?'

Robbie explained about Jack and his brother and the other salvage helpers.

'What extraordinarily kind people.'

Robbie agreed.

'So you'll be in Whitehaven this evening?'

'One way or the other, yes.'

'Where?'

'Ah, well, not sure yet.'

'Right,' she said slowly, 'I'll ring you later.'

'Um…'

'I know, not charged and no credit.'

'Well it's charged but…'

'OK, I'll sort it out.' He started to thank her. 'Robbie,' she stopped him and there was a long pause, 'you're going to have to grow up and stop running away one day, you know.'

Down on the beach little seemed to have changed; a small crowd was still gathered, all staring out to sea. A few faces were familiar and Robbie was fairly sure it was the same people who'd witnessed his ignominious shipwreck earlier. He certainly recognised the young man with the vicious-looking dog. They were now standing guard over a pathetic, water-logged pile of his possessions, flotsam washed ashore from *Idler* and fished out of puddles and rock pools by curious passers-by and dog-walkers. Robbie approached the young man and the dog growled.

'Canna have your autograph?' Robbie found a stained beer mat and a cheap biro thrust at him. He looked in bewilderment at the young man who grinned shyly. 'I saw you on the telly.'

'Oh.'

There was a general stirring in the crowd. Robbie took the mat and pen, scribbled his name across the brewer's logo and handed them back. The young man studied the mat carefully and held it out again. 'Can yer put "Captain Calamity", that's what they called you on the telly?' The dog growled, Robbie obliged and the crowd muttered to each other happily.

Out near the gently lapping water's edge Robbie could see *Idler*, still heeled at a drunken angle but somehow swivelled so she now faced out to sea. There were lines splayed out from both bow and stern holding her in position and Robbie was reminded of a fly caught in a spider's web. He splashed out towards his boat where Jack, clad in patched chest-high waders, was fussing with the rudder. 'How do, lad,' Jack greeted him happily. 'All set, I reckon. This is our Willie.' A rough-looking man with kindly eyes, also swathed in rubber, splashed round from the front of the boat and nodded and grunted a greeting. 'That's his boat.' Jack pointed out to the deeper water where a smaller version of the fishing boat which had rescued Robbie in the Bristol Channel rolled gently. 'Tow line's already made fast, all we need now's a bit more water,' Jack said, rubbing his hands in anticipation. 'Have you in Whitehaven by opening time.' His brother grunted his agreement.

Despite the encroaching tide slopping wavelets into Robbie's sea boots, Jack insisted on walking him around *Idler*, gruffly proud of his salvage efforts. Robbie was astonished; the earlier tangle of broken spars, canvas, wires and ropes had all been cleared away, carefully organised and stowed. Sheets and lines were neatly coiled, sails were flaked and trussed into tidy tubular bundles, the broken rigging had been cut away and even the shattered mast and boom were tidily secured along the side decks as if that was their normal place on board.

'We checked her over,' Jack said, 'nothing we could see to worry you. Sturdy old girl she is.' He patted the weedy hull affectionately.

Robbie nodded and tried to stand on tiptoe as another wavelet spilled over into his boots.

Jack hooked a leg over the gunwale. 'C'mon, best get on board, won't be long now.' He helped Robbie into the cockpit. ''Fraid she's not so clever down below, had a quick look but there was more important stuff to do on deck.' He gave a sudden grin, 'And I wouldn't let Florrie out here with her polish and Hoover.'

'I bet she would have done too.' Robbie grinned back; the old fisherman's enthusiasm and cheerful optimism was starting to infect him too.

The cockpit, despite being pitched at nearly forty-five degrees, was as organised and sea-ready as the rest of the boat above decks. Robbie felt a twinge of shame when he thought of how messy and chaotic he usually let it get, and that on an even keel. 'I just don't know how to thank…'

'Oh, nay bother, lad, but you'd better have a look at the rest,' Jack nodded towards the companionway.

Robbie leant through the hatch and winced.

'Told you,' Jack said. 'We stopped up that broken porthole and done some bailing but a bit of pumping would help.'

'And the engine?' Robbie ventured.

'Nothing wrong that I can see,' Jack said. 'Except…' He shook his head in reproach, '…you had no diesel! Which means the filters are buggered too,' he added.

Robbie showed Jack where the little lever that worked the hand pump was and left him to it in the cockpit while he went below. There, he wedged himself against the stump of the mast and started trying to get the saloon into some semblance of order. There were quite a few breakages and some cushions and bedding were soaked through, but on the whole it wasn't as bad as it had first looked. Robbie's mood of optimism increased with every secured locker. He'd just finished wringing out his sleeping bag, and could hear Jack talking to someone up in the cockpit, their words obscured by the slapping of waves against the hull, when *Idler* suddenly gave a little shudder. Jack's head appeared in the hatchway, his eyes shining. 'Things are starting to happen up here, skipper, best you come and see what me and Willie and the lads are up to.'

Robbie came into the cockpit on hands and knees and

wedged himself upright against the coaming, just as *Idler* gave another grinding shudder. Then, despite the anchor lines, she started to gently slew her bows from side to side like a punch-drunk boxer.

'All going to plan, lad,' Jack said seeing the look of alarm on Robbie's face. 'I've got her just about pumped dry, stern lines are off and we'll pick up my old kedge on the way out. I reckon Willie's about ready to take the strain now.' He heaved himself out of the cockpit and made his way forward along the high side of the boat moving easily despite the almost constant movement of the hull. Once on the foredeck he bellowed something incomprehensible at his brother, now back on the little fishing boat, which immediately turned seaward butting into the low swell. In its wake a long bite of dripping rope emerged slowly from the sea, lifting dangling clumps of seaweed here and there along its length like slimy washing on a line. By the time Jack had regained the cockpit, *Idler*'s bows had stopped slewing around and were pointing unwaveringly out to sea. 'Not long now,' he grinned.

Robbie could hear the odd bang and thump from down below as the contents of cupboards and lockers rearranged themselves again with the changing angle.

Jack looked round the cockpit checking everything was in its place, nodded his approval and stroked the tiller. 'She's a fine little boat,' he said, 'you just need to… well, a bit of care and attention and a few repairs here and there and she'd take you anywhere.' He looked wistfully out to sea.

There was another lurch. *Idler* seemed to give herself a good shake and suddenly the deck under their feet was level, rolling gently with only the slightest occasional bump. They both looked out to sea where the towrope had sagged and dipped back below the surface. 'She's afloat,' Jack said quietly.

Robbie forgot about the broken rigging on the deck and the smashed crockery and sodden cushions down below. Just a few hours ago he'd thought *Idler* was gone, and with her everything he owned, however meagre. Now there was hope, something to build on… and he still had a home, however damp. Robbie had a sudden surge of affection and gratitude for this gruff retired fisherman and was reaching for Jack's hand, meaning to shake it, when the tow rope suddenly tautened, *Idler* surged forward and he was sent sprawling to the deck. The old fisherman grinned down at him from his position at the tiller and offered a helping hand. Robbie, still flat on his back, grasped the hand, rough and spatulate, and proceeded to shake it. Jack heaved him to his feet. 'All yours, skipper,' he said and put Robbie's hand on the tiller.

Robbie may have been the "skipper" but in reality it was in name only. It was Jack who coordinated the tow with Willie and who gently nudged the tiller from time to time to keep the tow rope taut. And it was Jack who supervised his brother coming alongside and setting up the complicated system of ropes that held the two boats tightly alongside each other. And as they slipped round the Whitehaven seawall and entered the marina it was Jack at the helm.

Once alongside a floating pontoon and securely tied up, again supervised by Jack, Robbie was left alone as the two brothers wandered off to sort out the formalities. Apparently the marina manager was a friend and all three returned about half an hour later smelling of drink.

Only Jack came back on board. 'Right, lad, that's got you a berth, you can stay as long as you like. Reckon that's me done, Florrie's on her way to pick me up. Been quite a day, eh?'

'I really don't know how I can thank you both.' It was the first time Robbie had been allowed to finish the sentence.

Jack just grunted and picked at callouses on his hands.

'Really, I don't know… would you like a drink?'

Jack looked up from his hands and grinned, then looked along the pontoon. 'It'll take old Florrie a while yet. Don't mind if I do, what yer got?'

They sat companionably in the cockpit as the sun got lost amongst the forest of masts and rigging of neighbouring boats and worked steadily through a half bottle of cheap whisky, which Robbie had salvaged from the below decks' chaos.

'So what are your plans, lad?'

Robbie looked around what was left of his boat. 'Well…' He suddenly stopped and looked at his watch. 'What date is it?'

'Eh?'

'The date, what date is it?'

Jack thought for a moment. 'Um, well, Thursday was the twelfth because I got me piles seen to, so it must be, er, the fifteenth.'

'Christ, it's tomorrow! I've got to be in Keswick tomorrow, I've got an appointment. Is it far?'

'What, you don't know?'

Robbie shook his head.

'Well… should be under an hour by car, bit longer on

the bus. Important, is it?'

'I don't really know.'

Jack shook his head in disbelief, then said, 'You stayin' on board tonight then?'

Robbie glanced at the gloomy companionway and grimaced. 'I suppose so,' he said.

'Plenty of B&Bs in town.'

'Mmm.'

'You skint?'

'Uh huh.'

As Florrie appeared at the end of the pontoon Jack quickly hooked a battered wallet from an inside pocket of his oilskin jacket and thrust a wad of banknotes into Robbie's hand. 'There's 200 there, that'll get you a dry bed, a bit of tea and off to Keswick for your "meeting".'

'No, I can't take that, I mean thank you but…'

'Bring it back when you're ready, you know where we are.' He patted Robbie on the shoulder and climbed onto the pontoon.

'But you don't know me, what if, well…'

Jack grinned down at him and winked. 'Don't you worry, lad… I've always got your boat!'

TWELVE

Claire had woken Dom with a non-too gentle prod and a mug of coffee. 'C'mon, it's the early bird catches the worm, you're in the country now.'

Dom groaned and opened one eye. 'Not worms again, can't we have cornflakes like everyone else?'

Claire threw a pillow over his face and got back into bed. 'It's your big day, remember? "…something to your advantage," I can't wait to see what it is.' She hugged her knees, 'Perhaps you've got a rich aunt.'

Dom heaved himself up against the headboard. 'I have, she lives in the Cotswolds, her cottage has burnt down and she's so scatty it probably wasn't insured.' He sipped his coffee and rubbed his forehead, 'God, what do you feed those pigs?'

Claire snorted. 'Your head's got nothing to do with what you ate, anyway, you know it wasn't one of ours… now. More to do with Dad's whisky, although admittedly you didn't get much choice; people he likes never do.' She leant over and kissed his cheek. 'You were great. And you know what they say…'

'What?'

'You only get one chance to make a good first impression.'

'And did I?'

'Bloody brill!' She kissed him again and leapt out of bed. 'C'mon, let's get going, better leave plenty of time – you might have to push the car again.' She whisked the duvet off the bed exposing a naked Dom, who instinctively cupped his bare genitals with both hands.

Claire smiled down at him and shook her head. 'Silly!'

After ten mud-spattered minutes of heaving the ancient Beetle up and down the potholed track outside the cottage, Dom's whisky-weakened limbs had had enough and Claire took over the pushing herself. It took another five minutes, but one last shove finally bullied the little car into life, and with Claire back in the driver's seat they were on their way. After a few minutes Dom produced the crumpled solicitor's letter and read out the address of the Keswick office given for his meeting. 'No idea,' he said, 'not the same company name as the headed paper though. I suppose they must be borrowing another firm's office or something.'

'Oh, I know where that is, no problem,' Claire said. 'So have you been to Keswick before… oh yes, you said, holidays when you were a kid. With your family, was it?'

'Not exactly, more like a sort of youth camp.'

'Oh yes, we get lots of those in the summer. Scouts or something?'

'No, I seem to remember it was more, sort of Goddy.'

'Ah.' Claire didn't sound particularly surprised. She put her hand on his thigh and chuckled, 'You didn't look very Goddy stretched out on that bed this morning!'

Dom stroked the back of her hand. 'I didn't feel it,' he said, and leant forward over the dashboard to look up at the huge mountain off to their right. He couldn't remember its name.

Claire showed Dom where the solicitor's office was and then took herself off on an unspecified errand for her mother. They had arranged to meet later at a town pub she referred to as "The Woof Bang".

'The what?'

'Woof Bang… The Dog and Gun, obviously, ask anybody.'

* * *

Gavin got back to his own room shortly after dawn, showered, changed and had an early and solitary breakfast at a table in the bar. Then he drove to Keswick, arriving about an hour before his appointed meeting time. After cruising around the outskirts of the town for a while, he eventually chose a street of Victorian villas, which judging by the numerous plaques were largely occupied as short-term holiday lets. Parking was obviously a free-for-all and he found an anonymous and unrestricted space outside a large grey stone house, which was clearly divided into apartments. Parked here, the car would be accepted as that of just one more visitor out on the fells or exploring the town on foot. It shouldn't attract any attention for at least a week, maybe two.

After getting off the bus in Ambleside the previous afternoon Gavin had decided to find somewhere for a drink amongst real people before returning to the prim correctness of his hotel. He found a pub near a busy junction, which was obviously a favourite of walkers and dog owners, who, glasses in hands, had filled the small front yard and were now overflowing out onto the pavement. Gavin threaded his way through the crowd and ducked into a low-ceilinged bar. It was quieter inside than out and he quickly got served, choosing a local ale with an innuendo-laden name, which he took to a quiet corner table. A wall-mounted television flickered in a far corner and with no other distractions Gavin's eyes were inevitably drawn there. It was showing one of the rolling news programmes, a change from football at least, and although the sound was turned down, a sort of ticker tape, red for more urgency, ran continuously across the bottom of the screen. Gavin suddenly froze, his glass still resting on his lower lip. The reporter on the screen was an over-animated young man with vertical hair and a sheaf of notes, which he kept thrusting at the camera. Nothing unusual in that, but it was where he was standing that made Gavin stare; it was the exact spot where he, Gavin, had been standing just a matter of days ago. There was no mistake, the reporter was looking down at the camera from the top step of the bank that Gavin had helped Billy and his gormless son to hold up. Their little "caper" had suddenly, for some reason, caught the attention of the national news people. Gavin focussed hard on the rolling transcript and managed to make out: *...unexpected development..., ...two men helping police with enquiries..., ...further arrests expected...* That was enough, leaving his drink where it was, Gavin turned up the collar of his anorak and forced a way back through the al fresco drinkers and hurried down the hill to his hotel.

'Oh Mr Wheeler, Mr Wheeler…'

Gavin pretended he hadn't heard and kept heading towards the lifts, but missed the doors by a second, and a young, uniformed woman quickly appeared at his shoulder smiling brightly. 'Mr Wheeler, I'm glad I caught you, there were two gentlemen here to see you at lunchtime. They wouldn't leave a message, and said it wasn't important so not to bother mentioning it to you, but I heard them say they'd come back later. I thought you'd like to know.'

Before stuffing his clothes and toiletries into the bag, Gavin carefully peeled back the base lining and removed a passport, a driving license and a wad of credit cards. Gavin Wheeler had checked into the hotel but it was Stephen Chambers who was now checking out.

All Gavin's instincts told him to head for the anonymity of London, and turning out of the hotel car park he'd headed south along the shore of Windermere. Stationary for a moment in traffic, he looked out over the lake at a scattering of moored yachts peacefully riding to their buoys in the evening sunshine, and thought about what had brought him here. He remembered the new mood of optimism he'd felt the evening before while watching the sun set over the mountains, and how the mysterious summons to an unknown solicitor's office in a long-forgotten town had been integral to that, and how it had suddenly taken on a new importance. At the next available lay-by he turned round and headed back north.

As he drove back through Ambleside he wondered who had managed to track him down. Who even knew he was heading for Keswick? Jacko and Bobbie of course, but surely they wouldn't… Billy, but he definitely wouldn't, several car hire firms, but he'd blurred that trail, and then the Shaggy Cracks, but they wouldn't even remember. Then, of course, there was the woman Annie.

Two minutes later he drove past the inn he'd seen her at from the bus window. Why not? He had to stay somewhere and anyway…

'Hello, you again?'

Gavin hadn't seen her sitting in the gloomy alcove by the huge fireplace. She had a nearly empty pint glass in front of her and was holding a book up to the feeble light.

'A coincidence or should I be flattered?'

Gavin gave a wry smile, 'I decided on a change of scenery.'

'At seven o'clock in the bloody evening after a day's walking? You are a restless soul.' She raised a cynical eyebrow and lowered her voice, 'Someone caught up with you?'

Gavin hesitated for a moment then sat down opposite her. 'Let me buy you dinner and I'll tell you the whole story.

* * *

Greg squelched into the reception area of the solicitor's office. He was twenty minutes late, unshaven, generally dishevelled and reeked of red wine. The seat of his trousers and the legs up to the knees were soaking.

He and Martin had slept fitfully, at best. Martin had belatedly remembered the rug at the bottom of the picnic bag and with that and the unused bathing towel wrapped round them, they had at least kept warm. The novelty of disappearing into the shadows to find ever scarcer firewood had soon worn off, and by dawn the fire was nothing more than a dome of powdery ash and a single wisp of smoke. They had woken stiff and damp with dew, the previous evening's excitement and optimism displaced by the reality of their marooning, at least for the time being.

'No breakfast,' Martin said.

'No, and I could do with a… you know.

'Dig a hole,' Martin suggested.

Greg grimaced. 'I think I'll hang on.'

They threaded their way back through the trees to the little beach where they'd initially landed. Each privately nursed a vague idea that just possibly, by some inexplicable miracle, their skiff might have reappeared overnight. It hadn't. A light mist hovered a few feet above the mirrored surface of the lake, dissolving as it rose to meet the brilliant blue of the early morning sky.

Greg stood at the edge of the little beach and looked down through the clear water at the green slimy pebbles on the bottom. 'Do you think it'd be safe to drink?'

'Probably best not,' Martin said.

'Haven't we got *anything* left?'

Martin rummaged in the bags while Greg scanned the lake for signs of life. 'We can't just stay here, we need to get home – oh God, Derek! And I ought to get to this meeting.'

'I know, I know,' Martin snapped and tipped the contents of the picnic bag out onto the gravel beach.

'A boat, there's a boat!' Greg started flapping his arms up and down in what was, although he didn't know it, a universal signal of maritime distress. 'Hey!' Greg yelled. The shape in the boat turned, seemed to study them for a minute then gave a perfunctory wave and disappeared into the mist. Few trout fishermen in the Lakes are familiar with international distress signals. Greg gave a last yell and threw a pebble after the fading shape.

'I've found a scotch egg,' Martin said, squatting amongst the picnic debris.

'Scotch egg!'

'Why not? Think of it as a neat way of eating bacon and egg.'

'Yeah, but cold,' Greg took the cellophane package, 'and it's haggis!'

'Oh sorry but we're right out of porridge and kedgeree. Don't be so picky, do you want some or not?'

Greg nodded sulkily. 'Anything to drink?'

'Red wine, half a bottle.'

'For breakfast!'

'Take it or leave it.'

Greg took it and promptly choked. 'Another boat,' he spluttered, 'there, a sail.' He thrust the wine bottle at Martin and started flapping again.

The dinghy sailor may or may not have been familiar with distress signals but either way it didn't matter because to the castaways' relief the little boat came ghosting in towards their beach. About ten yards out it changed direction, the sails flapped limply and the boat stopped.

'Morning.' A whiskery face and red knitted hat appeared under the boom. 'Won't come any nearer, too many damn rocks. You fellas OK? Not really meant to stay on the island, you know.'

'We were stranded.'

'Oh, well that's different then.'

The sailor cheerfully agreed to give them a lift back to Keswick but, he explained, they'd have to wade out to him. And it was going to be a bit cramped on board, he said, she wasn't really built for this sort of load. And there wasn't much wind so it would be a slow crossing, but never mind, eh, it was a lovely morning and they weren't in a hurry were they?

'Well actually…'

'We'll see what we can do,' the sailor said happily.

An hour and a half later they didn't seem to have done very much. Greg and Martin were squeezed together on a narrow wooden bench, sitting in a puddle created by their clumsy boarding. The sailor, who was now puffing at a foul-smelling pipe, had asked them not to move as it would affect "the trim", whatever that was, so as well as wet, itchy backsides they now both had cramp. Greg tried to alleviate his by wiggling his wet toes and rocking forward with little thrusting movements, willing the boat onwards.

Martin risked cricking his neck to talk to the sailor: 'Um, are you expecting any more wind at all, at any time?'

'Nooo, shouldn't think so.' The sailor exhaled a huge cloud of smoke at the drooping mainsail.

Martin sighed. 'That's a shame, I think we're going to be very late.' The remark was addressed to Greg but loud enough to ensure the sailor heard it too.

'Yes, a real shame,' Greg said, taking his cue.

'Urgent is it?' the sailor said after a brief pause and a couple of thoughtful puffs. 'S'pose we could get the engine out,' he said reluctantly.

'You've got an engine?'

Ten minutes later the little boat putted and flapped to a halt alongside a low jetty extending out from Keswick beach. There were hurried thanks and goodbyes, then Martin set off to collect the car and inevitable parking ticket before heading home to salvage their business, while Greg dashed off into the town to look for a public toilet and the solicitor's office.

* * *

It was the change in pitch that eventually woke Robbie. The persistent purring of his phone had failed to cut through the dense fog of sleep, but after a couple of minutes the device had helpfully vibrated itself across the bedside cabinet and started rattling against the empty water glass. The higher tone eventually succeeded in penetrating the combined effects of exhaustion, relief and alcohol, which had tipped Robbie into a coma-like sleep the night before.

After Jack had ambled off down the pontoon, Robbie had collected together some of his drier possessions from *Idler*'s battered saloon, secured her as best as he could and wandered the early evening streets of Whitehaven looking for one of the promised B&Bs. Exhausted, he'd settled quickly on a narrow, bay-fronted terraced villa just a few streets back from the harbour side. It proved to be just as shabby inside as out, but seemed clean, comfortable and friendly. He partially unpacked his bags, draped some of his damper clothing on the cold radiators and ventured back out into the town in search of a meal, "a bit of tea" as Jack had put it. A few streets away, after following his nose, Robbie found a cheerful-looking Indian restaurant. The decor was flock and fish-tank, the music more drum machine than sitar and the generic curry sauce would undoubtedly come out of a jar, but it was quiet and he found the lazy meanderings of the fish soothing. He ordered far too much food, drank far too much lager and red wine and by closing time had become the best friend of the waiter. The young man had confided that he was in the country illegally but it was OK because he was going to play football for Manchester United. Robbie said that seemed like a sound career move, forgot to leave a tip and wandered off into the night to look for his guest house. Once he'd found it and tackled the stairs and door lock, sleep had come quickly.

Almost fully conscious, Robbie checked the phone and found he had twenty pounds of credit and a message from Sylvia. The message was short and businesslike; in his hurry to leave, as Sylvia dryly put it, he'd left the solicitor's letter behind and she thought she'd better remind him of the timing and the address in Keswick. Robbie realised he only had a couple of hours and skipped shaving and showering, dressed quickly and dashed down to the breakfast room. He still had no clear idea how he was going to get to Keswick. While helping himself to the usual buffet array he tried to attract the attention of the only waitress, a girl of about twelve as far as Robbie could judge, who was exchanging shrieks and giggles with the only other visible guest, a plump, pinkish young man in shorts and near hysterics. The girl looked up and caught Robbie's eye. He waved, she waved back, the young man squealed and the girl collapsed in another fit of giggles. During a pause in the merriment Robbie coughed loudly through a mouthful of cereal and the girl took the hint and ambled over.

'Black pudding's off,' she said by way of greeting.

'Good,' Robbie said, 'can't stand the stuff.'

The girl giggled and Robbie ordered the full Cumbrian, or what was available of it, and dropped hints that he was in a hurry.

'Got plans then?' the girl asked.

Robbie explained he had to get to Keswick, and added that he had no idea how at the moment.

The girl glanced at her watch. 'You might make the nine fifty-five,' she said doubtfully, 'but probably best get the ten o eight. Have to change at Workington of course, but it's quicker, or perhaps if you...' She seemed to have an encyclopaedic knowledge of the bus timetable. 'I goes a lot,' she explained, adding proudly, 'got a boyfriend there. Doing all right he is, bought me this.' She jiggled her right wrist at him and Robbie caught a glimpse of a tarnished gold bangle.

'Very pretty,' he said, 'I'll have to get one for my girlfriend.' Robbie handed her back the menu and looked pointedly at the kitchen door.

'What, you got a girlfriend?'

'Yees,' Robbie said slowly.

'But you're so… oh, I get it, go on then, wha's her name?' she demanded, playing along with what she obviously thought was a joke.

'Er, Sylvia.'

The girl looked at him closely for a moment. 'What, for real?'

Robbie nodded.

'Hmm,' the girl still sounded doubtful. 'Bit old-fashioned,' she said finally.

Inexplicably, Robbie found himself apologising.

'So is she a *proper* girlfriend?'

Robbie hesitated. 'As far as I can tell, yes.'

'So you still… you know, *it*?'

Robbie leant round the twelve-year-old and looked desperately towards the kitchen door. 'Shame there's no black pudding but I'd still like…'

There was the loud "ping" of an impatiently slapped bell from the kitchen. Robbie sighed with relief as his tormentor reluctantly broke off and headed for the swing door.

Following his breakfast-time instructions, Robbie had just made the ten o eight bus and was enjoying the meandering journey across north-west Cumbria, when he found himself fingering the phone in his pocket. For no obvious reason his mood darkened and a sudden icy stab of loneliness prompted a curious kind of home-sickness; for where he didn't know. He had a sudden urge to hear Sylvia's voice and took out the phone. He didn't know what he'd say but started to dial anyway; he would thank her for her message, and the twenty pounds of credit, and… well he'd see. But there was no answer and Robbie arrived in Keswick inexplicably miserable and with only ten minutes to locate the solicitor's office.

* * *

'My client is a Mrs Bethany Morrell. She is a lady of some means, as you will see.' He indicated the envelope on the blotter with an arm of his glasses. 'She may also be considered by some to be, shall we say, somewhat unconventional,' He clearly counted himself among this number and coughed at his own indiscretion, 'melodramatic even.' He pushed the envelope across the desk. 'Please open it.'

Inside were five crisp fifty-pound notes and an unsigned cheque for £50,000.

'My client has requested, and she has stressed that this is not a condition, although I would suggest it would be wise to consider it as so, that you meet her personally, at which juncture that cheque will be signed by a representative of this firm.' He returned his glasses to the tip of his nose, peered over them and steepled his fingers. 'There is a mountain near here, I'm told...' his tone suggested he disapproved of mountains, '...called "Blencathra".' He swivelled his head, still peering over the glasses, to seek confirmation from a fidgety young man sitting slightly behind him and to his right.

'About five miles away, Mr Cockleweed.'

The older man frowned; his junior had not been invited to speak, a nod was what had been required. 'Quite,' he said coldly and turned back to the desk. 'My client has *suggested* that you meet her on the summit at twelve noon tomorrow, assuming you are willing and able, when and where' – he nodded at the cheque – 'a signature will be affixed and she will personally explain her reasoning and motives for this...' He was apparently lost for a word and fluttered his hand impatiently. 'Please do not press me on the matter,' he sniffed, 'my client has not seen fit to take me into her confidence. I myself will not be present but Mr Clarke here has assured me that he is capable of completing such a task.' He looked doubtfully at the slightly podgy young man who beamed and nodded happily. 'Assuming you agree, Mr Clarke and our client will meet you, along with three others, assuming they also agree, on the summit of this Blencathra at noon tomorrow.' He took off his glasses and polished them vigorously on his tie. 'Most irregular, melodramatic silliness,' he muttered. 'Assuming you accept this, er, *suggestion,* and I have no alternative instructions if you do not, then Mr Clarke tells me he is willing to act as a guide if required, but in any case, on his advice, these have been provided to aid you.' He opened a drawer and took out a yellow covered map and a neat little pocket book. 'Map,' he said unnecessarily, 'and a guide book.' He turned it towards him and huffed, 'by a chap called Alfred Wainwright, now there's a... anyway.' He tapped the cover. 'I gather Mr Clarke has indicated a suggested route and he assures me the weather tomorrow will be clement, but I'm told proper equipment is advised; sturdy shoes, umbrellas and the like, I dare say. The cash has been provided for that purpose, although I really cannot think that such a sum is...' He finished with a series of tuts, shaking his head at the profligacy.

This was essentially the way each meeting had gone for the four interviewees. The conversation had varied slightly for each, as had the reactions to the contents of the envelope, but all questions had been rebuffed and requests to be accompanied by a partner or companion had been strongly discouraged, with heavily veiled hints of potential embarrassment.

Dom, Gavin, Greg and Robbie, whatever other emotions they were now experiencing, were left more intrigued than ever. They had all accepted.

* * *

Dom found Claire at a small round table tucked away in what would have been called the chimney corner in an earlier age. She had a glass of red wine in front of her and was reading *Farming Weekly*, her face a picture of concentration.

'Get yer a drink, luv?' Dom said in a rough impression of a south London accent.

'No, push off,' Claire said without looking up.

'Charming,' Dom said in his usual voice.

Claire looked up and grinned. 'Oh, it's my bit of southern rough. You look pleased with yourself, tell all.'

'I'll get us a drink, you look at that, it's a bit more interesting than fertilizer ads.' He carefully placed the envelope on top of her magazine and turned to the bar.

Claire looked flushed when Dom got back to the table. 'What on earth have you done to get that?' She studied his face closely. 'It is… you know, legal, is it?'

Dom picked up the cheque and looked at it again. 'As

far as I know,' he said, and explained the "non-condition" of climbing Blencathra on the following day. 'That's when I'll get the full story, presumably. And the cheque signed.'

'Bizarre,' was Claire's judgement. Then after a large sip, 'It's all a bit... well, unlikely, isn't it?' Dom agreed. 'So will you go?'

'I don't see I've got much choice,' Dom said, now fingering the fifty-pound notes. 'Meantime,' he wafted one of the notes under her nose, 'lunch is on me.'

They sat almost touching, leant into each other over the battered lid of a reclaimed school desk, all four elbows propped amongst the litter of small clay bowls, which a short time before had been full of steaming Spanish *tapas*. Each held a large glass of red wine before them as if for inspection. Claire swirled hers. 'So what are you going to spend it on then?' she demanded.

Dom swirled too. 'Thought I'd treat myself to a divorce.'

* * *

Gavin's "interview" had taken a little longer than the other three. He had opened his envelope, considered its contents dispassionately for a moment then made a request that caused considerable consternation in the stuffy atmosphere. The openly suspicious solicitor had waffled legalese for a few moments, exchanged meaningful looks with his assistant, to whom they obviously meant nothing, and finally stalked into an adjoining room to "consult with his client".

He returned, obviously put out, and with undisguised

reluctance painstakingly wrote out another cheque, this one made out to the name Gavin had requested. Before the ink had dried he nodded to his assistant to pick it up from the blotter, as if not wanting to risk further contamination himself. Gavin, who had sat still and stony-faced through this performance, couldn't help a wry smile as the solicitor pointedly waited for him to slide the original back across the desk, only then indicating that his assistant should hand over the replacement.

Gavin had intended to head straight for London after the meeting with vague ideas of somehow getting back to Spain to see what could be salvaged of his business, but the sudden and unexpected possibility of banking fifty thousand pounds made all the difference. It was a long time since he'd been forced to think about money; in recent years it had just always been there, and plenty of it. But now, after the debacle in Spain and without Jacko and his computer at his side, Gavin realised he had no idea whether he was even solvent. He had no way of knowing how much his treacherous aide had skimmed off, or what had been confiscated or frozen by the authorities, or for that matter, how much Bobbie had helped herself to on her way out the door. Gavin could sense a net closing in around him, cast from one side of the law or the other, and he knew it made sense to present a moving target, but fifty thousand pounds was a lot of money, and probably worth a lot more to him now than say, three months ago. He decided to risk another twenty-four hours in Cumbria.

Wandering the streets of Keswick in outdoor gear with a rucksack over one shoulder and a holdall in hand,

Gavin looked like many other visitors to the town, but he decided it was time to get off the streets. He walked the length of the main street, shunning the big, busy tourist hotels, before finally locating a vaguely remembered, old-fashioned coaching inn tucked away off the main drag. It had been one of his under-age drinking haunts and judging by the clientele hadn't changed much. They had no problem finding him a room and promised his bags would be safe behind the bar until it was ready.

He drifted into the oak-panelled bar and settled into a red velour corner with a drink, which remained untouched while he thought; why should a complete stranger, someone he'd never heard of, or knowingly met, suddenly want to give him a very large sum of money simply for climbing a mountain?

* * *

The kitchen table was littered with screwed-up bits of paper, scribbled sheets of figures and bank statements. In amongst this debris were several half-drunk cups of coffee and Martin's elbows. With chin rested on cupped hands he looked miserably thoughtful, which is how Greg found him when he shouldered his way through the back door later that afternoon.

Martin straightened up and managed a smile. 'Hi, how'd it go?'

Greg placed a battered cardboard box on a chair. 'You all right?'

Martin's smile faded. 'I'm afraid we've got a problem.'

'Oh God, what's he done now?'

'What, who? Oh, you mean Derek, no, nothing… well, the cat's gone missing and Lisa is threatening to sue for sexual harassment but apart from that.'

'What! Sue *us*?'

'No, no, only Derek, apparently he put his… oh never mind.' Martin scooped up a pile of statements and tapped them edgewise on the table. 'I've been doing some number crunching.'

'So I see. You don't look very happy.'

'By some miracle I managed to get through to a human being at the bank, almost wish I hadn't. Did you know we had a "relationship manager"?'

'I didn't even know they did marriage guidance, I thought it was just money stuff.'

'Be serious, I've been working really hard at this.'

Greg patted him on the shoulder, 'I can see that, The Pitcairn?'

'Yes,' Martin nodded, and reached up and squeezed the hand still on his shoulder. 'But I must admit, I'm really struggling to make it work. She was very vague, but Harmony…'

'Harmony! How can anyone with a name like that work for a bank?'

'Yeah, I know, but anyway, she wasn't exactly encouraging.' Martin started stabbing at the pile of statements with a pencil until the point broke. 'What's that?'

Greg had lifted the box onto the table. He reached inside and produced a scuffed leather box with brass catches and hinges, then opened it to reveal a complicated looking instrument of brass, mirrors, lenses and knurled knobs, nestling in a moulded bed of faded purple velvet. 'It's a sextant, I saw it in a window in Cockermouth and went back for it.'

'What on earth for?'

'It's for the Bounty Bar.'

Martin sighed heavily.

'And so's this.' The solicitor's cheque joined the pile of papers on the table.

Martin glanced at it and froze. 'Oh my god, Gigi!'

* * *

Robbie was shaking when he emerged from the solicitor's office and needed both bannisters to negotiate the stairs. He'd barely uttered a word during the meeting, struck dumb by the contents of the envelope, and had to be prompted to confirm his willingness to attend the next day's extraordinary rendezvous, mutely nodding his agreement. Regaining the pavement he thrust a disbelieving hand back into his inside pocket and tried to re-count the bank notes without taking them out.

'Excuse me!' A large woman towing a shopping trolley and gnawing on some sort of pastie in a paper bag forced herself past Robbie.

'Oh sorry.' He took a couple of steps away from the middle of the pavement and collided painfully with a concrete litter bin.

'Hello, Robbie.'

Robbie looked up from the shin he was rubbing. 'Sylvia! When… how…?'

'First thing, plane and hire car. I thought you might

need this.' Sylvia held out the crumpled solicitor's letter. Robbie took it and smiled uncertainly. He knew that she knew he didn't need the letter.

Sylvia led the way back to the car park in silence.

'So, what are we doing, Robbie, where are we going? I mean, the airport, the marina, where?' They were sat in the stationary car, Sylvia gripping the steering wheel looking straight ahead.

'Would you like to see *Idler*?'

'Yes, yes, I would, we can talk on the way.' She turned in her seat belt and smiled at him for the first time.

On the way back to Whitehaven, Robbie told Sylvia about the meeting, as much as he could recall. He described the office and the Dickensian solicitor and the chubby clerk called Clarke (another Sylvia smile) and he told her how he was going to climb Blencathra, which actually made her laugh.

'But why? What's it all about, and all this stuff about "to your advantage"?'

Robbie slipped his hand into the inside pocket. 'We haven't been told everything yet, we're meant to find out tomorrow, but there is something else. I'll tell you, or rather show you, in a minute. Probably best we're parked. Just follow the one-way system round…'

'Fifty thousand pounds!'

'Fifty thousand, two hundred and fifty,' Robbie corrected, fanning out the five notes.

They were sitting in the saloon of *Idler* nursing cardboard beakers of cardboard coffee, the acclaimed "aroma" of which, was no competition for the pervasive smell of diesely bilge water and damp upholstery.

Sylvia couldn't conceal her shock when she saw the state of the boat, inside and out. 'It's a miracle you weren't hurt.' Robbie nodded and rubbed his left knee, then his elbow. 'Well, not too badly anyway,' she added. It was her warmest smile yet. 'And that,' she nodded at the cheque on the saloon table, 'will that be enough for all this?' She waved a hand at the wrecked interior of *Idler*.

'Plenty, I think, with some left over.'

'Good, I'm pleased.'

They sat in silence for a moment fiddling with the coffee cartons.

'You wanted to talk about us, I think,' Robbie said suddenly.

Sylvia was taken by surprise. 'Yes, that would be good. It's why I'm here really, you'd probably guessed that. The letter was, well…'

Robbie took her hand and squeezed it gently. 'I know.' Still holding her hand he stood up and tentatively kissed her on the cheek. 'Do you mind if we talk on the way?'

Sylvia looked startled. 'To where?'

'It's a place called St Bees, there's something I need to do there.' He kissed her again. 'Oh yes, and I need a florist. And some boots.'

THIRTEEN

The Cumbrian weather proved to be predictably unpredictable and by mid-morning the upper slopes of Blencathra were windswept and damp with fast-moving banks of clammy cloud regularly blurring the full extent of the summit plateau. An occasional burst of watery sunshine highlighted the few figures dotted around the peak, some crouched in the lee of any natural windbreak, others standing, hopefully looking into the ever-changing, cloudy middle distance.

Gavin was one of the crouchers. He'd set off intentionally early but found the climb surprisingly easy, if tedious, and reached the top with plenty of time to scout around. He soon found what he was looking for, a well-screened vantage point from where, visibility allowing, he hoped to spot his fellow travellers as they appeared at the top of the recommended route. He had no idea how he'd identify them, who they might be, or what could connect him to them, but at least now if he sensed any threat or trap he was ideally positioned to disappear back into the mist and down the mountain.

Greg's appearance at the top of the path gave Gavin a shock. Presumably unaware of just how close he was to the summit, Greg had paused for breath just yards short of the final ridge, then turning his back to the wind had swept his hood from his face and was now looking directly towards Gavin's lair. Greg had worn well over the years, something he was aware of in his vainer moments and reminded of occasionally when Martin wanted to flatter or reassure. Gavin was sure he knew this man, but from where, and when, and was he a threat? After a moment, and unaware of this scrutiny, Greg turned away, gave his rucksack straps a shrug and regained the path, leaving a confused and worried Gavin scouring his memory to try and find Greg's place in his past. He was sure it was many years ago, school perhaps, or maybe an early client or distant family friend, but whichever, something wasn't right and had to be more than coincidence. Someone, for some reason he couldn't even begin to fathom, had engineered some sort of meeting involving at least one person from Gavin's past. According to the solicitor there should be four of them, so assuming the owner of the familiar face was one, there were two more to come. Would he recognise them too? Gavin wondered whether to go back to the summit and see if anything was going on, but with half an hour still to go before the appointed hour he decided to stay where he was and resume his watch.

Dom had struggled. It hadn't taken him long to realise just how unfit he was, and about an hour into the climb, a tedious zigzag slog, he'd even given some serious thought to turning back. But the solicitor had been ambiguous, to say the least, about the chances of getting that cheque signed if he didn't turn up on the top of the mountain – could he really risk it? And then he thought of Claire sitting patiently waiting for him in the Keswick pub and her excitement in the little restaurant the day before, and he smiled to himself, put back his shoulders and set off uphill.

Gavin couldn't be sure, the crumpled figure had been hunched over into a high collar like a sulking turtle, and what he could see of the face was blotched and distorted by panting, but there was something there, a vague familiarity. Let the face regain a more natural colour, lose the jowls and add a bit of hair to the temples and it could be... who? Gavin had no idea but thought it might just be someone, like the other guy, someone he'd once known. This was almost too much for him; with suspicions whirling around in his head he seriously considered forfeiting the fifty thousand pounds and just getting the hell out of there. But fifty grand... and he still couldn't see the angle. It didn't make sense, anyone wanting to make a move on him wouldn't need to go to all this trouble and expense. He looked at his watch. Another ten minutes wouldn't make any difference one way or the other; he'd sit it out, keep watching, and then make a final decision at the last minute.

In fact Gavin had already missed Robbie. He'd passed unnoticed about ten minutes earlier, just another blurred outline stumbling through a particularly dense patch of mist and apparently part of a loud group of young men who'd happened to be overtaking him at that point. With companions effectively banned by the solicitor Gavin had been concentrating on solitary walkers.

At two minutes to twelve Gavin made his decision. He emerged stiffly from his craggy lookout and headed up the path towards the summit plateau.

Greg was sitting on his rucksack near the edge, sipping tepid coffee from a small flask and watching the mist swirl around the knife-edged ridge at his feet, which rose to meet the peak. The exertion of the climb had distracted him, but he was starting to get nervous now, and without realising it was twiddling the zipper tag on the pocket that held the unsigned cheque. God, he hoped this was for real. The appearance of the cheque on their kitchen table had with one fortuitous stroke filled the void in Martin's calculations and brought all their plans within the realms of possibility. Greg had never seen Martin so excited, and the thought of having to slink home empty-handed to admit the whole thing had been some kind of scam or elaborate practical joke was just too much for him to contemplate. Surely it couldn't be; after all, the solicitors had seemed real enough and…

'Excuse me.'

Greg started and looked up, slightly alarmed.

Gavin, realising he was towering over the other man, squatted down to bring them more or less face to face. He peeled back his hood and smiled. 'I… er, think I noticed you coming up the path. Have we met somewhere before, maybe a long time ago? You look, well, familiar.' He studied Greg's face closely, almost to the point of rudeness.

Greg instinctively pulled back but a brief inspection of Gavin's tanned face was enough to convince him that at some time, somewhere, he and this man *had* met before. And he agreed with Gavin, whenever it was, it was a long time ago. Greg delved cautiously into his memory. Which chapter of his life could it have been from: school perhaps, or that youth club his parents had made him go to, or one of the many other clubs that came later… before he'd met Martin? 'I think you're right,' he said, 'but for the life of me… sorry.'

Gavin dismissed the apology with a shake of his head. 'I'm sure of it now, just can't place you.' He smiled again. 'I guess names might help, I'm…' he hesitated for a moment, '…I'm Gavin Wheeler.' He held out his hand.

Greg looked thoughtful then took it. 'Greg, Greg Barnes. And your name does ring a bell.'

'I think yours might too. Look, are you here because some firm of solicitors asked you to be, with the promise of…' Gavin's habitual wariness kicked in, '…well, an inducement?'

'Yes, yes, I am.' Greg flicked away the dregs of his coffee, screwed the top back on the flask and scrambled to his feet. 'Do you know what it's all about? I'm worried it might just be some sort of stupid scam, but now you're here too…' They both turned as a bulky figure in ill-fitting waterproofs approached through the thin mist.

'Um, excuse me', it was a cultivated Home Counties accent, 'I've been waiting over there and couldn't help noticing you. You seemed to be introducing yourselves – sorry if I was staring – it's just that I'm expecting to meet up with some strangers here too, and was just wondering whether you might be here because...' Dom hesitated and looked from one to the other realising how ridiculous his next statement was going to sound, 'well, because some solicitors asked you and promised "something to your advantage".' He shrugged. 'Probably a complete con and waste of time but...'

'Well, if it is, then all three of us have been had.' Gavin put out his hand again. 'Ste... Gavin Wheeler, welcome to our magical mystery tour, and this is...'

'Greg, Greg Barnes.' Greg moved forward, hand outstretched, and peered under the peak of Dom's hood. 'We think we've met before,' he said, nodding towards Gavin without taking his eyes off Dom's face, 'and do you know, I think I've seen you somewhere before as well. What colour was your hair before... when it was fuller?'

Dom removed his hood to reveal thinning light brown hair with some unprotected wisps plastered to his temples.

'It is you! Don't tell me, it's... Ron, no, Don.'

'Dom, Dominic Cartwright,' Dom said, not sure whether to be pleased or not at being almost remembered.

'So where was it we met?' Greg shook his head in frustration.

Gavin looked at his watch. 'Ten past, that solicitor bloke was meant to be here by now to, you know, complete the business. And there's meant to be four of us isn't there?'

'I just want to find out what's going on, get the thing signed and get down off here,' Greg said. It was the first time any of them had referred directly to the cheques and glances were exchanged.

'There's someone else over there.' The summit was unusually empty, even allowing for the weather, and there was just one other figure visible. He or she seemed to be looking intently in their direction, and as they stared, started moving slowly towards them.

'Doesn't look like the solicitor, not fat enough,' Dom said, his disappointment obvious.

Robbie approached hesitantly and stopped a few yards short of the group. 'Are you here for a meeting?' he demanded. He hadn't enjoyed the climb, his waterproofs weren't, and his new boots were pinching in more places than he could count. He swayed slightly, easing his weight from one foot to the other.

It was Dom who replied. 'With a solicitor? Yes, we are, at least we hope we are. You too?'

Robbie nodded. 'Yes. It really is going to happen then, is it?'

'We don't know any more than you,' Gavin said. 'Just told to be here at twelve to meet that clerk bloke from the solicitor's office, when all would be explained and…' Gavin still couldn't bring himself to refer directly to the payment, '…things would be signed off. We've been hanging around for a while now and there's no sign… you've got to wonder, haven't you?' He looked at his watch again, 'I'll give them ten minutes then I'm off.'

Greg had been distracted during this exchange, mentally placing Dom and Gavin in all sorts of situations to see where they fitted into his memories. He thought there might be something about this latest addition to the group too, but wasn't so sure. 'What's your name?' he demanded. It came out more aggressively than he'd meant. 'Er, sorry, I'm Greg Barnes.' He held out his hand.

They all listened as Robbie introduced himself.

'Cox-Robinson, I know that name,' Dom said thoughtfully. 'We're fairly sure we've all met before,' he explained. 'What do you think? A long time ago,' he added.

Robbie looked from one to another. 'How long?'

'No idea,' Greg said. 'If we could remember that, it might explain why we're all here. There must be something to connect us.'

They started by discussing schools, but it turned out they'd all been raised in different parts of the country and couldn't have met there. It was the same with universities, and in later years they'd all pursued different careers and hobbies so there was no workplace, team or club to connect them. There didn't appear to be any common denominator.

'It's quarter to one,' Greg said suddenly, interrupting the debate. He thought of Martin waiting at home with all his plans and dreams. 'They're not bloody coming, are they?' He fingered the pocket zipper miserably. 'It's a bloody scam!' he burst out 'I knew it was, they've got us up here, God knows why, and now...' He petered out in near despair; he didn't know what now.

No one said anything for a moment, all trying to make sense of the situation and nursing their respective disappointments.

Gavin glanced unnecessarily at his watch. 'I think you're right, we've been stood up.' He picked up his rucksack and started slipping into the straps. 'Next stop that fucking solicitor's office.'

Dom gave a resigned sigh but didn't move. 'But why?'

'I bloody near got killed getting here,' Robbie said bitterly. The others looked at him. 'Nearly drowned,' he explained, 'and more than once!'

'I've picked up a divorce on the way,' Dom said, 'and hard to believe, I know, but I jumped off a moving train. On the other hand though…' he added thoughtfully.

'I had a baby,' Greg said proudly. 'Well sort of, it's a long story. Then we ended up stranded on an island overnight and decided to buy a hotel.' He fingered his pocket zip. 'Or at least we might.'

They all looked at Gavin. 'You don't want to know,' he said, adjusting his rucksack, 'but a bank and a drug-crazed punk band come into it.' He thought of Annie. 'And a chimp rescue centre. Let's leave it at that,' he grinned, despite himself.

No one moved, even Gavin who was already reconsidering the wisdom of a showdown in a solicitor's office. None of them was quite able to bring themselves to leave; to leave would be to abandon all hope, it would be over.

'Hang on, there's someone over there.' Dom couldn't hide his excitement. 'Oh it's a woman,' he added, his voice flat with disappointment.

'There's meant to be a woman, isn't there?' Greg said, 'something about their client.'

'You're right, and she's coming over.'

'Gentlemen, can't apologise enough, bloody tough mountain…' A fit of coughing cut off the end of the apology.

They all turned at the sound of the rasping voice. Distracted by the approaching woman none of them had heard the little clerk scrambling up behind them, and now, as they watched, he suddenly bent double, still gasping hoarsely, and stayed there for what seemed like a long time.

'Do you think he's all right?' Greg said quietly to no one in particular. His concern was understandable – the clerk's plump face was a livid shade of red, the eyes and nose were running and the jowls were wobbling with the effort of breathing. But the voice, when it came, had steadied. 'So sorry, bloody tough,' he repeated. 'Been training for weeks taking the stairs down the Tube but it's not the same, is it?' He managed to straighten up and catch a few deep breaths. 'Apologies again and thank you for waiting.' He coughed and sniffed wetly. 'And all here, I see,' he added, nodding his approval. 'Ah, and here's my client.' He was looking past the four men and they all turned to see the woman a few yards away.

The clerk positioned himself next to the woman and fiddled with a clipboard he'd taken from his rucksack. The woman had yet to speak but carefully studied the four men now standing before her, and they in turn appraised her; a slight figure under the bulky walking gear, she looked to be about thirty with light brown hair and gentle grey eyes, which seemed to be smiling even when her mouth wasn't.

'Ahem.' The clerk cleared his throat and tapped at his clipboard; this was clearly his moment. 'Mrs Morrell, these are the gentlemen you asked us to trace, er, contact, and gather together.' He consulted the clipboard. 'And we have... and excuse me if I can't put names to faces, never could, hopeless, anyway, in no particular order,' he chuckled, '...we have a Mr Cartwright.' Dom had to stop himself barking a schoolboy "here" and instead raised his hand slightly and said a quiet "hello".

'...then we have Mr Cox-Robinson.' Robbie made a sort of Native American "how" gesture.

'...then Mr Wheeler...' the clerk cleared his throat again, '...or Chambers.' Gavin nodded.

'...and finally, and I'm sure by no means least,' the clerk chuckled again, 'a Mr Barnes.' Greg smiled and mouthed "hello".

'Now, I've got no idea what this is about either,' the clerk burbled happily, 'so I'll let Mrs Morrell enlighten us all. If that's OK with you, Mrs Morrell,' he added quickly.

The woman ignored this last obsequiousness. 'Hello, my name is Bethany Morrell.' Her voice was deep for a woman and slightly hoarse. 'You're probably all wondering...' she was obviously very nervous and there was a long pause, '... well firstly, thank you, thank you all so much for coming.' She sounded like an inexperienced hostess welcoming friends and family to a celebration or party and didn't seem to know what to say next. The little clerk coughed for attention and she turned to him, clearly grateful for the interruption. 'Ah yes, Mr Clarke, perhaps before anything else you would...' She gestured at the clipboard.

The clerk beamed and nodded his head. 'By all means.' He produced a pen from an inside pocket like a magician with a bouquet of paper flowers. 'Gentlemen, I'm sure you've all brought the requisite paperwork.' He gave a knowing chuckle and there was an excited gleam in his eyes; he probably didn't get to sign cheques totalling two hundred thousand pounds very often. He held out his hand to Robbie who was nearest. 'Let me complete the process.'

Robbie fumbled in the pockets of the unfamiliar anorak and produced his cheque which the clerk smoothed out on the clipboard and signed with a flourish. Dom, Gavin and Greg followed, with only Gavin resisting a surreptitious glance before tucking his cheque away again.

Bethany watched the process impassively. No one, least of all the four men now standing looking at her curiously, would have guessed that in the last few minutes she'd given away nearly quarter of a million pounds to four complete strangers. The clerk magicked his pen away, snapped the clipboard shut and looked at his client expectantly. It was his reluctant acknowledgement that his part in the drama was now over.

Bethany took a deep breath. 'Again, thank you for coming, not just all the way up here,' she indicated the now empty summit, 'but up here to Cumbria. I'm told it's been a long way for some of you, I hope you feel it's been worth it.' She paused and looked at the four men one at a time, then gave a small smile and continued, her voice strengthening with every sentence. 'You must be wondering why I've gone to so much trouble to trace and contact you all – or at least Mr Clarke's firm has on my behalf – and then to ask you to meet me in these rather unusual circumstances. I'm sorry if it's all seemed rather mysterious up to now but I hope you'll understand. And this…' she swept her hand around, 'this must all seem a bit, well, melodramatic, but somehow it seems appropriate and I even hoped it might jog some memories. That needs some explaining.' She looked at the four very different expressions on the faces ranged in front of her and gave a nervous laugh, 'I've got quite a lot of explaining to do, haven't I?'

No one said anything.

Bethany's eyes rested on each face for a few seconds and she knew the time had come.

'Gentlemen, I asked you to come here because… because I believe that one of you is my father.'

The silence was eventually broken by the rasping cry of a crow which came skimming up the mountainside and whirled over the summit. Gavin and Dom both turned to watch it and the spell seemed broken.

'Well…' It was the solicitor's clerk.

Greg just stared at the woman open-mouthed.

Robbie shook his head in apparent disbelief, or denial: 'What on earth makes you think one of us…' He just finished with a shrug.

Dom turned back to the group and cleared his throat as if preparing to speak but didn't.

'…just madness,' Robbie continued, 'it's like something out of a crap movie.'

Greg came out of his trance. 'I knew it, I just knew it. This whole thing was always going to be something… unbelievable.'

'I should explain.'

Gavin spun round and glared at Bethany. 'Yes, I think you bloody should.' He turned his attention to the clerk. 'Is this some kind of a joke, a stitch-up?' The clerk went wide-eyed and started to mouth soundlessly. Gavin patted his pocket. 'And this had better be real.'

'It most certainly is,' Bethany snapped, 'and no, this is not a joke.' She looked at him steadily for several moments.

'Go on then,' Gavin said eventually.

Bethany nodded. 'OK. It might sound extraordinary but this is how we got here. My mother had me when she was very young, she was unmarried and never told anyone who my father was, including me. Many years ago you were all friends of my mother. You probably don't remember now but you did all know her. Her name was Mary Wainwright.' She paused for them to think about this.

Greg slowly raised a finger and tapped himself on the temple. 'I remember that name, and I remember her, a pretty girl.' He glanced at Bethany and gave a little nod, 'and it was here… that's it!' He spun round to face Dom, Robbie and Gavin. 'That's it, that's where we've met, it was here at that weird camp by the lake in Keswick, when we were kids. You remember, with the church and youth club people, canoeing and sailing and walking and stuff… and the dodgy preacher and the Hell's Angels in the town?' he finished with a laugh.

Dom was staring hard at Greg. 'You're right. I remember you now, you were the really keen walker, and yes,' he turned to Bethany, 'I remember Mary Wainwright, er, your mother.' He paused then added, 'And yes, we were friends.'

Robbie joined in: 'I remember that camp; never enough to eat and they liked us all to pray a lot.' He turned to Bethany. 'I'm afraid I don't remember your mother though. There was a big gang of us and she might have been part of the crowd but all I was really interested in was the sailing…' Robbie tailed off and looked away. 'We both were.'

'And you, Gavin,' Greg said, quite enjoying himself, 'I remember now, you used to flog the tourists any canoes or other kit left lying around.' He laughed. 'Quite the entrepreneur.'

Gavin had kept quiet throughout these exchanges, throwing glances between the three other men. Yes, he could see it now. Robbie had changed the most, but Dom was recognisable, Gavin remembered him as one of the regular curfew breakers keen on the town pubs, and Greg seemed almost unchanged. Then he looked anew at Bethany Morrell and remembered Mary. In fact he'd never really forgotten her; she'd had something special, something he suspected her daughter might have too. Cutting across the reminiscences he said: 'OK, so we've established that we all met years ago when we were kids and we remember Mary Wainwright, your mother. Or at least us three do,' he nodded at Dom and Greg, 'and he might,' he added, pointing at Robbie.

'So you remember her too?' Bethany said quickly.

Gavin hesitated. Absorbed in his memories, the acknowledgement had just slipped out. He met Bethany's eye and nodded. 'Yes.'

No one said anything for several moments: Gavin had seemingly lost his thread, Robbie, standing slightly apart, stared distractedly into the murky distance and Greg and Dom seemed lost in their own thoughts. Bethany stood patiently looking from one to another and ignored the solicitor's clerk who fidgeted at her shoulder.

It was Dom who broke the silence and he sounded

nervous. 'OK, so as Gavin here has said, we all knew each other and we knew your... Mary Wainwright, but it's a very big leap from there to making the claim that one of us is your father. There must have been other, er, friends, in your mother's life, what makes you so sure it's one of us?'

There was a grunt from Gavin, Greg nodded his agreement and Robbie, who'd been listening from the edge of the group, re-joined them looking pensive.

'This whole thing's just not believable,' Dom continued, flicking a dismissive hand that took in the mountain top and their six dripping figures. 'And all this... this melodrama. Your word!'

'And there's something else I don't like here,' Gavin interjected. 'How did you know where to find us, or even where to start looking after all these years?' He had a sudden thought. 'Or for that matter, who gave you our names in the first place?'

'My mother,' Bethany said simply, 'in this.' She'd obviously been waiting for this moment and held up a small red leatherette book, the covers curled and scuffed. 'My mother died nearly a year ago of a rare brain cancer, which gave her dementia-type symptoms.' She caressed the little book. 'But in one of her lucid moments just before the end she gave me this and told me where to look. It's her diary. It would seem she'd always kept one, and it's remarkably detailed.' She riffled the pages. 'Where she went, how she felt, even what she ate.' She stopped riffling, 'and perhaps most importantly, who she met.' She paused and looked at the four men. 'She also describes her relationships with those she met and is remarkably frank.

She obviously enjoyed the company of men, boys, and… well, she liked sex.' She tapped the diary. 'She makes no bones about it so nor will I.'

Dom gave a little cough. 'That was sort of my point,' he said apologetically, 'we weren't her only… friends.'

'No, you're right, but you were the special ones, the four of you, her favourites, and she talks about you a great deal in here. I could almost recognise some of you from her descriptions. My mother even had a name for you, she called you her "boys", her "Wainwright Boys".' Bethany gave a little laugh. 'The Wainwright Boys, the special ones.' She looked slightly embarrassed for the first time. 'And I'm sure you must all remember just how special.'

'OK, so if there's so much detail in there,' Gavin demanded, 'why all this charade? Which one of us is it… and when was it supposed to have happened?'

'Well that's it, she doesn't actually say by name which of you it is… was.'

'What!'

'It seems, for whatever reason, she didn't want anyone to know who my… the father of her baby was, including him. And I think she was perhaps worried about someone reading her diary, so instead of putting it down in black and white she left a clue, a sort of process of elimination puzzle, which can only be solved by the four of you. Hence this.' She spread her hands to include them all.

Gavin shook his head in disbelief. 'So we're all here on top of this bloody mountain in the pouring rain and a howling gale to play some bloody game! Well…'

'Yes, but with a very generous prize and no losers,' Dom interrupted. 'We've accepted this lady's money so

I think the least we can do is hear her out… civilly.' He looked pointedly at Gavin.

'And I think there's something else we're overlooking here.' Greg had been an observer for some minutes but had their attention now. 'If this lady, er, Bethany, is right, then one of us is her father. Think about that, one of us has a child we didn't know we had, this young woman, and it might be a bit of a, well, shock, but isn't it also rather… wonderful?'

From under her hood Bethany gave Greg a quick smile and looked round the other three faces. Gavin didn't look convinced but his face had softened, Dom shrugged and smiled uncertainly, while Robbie still seemed preoccupied, not fully engaged.

Dom half lifted a hand, as if asking permission to speak again. 'When are we talking about here? I mean, when did… you know, it, happen?' He smiled apologetically at Bethany, 'I suppose that's sort of asking you how old you are.'

'I'm thirty-two and it was 1976, a very hot summer I gather. You were all here at what was called the Keswick Gospel Brotherhood Camp, and so was my mother.' She looked at the four men in turn. 'And at some point she made love to each one of you.'

Dom looked slightly embarrassed. 'So in that case, how can you really know… for sure, you know, without DNA and things like that?'

'The clue, the process of elimination I mentioned, if I hadn't been sure about that I wouldn't have started this whole thing.' She looked sad for a moment then tapped the little red book. 'My mother knew who, she had no doubts, and her diary is very clear.' She had their full attention now. 'There is one critical date from that summer which completes the process of elimination, August the 20th to be exact. On that day three of you stood on this mountain with my mother. The point is she doesn't say which three, so I needed to ask you.'

'And the one who wasn't here?'

'That was... is, my father.'

Even the blustering wind, rain rattling on waterproofs and screeches of wheeling crows didn't seem to penetrate the silence that followed.

It was Greg who finally broke it. 'I remember that day. We came up that ridge over there, I was looking down it earlier. God it was steep, scary in places too and stinking hot. Loads of people turned back, I remember that.'

'Yeah, I've got it now,' Gavin said slowly. 'You're right, there weren't many of us left by the time we got up here. I remember Mary being here, and another girl, I think she had a bit of a thing for me, and then a few of us boys. And I'm sure I remember you, Greg, like a bloody mountain goat you were... oh, and that black guy, he was the sort of leader, wasn't he?'

'A boxer,' Dom interjected, 'from south London I think. Nice bloke, not too Goddy and not always trying to get into the girls' knickers like some of them.' He glanced at Bethany. 'Yes, I was here that day, and I remember Mary, your mother, being here too. She was always ready to join in, good fun, but now I think about it, and it's a long time ago, I do seem to remember she was a bit quiet that day, things on her mind I think.' He looked thoughtful. 'I suppose if she already knew, or suspected that... well, it's not surprising then really. I think her parents took her home the next day.'

Bethany flicked open the diary, found the right page and read: '"...*Mum and Daddy came this morning to take me home. Stopped for tea at Aunt Jane's. Daddy got a puncture and got cross. Got home late but have still written four pages. I hope he is missing me like I miss him. I love him. Still not going to tell him though. Ever. But I hope it's a boy. Night night diary.*"' Bethany shut the book.

'So what does she say about the day we were all up here?' Gavin asked.

'She mentions everything you've described; the steep ridge, the heat, people turning back, the black man – she liked him – and the other girl. And yes, she did know by then she was pregnant.' She looked at Dom. 'You mentioned she seemed quiet, no wonder, it would've been quite a scandal I imagine. Oddly, she doesn't say anything about that in here,' Bethany tapped the diary, 'but my grandparents must have been horrified, furious.'

'That day's entry is a long one but I'll read you this bit.' She already had her thumb in the place. '"...*got to the top finally. V V hot. Three of my boys came too. They are lovely and Barry very nice too but wish He had come. I wanted to stand on the top with him and look down to where it happened. I know it's him, it can only be him and I am glad but will never tell. Home tomorrow. I will miss my Wainwright Boys but specially him of course. I love him. Hope it's a boy.*"' Bethany gave a wry smile and shut the little book like a vicar concluding a reading.

'Well...'

The clerk was ignored and a long silence punctuated only by nature settled again.

'I wasn't here.' Standing slightly apart, staring into the mist, Robbie had until now seemed almost disinterested, taking no real part, and it was the sound of his voice as much as his words that made them all turn and stare. 'I wasn't here,' he repeated.

The clerk let out a sort of sigh and the other three men exchanged glances. There were a few murmurs, whether of relief or disappointment wasn't clear, not that it mattered to Bethany, her full attention was now on Robbie, her eyes locked on his.

'You didn't seem sure,' she said, her face impassive but the voice shaking slightly, 'I mean you didn't even seem to remember meeting my mother, but you must have… you were lovers,' – she held up the little red diary – 'she says you were.' The impassiveness was starting to crumble.

'I wasn't here, I've never been on this mountain before and…'

'But you must remember, please!' There was a quiet desperation in her voice now.

'…I wasn't here, I mean I wasn't here in 1976.'

'What?' Her eyes were still locked on Robbie's. 'Are you sure?'

Robbie nodded unhappily. 'Sorry.'

Bethany spun round to confront the clerk. 'What the hell have you done?' she snarled.

The little man wilted, all bumptiousness gone, and started frantically leafing through the contents of his clipboard, muttering, 'Cox-Robinson, Cox-Robinson…'

'How can this have happened?' It was almost a plea after the anger. 'The wrong man, your firm assured me, and after all this…' She was close to tears.

'You see, it wasn't my turn.' Everyone turned back to Robbie. 'I was odd numbers, my mum and dad couldn't afford to send us both every year so I was odds and Rickie was evens. He was here in 1976. I remember, brilliant summer he said, not much wind but in and out the pubs, lots of girls and, well, it all sounded pretty wild. Yes, he was here in '76.'

'Did you say "Rickie"?' Bethany said.

'Yes, my brother, Rick, Rickie, Richard if he was in trouble, which he often was.' Robbie gave a wan smile and quickly looked away.

Bethany started rapidly turning pages of the little diary.

'I remember a Rickie,' Greg said suddenly, 'not bothered about the walking but mad keen on sailing.'

'Me too,' Gavin nodded, 'one of the good guys. And you're right, it was all about the boats with him, you'd never have got him off the lake for long enough, I'm sure he wasn't up here with us that day.'

'Here it is.' Bethany prodded the open book. '"*My Wainwright Boys,*"' she read, '"*Dominic Cartwright, The Beeches, Randal Road, Surbiton. May twentieth...*" – she had all your addresses and birthdays – "*Gregory Barnes... Gavin Wheeler...*" and yes, "*Cox-Robinson, Rickie Cox-Robinson...*"' She looked coldly at the clerk. 'Not *Robbie*, "*...17 Helford Road, Falmouth. April twenty-third.*"' She slapped the book shut. 'The wrong brother, you've traced the wrong brother.' The clerk mouthed soundlessly. 'Your firm has a lot to answer for,' Bethany said slowly.

'Well, yes...' the clerk finally spluttered, 'but at least

now you sort of know, we've just got to talk to the other er...' he consulted his clipboard, '...Mr Cox-Robinson and...'

Bethany ignored him and turned to Robbie. 'I'm so sorry you've had to... well, all this,' she spread her hands. It was Robbie's turn to look close to tears.

Dom cleared his throat. 'He's got a point, you know,' he said, almost apologetically, 'Mr Clarke, I mean. The three of us are all sure we were here that day, with your mother, all those years ago. And the right year,' he added, 'and we all remember Rickie and are sure he wasn't up here that day, so it would seem, well...' He spread his hands and shrugged.

Bethany turned to Robbie who stood, head bowed, slumped and crumpled in his over-sized waterproofs. 'I'd very much like to meet your brother,' she said quietly. Robbie's head remained bowed and he shook it slowly. She reached out and touched his arm. 'Please, I mean after all this... do you know where he is, will you help me?'

Robbie lifted his head and met Bethany's eyes. Tears poured down his cheeks, 'Don't you see, it's too late, he's dead.'

Nothing seemed to happen for several long minutes until Robbie, as if waking from a dream, turned and walked away, stopping at the edge of the summit plateau. The rest of them, silent and unmoving, stared at his hunched back until Bethany quietly walked over and stood beside him. After a few moments she put her hand on Robbie's shoulder and he started to talk.

'It was an accident... sailing, it was what he loved and

it killed him. Down there, Derwent Water, summer 1980.' Robbie shrugged. 'Just bad luck really, probably pushing it too hard, Rickie always did,' he smiled through his tears and there was pride in his voice. 'And over they went, three went under and only two came up. Rickie had somehow got tangled in the rigging and... well...'

The two of them stood in silence then, each lost in their own thoughts of what had been and what might have been. There was nothing more to be said. Then the clouds parted fleetingly to reveal distant slivers of the lake, Derwent Water, and they looked down together as so many others had before them.

EPILOGUE

Dom became a Cumbrian farmer's husband and amateur gamekeeper. He organised informal shoots and over the coming years helped to raise enormous sows, prize-winning tups and three boisterous sons. He never mastered chutney making but his marmalade became famed across the county.

* * *

Gavin went to prison. Then he went to Florida where he bought a gun and nearly went to prison again. He briefly returned to Spain, via Gibraltar, before moving on to East Africa where he developed and ran an exclusive safari lodge, donating the profits to conservation projects and local charities

* * *

Greg and Martin bought the newly named Pitcairn Hotel in Cockermouth. When the law allowed they got married and after years of bureaucratic hoop-jumping adopted two children, a brother and sister, toddlers orphaned by the war in Syria. Ben and Cat stayed firm friends and the two families often holidayed together.

* * *

Robbie returned to the Isle of Man where he refitted *Idler*, helped to run Shakespeare & Co and enjoyed freewheeling beach parties. Unannounced, he and *Idler* disappeared one day and were last reported in the Canary Islands apparently preparing for an Atlantic crossing. He was never heard of again.

* * *

Bethany married a naval officer called Walker. They had five children and returned to the Lakes every summer, renting a farmhouse on the shores of Coniston Water where the children learnt to swim and sail and cook on campfires. In time they were allowed to camp on one of the islands and every holiday became an adventure.

This book is printed on paper from sustainable sources managed under the Forest Stewardship Council (FSC) scheme.

It has been printed in the UK to reduce transportation miles and their impact upon the environment.

For every new title that Troubador publishes, we plant a tree to offset CO_2, partnering with the More Trees scheme.

MORE TREES
LET'S PLANT A BILLION TREES

For more about how Troubador offsets its environmental impact, see www.troubador.co.uk/sustainability-and-community